Fierce Companion

Thomas H. Windham IV

ISBN: 978-0615471976 (Fierce Companion)
ISBN-13: 0615471978

CONTENTS

1   The Pit Bull Smiles   1

2   A Stranger in the World   9

3   Children of the Peopocalypse   29

4   John Flint   50

5   Burning For Steam   63

6   Petting Dead Dogs   87

7   Mimosa Day   114

8   Grandiose   138

9   Washed   154

10   Sapience   195

11   Too Far (Poem by Tom Windham III)   210

12   The Face of the Blue Beast   232

13   A New Beginning   254

"From out the primordial bog, red fanged with honest savagery, we come through sanguinary eons of development, through alternating fits of war and council to abolish war, with never ending layers fraught with hate and guile and cold futility." – Thom Windham II

1. THE PIT BULL SMILES

The pit bull smiles with smug contentment. Smug in the face of the fact he has become utterly useless in this world, smug in the face of a world with no use for him. His quality is hidden; he no longer displays any of the traits of his extensive breeding. He smiles smugly, displaying subtly in his grin the quality he knows he posses and others lack. He is game. He knows they can do nothing to make him stop, to take away his will. He looks up at the world in a veiled contempt. His eyes look up to the side and his head stays down, holding on to his seemingly useless gift and waiting for the day when the world needs it, needs him again.

Lapdogs sit panting, pretty and pissing themselves at the first sign of rebuke. They have earned their affection through the trait of cowardice, limping away with tails between legs and passing their gift on through generation upon generation, leaving the remnants of independence behind ages ago to eat from the hand of their masters. They have no skill to trade, no protection to offer. Only the promise that they will never bite back gets them by, keeps them full, inside by the fire with the lady of the manor.

They, like the entire world around them, have become dependent, accustomed to the softness and ease, waiting for the next free meal. He wants to eat them all, tear them apart. He wants to show them just how useless they really are in a world of savagery and survival. He could do so at any minute he chooses, but he waits. He waits with lowered head and eyes looking up for the time when they will need him. He has found a way to adapt. With his head tilted down and his eyes cocked back, his means to adapt is in every measured motion of his spring loaded body.

They say he is not smart. He surrounds himself with fierce men, communicates in grunts and flashing eyes, with penetrating glares communicating something no one understands anymore. They see him and don't understand and assume he is saying nothing. They think he isn't smart. Only he knows that they could not survive a day in his world. Only he knows his quality *is* of the mind, his mind's uncanny ability to defy its own self, to neglect the pain in his own body, to will his body to fight on past any reasonable hope of repairing himself. They think he is not smart, because they have no way to fathom that which he knows.

Oh, and traits have passed him by. His ability to compromise is lacking. He has not cultivated the skill of flattery; he gets nothing for false adoration and platitudes. With all the things he is missing; he just looks at you with those quite eyes saying; "You are what you are" and "Here I am." It's just him, with the quality we can't see, the thing we never name. He knows he has it yet cannot explain the complete indifference to personal pain.

But oh, the compassion! Although indifferent to his own pain, the empathy god dealt him in overwhelming amounts makes him care so much for the pain of others. He is sensitive to it. He feels it like a hot iron fresh from the coals being dug beneath his skin. The pain of others he feels. Like a super hero with a useless power, he looks around himself and finds no use for his trait. A world of easy paychecks, insincere loves, and veiled vanities surrounds him. He sees no use for himself, but knows his trait is valuable so he holds it. He holds onto it and he waits, patiently simmering like roux for the time when the world needs him again. He finds a way to survive, he waits for his time, and she is his daughter.

THOMAS WINDHAM

2. A STRANGER IN THE WORLD

"There is no need for this. There's no need to be fighting every step of the way, like Salmon bouncing off of rocks upstream to their deaths. There is no need for this: A moshpit of flailing bodies in a dark room, people's hands swinging wildly over their heads as they blindly bang into each other and bounce off of one another like popping corn kernels. There is no need, when you can simply go with the flow. We have it all figured out for you. It's very easy, and in fact, there is actually very little thought required on your behalf. To avoid the uphill fight, there are a few things you must do first. Number one: Learn your place.

We have a very simple program for you here. Your first step is to stand in line. We will take you to the cafeteria where you will eat, but first, you must stand in line. Your place may not be in the front or the back, or in the middle; you just never know. Your place is there where we put you, sorted according to the alphabetical order of your last name. You will stand facing the back of the person in front of you, and then we will orderly follow one another to the cafeteria. You may cut in line, if you can get away with it, but you must *never* step out of the line. Once we have learned this *very* simple step, we can move on to other things, and it appears we *just may* have a place for you… yes, we will fit you in, somewhere.

There are many elements which should take care of themselves first. Your peers, by this age, have already come to understand that uniformity is a must to function as a group. Your mother should know to buy you new clothes. We also must require one list of injections, three forms of inspections, and a few strongly recommended corrections. This child may be prone to loosing attention in geometric lessons, it appears to be genetics, but we have a pill for that. Do you think that psychotropic prescription medications may be appropriate for your little fish?

In order to assess a proper diagnosis; we've orchestrated a display of semi pseudo violence. Through the glass, in the tank adorned with artificial plants, we will see how they swim. Notice there the one of the different stripe, swimming off away from the school which has grouped together. It's been observed many times that the one that doesn't fit in, the odd one out, he will be picked at from each angle. The school's members will make frequent passes, nipping a little off of each fin here and there with each pass until, eventually, he can't swim and will begin to list. You can already see what happened to him… over there floating on his side in the corner of the tank…"

The boy's first day of kindergarten is a big wake up and induction to a starkly different life from what he is used to. The wide-eyed kindergarten student has never been faced with the choice of clothes, what he's supposed to wear or what he's supposed to think. He's never had to consider who he stands behind of or of whose place it is to always go first, second, and last. He did not know in his childhood bliss that someday soon someone else would tell him how it was supposed to go.

A dumbfounded, blank look holds to his face as he watches all the other kids falling into line automatically, as if they had been trained from birth for numbly going where they were supposed to go and doing what they were told to do with a blank smile. The trip continues through the strange day, down halls and into lines, until the children are being herded to their busses.

"How do they know how to do that?" he thinks as a stare comes over the boy. An older boy in a group walking past him notices the fat faced youngster with his hands frozen in a contorted position. He looked confused, his lips slightly curled as if he was trying to identify a smell he didn't like. Trying to wrap his head around it, he is startled from his daze.

"Are you trying to find your bus?" the freckled fourth grader asked him. He was tan, with Sun bleached hair, blue eyes, and a big gap between his new front teeth.

The kindergartener still seemed perplexed. Something about the big bus before him scared him. He sees the blue banner in the window and understands that this is where he is supposed to go. The only thing his mother had told him was,
"Davey is riding home with his grandmother. Don't ride with any strangers, and don't let anyone make you do something you feel uncomfortable with."
He was being urged on to board through the strange door of the foreign yellow bus. 'Not me', he thinks, 'I can fight it.' As his eyebrows descend over his now angry eyes, he makes his decision. He knew better, he had been taught differently.

"No."

"Well then, come on. We're all going to walk," says the freckled forth grader, pointing at the group of children who were just to the edge of the play field, waving him to hurry up before they cut through an opening in the brushy fence line.

Children are running towards the busses lined up in front of the school, prodded on by the adults with whistles. The younger children have had a piece of colored paper pinned onto their shirts. On the busses, the corresponding colors were displayed in the windows. Some confused ones are directed and gently nudged towards the correct orderly line forming outside of one of the bus doors. Other children, older ones, already know where to go, but the whole encounter reminds the strange boy of a bad dream spurned by a movie he never should have watched. He runs towards the others across the field beside the playground and beyond the lined up yellow busses, but loses sight of them by the time he reaches the other side.
The five year old child tries to remember the roads through the suburban neighborhood around the school as he navigates the streets for his first time, trying to find his house. It is an older neighborhood in Beaumont, quaint with brick houses and giant, swaying trees in the neatly trimmed, bright green grass, which was

divided evenly by cement edges of sidewalks and driveways. While walking home from school, he comes to a yard of one of the suburban homes lining the cracking paved street which is different than the rest. It has a coble-stone driveway and the foliage is tropical, with long flowing leafs making it look more like a rain forest than a front yard.

Every square inch is covered in trees and shrubbery, making a dark cave in their canopy, and a red stone trail leads from the driveway into its darkness. The cave presented under the enclave of Magnolia leafs and twisting ivies is inviting in its apparent cover from the view of the foreign streets, yet spooky from the darkness at the head of the trail.

Once inside, the neat row of houses lining the sidewalk disappears in a hidden world separated by foliage, completely blocking any view of the outside world. Strange birds with orange and blue feathers squawk down at the small, wide eyed boy from low hanging branches of ornate trees in the surreal daytime darkness of the miniature rainforest. To the outside world he tries to listen, finding himself in another dimension. Everywhere he looks he sees twisting ivies, vines and branches intertwined to create solid walls of foliage. He hears no cars passing by, and he knows that no one can see him.

This is a dark world, completely separated from the outside. He knows that people driving by provide him a degree of security and that if the person who made this tropical maze of intricately twisted vines were to come outside and find him, no one would be around to help him. He feels safe, he is confident that whoever made this place is of no harm to him. He slowly walks down the enveloped path through the yard, trying to understand the vines winding up the trees and feeling lost in a fantastic world just feet from reality.

As he emerges into the afternoon's Sunlight at the end of the trail on the opposite end of the lawn, he is emboldened by his victorious march through the unknown, confident in his decision to stray off from the other children boarding the busses. The maze of streets seems simple and he casually walks the rest of the way home, lost in thought up to the moment that he pulled the handle of the old screen door leading into the familiar kitchen of the cozy brick house where he lived.

"There you are! I was worried sick about you," says his mother as he enters the kitchen, with her overly caring smile and eyes quivering in joy for the love of her son. Her slow Beaumont draw was so eloquent as she drew each syllable into a song. "I was at the school to pick you up, then I drove around the neighborhood looking for you, but I thought: he's never been around here before. I was almost worried sick because Mrs. Walker said she hadn't seen you get on the bus, then, something told me I should come back by and check at the house. And, Bingo! No sooner do I park the car and come in the front door, than do you come walking in the side door! Where have you been?"

"I was probably in the jungle when you drove by," the child responds to her, with his big, innocent eyes shining up over the baby fat on his cheeks. The surprised mother queries deeper into the child's strange story, puzzled.

"Did the jungle have trees? Was it a real jungle, like with snakes?

"No, but there was a big bird, it was Red."

"A big bird? Do you mean like a parrot? Where was this jungle?"

"On the side of the road, the one that comes home…"

The mother looks befuddled and asks,

"Are you sure Deana didn't bring you home?"

"No, I walked home."

"Honey, if you're going to walk home, you need to walk with the other kids. Okay? How was your first day of Kindergarten?"

"I don't know," he says. Now that he is safe in the dim den of his home with the florescent light on the ceiling back shadowing his mother in the kitchen, the events of the day start to replay in his mind. As he tries to fit it into context, another blank expression comes over his face and he appears to be gazing deep into the distance towards the draped window in the living room. A muffled light coming through the drapes gently moves from wind swaying the trees outside, the Sun's ambassadors complete their long journeys through space and clouds by finally passing through the openings between branches and leafs to reach the outside of the covered window. Dots of light are softly outlined and silently move up and down. Looking at the boy, who was suddenly in a deep trance, the mother began to be a little worried for him.

The boy was in for a long trip, a hard ride, a tough go at it. At an age when conscious decisions are based on little past one's natural instincts and the few lessons ingrained in his youth, he made his choice that would affect the outcome of the rest of his life. His mind was set like stone.

With his chubby face and helmet cut hair, fashioned meticulously by his loving mother, he seemed so innocent. He looked like a poster boy for baby food in a striped shirt and brown corduroy pants. He had big eyes, deep brown and softly blended into white around the pupil's edge, and with them he looked at people and things in long, dazed stares. The big eyes absorbed all that was there, like panoramic lenses connected to a giant computer, filing, processing, and storing everything he saw. He asked many questions, and after receiving answers he sat silently for hours, pondering and processing, rolling each new concept and thought around in his head until he was sure he had grasped every angle of it. Sometimes his long stares and periods without responding to the world around him even led people to think that he may be, just a little, slow.

His parents were delighted when the aptitude tests from the state came in the mail from the public elementary school. He scored higher than 98.9 percent of the children to take the test. His problem solving, reading, and identification skills were far beyond his years, and no one really knew where they came from, especially because he seemed to loose concentration for exercises in the classroom so quickly.

His parents had read to him, even taught him to read before sending him off with his cartoon adorned tin lunch box for that fatal first day. They had studied the Bible beyond memorization of verses and had taught him what the proverbs and stories within it meant, what they were trying to convey to him and why.

"Understanding is the key," they told him, "wisdom is a virtue, and it is better than rubies and gold."

When they read to him about Daniel in the lion's den, they strived to teach the young boy the intricacies of the story and the reason for each character's plot as related to the whole. They painted the picture of the young man cast into the lion's pit for praying to his own God to be eaten, and of the surprise to the spectators when they found out that the hungry lions would not eat the man as he continued to pray in the pit. They had brought all the Biblical stories to contrast with everyday situations, expecting the boy to understand the paradoxes before he was able to even formulate his questions into words. One day, they showed him tweezers and the electric socket and learned a valuable lesson about the wide eyed boy.

They told him only: "Whatever you do, do not put these tweezers in that socket."

The moment they both left him alone to join in a shower together, he did exactly that. When they found him with black charred skin next to their bed, with the sheets on fire and his hair standing straight up on end, they learned a painful lesson about rearing their strange child: If there was going to be a rule, it would have to make sense to him.

His forehead became like a hardened hammer. He would be prone to bang it wherever he went. As they moved from city to city every year, he would find plenty of opportunity for molding his blunt striking object. An artist, his father had been a boxer growing up. Dad would revel in those days over scotch and milk, which he fondly referred to as 'Scuds', and begin reliving and acting out the trials of his glory days for the boy who looked up at him, standing barefoot on a cool linoleum kitchen floor in the evening. With his hand popping a gust of air as it snapped just before the boy's face, he would snap jabs out and make the sound effects for him while recanting the stories.

"I was legally blind, couldn't see a thing. But my trainer, Bobby, over there in black town, he would tell me, "Tom, when you feel your head snap back, you know they're in range. Then you snap out that jab." But bwoooy, that jab of mine! WHOOP! WHOOP!"

He would extend the jab out inches before the boy's face, making the air pop in its sudden whoosh like a snapping whip. The boy instinctively refused to move away from the big man's punches and seemed distant as he stared up at ol' dad. The stone glazed stare was not induced by fear; he knew his father would never hurt him. He was studying the form.

"You punch straight, from the shoulder, like this!"

His father taught him how to throw a punch, and he also taught him how to be a man. "Life's not fair." Was one of his favorite lessons to impart on the boy, as well as , "Men don't cry, you got that son?"

"It's the holes we shoot in our feet that keep us from walking on water," and "No one can defeat you except yourself."

He always remembered the familiar lesson from one of their many fishing trips to the jetty. His little brother tripped over his fishing line while he was trying to bait his hook, causing the barbed fish hook to sink deep into his flesh instead of the squirming minnow in-between his soft little fingers.

"You little son of a bitch!" he yelled at his little brother, Crockett. "Argh!"

"Don't be such a pussy!" the unreasonably brave little brother told him, "just take it out."

"It's stuck in there, asshole, the barb won't come out!"

"Here, I'll cut it out for you." said his father, whipping out the old pocket knife with the aged yellow handle. That meant: 'It's time to stop whining.'

"No thanks, I got it", he responded calmly. Then he worked the barb out himself, yanking out the flesh in his sensitive finger tip slowly and methodically, while ignoring the pain it caused him. At one point, frustrated that the barb would not come out easily after working it back and forth and angling it around for what seemed like eons, he asked his dad for the knife. He held the knife in his right hand, the one he used the least, and decided he just couldn't do it. He walked over to his dad, who was patiently untangling a line for his four year old sister, and asked him to do it.

The father was distraught. He had whipped out the knife before for effect, always recanting his own father's words of machismo toughness, but never planned on actually having to use it for minor surgery. Before ol' dad had to figure out what to do, young John changed his mind and decided to do it himself. He sat back down on the wooden plank dock and went to work, slicing off just enough of the sensitive flesh around the hook still stuck on his finger to remove it.

As he grew up, he learned to make a mockery of others through his indifference to pain. Putting cigarettes out on each other's hands, punching each other's jaws for sport, while driving, for fun; his friends would need to be willing to enjoy a little pain to have a good time. Shunned by normal society in their inability to adapt to the norms, they gripped indifference to pain as a major tenant of their identities and wasted no opportunity to prove it.

Of course, his stubbornness and toughness did not help him at every turn. Neighborhood bouts won him respect from his peers. He was known for standing up to anything, even adults, amongst the other kids, and they looked up to him for it. His authority figures, however, had a harder time accepting his unbending will. He was a little too smart to trick into doing what they wanted him to, far too fearless to scare or intimidate, and too impervious to punish. They grappled with ways to deal with him, to bend him, to make him conform.

The school's staff tried to bore him with solitude and detention, watching daily through one-way windows as they waited for the day when sitting in a confined cubicle would drive him crazy, and they found themselves confounded when he seemed to enjoy it. Instead of growing angry or depressed, he showed no care and constantly doodled the day away on pictures of army men propelling down cliffs to avoid incoming missiles from helicopters. To him, being stuck in one room was just the same as being stuck in the rest of the school; it was just something he had to do. They would see that he was enjoying himself drawing the day away and take away his pencils. They tried diligently and endlessly to break his defiant will with all their tactics to no avail. Eventually, they just ended up hating him. It wasn't that he was a particularly bad child, they decided, he just had a horrible attitude.

Occupying his time with his own thoughts got him through the years; he learned to keep his head down. He made sport of the teachers who insisted on breaking his solitude during the monotonous classes he sat through. "The person who gets mad first, looses," his dad had once told him. Precision guided words and glances waited for the perfect time to inflict the most damage, and often sent his teachers into emotional tantrums aimed at the boy. The feuds would continue daily, like an emotional chess match, and in each period of the school day he would formulate his battle plan upon arriving at class. Like a seasoned general drawing his enemy's army in and then encircling their forces, he won his battles through patience and managed to piss them all off.

One frustrated teacher, a football coach, totally lost his composure at the child's smart remarks and grabbed the boy by the shoulders and shook him while shouting profanities at the juvenile miscreant in the classroom where he taught Geometry. His outburst was quickly interrupted by stunning blows to his face from the 13 year old boy, stunning in their accuracy and quick delivery. The punches had flown from the brash student like second nature; after all, he had been training to deliver them since learning how to pee in a toilet. They sent him to the principal's office and suspended him from school for a while, but they already knew that wouldn't work. There was really no getting through to him.

There was no way to win him over. Platitudes fell short. The few adults who had broken through the defensive shell with the twinkling in the eye and the practiced look of understanding over the years, eventually showed their true colors to the boy. Disappointments left him hurt, and he set himself up not to be disappointed any more. He learned to let no one through his invisible wall.

There was the kindly small engine mechanic who had helped him build a tree house one summer. He worked behind the trailer in a small wooden shop, far removed from his wife. Kurt Yawn would let him drive the go-carts after he repaired them, just to test them out, knowing the joy it brought the young boy who never had owned one and thought them a grand display of opulence. In fact, John had always saw other kids with them growing up and had never even been allowed the privilege to drive one before then.

On top of letting him test drive the go-karts, Kurt even let him use the lawn mowers and weed eaters he fixed to start his first lawn route in the 5th grade, where he earned candy bar money from the sweet older people in the community. The twinkle in Kurt's eye always told a joke without speaking, and when he did tell a joke, it was always funny. John washed his truck and learned how to do things right, Kurt even taking the time to discipline him and make him go back and scrub the wheels before giving him the five bucks. He felt a strange feeling, being used for the first time, not knowing what was really going on. He did know that 5 bucks was worth a few Payday candy bars at the old corner store in old town. He did not know that the four hour wash and wax job, including scrubbing and polishing the rusty chrome wheels, should have cost about 20 dollars, at least, but he had a suspicion all the work was worth more than what he got in the end.

He had made a friend in town whose parents owned a restaurant and also a snow-cone stand. The boy had a video game system hooked up to a black and white TV in the snow cone shop where they worked together. John spent that summer's days playing video games and eating snow cones while pausing for the occasional interruption to shave some ice into a cup from the old machine or to go down to the corner store with a red wagon and cart back a big block of ice. He was happy to be hanging out in the snow cone stand, playing video games. The boy whose parents owned the stand invited him to spend the night at their house a few weeks later. The two boys spent the day playing with toys and shooting frogs with his fancy pellet gun and the night passed watching soft core porn on cable TV and munching on sugar snacks.

It was a whole other world, almost unknown to the boy. Refrigerators full of sweets and candy for every fancy in the kitchen and garage, automatic sprinklers in the manicured lawn, and two adults too preoccupied with whatever they were doing to worry about what he was doing, were all new to the juvenile. Cable TV bringing every room anything you may want to see, any video, any movie. Toys only seen on television adorned him, his parents had even bought him the most powerful, Carbon Dioxide compressed air powered, 357 magnum replica pellet gun.

The next day they brought the air-gun with them to the drainage ditches lining the back of the subdivision and shot at cans, bottles, and whatever a boy might find to shoot a pellet gun at. John always liked frogs. He would catch them in his back yard and examine them, he liked to watch them eat bugs with their stealthy tongues. When his buddy started shooting the frog they found along the ditch at point blank, he thought something must be wrong in the joy the little boy got from it. Watching its little pink guts bulging out as he reloaded several times and shot it repeatedly, John was bewildered. He felt obligated to alert the parents, an overwhelming sense of alarm had overtaken him when he realized the boy was killing for fun. The parents looked at him like he was crazy, and he was never invited back again.

Then, a short time later, he was invited to Kurt's house where he was mounted atop a riding mower and set to mow the vast lawn of Kurt's church. When they were done there, they loaded up and went to mow Kurt's lawn. He met Kurt's beautiful, young, brunette wife and felt he was in love with the wonderful woman. She had radiant brown wavy hair and wonderful breasts. Pre shame and pre pubescent, his little pecker swelled at the thought of her supple, soft breast pushing on her bra beneath her soft, fuzzy sweater. It was years before he began to understand men's depravity and the lengths they would go to in order to satisfy their selfish desires.

Only days later, behind the railroad tracks near his house, just past Kurt's shop, he found the body of a transient. In a cold, forever sleep, the vagrant sprawled across the steep slope of jagged rocks by the wooden ties. A cheap bottle of wine in a little paper bag still rested in his grip. There was a bag of items apparently stolen from a nearby shopping district still hanging from the old man's other hand: little metal castles, snow globes and trinkets filled the plastic sack. Perhaps the dead man had planned on giving them to someone he cared for; a daughter or a long lost love. Maybe he meant to be hit by a train and passed out and died of a heart attack beside the iron rails before it arrived? The morning was cold and the spot made John think of himself walking in the man's old, faded white tennis shoes down the lonely railroad tracks in the middle of the wet night. He thought of the man's daughter, his wife, and his parents. Would they ever know?

It was also not far from there he found his first porno magazine discarded on the railroad tracks. There was a short, platinum bleach blonde haired woman on the cover, on the inside were spread vaginas and throbbing penis's displayed under studio lights in sweaty glisten. It made no sense to him then, having no grasp of man's depravity. It seemed so disgusting.

Shortly after, his parents divorced. They moved away from the little trailer park, like they had moved almost every year of his childhood. In the absence of his father, his trust for adults vanished completely. Even in ol' Kurt, who showed up at their house with flowers once dad moved out.

There was a tear; a permanent break in his naive perception of men after the events of that year, he would never trust anyone again. His friends were made through domination and he adopted a policy of trust: Trust people to be what they are. Trust that people will lie, cheat, and stab you in the back. Expect nothing more, and you're in for no surprises, no disappointments.

He ran a hard line. The thread between a desire for acceptance and a general hatred of those around him was thin. Their fancy clothes, 100 dollar tennis shoes, and knowledge of popular culture all set him aside. Late one night in his living room, he saw a Kung Fu movie where a fighter made his hands and legs into rock hard weapons through abusing them against wood and steel. He made this his hobby, taking his anger out on standing trees and plastered walls.

Teacher's did not know how to react to him. The few who tried mocking the outcast were met with surprising blows, he earned a reputation for fighting and people began to leave him alone. "I have friends and people I have not beat up yet," he would say.

In his solitude, he began erecting pillars of thought to support the shell of a world he was constructing within his own mind. He had already accepted himself as the outcast, an outsider, and had now no reason to follow conventional patterns of thought. Every teacher's lesson was considered in terms of "what if", and "what really probably happened", and, "how it could have been different had this person done this certain thing on that particular historic day?" His hours in the classrooms were spent in daydreaming and imagining, only using the lessons as fuel for a million possibilities and stories of his own endings and plots. Even mathematics, where they taught the process of copying formulas and working through them in certain ways, were only fun to him when finding another way to reach the solution.

He rarely took out a pen in those classes, choosing instead to see how far he could work the problem from his head. When told to take notes, he would take out his pen and begin drawing pictures, drifting back off into his fantasy world of naked blonde headed women hanging by their wrists from chains with their large breasts exposed in a deep, secret dungeon where he would rescue them through a series of sword fights and gun battles and then nestle his head into the rescued women's big soft breasts.

Occasionally, he would look up at the board and the algebraic equation presented.

"If this is greater than that, and the square root of that equals this, and the sum of these two makes up a number less than this one, what number does "x" represent," the question would say in some cryptic code.

"Who cares?" was his usual first reaction. Then, just to show the world and himself that it was simple, he would deduct the answer in his head through a series of eliminations and equations, in the total opposite form of the method being taught to the brain straining students around him.

The teacher would see the pen hanging out of his mouth as the blank stare caught her attention and ask him the answer, trying to catch him off guard. With a slight pause, he would answer the question, usually correctly, satisfying her that he was diligently working out the problem on the paper and had only quit because he solved it before anyone else. He would then put his head back down to his desk and continue his illustrations of candles melting wax down into drops forming the shapes of women's supple breasts and sharp teethed demons devouring flesh, as the other students continued doing the same problem with different variables over and over again for the rest of the class. X's, O's, numbers, dates... Somehow the information settled on him in each period, although he never paid attention or wrote any of it down. He aced nearly every test.

Of course, by this point, he had realized that acing the tests was not the reason he had been brought here, it was not the useless information they wanted him to learn. It was the order of things, the way to conform was what they were trying to impress on him. Usually, he went along. He learned to keep some ideas to himself and learned who he could trust to share them with. He let most teachers think they were smarter than they were and most authority figures think they were in charge. However, some of them saw through his veil of indifference and seemed to take the matter very personally.

He kept to himself, always talking and smiling, but rarely revealing his thoughts. He made friends with other miSunderstood throw-backs of a distant age who were as lost in the world as he was. Boys that saw toughness and grit as a quality, those who retained somehow the warrior's spirit; they made up his band of friends. Many of them were new kids who came to the school and were forced to get tough or act tough. He befriended them by taking their side against bullying and hazing, by sticking up for them. The friends he made would defend him fiercely at any time.

That was the way he met Peoples. He was confronted by him in his government class. The new kid came into his world with a neck brace and a story, describing the fight which had left him temporarily handicapped with great emphasis on how the other guy ended up much worse. At first, the strange boy was intimidating, then funny, then downright inviting in his jokes and attempts to win over the established boy sitting next to him.

They kept a professional relationship, never showing weakness or respect for the other as they passed in the halls and sat next to each other in the US Government class where they both made a mockery of the institutions and the order they were supposed to care so much about, while easily acing the quizzes and tests. Then one summer night they met outside of school unexpectedly, awkwardly pacing in front of a house in a sleeping suburb.

When they snuck away from the group of John's friends earlier that day to frolic, the girl had told John that her grandmother was in town and that the old lady would be staying in her room late that night, and that he should wait to come back over until after midnight so they could be alone. As he ate at a late dinner in a diner with some friends, a couple who were in love with one another, he described the girl's strange request.

"She's probably got another dude coming over first," Tonya told him as they ate.

"You're probably right!" He acknowledged, although it didn't matter.

At precisely twelve o' one he climbed her fence and knocked on the backdoor to her bed room. There was no answer, so he knocked again, just a little bit louder. She finally came and cracked the door slightly.

"My grandma's still here, come back in 20 minutes."

The loud snores coming from inside seemed strange to him, 'mighty loud for a grandma', he thought. Yet he returned in 20 minutes, anyway. The story was the same, and the snores were still persistent, so he returned again in 20 more minutes, and then again as she kept telling him the 'grandmother' would be leaving soon.

On his last trip towards her door from the car parked in the street where he had waited with his teeming teenage hormones keeping him concentrated, he was confronted by an unexpected sight. Justin Peoples was coming his direction, leaving her parent's back yard.

They both figured it out. A moment of awkwardness passed into a shared shit-eating grin. After that, they sat in his car and smoked weed from a plastic bong as they laughed about the girl's devious plans together. From that moment on, they were inseparable friends. By banding up with John, Justin had joined a group of outcasts, kids from other places with other values who had banded together, attracted to one another subconsciously, naturally, like the orbit of planets. They were the tough kids from Philadelphia who were set apart by their accents and decided meanness. They were the strange faced kids with hanging foreheads and protruding cheek bones who could not muster a kind word for the people they just did not like. They were the outcasts; they would make their own rules.

Before they began chasing girls, they played games in the woods. Their favorite game was called "Hunter." One boy would hold the stick, the "spear," and count to 500 while other boys fled and found hiding spots amongst the trees and bushes of the large forest. Imagining yourself a hunter, you wielded the weapon and stalked through the woods, hunting your hiding prey while trying to guard the safe 'home' spot where you had counted laboriously. Upon finding the others, a thrilling chase would begin and the hunter would have to touch them with the spear to "kill" them before they reached the counting spot. Upon being "killed," they would return to the counting spot, "dead". The last one to get killed was the new hunter in the next round. Often, the game would become a race through the thicket as one boy ran for his life from the hunter to reach the safe spot of the counting area. Maneuvering over fallen logs and pits at full speed, he imagined the stick a real spear while low hanging branches slashed at his face as he dashed through them.

With adrenaline pumping and eyes wide open they ran all out through the woods, disregarding the stickers cutting through the thin skin of their legs and arms as they plunged through the bushes fearlessly. They dove on their stomachs under foliage into beds of pine needles, unconcerned about the bugs and thorns there to meet them. They scaled trees like stunt men and leapt across wide ravines over deep gullies to creeks strewn with dangerous Cyprus knees which made vertical spikes from the ground below, avoiding certain death by reaching the other side after their blind leap through the air and clinging to exposed roots and branches as they clawed their ways up the other side.

Scrapes were signs of toughness which they all strived for and compared in warrior's pride between their sessions. Their games soon evolved to backyard boxing and no holds barred team fighting for pride and a small amount of change they had placed into a shoe in the yard, which was to be the spoil of the victors. Insignificant sums of money would be spent on candy and baseball cards at the corner store after the matches, which only ended when each member of one team had given up, or called "mercy."

They were the tough ones, the ones whose lives had tested every grain of their grit through innumerous damaging blows trying to bring them down. Pressures that made normal men crumble and cry for mercy only made them stronger. In a world that spits in their face a thousand times, they smile right back, displaying the strength, will, and courage to stop breathing before taking their last breath.

Gravity held them together, chemistry and physics. A contradictory world told them to be strong, yet feared their strength and tried to bring it down in numbers. Quirky traits of fierce loyalty and self reliance scared those around them, increasingly trying to find ways to place them in the back. Somehow, someway, their parents had held those qualities and passed them on, in some places even nurturing them. The quality kept them at constant odds with the functioning society, yet they knew it was a quality and they kept it like a kindled flame of fragile embers, protecting it constantly from perishing in a surrounding swamp of despair.

They thought they were special, perhaps the only ones of their kinds. There was no apparent sign to their inexperienced minds of similar consciousness elsewhere. However, throughout the suburbs, neighborhoods, and countryside, the story was playing out. Some of them were just warriors. They banded together and shaved each other's heads and sparred with each other in the yard. They arm wrestled each other and all agreed that they would never back down. Wiser with years, they started seeing the same traits everywhere they went as they grew older. The North Spring Posse, The Dove Springs Posse, the South Cove Boys; it was the same everywhere they went as well as everywhere they never imagined.

Although they eventually graduated to the sport of chasing the high school girls and playing more conventional sports like volleyball, where they could find them on the sandy courts and neighborhood football games in the park, the group still kept an affinity for running all out through the woods like a band of warriors. They would meet at an apartment on one side of the thicket and roughly map out the forest with sticks in the grey dirt, assuming which direction would spit them out on the other side of town. Then they would race there in an all out run to test their grit and endurance against one another and themselves.

It was one of these trips that brought them out at the creek after a long run through the woods. That they had hit the creek in this specific spot was a testament to blind faith, for it was exactly where they had hoped the 5 mile trek would land them. The creek was swollen from a few days of hard rain, reaching far up the familiar sandy embankment. The tired boys knew it was dangerous, but the jubilation of the successful journey's completion was urging them to take a swim. Never outdone, the overzealous John jumps into the creek in a running leap at the end of the epic race, determined to swim to the other side and counting on the giant leap to put him far enough into the swilling currents to do so. The muddy water rushes over his head as he lands feet first and immediately begins swimming.

Futility is defined by fighting a force with no effect. As water pushes against you, you push it behind you with the scissoring of your legs and pull at it with your arms as hard and as ferociously as you can. You know you must make it across; your very life depends on it. You feel the fatigue set into your muscles as you try harder and harder to move forward through the water, but find you are not moving at all. You are now struggling just to stay above the surface as it pulls at your wet clothes and tennis shoes; you contort your neck to keep your nostrils above the water as the swollen river laps up over your face. You try to fight it, but know you can't. You think to yourself, "this cannot be the way I'm going to die." As you look to your friends who are helplessly watching from the bank, you feel the pain in your tired arms subside when you quit swimming and begin to sink down. You now have a choice: fight to the dying last breath, or just let it happen.

There under the water, John decides to open his eyes. All he sees is a murky darkness. It is there the voice comes to him,

"I'm not going to let you die."

He feels a calm coming over him and does not know what to expect. He knows it will work out, somehow, and just lets the water's current carry him. The murky water seems to get darker and darker. Just as all goes black, he feels something at his feet. It is a

26

tree submerged beneath the rushing creek. He grabs it and hangs on, stabilizing himself with it and poking his head above the water to his comrades searching for him with their eyes from the bank. He is right in the middle of the creek and hollers at them from the submerged sapling which is stabilizing him in the water. The numbness in his arms and body is replaced by a burning rush of blood pumping oxygen back into his extremities. He gathers his thoughts and his strength, and eventually decides to swim back to the side from which he jumped. He rides the current instead of fighting it, letting himself be washed downstream while gradually working his way back to the shore, which he finally reaches 50 yards down creek at a low, muddy bank.

Climbing up to the dry sandy embankment, he realizes how much he loves life, feeling he has been given a whole other chance to utilize it and knowing he could have been dead. He falls to his knees in the tall grass and grasps it with his hands, lowering his forehead to the soil and literally kissing the ground, thanking the unnamed entity in the water.

As he walks back over to the area where his friends are, he looks to the sky. The surreal moment seems to be trying to tell him something. Everything is okay; everything under the sky is in place. The birds are still singing, the Butterflies are still flying around and the trees still sway gently in the wind. He realizes that it would still be the same whether he had died or not.

"Dude, I almost died" he tells them, walking back up the sandy incline towards them, soggy and winded.

"Whatever, don't be such a wimp" says Robert in his thick, Philadelphian accent.

"Yeah, don't be such a wimp, pussy" the chorus begins.

"Shut up, I'd like to see you try it." he responds.

"I can do it, easy" says Robert.

Robert is Joey's big brother. He is older, tougher, and often prone to be right. Like his brother, he is stout and handsome, with a perfect smile barley marred by the few crooked teeth from his various brawls.

"All the way to the other side? Yeah right. I'd like to see it, but trust me, don't try it," he tells him in sincere concern.

Robert says, "Okay, watch this," as he takes off his shirt.

"Man, don't do it," he repeats, amazed that he might be so foolish after watching him almost die and sure that he was bluffing.

"No problem, tough guy, I got this." Robert responds calmly. He then walks about 30 yards upstream, down to the lower embankment, and starts swimming across, riding, not fighting, the current.

To the near drowning victim's amazement, Robert reaches the other side just at the point he, himself, had been struggling to reach. A life of fighting against the flow had trained John to go straight forward into adversity, which he deemed the water to be. He had been fairly successful in fighting the flow in life. No stream of thought or persuasion seemed too strong to him, having met nothing capable of changing his direction. That day he learned a valuable lesson: You can fight the institutions of man and society, but you can't fight nature.

Robert looked back at him from the other side, smiling to flash his white teeth from across the creek. He didn't say anything, but catching him in his stare, he knew he had taught him a valuable lesson. Even Robert, the determined tough guy who always did his own thing, knew how to go with the flow.

3. CHILDREN OF THE PEOPOCALYPSE

"This place is hell, man."

"It's fine, John," says Peeps in his slightly concerned, slightly mocking voice. "You got it jus' good as anyone else." Peeps is a lot more accepting since he has been out of prison.

"Man, look at this toxic sludge all around us. Who knows what the hell chemicals are in this mud. Look at it, it's glowing. It can't be good for you, hell, it says the shit's cancerous on the label of every goddamn container we use around here! These name tags turn purple in the presence of Phosgene gas. They turn purple and we'd all be dead! This is bullshit."

As they stand there relishing a cigarette, they observe the piping helpers bending conduit. They appear extremely disgruntled as they continue measuring and bending the small metal pipe which would be housings for thousands of miles of copper wires in the big chemical plant.

"Man, you're in there in the cold AC, you're an Electrician's Apprentice," says Justin, "what do you have to complain about? Just do your work and you'll be fine."

"This place is hell, man. This is bullshit."

Justin Peoples, 'Peeps,' knew his best friend was right. He didn't really care, though. He had a good way of dealing with that already in place. On the way home, they stopped at the first gas station at the end of the remote road leading into the gigantic plant they had just left, as usual, to buy cold cans of beer from the ice filled display by the door. The Hindi man knew they were underage, but let them buy it, anyway. On the hour long drive home they would drink them, relishing the cold can as they let the open window's wind cool they're bare, sweat crusted chests. Peeps was a great back seat driver.

"Watch out for that car!" he would yell as he slammed the outer door with his hand hanging out of the window.

Ass hole. The therapy of cold beer, frothing and fizzing in your mouth before the chilly liquid goes down, is heightened in the raging teenage mind by the fact that drinking it while speeding down the road is illegal. Banging on the door, pointing to a spot for no reason, these were all games they played with each other to try and piss the other one off. They played a game at that time called the jaw game. You've reached a certain level of endearment when you begin jacking each other's jaws for sport.

"Surprise!" you hear as you look up from your J.R. Tolkien book, while sitting on the toilet, to see a closed fist coming through the bathroom door to rattle your chin and clang your teeth together. It really was funny but, *please* man, not while I'm driving… In other circles, some of their games must have seemed very weird. Imagine being at a party, lounging on a plastic deck chair with a cool plastic cup of keg beer, and seeing a group of people you don't know start punching each other and laughing about it hysterically.

Peeps rolls up the first joint of the afternoon as they speed down a six lane interstate past the gentle landscape of green fields and pine trees, pushing 90 in a tiny Toyota Tercel. He is holding a Kool Menthol cigarette in his loose mouth and making ridiculous comments about everything as the open window emits the cool air of a setting Sun. The orange haze of a thick, Southeast Texas evening began to paint the clouds purple and bright gold. It was as if the Sun was painting its last picture of the day upon the sky-scape, and the clouds were giving a standing ovation as they reflected his last lights in brilliant gold and pink violet applause. The outburst of colors rang out like a silent symphony in crescendo.

"Bill Clinton is gonna cut wages for everybody." Peeps begins his diatribe as his eyes start to squint, "They've got this car that runs on Banana peels, like a time machine, but the oil companies keep buying all the patents. This guy had one, and he wouldn't give it up, and they killed him. That's also why they killed Lennon."

"You're crazy, man."

"Yeah, I'm fucking crazy. In China, where the government runs the medical services, anyone who dissents to the government they just diagnose as 'crazy,' then they lock them up in mental wards. After they fry their brains with all kinds of drugs and electrotherapy, the people just come out drooling and everyone thinks they're crazy, anyway. They'll do anything to stay in power. Really, that's what we do all day working for these oil companies, just keep the ruling class in power. You can't overthrow the people, man!" His voice grows to a roar as his rant continues, "Because the people are going to fight back! We were not put here to be ruled by these crazy demons from another planet! That's why the pyramids are so crazy. You ever wonder how they got them so perfectly straight like that? *IT'S BECAUSE THEY'RE ALIENS!*"

It fades off as the sky sweetly sings, Justin's voice fading into background noise like the low humming of the small spinning wheels on the pavement below them. The joint burns and they slow down a bit; Justin's rant subsides as a content looseness begins to tug at his face. At that point in the trip they would turn on some weird music, turn it on real loud, full blast, hang one leg out of the car's window, sit far back, and enjoy their journey home. A seat leaned all the way back while the wind rides up into your pants leg as one foot hangs out the open window is therapy, absolutely. Peeps' ritual does not stop there, however. In the tub he'll smoke another dooby; the resonated roaches of his joints litter the side of the bathtub constantly, wet and stuck to the porcelain. By his nightstand is another one already rolled for when he wakes up, not just in the morning, but in the middle of the night, to smoke. He really doesn't care how much meaningless filth his job consists of or how filthy his room is, but take away his weed and you've got one discontented, pissy son of a bitch.

"Hey man, you got a cigarette?"

"A Kool, cool."

"Got a light?"

"Goddamn, you want me to smoke it for you, too?" Like this they would pass the hours away when off work. A constant game of one-upmanship and joking jabs kept them busy. Justin lived in the world of drug strewn confusion, he maneuvered well in it. He developed catchphrases that he would use repeatedly as the situation arose so he was never at a loss for words:

"Got a light?" John would ask.

"I am the light, John, what you seek is fire," he would say.

"Just shut the fuck up and give me a lighter."

Two weeks after they started the job, John was in jail. He was not going to climb that ladder, as it had so seemed. They had taken IQ and drug tests for the giant contractor to work in the filthy plant, and thought they were making damn good money. They thought it was money well worth driving an hour each way for as they stepped into the office, where they daily clocked in with their fancy Phosgene sensitive badges by swiping them through the blue box affixed to the wall. Confidently smiling and joking with the receptionist, they were not thinking of the day when they had sat and hoped their urine was misleading on their first visit to that same office. They certainly did not feel confident that day, although they had no trouble with the multiple choice evaluation. This one wants a "C.", this one wants that one. As line after line of puzzles asked which puzzle should appear next, they wandered the results of the other test, their drug tests, with hidden concern.

When they got their assignments, Peeps congratulated him. 'Electrician's Apprentice,' that was a pretty good assignment. It looked like he would do well there, being appointed to the cushiest job in the place for a starter. He liked the title, and he was happy about the hour long drive to work with his buddy. Confident he would thrive in this realm, he even sought to join the company soft ball team.

"Just not this weekend, guys, I have an important appointment in Houston this Friday," he told them. When John went to Houston to pay his probationary fines late that Thursday afternoon and completed his final meeting with Larry, his probation officer, he thought everything was going fine. He was ready to fulfill his duties and spend the rest of the weekend partying with his buddies. It was to be his last urinalysis for the city. After drinking nearly a gallon of water during the two and a half hour drive, he arrived at the probation office eager for the 'piss test.'

He told Larry that he did not have the rest of the money for the fines he owed, but that he would be getting paid tomorrow and would borrow the last 237.00 dollars from his mother if it could not wait until the next day. He was surprised to learn he did not need to take a drug test on this last meeting, and his probation officer told him it was no problem about not having the money today, all he had to do was take the papers to the court house the next day with his check. John was surprised by the civility and smiled as he casually crossed the Sun laden parking lot, got in his car, and sped off in search of the nearest restroom.

The next day, after the complicated nightmare of parking near the justice system complex downtown, he arrived at his appointment on time and was shown to a room. It seemed friendly. The cute, red haired secretary smiled at him as she rose from behind her desk and led him down a hall. As she took his name, she scrolled down a hand written list on her clipboard.

"Oh, yes, right this way," she said with a smile, looking up from under her eye lashes. Her eyelashes did not flutter. They covered just enough of her eyes to hide her intention, slowly squinting with precision.

Following her was instinctive. Walking down the hall and following her into the room to the right was an automated response; he followed her like a dog following the scent of sweet barbecued chicken. The thought of not following her never even crossed his mind. She exits silently as the door shuts behind him and he is left in a small room, standing before a standard, red stained wooden desk.

"This is hairy," he thinks to himself.

Two men in plain grey suits are standing behind the desk, on either side of the man who is sitting down as he receives the check for 237 dollars. The balding, heavy set man takes the check and hands him a receipt across the polished wooden desk. He had expected to just walk up to a window and hand over the check to a cute, red headed receptionist. To his half dazed mind, it's one of those times when it just doesn't feel right.

"Why are these two guys standing there while he takes my money?" he asks himself.

"Here's what's going to happen," says the brusque, fat man in the middle. "These two men are taking you to jail."

"For what?" he asks, his voice raising an octave in surprise.

"For delinquency on your fines," replies the man in the blue suit. "You have been issued a warrant for delinquent payment as of 12:00 AM today. You can show this to the judge," he states flatly, pointing at the pink paper receipt.

John folds the receipt up and tucks it in his sock, the only place he knows he'll be able to keep it safe, and wanders what in the hell is really going on. He'd been through this mess three times, sleeping with the crack monsters and car thieves in the 30 man cells and piss stained floors of the numerous processing tanks. It seemed like a big ordeal over two hundred something odd dollars. Turned around by his arms and handcuffed, he is escorted to an elevator in which they descend below the ground floor. The door opens to a familiar sight: cinderblock walls, metal doors and guards. After a quick signing in, he is led down a maze of halls, ever descending downward into the Harris County Correctional Complex. Muscles on his arms concentrate to hang completely limp. The springs in his fire hot neck fight themselves not to quiver. There is only one way to survive now, at this moment. He knows now that he is walking under streets and major intersections, beneath giant downtown structures, on his way to the processing tank.

"Here we go again..." Pale blue lights adorn the pale yellow cement walls of the tunnel's corridor. The slant of the walk is so subtle that you almost don't notice that you're descending as you plod slowly down the corridor. But as the oblique mirrors mark the end of each hall and you turn around to go the other way, the gradual decline becomes evident. It seems they've taken great measures to hide the fact that they're taking you deep underground. With hands bound behind your back in cold steel, for effect, you lower your head and just walk and wander why they would attempt to hide the decent, as if it matters, as if there is something you can do about it. Once you're down there, there is no one who can help you.

"Boy, I will beat your fucking ass!"

"But I'm not supposed to be here."

"Lower your goddamn hands!"

"I'm supposed to be walking with them; the judge said I was to go."

"Shut the fuck up! I will beat your fucking ass!"

He had seen the poor black boy drug down the hard cement hall and beaten the whole way. The eerie sounds of an 18 year old kid screaming and pleading for his life, echoing off the cement walls as he was drug down the hall behind mechanical steel doors, had haunted him. The stories on the news of people dying inside the complex took new meaning as the mentally blank guards took vengeance for their meaningless existences out on each case they could, right in front of anyone who may be around to see it. They were a uniform lot, crew cuts and pink necks lopping over the collars of their uniforms of blue shorts and button up shirts with the sleeves rolled up over their unnaturally fat arms.

In his cell, he made some new friends. Expecting to be free the next day, he had let his girlfriend paint his toenails sparkly, shinny orange the night before as they enjoyed each other's company and frolicked on the couch. Now exposed by the orange rubber flip-flops he had been assigned during processing, his toes began to present some concern to the other criminals sharing his cell. They were mostly car thieves and crack dealers, not violent offenders, really.

"Why the fuck are your toenails painted, essay?" the young Hispanic asked him from his table, surrounded by the rest of the Latinos sharing the cell. He was standing before the seated white boy with his out turned forearms displaying elaborate tattoos of mother Mary and pit bull dogs with his black hair slicked back.

"Because I'm a fucking faggot!" John yelled back, seated on the concrete bench of the table looking up at him. He held a maniacal, dead set stare on him for a moment, until the look of surprise had begun to turn to that of a group being challenged when he added, "Just kidding, man, my girl friend painted them last night. I didn't know I was coming in here! I mean, just last night, well like two nights ago... Shit! How long does processing take? Like a fucking week! It seems like just last night, at home on my couch with my sweet girl, watching the late show in my living room. What day is it, anyway?"

"It's Sunday," said the apparently slow boy in the back.

"Oh shit homes! We thought you were gay!" said the one in front.

As he grinned, laughter erupted amongst the group and the toenail polished boy fell into his normal routine of befriending everyone in the cell. It was like a summer camp to him, a chance to get three square meals a day in and catch up on some rest. Three days later, in front of the judge, he holds his tongue.

There seems to be some sexual relation between the thin man behind the bench and his young secretary who brings the folders containing each case before him. In his orange jump suit and rubber, jail issued flip flops, John feels the goose bumps on his skin and his nipples hardening in the frigid cold air of the courtroom. People in the seats behind the wooden wall dividing the proceedings from the audience are dressed in suits and ties to see the sentencing of their loved ones. He looks hard, but already knows that there is no one here who he knows. Handcuffed with his hands behind his back like a dangerous animal, escorted by a burly guard who holds him firmly by the arm, he enters the court room.

The judge has the unmistakable shiftiness and jerking movements which, combined with his happy arrogance, tells John that the man is on Cocaine.

"When I was a boy, I did some partying myself," the judge tells the boy before him. "But I straightened out my ways, and you should, too." He lifts the folder and says to himself, "Now what have we got here..."

John thinks about pleading his case, how the crime was never really his crime, how he was a good kid, the whole story, but he'd been through that too many times with no avail.

"I've got this." says the defendant, producing the receipt from under his shirt and holding it up hopefully.

"Let's see that," says the judge, nursing the small urge inside himself to find an excuse to be happy and reaching out for the folded up paper, which the prisoner has been hiding on the waistline of his orange jump suit for the last several days, since they took his socks and shoes.

"Paid in full," he reads out loud while peering under his glasses and over his Ned Flanders moustache, "Good job. Your case is dismissed."

Over 48 hours later, in the last holding cell, where people are being taken out to their freedom three at a time for processing, he watches the others stand before the last guard at the desk, through a gap in the metal door. The young guard chastises many of them before allowing their final release from the detention complex.

"What's with that earring, boy, you a faggot?" says the guard to the tall, thin, ebony skinned boy.

"No sir," he replies.

"Then why the hell are you wearing that gay ass earring!?" the guard thunders at him from behind his pulpit.

"Man, I don't got no time for this," he says, embarrassed and wanting to look tough as the female inmates stand in a line against the far wall, giggling at his predicament.

"You talk back to me, boy?" the guard demands in a roar, his hot breath rushing over the soon to be freed inmate as he leans over the tall wooden divider between them.

"Naw, I just..."

With that, before a clever remark could exit his mouth, the boy is taken from behind by surprise. As he jerks, he is smashed by a baton and wrestled to the ground, hog tied and drug down the corridor behind a slowly closing mechanical door in the punishing grasp of three guards. His screams begin to echo and resonate from behind the door, growing quieter and more distant as he is drug away. Standing before the same guard ten minutes later, John is asked if he is affiliated with any gangs.

"I don't believe in that shit." he replies. The guard's eyes raise from behind the paper with a credulous look in his annoyed face, as if this insolent prisoner is trying to make him out for a fool, and he says,

"What the hell do you mean, you don't believe in them?"

"I have to worry about my sisters and mother; I don't need to get mixed up in any of that stuff." He responds, as his penetrating eyes disarm the guard. He does not know that the jumpsuit clad inmate is practicing his form of mind control over the guard, excreting the juices in his own mind of serotonin and endorphins that cause the guard to feel instantly at ease and calm as he stares into his eyes.

"Well, that's good," he says. "I hope we don't see you back here. So long until next time," he mocks.

"I won't be back, I'm never coming back," he says plainly, as if reciting a simple math problem.

Again the guard's eyes raise alerted from the paper and, again, he is met by a measured smile that amounts to a wink. The gesture instantly makes the guard feel he is on the same side and page as the young criminal before him.

Out in the real world, John rejoins his old clan of buddies, finding them holed up in a familiar house in his old neighborhood, doing drugs. The lost youth of his time are not really so lost, just self proclaimed outcasts from a world they don't like. They are really the only ones with half a brain, mounting their own rebellion in their personal destruction, living in a self induced daze that keeps them from operating in this strange society. It wipes clean all their preconceived notions and leaves them free to see the world through a stranger's eyes. They reject the notion that their existence is for the sole purpose of operating as functioning pieces of this institution. They rebel against it in every way. They find music that is not music, joy in pain, and violence in sex.

Peoples is there, he is the ring leader of it all. John's arrest had also suspended his ride to work; they had both lost their jobs. Sitting on the floor in front of a litter strewn coffee table as he concentrates on rolling a joint, dim light reflects from his clean shaven head, which is large and symmetrical. He calls them all his brothers and seems intent on letting none of them join the workings of that big machine they all sense they are being groomed to operate daily by school classes and television ads.

They can see it all around them, it bombards their daily lives. The lines at the grocery stores where they buy their food are laced with insidious references to a normal life, one of consumption and high vanity. The products tell them that a pimple makes them unattractive, an old shirt of a past fashion is a sign of a weak mind, and that the reading of books is the sign of a weak body. Music portraying love is considered weak; the accepted musical taste for boys is in songs depicting strength through taking advantage of the weak around you. For girls, the mainstream of music focuses on sexual promiscuity, of finding multiple mates who drive certain makes of cars, of men who are dressed in certain ways to go to certain bars, of shoes and bags bearing certain designer names. Nothing points to individuality.

For Peoples, however, individuality is never a choice. His weirdness and stubborn mind guide him daily. He never could afford to judge himself up against standards of normality. His tough exterior fits him perfectly. He seems invincible as he takes blow after blow through life. His thick legs like sturdy oaks, his skin like hardened hide, sarcasm gets him by. He wins his friends over with a morbid humor while illustrating the futile hopelessness of their meaningless lives, urging them to strive for something more by constantly pointing out what they are not. Those weak ones around him fall into despair quickly and find their ways, badly tattered, back to their school and swim again with the other fish. Others, like the people now sitting in the dark room with them listening to instrumental music and playing video games, find a strength they never knew they had and begin to cultivate it and their own toughness through his cruel tutelage.

They forge ahead, doing nothing to better their positions within the machine, but opening new doors that will guide them through this foreign world mentally for years to come. They care not what people think of them and choose clothing that shouts that statement loudly. They wear golf pants and baseball socks, old bowling shirts and trucker's hats. They begin to understand each other without speaking, hours of mediation and together revealing the deepest crevices of their minds unto each other. They learn first telepathy, then to control their own minds, and then to influence the minds of others.

"It's not the drug, it's the juices from your own glands coming out. Did you hear about the lady who lifted the car off of her baby? She just picked it up; they say it was her adrenaline glands that made her 100 times stronger than normal. Then there is the serotonin gland, it produces something that makes you feel better, happy when you're sad. Everything from your sleep cycle to your appetite, to your body's tendency to age, is controlled within the mixture of your glands, even your sex drive." Peoples is speaking to the big, black eyes humorously as his reflection distorts within the dilated pupils.

"You feel that drip in the back of your head? That's adrenaline from your adrenal glands. If you rub your head right here... like this, let me do it for you... those are your serotonin glands and endorphins... doesn't that feel good?"

He grabs the skull of his tutor in his fingers and begins to massage. The captivated boy's eyes roll back as he feels a tingle of sensation running down the back of his head and into his neck like cold metallic liquid dripping down within him.

"There are glands that make your brain more susceptible to impression when you are a baby, they help you learn about your surroundings more quickly and help you survive. If you touch fire, you will remember it, and always remember it. Those glands go dormant after about six years of age, but they are very active right now. The poison placed inside you is poison to those glands, and they are expelling all of their juices simultaneously to wash the poison out of them. All of your endorphins and adrenaline and everything else is mixing together to make these sensations. As you come down, each of the glands will begin to run out of fluids. If you concentrate, you can feel them within your body as they peter out. There's one that makes you not notice your own smell, you will definitely notice that one later because you are sweating like a pig right now. The oil glands in your skin are even going nuts, look how shiny you look..."

The disciples of the mind soon learn that the chemical reaction born by mixing these secretions within their bodies causes a change in the pupils of the eyes. That is where the chemical side of falling in love comes into play while looking into a chemically compatible mate's eyes. That is where your internal fear makes your enemies more confident and your lack thereof makes them afraid. That's why they say to look at the eyes to learn if a person is lying to you. The chemical reactions taking place in your brain are displayed within the pupils, they signal primitively the flag for reactions that should be occurring in those around you. They work on the sub-conscious nervous system, the one that causes you to blink and flinch, to laugh and smile.

"The next step is to learn to activate these glands within your own mind at will, based on conscious command instead of just to the reaction to external stimuli. Try it while driving to work with a hangover or doing something you don't want to do, like driving to work. Touch the place where you felt those fluids secreted when you were happy and ask them to come out. Try this in every situation; make a habit out of forcing your brain to do the opposite of what it wants to in every situation. When you are nervous, be calm. When you are scared and your arms shake in apprehension, when you want to fight and lash out, calm yourself at the innermost level and let it move throughout your body. Regulate your breathing. Once you have mastered this, you have mastered your own mind. Now you know that your chemical reactions spurn the chemical reactions in the minds of those around you. At a subconscious level, flashes of information passed on by your eyes, telling the chemical makeup of your mind's very thoughts, guide the way people will react to you on a daily basis.

"Try it. Go into a gas station and force your brain to secret the adrenal and other glands associated with fear and panic. Don't say anything alarming, act normal, but feel those juices secreting in your brain. See if you notice the nervousness of the attendant as she is growing very apprehensive. Now, try the opposite: Calm your every though, let those endorphins roll out, but act the same way. Let the attendant get a flash of your eyes and see her worries melt away as she instantly, inexplicably, feels safer. See if you can make her slow down. See if you can get her high by swilling the juices in her own mind." His fingers twiddle above his head like fizzing sparklers.

"Try to get her really feeling good. Maybe she'll lose focus, turn and look out the window in a short moment of bliss spurned by the Sunlight coming in from outside, pouring into her now opened mind. It mixes with the chemicals swilling around in there like a burst of cold air. She reacts like a baby boy, peeing as soon as you take off his diaper, momentarily overwhelmed by the rush of sensations.

"You must practice to use your mind state to affect theirs, and you are learning the art of mind control. Now you can grab that pack of cigarettes from the display and calmly place them in your front pocket as she dazes out the window in a natural state of euphoria."

They practice their new tactics on those around them and each other, honing their skills in a game of one-upmanship until they can take it no further. With the presence of beer, the games grow from there...

"Yeah, you got it all figured out, but what about this?"

"What?" Peoples asks as he looks in the direction of Pickle's pointed finger, distracting himself from his video game.

As he turns to look back in his friend's direction, wondering what he was pointing at, he is met by Pickle's fist colliding with his chin.

"Mind control that, mother fucker!" the skinny Pickle yells triumphantly as he jumps from the edge of the bed away from the much larger man, fearing instant retaliation.

People's is far too lazy to chase him, but knows, in patience, his time will come. They have now taken their game to a new level; of training the mind against reacting to physical pain. The skill of controlling one's mind is refined to absorb pain without reacting, waiting patiently for the time of maximum revenge. It soon becomes their game of choice in most gatherings. The next morning, while Pickle finally sleeps, Peoples pees on the soft pillow where he rests his head.

They walk the street together as the morning Sun begins to illuminate the sky, roaming through high, dew moistened grass among the droids in their shinny cars lined up at traffic lights, who are trying to get to work on time. The clan is far removed from any sense of their realities. Each one consumed in their own little world, with their own super important deadline to meet and people to greet, planes to catch and coffee to fetch. Each one in their own world of supreme importance revolving around themselves. The outcasts listen not to the long stories about the heroic acts or comical tragedies played out by fast talking peers as they relate their vicarious lives they have lived through television programs the night before. They understand none of it; it is like Greek to their ears. They pass their days seemingly unnoticed, they are the children of the Peopocalypse.

By law, they are still required to go to the public schools. They do their best not to tolerate it, and get a never ending catch twenty two in return. Better acting under mild stimulants and sedatives, they find an easy way through the hours long days spent under humming florescent lights, under heavy medication. Gavin, who was just another one of them lost on the same trip, found his allegiance out of place with the students standing next to their desks with one hand over their hearts in pledge of a flag hung at the front of the room, as he sat atop his school desk and chanted to Satan in his own humorous rebellion.

His mind blown with hallucinogens, his desk becomes a boat upon confrontation by the teacher and he flips it over to begin paddling it out of the room, kicking with his legs and skating it right out the door to the polished floors of the main hallways and into the auditorium where the local police, by sheer coincidence, are giving a demonstration on drug awareness amidst the good students and school administration.

"I love Satan!" he yells in triumph, kicking the flimsy desk-chair down the aisle as the guards and police join in chasing him down and tackling him in dramatic fashion. He is scrambling, not to evade the officers, but to catch his desk-boat rolling down the stairs of the auditorium.

He kicks and cusses as he is brought to the floor by the five big men and one stout woman, who first handcuffs him and then electrocutes him with taser a gun.

"You're being tased!" she yells triumphantly, squeezing the

trigger with both hands.

As the battery runs out on the hand held device, Gavin begins spiting cerebral fluid from his mouth in unmeasured convolutions and seizures. The lady cop is still clicking the button, trying to activate her device for another light show, but is now realizing she's used the entire charge up on her yellow plastic tazing gun.

"Whew!" says the stalky woman in the red necked voice of a man who had just caught a big fish, "That was a live one!"

The administration couldn't have planned a better example of why they needed to keep drugs out of the school than the one who came in right on time, riding a school desk raft into the belly of the beast he lived in. The belly, tickled by the fire, had spit him out. He was not coming back to the campus. He wouldn't have to worry about officers coming to his home on the days he skipped school anymore; they did not want him there. Now he would be free to spend the days as he wanted, comforted by the surroundings of his buddies and dazed into forgetfulness by hard drugs.

Filtering through life the things they discovered, the band of adolescent friends drifted apart through time. Many would end up dead or in jail. Some would start families and conform to the rigors of everyday life, taking jobs and getting up early, forgetting their high hopes and idealistic rebellion each night as they retired to bed. Some would grow weary of the uncertainty of a place to sleep and seek peace, returning to their families or relatives in distant cities and opposite ends of the same towns, separating themselves from their faithful chorus of backup singers and taking on new identities amongst their new friends, assuming new roles in society. Some would get good jobs, some would get new boyfriends, and some would drop off the face of the earth and never be heard from again. Many would go un-remembered until an unfortunate event such as an early funeral would bring most of them together through a web of contacts which was too spread out for them to see and they would conjure among themselves memories of the days which seemed so long passed, as if another life had been lived in their drug induced haze only a few years prior.

John Flint was just another lost child of the Peopocalypse. Most days he opened his eyes not knowing where he was. Usually it was a small hotel room with the curtains pulled tight over the windows. The curtains were so effective in blocking the light, he usually couldn't tell if it was day or night until he drew them back.

He would lie in bed, trying to remember what day of the week it had been when he went to sleep and guessing what day it was now.

One day, upon awaking, his eyes refused to open. They were crusted shut by a layer of sleep that had formed on them, sealing them together during an epic nap which may have lasted for days. He knew he was awake, but he did not know where he was and he could not open his eyes, so he reached his hands up to his sealed sockets to find the rigid layer of crust over them and picked the hardened gew from his eyelids, digging it from the corners of his eyes.

When he opened his eyes, he saw a light coming in from an outside window, moving against the glass of a large sliding glass door. The luminous spots on the window moved in waves, steered by the wind directing shadows cast by the swaying leafs of trees, which the afternoon Sun's rays where passing in-between. The air outside was clean and the layers of swaying trees outside the window moved in a silent rhythm, making him feel very tranquil as he could see the motion in the gently moving spots of Sunlight on the window.

He had left the city, traveled across the country, and landed in the remote Southeast Texan Cyprus knees and Pine trees at a house along a rural highway. As the light played on his waking eyes, it started coming back to him. He had moved in with his grandmother after having all he could take in New Orleans. While carrying contraband to the towns along the highway corridor and living in a haze of uppers and hallucinogens, he had accepted the necessity to carry a gun. The valuable contraband had been driven down the long highway at night by white knuckles griping a rubber steering wheel and a steadfast devotion to the speedometer which was kept exactly 2 miles over the speed limit to avoid any attention from the I-10 Task Force on the arduous trip.

A fake name had been assumed to avoid the relationship being drawn by undercover cops, which he had began to suspect everyone of being. No one new who 'John Galt' was. Through his various dealings at raves and night clubs, he met hundreds of strangers and the suspicion grew into paranoia as every eye seemed to be secretly looking at him from behind and his every move seemed to be watched. The knotted pain in his stomach grew with his hunger, but the drugs and the stress would not let him eat as he tried to force the food down, chewing it and trying to swallow to no avail. The bread went dry in his mouth, it tasted like cardboard.

They stayed in hotels and slept through the day, then went into insane parties at night to sell their commodities in mass amounts, one at a time, to hundreds of strangers per night. The people at the parties wore outrageous outfits, fishnet stockings and masks, and crowded into the dark buildings to create their own reality while shrouded in flashing lights and fog. The revelers were deafened by the continuous thumping of subsonic bass for many, many hours as they walked in circles in the dark and painted the scene with their own imaginations. Negotiation became a master art.

"These pills are no good, they don't work," a highly fucked up individual would tell him.

"Ok," he would say, not arguing with them at all.

He had a fool-proof way of dealing with this familiar incident. "Do you want your money back, or do you want more of the pills?" Confused, the invariable answer would always be,

"We'll just take some more pills," to which he would respond;

"You stupid idiot. If the pills are no good, why do you want more of them?"

A dumb look would come over the disgruntled customer's face as he thought of an argument.

"Tell you what, how about I give you two of them for 30?"

"We don't have 30 dollars," they would say.

"Well, then go find it."

The pills might not have been spectacular, but they definitely were not free. If not for cash, they could use them to barter for other drugs. Pot was the greatest commodity and the hardest to find. Usually it was Peoples who did the bartering, popping up with rations of this and that, always just in the nick of time.

"Check it out, man," he said as he produced a big bag of horse tranquilizer from one of the oversized pockets in his jeans.

"Give me that."

Feeling sure that there were undercover cops in the bathroom and eager to feel high, John devised a quick plan.

"I'll just snort half of it out of the bag with this straw and you can do the other half," he told his friend.

"I don't think you want to do that."

"Just give me the damn bag," he demanded.

He inserted the rolled up dollar bill into the baggy and took what he thought would be a modest snort of about half. The powder proved to be deceptively light, for when he removed the makeshift straw after the mighty snort, the baggy was empty.

"Damn!"

He felt good as he strutted out onto the dance floor amongst the freaks in costumes swimming in the sea of vibrating subsonic bass. He began to feel as one with the people there as the waves of sound began to feel more and more like waves of water and the perception grew that they were all in the ocean together, swimming to the drowning beat.

A girl began to transform as he watched her dance. Serpentine movements of her arms guided the snake's heads which had become her hands as her arms grew longer, waving out before her like searching beasts of the sea. Gills and scales adorned her body as she turned reflective green and blue of oil slicked on water, reflecting the flashing light of the lasers. Another dancing teenager became hairy and orange, lifting his giant paws of feet up and down to the ground as he danced to the music, marching in place. Noticing the eyes upon him, he turns his head to glare back at the onlooker with a menacing grin, displaying rows of sharp, curved teeth in his giant monster mouth.

"Join the party," John thinks as he begins moving to the music.

His arms feel like long ropes of water-hoses being swung beneath him. Looking down, he sees that his own hands have grown mouths and become the heads of serpents, and that his fingertips have become long, sharp fangs.

"Fuck it. I always wanted to be a monster," he thinks, feeling his beastly form could take on anything.

At some point, after he has transformed into a completely serpentine animal and began slithering on the floor, he is collected and flown to the top branches of a giant tree by an Eagle which dwarfs him in size, and deposits him amongst the high hanging leafs upon a tree branch. A strange, internal panic grasps him as the thought stimulus to his hands goes unanswered. He tells his arms to raise and push him up from his fetal position, but they do not respond.

"I'm a snake," he remembers, "I have no arms."

Around him are giant birds of prey, contemplating his fate as they look down on the curled up figure. They see a vulnerable white mammal, fresh from the womb, unable yet to open his eyes. A giant blue bird hops back and forth, angrily rallying the others in chirps and cackles. Another black bird sits on a higher branch silently looking down over them, occasionally darting his yellow eyes around as if waiting for the best time to swoop in and gobble up his prey. The Owl is directing the others as to what they should do with their helpless meal. They all want to eat him. Of course they want to eat him, he is a snake.

Awaking in a dream while still dreaming, he realizes that he is lying on the floor in the lobby of the theatre. The birds of prey are actually some girls looking at him, unconcerned as they pass a glass weed pipe to one another. He rises and feels now more like a monkey or human primate in the rising Sun coming through the front doors of the theater. Around him, others appear as monkeys, too, walking with their shoulders slumped and their knuckles hanging loosely by their sides, scraping the ground as they file out towards the daylight penetrating the doors of the State Palace Theatre lobby. John pats himself down, feeling for his gun in the front pockets of his oversized jeans and the roll of cash in the back as he joins the progression.

The disoriented crowd migrates to Fontainebleau State Park the next day. With no sleep in sight, hundreds of them descend on its grassy landscape by the river and sit in circles talking gibberish or walking around in circles grunting unintelligibly like animals. They all stink and have lost the ability to ignore their own scents. Upon finding someone with weed, Peoples borrows the keys and runs to the car for the pipe. Just as he shuts the trunk of the vehicle, with the colorful, two foot long glass pipe in his hand, he is surprised by two horse-mounted park rangers riding up behind him.

They tried to get Peeps to stop as he ran through the river front park, but they couldn't catch him once he got into the trees and began weaving through the masses of people. He makes it back to under the big tree, where his buddy is waiting, and tells his story.

Upon hearing this, John begins to fret compulsively. There is only one exit from the park and he is convinced they will surely wait for him to leave and pull over the car on the way out. In the confines of the crowd, they debated what they would do next until he had made his decision.

The gun, the drugs, and all the money except for 500 dollars were snuck into a car Justin would ride in while they thought no one was watching. Their plan had been to meet in the next major city on the way back, Baton Rouge. After a little trouble finding his way back to the interstate and hours of driving over the Louisiana swamps, John arrived at the rendezvous point. He had waited at the gas station and called the number of the other driver repeatedly for hours before giving up. Alone, confused, and very hungry, he drove back to Texas.

The long, straight, and monotonous drive across the swamps of Louisiana lends itself to introspection, especially while alone. He did not have a clear thought in his head as his loud mind drowned itself out in fear and confusion, but a survival instinct finally took hold and he decided he would stop for good as soon as he crossed the Sabine River and live with his father's side of the family in Southeast Texas.

When the crust came off and he began to see things more clearly, his thoughts began to come back together, as well. His grandmother's house was frequented by visitors who came to drink coffee and tell stories. Old people who had seen it all treated him kindly and with great understanding, giving him kind, knowing looks of caring and wisdom in place of his blank stare when they looked at and spoke to him. Mostly he just listened. The daily breakfast and words of wisdom nurtured his body and spirit back into health over the coming weeks and months.

He eventually got word from his old buddy, Peoples. It turned out that he never made it to Baton Rouge; he had been arrested long before he got there. It seemed they were actually watching them make the transfer between cars and knew to yank the other car just a few miles from the park. The adrenaline, combined with the hard drugs, had proved too much for the compadre when he was arrested. In the back seat of a police car, handcuffed, he kicked out the window laying on his back and then used his head to break the other one once the police had hogtied him. The collect call came from Peeps' new residence at the Louisiana State Penitentiary.

Surrounded now by a new crowd, in a new world, John adopted new ways, their ways. He began to form bonds with people he met through his cousins, making new friends and starting new bands of comradery. He picked up a job at a local chemical plant in Port Neches. Not realizing how fortunate he was to have survived the maze which was his former life, he saw his thoughts transform among the spread out terrain of endless Pine trees passing by him on the roads as he looked out passenger windows of cars speeding down country highways. His mind had become functional and lucid, however, the car windows still seemed like movie screens and the reality of nature surrounding him seemed unreal to him. He did not realize that he was on a permanent trip as his mind continued to adjust and adapt to functional levels around the holes he had burned into it.

4. JOHN FLINT

John Flint was hot. The southern summer Sun was really coming down on him, on all of them. He looked up at the huge maze of metal pipes bouncing the Sun's energy off of their reflective gleam. It was a good n' hot day in August and he and the other refinery workers stood around the muddy area covered by wooden pallets and smoked cigarettes, talking about little to nothing but women, cars, tools, and fishing. The subject in these break circles always goes back to work in one way or another. There were different types of people who assumed the role of bringing the conversation back to the current or upcoming task. Daniel, the burley young welding Forman, had a great way of doing it. A lot of guys in his role would simply say,

"All right, back to work."

But Daniel would wear his white plastic hard hat all through the break, enduring the heat trapped beneath it, while signifying his position of foreman to the other men whose yellow hats hung by their sides in their hands. He would say very little, in fact, next to nothing unless you brought up fishing-poles, which would send him into a list of specs and models and how he used them yesterday out on the flats, catching Flounder, that Gar was good eating, some say, but he didn't like it, and so on. Towards the end of the break, he'd methodically lift his white plastic hard hat, revealing his matted blonde hair, and wipe the sweat from his reddened forehead with the back of his dirty hand.

"Weeeell,…" he'd say, "What was it we were doing?"

One of the less experienced hands would inevitably interject with,

"Oh, oh, we needed to get that coupling from parts and we needed Old Man Hodges's permission for that!" Then Dan would say,

"Well, why don't you go find him for that? We'll all have to wait to start back up until you get back."

Prompted by his own eagerness through a slip of the tongue, the lucky guy would be sent on a wild goose chase around the refinery, up ladders, over rafters, down man holes, climbing over pipes like some Spider Man for opening his big mouth. This time it was John. He should have known better and kept his mouth shut if he didn't want to be sent out on the chore. But, it turns out that John loves this sort of thing.

Sitting in front of a pipe joint, sanding and prepping, then waiting for the welding to be done by the welder, is exactly how most of these guys like to spend their day. The heat is oppressive, so exerting less energy becomes a survival tactic spurned by instinct. You must wear a flame retardant, one-piece suit, boots, and gloves to comply with safety regulations, as the Sun keeps the Southeast Texas humidity steaming above you in mirages of water everywhere you look. The moisture in the humid air becomes steam and water again, resting in an in-between state of matter mixed with airborne chemicals giving it a purplish glow. 'Take it easy' is definitely the course to be recommended. Stay hydrated, don't sweat too much, try not to breathe too hard.

John feels power in his wiry arms. He likes to grab the hot metal pipes made for bringing their gaseous mixtures from one vat to the next with his bare, callused hands, and lift himself over one pipe to stand on the next in order to take the fastest route to the top of the structure. He wears his harness, as required by safety regulations, but he never ties off. He could hear the old man's voice in his head,

"Just mind where you put your feet, somebody died last week when they fell into the cooling tower. A gruesome death, breaking every bone in his body as he spun and bounced off the web of steel pipes on his way down, they say he was dead before he hit the ground. He was wearing his harness, but he wasn't tied off..."

John gets to the top in record time. Mr. Hodges signs the perfunctory sheet allowing the parts depot to release the pre-manufactured valve to the certain department of the construction crew, as he is pestered about which pipe does what, where it goes, why it mixes it, and so on by John. The questionnaire can only be answered so far by the construction foreman; anyway, the rest is for the scientists and chemists. John takes a look around himself.

From the view on this diamond grated flooring at the top of the structure, the plant starts to make sense. There are the vats for the raw crude; those long pipes bring them here. Below you are the smaller vats where pipes bring different solutions and chemicals to mix at specified temperatures. By-products roll off there; here the pipes shoot up horizontally to shoot their flames high into the air, burning off their toxic mixtures safely above head. The heated water rotates up the vats in the spiraled pipes that eventually lead to the top of the cooling tower where, like a giant radiator for an automobile, the water is cooled by air as in runs back down the towers propelled by simple gravity.

He studies his surroundings for a brief moment and tries to take it all in. He can see the marshes out over the horizon where the inner-coastal canal runs its windy path to bring the barges and boats from the refineries to the vast oceans, then back again. His eyes squint to see the furthest point of the horizon. As he strains his eyes to focus, he dazes off for a moment, forgetting where he is. Then he gets back down to find the rest of the guys finishing up another cigarette, disappointed he had made it back so soon.

"You got the paper signed?" asks Dan.

"Yes'r."

"It's the right one, for the 4803 B?"

"Yep'r."

"For the four inch galvanized?"

"Yep."

"Good, now go bring the form to the parts depot and get the part."

The work field is mostly a mud pit. Not black mud, or even dark brown, but a gravely orange. The puddles coalesce and shine with a rainbow of chemical swirls, broken up by forgotten bolts and disregarded insulating tape partially buried in the sledge. By the end of the long day, the men are all tired, no matter how much shade they sought throughout the day. They all gather by the water troughs and strip away their protective suits.

It's a hilarious sight: A bunch of gruff men stripped down to boxers and work boots, grunting short jokes and insults at one another. Their naturally rounded body shapes contrast against the geometric surroundings and their pale, sweat cleaned skin to the grime all around them. John thinks about his project now, his painting at home. It's of her, lying naked with her sweet, 17 year-old breasts displayed proudly. He thinks of the curves and is suddenly taken to the beach. As the other guys joke and squabble over some missing tools or boots, he is somewhere else, totally away from them.

The next day, he goes to the beach. He rides the ferry across his familiar path and watches the big barges rolling out to sea from the upper deck of the boat. They are lonely, like a ghost ship going over the water, like a lone wolf crossing a barren dessert. He is surrounded by people on the deck of the public ferry boat, but in a daze watching the slow moving barges on the water and feeling comfortably alone.

Quietly, slowly, the cargo ships embark on their own path, leaving behind all familiarities of home, of land. He watches them quietly push towards the horizon in a disappearing line from the top deck of the ferry, which is pushing headlong into the brisk, whipping air. He sees the birds flying around him, keeping pace with the boat as they are dipping and rising on the invisible current of the wind. The fish jump from the water then submerge again. He feels his hair move with the breeze, stirring shivers on his arm and up the back of his neck. A bird floats beside the moving boat, effortlessly riding the wind. It glides parallel with his head, ten feet apart from him and hovering above the tumultuous sea as it flies alongside him. John decides that he wants to be like them.

"Wind is their play toy," he thinks, and begins to ponder in deep meditation.

"If evolution really did happen in the way they say it did," he thinks, "what thought process led to learning to fly? If it is true that your actions are dictated by your thoughts, when did birds of flight start thinking this way? Furthermore, what types of thoughts led to this? To their complex understanding of aerodynamics and their effortless ascertaining of their understanding? Surely the urge, or tendency towards free will, would spurn organisms in this direction, some primordial drive to leave the confines of earth and join the air, some primitive understanding of how the forces of nature work. An instinct for aerodynamics, a propensity towards physics, a basic understanding of the laws of inertia; surely they were born with them? The way each thought dictates the next thought, how these thoughts are transformed into circumstance, into being brought forth from the application of aptitude wrought from these circumstances presenting new decisions which require, in turn, new thoughts to answer new choices, has made them.

"Over thousands of years of 'evolution,' one singular, underlying theme in these culminating thoughts must be present, to dictate the decisions so homogonously in line with each other through thousands of generations in their direction until the being, through precision angling of choices made tangible, flies."

The questions of evolution run through his head, passed through a filter of all he has known and seen as he tries to figure it out.

"Hell, that's how Newton did it," he thinks.

Just then, as a cloud moves from around the setting Sun, the glow of the light's reflection laminates the horizon, making a straight line into the side of his watering eye, as if sent to wake him up.

He has been standing still with a limp face and steady stare for several minutes. Looking towards the light, it appears that the beam is making a straight line towards his squinting eyes over the water to form an arrow pointing at him. Silent voices speak to him. The light casts a setting of purples and blues, yellows and orange, in wispy streaks forming fingers that wish to envelop him, stretching across the sky. He feels the tingle within his skull as the cool ocean air rushes through his head from his nostrils and the wafting wind lifts his hair, gently rustling it about his head. His eyes glaze over, he stares deep into the Sunset and sees nothing as his mind becomes quiet, oblivious to the people around him who are wandering around and pointing at the fish in the water and throwing bread at the birds, as he feels the spirit consume him and fill his body and being.

He is one with the air, the wind, and the currents that move it. He is a piece of the direction, a speck of the matter representing the energy which is endless, perpetual, with the entire scope of existence. He is tiny in comparison to it, huge in his connection with it. It is giant and unending as at each end of the line there is a connection where it all comes back together. The universe is never ending, never beginning. His spirit begins ascension as he is lifted off the ground, feeling as one with the birds as he feels the wind wafting under his cupped palms and scooping upward at the back of his neck, making his skin tingle.

As the energy rushes down him, as he envisions it coming down through his head from a point on the top center, through his brain and neck, down the nerves running through his spine, and out towards the tips of his fingers. He imagines himself spinning through the air. Through the bottom of his feet, he feels the boat's upper deck moving beneath him and the reality sets in that, by gravity, he is tied to the platform and he opens his eyes.

The boat has reached the dock and is bumping the bobbing pylons in the bay as it is about to touch land. On the way down to the car, he remembers his last conscious thoughts of evolution. Considering what he has just experienced, the continued direction of his decisions and line of thought leads him one brick closer to laying the road based on what he'd already known.

"There's no denying it," he thinks to himself, "evolution is bullshit. God made the birds fly."

Upon arriving at the peninsula's end, the line of cars proceeds slowly out of the boat to the dock worker's waving baton. The people in the exiting cars pass the patrol cars stationed at the loading docks but do not look at them, choosing instead to look at the cars lined up the other way waiting to get on the ferry.

Driving down the old highway, past the old light house on the concrete road seemingly paved through the middle of cow pastures which are occasionally edged by small stores, motels, and restaurants, always brings John a sense of nostalgia. This is a trip he has made many times. He recognizes all of the neighborhoods, each of the faded signs in front of the subdivisions in-between the highway and the beach. All of the small hotels and convenience stores along the rustic path are familiar landmarks for him. He knows it is less than a half of a mile to the water on either side of the highway.

In high school, he used to bring her out this way to see her parents, spending the weekends on their couch and following her around the beach community. They walked on the beach and laughed freely, dragging their bare feet through the bubbling waves which were striving to work their way up the sand to the dunes separating the ocean from the houses and cars of the small town.

The water seemed so big, endless in its depth under the high

Sun, as she would tell him stories about her past and of the adventures she had experienced with the crazy people who lived in the beach community. As he looked out onto the ocean in contemplation, feeling as small as a single grain of sand in comparison to the vast expanse displayed out before him, he would listen nervously; worried he might say something that would make him sound stupid in response.

She was five foot seven with soft olive skin made into the color of honey glaze by the gentle kiss of the coastal Sun. Her slightly wavy hair was brown and she pulled it back into ponytails frequently, raising her elbows above her head to tie the knot. Each time she did, she secretly made sure her shirt rose above her mid-drift, exposing her beautiful, supple little belly. Her breasts hung like jeweled ornaments just behind her shirt. They were captivating to him, like a hypnotist's watch swung before his wide eyes.

She smiled as she talked, zealously explaining things in subtle expressions that she had become accustomed to him catching, as he was always watching her like a hawk. The curve of her eyes was set under her delicate eyebrows as she looked high and to the right and formed her lips into inviting curves when she laughed the days away with him. He just watched, listening to the words but not hearing the story.

Her ways were enchanting to him. Her active mind and spirit raised his consciousness, making him aware of every breath he took as he concentrated on how it felt, how it sounded. The moon was held in gravitational pull to the orbit of the earth and Sun, and he was her satellite, bound by her gravity as he felt an immense weight in her presence. The limbs of his body felt heavy as they sat together for hours in total silence, watching movies or riding in the car. The air felt heavy and the strange force even seemed to affect the mysterious march of time. Everything slowed down and became concrete for him under the spell of her intoxicating, wondrous ways.

She didn't say a lot of words to him, but the things she said stood out in his mind as he replayed them over and over in her absence. Some nights they would find themselves stuck some place, sharing a bed or a couch, and he would snuggle up behind her nervously, trying to regulate his breathing and control his raging hormones as he awkwardly tried to find a good place to rest his arm around her little body. She would sleep and he would lay awake throughout the endless night, looking over her and trying to muster up the courage to give her a kiss. He would follow her anywhere.

She felt safe with him. She gave her love freely to whomever she might please and he watched in silence as she dated other guys over the years, pretending his best not to be jealous, but going out of his way to prove some form of dominance over her lovers with every chance he got. She knew he would never hurt her. She knew he loved her, she knew his secret. Everyone did, it was all but evident by the way he spent every spare minute he could find escorting her around from the time she captivated his heart by the lockers next to the detention center in high school. It was a moment he would never forget.

She wore oversized men's plaid pants, which hung loosely from her shapely hips in a mockery of contemporary fashion. A stretchy, tight, sleeveless shirt contrasted her baggy pants and outlined her curvy torso. Long, brown, wavy hair hung over her tanned shoulders and onto her slender arms. The curve where her forearm connected to her wrist bone was exaggerated. It was an elegant portrait of design following function in his eyes. One hip stuck out further than the other as she rested her weight on one side, making a gorgeous curve out of her hips. He would never forget her in the hall where she stood smiling at him, with teeth showing and happy eyes beaming. He felt as if he was looking into a beautiful light, and from that point on he was captivated. He broke up with his girlfriend and spent his time trying to chase her down.

It was as if he had chased a rabbit down a hole. The maze twisted one evening into the deep piney woods behind her house. They walked through the shaded canopy in the late summer evening, sharing their minds as they spoke freely. He noticed his mind changing around him. Everything looked prettier, the butterflies were flying in a complex pattern around one another, the trees intertwined and wrought out fingers, crossing each other to form intricate patterns of black lines. The Pine trees were silhouetted by the pale yellow haze of distant sky light behind them. The soft layer of brown pine needles below them opened up to expose paths of fine sand under the bed of needles, leading down another corridor, deeper into the dimly lit woods.

The feeling of being displaced from his body was totally

unfamiliar to him. It was as if the air on his skin had become a drug, a soothing narcotic, stimulating him to exhilaration. It was as if he was living his purpose, as if there was nothing as exciting as life, and that his only part of it was just to be. He was in the moment, fully present, alive with all the possibilities and function life now offered. This was the simple pleasure that Zen practitioners yearn to find by writing books and training their minds. This, however, was nothing you could write a book about, it was nothing one could train for. It would be like writing a book teaching a seed how to grow. She had taught it to him with a smile.

Patiently it waited. The tiny roots sprung forth and probed downward for soft soil as the first green bud dug through to the topsoil towards the surface air. As the planet circled around the orbit, it collided with another planet and stopped. Chunks of fiery rock the size of California plummeted through space as entire existences of populations, complete with all their cares and worldly desires, incinerated into nothing but noble gases, free to float around without purpose or direction.

No one heard it explode, they were already consumed by the fire when the boom bounced back to them from across the cosmos and sent its subsonic waves outward into space. It was like a tiny collision of planets when the bud sprang forth, when the lifeless seed clicked like the hour hand of a watch. Life sprang forth. Every thought they shared fed the growth of the fragile thing as it anchored itself slightly more so, gripping into the fertile dirt like fingers clinging to the soil, while the inertia of a spinning planet tried to pull it away. Trust was established and built upon through shared secrets, souls were exposed as the pliable bonds hardened, and a rough, protective bark formed around the body of their tree.

The bonds they formed were too important to be jeopardized. In moments of lust they held themselves in a great imitation of chastity, saving their animal lusts for the people they felt the least close to. They watched each other amuse their desires with others while remaining close friends through it all. As others drifted apart, pulled by gravity away from their universe, they kept the bond.

Before it all came to its potential end, he had held her in his mind as the ideal to be achieved, ignoring their other relationships and rationalizing everything in his own mind. While he drove down the highway of the peninsula, he thought of her and how happy she would be to see him. It had been months…

The bar where he thought he would find her was full of locals, most in cut off shorts and sleeveless t-shirts. The people of the beach, always tanned and seemingly worry free, were in the same place they always went, doing the same thing they always did. They were tossing back a couple of beers at their local bar. John, barely 19, was doing something he had never done: sitting in a bar and being served beer. As he waited for her to show, he made some friends. Talking about whatever they wanted to and just being happy to drink beer in a bar while underage came naturally to him, as if it were a hobby he had been practicing for many past lives. They talked about the football team, fishing, the local police, and everything in-between while they shared platitudes and laughter.

He became increasingly buzzed with each round, spending his money to buy shots of whiskey for the new found friends and for familiar songs in the juke box. The afternoon became night as the daylight disappeared without notice. The long blonde haired man's wife became more attractive and unfamiliar every time she passed by his spot at the bar, her swaying hips beckoning as she passed, and his teeming hormones led him back to thoughts of the girl he had come to see. He began asking about her. The bartender knew her, as it seemed everyone there did. Of course, her parents owned the place. When his mouth began to ramble without control, he started catching strange looks from the people around him.

The last thing he remembered saying was,

"I'm only 19,"as the beer was yanked from the sticky wooden bar in front of him and it became evident that it was time for him to go.

Once in his car, the strange reality that he was in a remote beach community, where he knew almost no one, began to set in. The car key seemed foreign to the ignition as he fumbled it into its hole. He turned the switch to 'on' without starting the car in the sandy parking lot next to the bar and the radio began pumping music through the speakers. Where was she? There was no way to know. He thought about driving to her mother's beach house, but decided against the possibility of showing up unannounced and finding her off somewhere, probably on a date. His head felt light, he was drunk, and he rested back into his seat and began to fade into a restful nap.

BANG! BANG, BANG!

The pounding on the window wakes him as he shoots up in his

seat, thinking he is still in the dream where submarines are launching rockets at his ship. He looks back and forth in confusion until he realizes he is in his car and sees Peoples banging on his window in the parking lot.

"Whaaat are you doing?" Peoples asks in a puzzled voice, peering through the car window with a cocked head as John rolls down the window.

It had been over a year since they had seen each other. Peoples wore his patent smile of mischief and curiosity as he looked at him strangely. Some of their old friends were there behind him with a few unfamiliar faces who were looking at him as if some violence was about to go down. Their worry turned to glee as John responded,

"Man, what the hell are you doing here?"

"We came for the rave, on the beach." Peoples said simply.

"Cool! Where's it at!?".

"Well it's not gonna be no-where with this big storm coming in," replied Peeps with a tone of sarcasm.

"Man! When did you get out? I had no idea. Cool! Good to see you! So, no rave? Oh, well, what's the deal?" Said John, eager to band up with someone he knew and reminded of the old times by the presence of his old partner in crime.

"I don't know. We could all drive back to Houston. OR, we could go see what Francis is doing?" he proposed.

The thought of going there with a bunch of people seemed like a much more victorious idea than showing up alone like an orphaned puppy after she failed to meet him at the bar as planned, so he agreed. In a line of cars, they caravanned the familiar path to Francis's mother's house. When they arrived, it seemed some others from the old days had gotten the same message. Cars were lined up down the sleepy neighborhood street in front of her mother's beach house. She comes outside and greets them as they arrive.

"I wanted to come, but I've got all these damned people here!" she exclaimed, excitedly greeting her new guests.

The downstairs of the beach house had once been used for showering up after fishing trips and cleaning fish or cutting bait. Now, it was the spot for the kids. There were three double beds on the concrete floor and another pair of bunk beds against the back wall. A TV against the wall was the typical focal point, as boys and adolescents beginning to show pubic hair under their arms waited their turn to play the video game. As the entrenched youngsters watched unflinchingly the fighting characters on the screen, the new arrivals waited to be introduced to one another. It was easy to distinguish those who had been drug into the madness for the first time.

Being the one who had been away; they all wanted to know what Flint had been doing. He told them about the great machines he'd been operating and the strange new way of life he had adopted with the guys in the small town. Peoples's new young disciples sat quietly in reverence of his old best friend, hanging onto details of the stories of glory which they shared in memory throughout the night. Of course, Peeps had brought drugs to supply the rave and was now completely overstocked. The black paper squares with the white bubble patterns printed on them came out after the beers had loosened inhibitions, and loose deals were made to pass them around.

Everyone got to participate, even the dog got some. Francis's little brother and the strange kid who seemed too young to be there both got their first try at the mind altering drug. Forgetting the concept of time in the whirling sensations of streaking light, they all walked down the crudely paved road to the beach in the dark night, hollering at the moon and each other as they scampered barefoot and careless down the sandy road to the water's edge.

The night air blew furiously on them from across the water. A gigantic storm was out in the gulf, approaching over the black waters of the night towards their sandy shore. Looking out over the ocean into the darkness, the still night's sky opened up to a semi circle of clouds wrapping around them. The storm was coming in over the water towards them. It looked huge in the great open sky. Its high clouds, occasionally revealed by lightening, rose up like walls pushing towards them in an ominous stance. Peoples, Francis, and John walked past the rest of the group as they trotted down the beach, trying to share thoughts as the others kept catching up and annoying them.

The long, empty beach stretched out before them like their very own playground in the night, as the group kicked the sand carelessly and frolicked along the shoreline. The scene conjured abstract thoughts about existence amongst them, which were constantly interrupted by the others running up and to them and asking questions about what they should be doing, where they were going, and what was going on. While the three of them got a ways ahead of the others on the beach, they found the solution to their problem. They had it all figured out when they decided to walk out into the ocean.

There was no room for questioning safety in their minds as they waded out into the dark water. They felt fish brushing up against their jeans as they trotted out, the water slowly edging up their legs and crashing higher on their bodies with each wave until they reached a sandbar where the water was only a few feet deep. 50 yards out into the water, they sat on the sandbar and looked back to the shore.

Their friends were running back and forth, trying to find them and confused as to where they had gone. They could not see them there in the water under the veil of night, even if they had thought to look out towards the ocean. Now they were free to share their thoughts with each other silently, just the three of them who where sure that they understood the best that they could. The lights of the stars shone lucid in the sky, sometimes moving and pulsating with the will of their imagination. They looked out into the ocean's sky and watched the storm shoot lightening into the water in the distant horizon as it formed around them.

"This is our island! We can live out here, never have to go back and deal with their bullshit!" John proclaimed, watching the others run up in down the beach in utter panic from the sandbar, where they sat amongst the black waves beneath the oncoming storm.

Like cartoon Greek gods in the sky looking down from a cloud, the friends could hear the others and see them, though they were unseen and their voices were masked by the waves crashing onto the sandy beach in the black night. They shared the moment in some subtle reverence as the lightening crashing across the gulf occasionally lit up the night, not knowing it would be their last shared moment for a very long time. They had no way of knowing that the storm's brilliant display served as a symbolic goodbye to their careless youth.

Walking back to the beach house, John manages to catch her in his eyes, holding her in a long silent stare. A flashing light from the arching lightning over the water flashes in her eyes, revealing their brightness and the light that seemed to emanate from within them.

"This light is mine; I'm going let it shine," John sang.

5. BURNING FOR STEAM

As your eyes begin to flutter rapidly under closed lids, a force propels you, something beyond your control. Flying through ascending clouds, you grasp at rushing air passing through your outstretched fingers while plummeting downward at unbridled speed. As the wind lifts you by your outstretched arms, you see an airplane flying next to you, so you land on its wing and look inside. There you see your lost love, the one who really understands you, and you share a brief, sarcastic smile with her.

You decide to go into the plane. There is a wide array of people in here… Why, that's strange, there is your aunt. And what is your brother doing here? You shuffle through the aisles looking for something, you forgot what. Just as she comes to your mind, she appears in the row ahead of you. Good, you've found her now.

The craft you are riding in is traveling a vertical line from the earth and you can feel your body becoming lighter as it ascends, carrying you spaceward at an insane velocity.

Now the dream takes a strange twist. The plane is spinning around as it rapidly descends from the atmosphere of space, leaving the moon and blackish blue of space-sky behind as it plummets to the earth. Your body feels heavier and heavier until the pressure of gravity feels as though it might crush your skeletal frame. Your guts seem to be rising up in your body as you fall through the sky within the aircraft. Abruptly, the airplane levels off and you feel your stomach settling down into place as the plane pulls up over a big lake.

The landscape is serine, green pine and fir trees outline the edges of the deep blue water under a still, cloud dotted sky. You feel at peace, although the airplane is still speeding furiously and the people inside are strapped back to their plastic seats by the centrifugal force of speed pinning them like bugs on a windshield.

It was all a vacation, a field day, that's all. Now that you can see you've landed on the lake by the school playground, you know that it is time to go back to classes. The seat you are in is like a giant plastic booster chair, hollow and industrial with some stenciled numbers painted on the back in black. You are buckled in, safe, with nylon belts crossing your chest and pinning your legs.

"Good to go? Alrighty, then! Off into the water with ya!" says the bus driver.

Once tossed into the water, you bob and float to the shore in the big chair, in an organized manner with the others who you strain and twist your neck around to see floating in line behind you. Bobbing in the water, safely strapped to your giant, hollow plastic chair, you can see the familiar sight of your old school building ahead on the shore.

Upon reaching land, you are let out of the chair and find yourself on the side of the school building where the busses drop you off every day. You recognize the familiar schoolhouse. You know what to do so you drone towards the entrance where the other children are herding together, bottlenecked by the single opening on the long, tall brick wall. Upon filing inside the yellow cinder block walls through the pale blue painted steel door, they direct you all to long tables in the cafeteria.

"To find your assigned table, just match the color of the card we gave you to the color on the table... Oh... A crimson one? We don't have many of those..."

He wakes in a cold sweat. As he opens one eye, then the other, he realizes he is back in his little house, looking at the artwork he has done through the years and pictures of his high school friends on his bedroom walls. The wallpaper made from speeding tickets, newspaper clippings, photographs, and flyers covering the bedroom walls from corner to corner, reminds him that he is in the bedroom of is own home. He's not a kid in elementary school anymore, and he is relieved to know so. In the cold morning, it is nice to have the two big dogs pushing their backs up against each side of him.

The two heads of the same dragon are arguing again, as they do each morning when they wake him through the tiny speaker in the alarm clock. A quick slap of the snooze button shuts them up. Trying to return to the world of his dream, he quickly falls back asleep until the voices blare through the speaker again 15 minutes later. Comfortable and seduced by the softness of his warm sheets, he resists the temptation of going back to sleep one last time and rolls onto his back, pushing his legs and arms out in a gratifying stretch, and sits up.

"Get down dogs, let's go outside."

As he opens the door to let his companions into the backyard, a frigid chill gusts in on him and he closes the door quickly in order to keep out the cold air. The voices continue to blare from his alarm clock. They are talking about an elderly lady who had been pulled over and subdued for 'resisting arrest.'

'Well, Sam, don't you think the woman had some rights?'

'No. I don't think she has any rights. When an armed enforcer of the law directs you, you do what they tell you to do, that's all there is to it.'

'I don't know Sam; it might be sending the wrong message. Okay, on to our next caller, Gene, You're on KLBS.'

"Hi, Billy Bob, great listening to you guys. I just wanted to say, if that old lady didn't want to get tazed, she should have done what the police man told her to do. I mean, what kind of 73 year old woman thinks it is okay to do whatever she wants?'

'Good question, caller, it's hard to argue with that.'

John goes to his bathroom where he looks into his mirror as he gapes his mouth open, leaning over the sink close to the mirror to look at his broken tooth as he scratches his scrotum in a drowsy morning haze. Abruptly, he yells loudly in utter pain, emitting a battle cry that turns into the dragging moan of an approaching fog horn. The muscles pull tight around his jaw, jutting his bottom teeth forward to emit the cold morning air into his mouth and rushing the chilled particles across the exposed root of his bottom back wisdom tooth. It sends a dull pain through his jaw, into his ear, and pulls at the muscles around the back of his neck tight in tension.

'Well, there's no arguing with it, you just can't argue with the law. Besides, it probably just charged up the battery on her pace maker. We'll be right back after these messages!'

'They're lucky it wasn't my grandma,' he thinks to himself.

He goes back to his room and turns off the small electric space-heater, then into the kitchen where he tears a fresh swatch off of the paper towel roll to fashion a coffee filter, then measures out a few scopes into it and starts his coffee. He turns the griddle up to just past medium and pulls pan sausage, eggs, and tortillas from the refrigerator. He takes a quick shower, eats the breakfast while watching the morning news on television, shaves his face, ties his tie, and goes to work.

Next, he drives the few miles down the country road to the highway where, cars are already lined up waiting to turn onto the congested road feeding into the freeway, before remembering that he forgot to brush his teeth after he ate and uses a toothpick to clean the crevices of his sturdy front teeth. How many minutes are in a day? He turns on the radio.

"In other news this morning, a Chinese flag will be flown over the Whitehouse today in honor of the People's Liberation on this day in history and the accomplishments they have achieved since that time. The president has announced today local deputies and sheriff's offices will no longer be free to do as they please." The news clip breaks to a cut of the president's voice.

'We realize that there is a need for accountability and uniformity in the dealings of the law. That is why, for the first time ever, local law enforcement agencies will be working directly with the international enforcement agencies to ensure consistent delivery of the laws we have enacted.' Abruptly, the anchor woman's soothing but direct voice cuts back in.

'The stand off with the 'Children of Abraham' cult came to an end in the early hours of the morning when their compound burned to the ground. According to authorities on the scene, none of the 60 plus residents survived. Here's Kevin Shimick with the weather and stay tuned for traffic updates. Kevin...'

Once on the huge interstate highway, he plods a few feet at a time for the next hour on his way into the city, surrounded in a sea of marooned automobiles. People smoking, women doing makeup, someone sending her boyfriend a last minute text message on her cell phone about where she was last night, another calling his boss to say he'll be late, again. This damned traffic!

They all share a similar trait: they don't want to be here. Some come from even farther away. Who knows how much time the millions of people who make up the working class spend commuting to work every day in the city? It's hard to say, but for easy math, let's call it an hour each way, times five days a week. That comes to 10 hours per week, which, multiplied by 52 weeks, equals 520 hours every year. It's a good thing we learned to stand in line during our first day of kindergarten, looks like it's prepared us for how we will end up spending 25 thousand hours over the next 50 years of a monotonous life.

'Lisa, tell us about traffic.' From the car radio, the beating sounds of a helicopter backdrops the young, attractive sounding voice of the announcer.

'The North South Interstate is backed up from Aquafine, all the way into downtown, it's bumper to bumper. Expect a one and a half hour commute coming in from the loop. Also, if you're heading westbound, you might want to consider an alternate route. It looks like if you're just getting on at Granite Rock, you'll be there for a long, long time. Up next we have Deuce Schmuckerman with Your Eye on Sports."

The woman in the little, beat up, black and grey Honda in the next lane is really there today. She's looking damn good, her hair teased up and groomed with every strand accounted for, plastered in its proper place. Her lips are red as blood, her facial features all perfectly accentuated by her expertly applied make up. From the view of her through the car window, she looks to be wearing a nice business suit. It is conservative and business like in navy blue and cream pinstripe, with just enough cleavage showing to please her old, perverted boss.

He watches porn routinely and saves money with his buddies for their bi-annual trips to Vegas. His girlfriend doesn't know that it's not his boat, and his wife doesn't know that his secretary's roommate is making a new hobby out of pleasuring him in increasingly public places. He drives a Beamer and pays the lease. His watch is fine and he smells clean, of expensive cologne and professionally cleaned shirts.

Damn the cold. It makes John's teeth ache in its frigidness.

Each of the blackened caverns through the soft tooth pulp in the three broken teeth are lined by razor sharp ridges of jaggedly broken tooth enamel and end at the top of a long nerve. One of the exposed nerves travels up to his eye under his face, the other carries a dull throb of crushing weight, like a foot standing on his bones, down one side of his jaw. The root ends at the terminal of the stimulus-sending pipeline which extends down his chin bone, connecting to the root of the rest of the lower teeth, which makes them feel as if they were also aching. He thinks about the mean little dentist with his fancy spinning tool in disgust and contempt as his eye twitches in pain. It has been 10 years, but he remembers it like yesterday.

"I've set you an appointment through Medigiv, you're going to be there, right?" she said. Although they lived on separate ends of the giant city, she still tried to ensure he took proper care of his health. The warm sound of his mother's voice still touched him in those lost days of adolescence.

He would never forget the office built into a stripmall in the sprawling outer metropolitan reaches of the city, where teenagers practiced sex for sport and small infractions and tiny tragedies went unnoticed. From a bird's view, the rooftops stretched out for miles. Squares of burnt orange shingles were orderly arranged within white outlines of pavement streets, blurring into a dotted pattern as they stretched out towards the horizon. Each block within the grid represented a microcosm; beneath each roof was an all important struggle.

Stepfathers were molesting daughters with full consent. While a father watched Eastern European sex slaves being raped via internet on his monitor for free, his daughter was upstairs experimenting with methamphetamines via hypodermic needle. In the maze of subdivision streets, there were mothers rushing to hospitals where son's mangled bodies from car accidents clung to life via artificial respiration. There were one million tragedies in a one mile radius amid the suburban sprawl.

A magazine in the lobby from a few months ago, a window to an office with a clipboard of sign-ins on a narrow shelf in the window, dull florescent lights and fake Palmettos; it was like any other dentist's office. At that very moment, one looking down from high in the sky would see it within a maze of buildings and intersections. Statistics would tell him that within the metropolitan grid consisting of a few hundred square miles, there were hundreds of teenage daughters having sex with their boyfriends before their parents got home from work. Countless youth were getting high and thousands of middle aged men and women were hiding from Sunlight in dark bars. Someone was being arrested, there were people being robbed, and, in the span of a breath, someone would surely die. There were a million soap operas going on at once, but only one at a time in the tranquil dentist's office.

Stealthy, the pretty young attendant escorted him back to the room, where her gentle persuasion had him laying in a contoured chair, on his back, without resistance. He looked up at the swing arm of the unlit light above him, noticing the shiny reflections of the metal and the precise machining of the rounded joints at the pivot points in the placid operating room. The cool leather of the chair was all it took to relax his sleep deprived body after the last few days he had spent running around and enjoying his youth, perspiring in the humid Houston nights.

A natural meditative stare of pre sleep was overcoming him when the slanted eyes abruptly seemed to appear from nowhere above him through the thick glasses. His eyes seemed grotesquely oversized behind the lenses magnifying them. The little Asian man gave allusion to a mad scientist in his white draping jacket, which was far too big for him, as were the frames of his glasses and his ears. With abrupt commands, he had John's mouth agape and his head leaned back over the contoured cushion. He poked and prodded at John's mouth with a carbon steel pick, pushing it deep into the teeth each time he probed, making concerned observations to himself.

"You need bwaces." he stated.

"I don't need any damn braces. I like myself just how I am. I'm a naturalist," responded John, shocked that someone would try to sell him a medical procedure like a paint job on a car.

The medical aid program his diligent mother had enrolled him in guaranteed payment from the government organization which funded it, anything the ambitious immigrant doctor could get the juvenile to agree to would be paid for without protest or delay.

"Is almowst the yeh 2000, the yeh of the pafac pason. You

down juan new go inew the new miwinium wiff teef like dat, do you? Dwo you know any won who has bwaces? No? And why do you fwink that is? The popuwah peopew at your schew, do they have stway teef?" The south Asian dentist's lackluster attempt at a sales pitch, made worse by his almost unintelligible accent, served to make the rebellious teen even more mad.

"Man, I don't need you trying to sell me something when I come in here to get my teeth checked up. Is that what you do? Just do your thing that you're supposed to do and let me go. I've never even had a cavity, my teeth are fine," John tells him brashly.

"OK," he says, "I do the queening, way bak down, way your head bak now."

With that, the little man goes to work. His pneumatic tool spins the abrasive edge of his cutting utensil, easily sinking into the tooth, making the hard enamel seem like melting plastic under its precisely focused power.

"Ouch! What the hell!" John grunts through the stints and cotton balls in his gaping mouth.

The dentist settles him and commands him to relax. Again he penetrates another tooth with his tool, then another, trying carefully to sink his hole just below the enamel of the newly forming wisdom teeth. He tries not to rouse the boy's contention while he works. The vindictive little man laughs inside at his evil scheme. His personal revenge was finally serving him well now, 10 years later, as John plodded down the highway to work and rued his aching tooth.

The immigrants riding alongside him in the back of the multicolored pickup truck are probably really starting to feel the moisture in the frigid air, now that the traffic has started moving. Bundled in scarves and blankets, with only their eyes showing as they pass in the rusty truck bed, their glares are set like warriors on the way to battle. The orange back fender and green front fender of the beat up white pickup truck are like swatches of a Calvary flag celebrating their heritage, leading the battle cry on the march to some dirty place to do battle like Scottish savages; their axes and long bows being nail guns and jack hammers.

Wondering if the bundled men have any holes in their teeth, returning the blank stare, John imagines he is behind the man's eyes, looking out at himself. He waves at them to say 'hi', but they just stare at him as if a wave were a language they did not understand, some strange, foreign tongue. After a moment, one raises his hand and waives back, holding steadily the emotionless gaze.

His mind is not with you, or even concerned with any of this. He is thinking of her as he lays his mortal body down in a soldier's servitude; of her young, supple face, her innocent, delicate vulnerability. She is back there, with her ailing mother. She is raising their child alone in a world where the polite platitudes towards the vulnerable are not so common as they are in this fluffy world of plastic debit cards and expensive but cold coffee.

It's better for her here, safer. He wants to bring her here. That is why he sleeps on the floor of a filthy dwelling and wears the same three outfits all week long. That is why he does not smoke cigarettes, he does not eat out or join his friends at the titty bars on paydays. His only diversion is a payphone and green plastic international calling card that he buys from the gas station on payday. He works for a wage John would never dream of working at and he works harder than anyone. He will work mechanically in the hot Texas Sun or in the wet sludge of mud that pulls at his boots until the Sun descends and they take him back to the crowded apartment where he sleeps. He doesn't care what joy his body finds here, he really just hopes she's okay.

His life is not important to him; his body is just a vessel to forge a little further on. He doesn't really think of the people who will dwell in the apartments he frames, nor place any symbolic significance on the structures he builds. The giant buildings quickly go up, providing a rotating dwelling for thousands like him in the years to come, but he holds no delusions of grandeur. He is numb as he rises daily to wait for the truck to pick him up, deadened to the piercing stares of those around him who shoot nails in his skin with their condescending looks. A life spent in sacrifice is what is expected of him now, and it alone is his great accomplishment.

He does good work by his boss. He is good with a nail gun and operates it unflinchingly, as he fires off the rounds with rapid accuracy. Bang, bang, bang! The .22 caliber rounds fire the nails into the two by fours, wedging them firmly to the boards behind them. Bang, bang, bang to the other, quickly the structures are erected as skeletons awaiting their skin, with every internal function accounted for in the skeletal frame of the housing unit he is erecting.

There are the marked beams to carry electrical wires along them, the places for the light fixtures, appliances, and plumbing. There is, of course, the spot for the air-conditioning. It has vents that run through, shiny and insulated versions of arteries and ventricles. The ventilation system is the heart of the building, the building is the heart of the machine.

The people living here will turn the all important wheel; they will all make it go around. They'll file through the corridors of it like marching little ants as they busy themselves with their daily doings for years to come. They will do their laundry, cook their food, and wash their dishes here, before they find time to talk on their phones and watch TV. They will go to work and stock grocery shelves, fabricate airplane wheels and unload cargo shipments. They'll turn hamburger patties off of microwaved Styrofoam onto the toasted, sesame seed buns and add your tomatoes and lettuce. Do you want a combo with that?

You will take the food with you to your various places as your tight schedule requires. To the office as you eat in the car, to the car wash, to the construction site, you'll eat that food and you will hurry to do what it is you're supposed to do. You'll burn that energy entering data into computers, counting the deposit for the bank, and connecting calls through the network like electrical thought stimuli of a brain transmitting through the body. You'll push like blood through the corridors, supplying vital components to some limb of the body and allowing it to move with purpose.

The purpose is life or death, always of upmost importance. Those numbers need to be in by noon in order to get the deposit to the bank, the inventory must be completed on time so that the order can be placed for the pickles. If not, we will go without pickles for the whole day, causing hundreds of people to miss out on pickles, and it will all be your fault. Something tells the heart to beat. It must beat so it requires fuel, sugar, carbohydrates. It must have a way to convert that raw food into energy it can use.

The entire life cycle of a pickle contained in your snack. From the storage of the seed to its eventual packaging and distribution on automobiles and trains, their roads and tracks forged through forests and mountains to the place where they will be planted into the ground. In the soil, the seeds begin the process of absorbing nutrients from the dirt and energy from the Sun and spreading out along the ground as happy, fuzzy little vines, soaking up the water around them veraciously and storing it within until the time when the flowers begin to emerge. Bright Yellow, delicate pedals fan out and slowly show the culmination of all their hard work as they produce the fruit of all their labor: the hearty Cucumber. Someone must be watchful and careful to harvest the green gourds on the right day. If they are taken off too early, or a few days too late, they just don't taste right. Shudder to think of the hands they touched in the bottling, slicing, and prepping of the three little pieces of that precious little fruit hidden between your meat and your bread.

Don't think too much of it. You need a good meal. You need to work all day; you've got a lot of bills to pay. At supper you'll have something better, maybe a steak. You spend your day responding to a strand of emails and answering a constant barrage of phone calls and requests. You walk between the offices and bring messages of this or that, you laugh and you joke, you enter some inventory into a database.

On the way home, watching the Sun go down behind the brilliant array of colors silhouetting dark grey clouds, you pull off from the bumper to bumper traffic of the highway to get some gas. You put in half a tank, just 20 bucks. In the men's room, you watch yourself peeing in a trance brought on by the sound of water running into the ceramic bowl. It's disgusting. Dark yellow sediment looks up at you from the toilet bowl, slimy and glistening. Raising your eyes from it, you look at the glossy advertisement on the wall directly in front of the stall:

A smiling young man stands with one foot on a yacht and the other on the dock as he helps a woman onto the boat. She is wearing a string bikini. Her long, slender legs are tan and her blonde hair is fluffed over her grateful smile as she holds the man's hand. Behind them, the beautiful lake reflects the Sunset. At the bottom of the picture is a caption reading:

"Call the Royal Yacht Club for 'your' boat today;" followed by some contact information. At the top of the picture in bold letters the banner reads:

"SHE'LL NEVER KNOW IT'S NOT *YOUR* BOAT."

The six-pack of beer and the gallon of milk costs you another ten bucks, not to mention the gasoline and the self congratulatory pack of cigarettes. You can do okay, you deserve it. You bring home about 100 bucks a day, after your taxes. That was 40 of it, but I wonder how you'll spend the other 60? Perhaps some entertainment with your lady could put out the fire in your pocket?

The boy at the counter of the movie store is in high school. You look at him and remember when you were that young. You were working until after midnight each night and getting up before 7AM to get to school. Wow, you've come a long way, you just made minimum wage back then and it seemed you were always working, never doing what you wanted to do, running like a hamster on a wheel. Ah, those were the days.

You look at your girlfriend as she stands there looking at popcorn in her sexy little outfit, and wish she was not going out tonight. It would be fun to watch the new movie with her, but she's already made plans. Her and her roommate are getting really dressed up and going out. Apparently, it's a big social event for her best friend's work which is invite only, and it's all being thrown by her friend's boss, so everything is paid for. She says she would have told you sooner, but it totally slipped her mind. That's okay. You'll just stay home and watch the movie alone.

At home, you finally get that good meal of the day. It comes in a generic box that say's "Cheese and Mac," and you even mix it with a can of Salmon. As you fall asleep on the couch, you think about the coming weekend. The two of you will spend some time together, maybe go shopping. Did she say that Saturday she is going to the lake, something about a boat? Otherwise, it's the same as last week, as well as hundreds and hundreds of weeks to come.

When your eyes close, you find yourself pulling through tiny corridors of pipes and wires. You are escaping a great raging fire beneath you as you ascend up through the maze-like tunnel and emerge on the deck of a wooden planked boat. There, you join the others in pulling the giant oars by the handles coming into the boat. Rowing this boat is your life; you put your soul into it! You pull it with all your might, you don't understand why those around you seem to hate the simple labor so much as you begin to enlighten the crowd and try to bring them up to your enthusiastic state by starting up and singing a song. Don't they know it's better than what's down there? That raging fire, hungry to consume your very body awaits there below, you've only just escaped it.

The bald headed man has stopped rowing as a glow is growing around the black night sky and, as you look at him, he points his finger down to where he wants you to look, off the side of the boat. You peer between narrow openings in the high wall of the ship's deck, expecting to see dark waters of the sea below. Instead, your eyes widen as you see the molten seas circling there beside you. The oars of the boat are going down into a circling funnel of flames. Your own turning of the oars is generating the twirling motion of the whirlpool, the boat riding lower into the funnel as the water turns to fire. You were the one who had Sung the song, carried the flag, and tried to lead the others in turning the oars. Now you see that the oar you row is fueling the fire below. Vivid images of flesh dripping off of bones in the fire and the faces of people burning and screaming is the last thing you remember seeing as you awake.

Happy to be alive, you arise once more to spend that precious life force in your tiny, feeble task of barley propelling the giant wheel with your weak, insignificant contribution. You do it with passion. You are the heart's blood.

The lights flash behind him as he pulls over to the edge of the highway on his way to work. The new edition of the ONE patrol vehicle looks like a motorized beast in his rearview mirror. The beast's windshield is like a reflective visor; its eyes are unseen behind it. Still, he knows that the machine's eyes are on him, in there somewhere. Behind the glass of the windshield is a camera which is attached to a computer. The computer is one mind with its master as it automatically scans and registers the plates of every passing car from the side of the highway, simultaneously displaying the record associated with John Flint on a screen built into its console.

That gives him a few more moments to worry as the cars speed by him, whooshing by his car with a gust of wind that shakes it each time they pass. He knows that there are seven different counties threatening to arrest him for not paying the fines he's already accumulated, and he knows from his last ride in the back of one the cars that the screen is displaying numerous pages of offences for the officer to scroll through.

The familiar catch twenty two continues into John's young

adult years of life, where mounting fines he can't afford are expecting to be paid before the cost of registering his vehicle to avoid the fines. The fines would amount to half a year's salary, as he struggles to make it to the next paycheck.

"This is going to be real bad," he thinks out loud, eyeing the sinister vehicle in his mirror.

The tapping on the passenger side window surprises him as he peers through the mirror mounted on the driver's door. He is even more surprised when he looks over to see a State Trooper's badge gleaming Sunlight into his eyes below a cream colored cowboy hat. He cannot see the trooper's eyes, only his own reflection in the cop's reflective aviator glasses as he rolls his window down.

"I'm going to have to see your license and registration," the trooper tells him, in a professional southern drawl.

"Is it okay if I get out, it's in my back pocket?" asks John as he points to his seat.

The cop's hand moves instinctively to rest on the butt of his gun at his waist as he holds a silent stare in response to John's question.

"Oh, here, I'll just... I got it. Here you go," John hands him his driver's license and say's, "Listen, I might have some unpaid tickets, and I know I shouldn't be driving, but I just got to get to work. If I don't, I'm going to get fired."

The officer stops walking towards the patrol vehicle and circles around the front of the car to the registration tags.

"Are those right!?" the officer snaps, pointing the back of his pen at the Sun faded registration stickers which are nearly three years old.

"Yes, I'm afraid so," responds John, gritting his teeth and pulling his cheeks back in a mimicked expression of pain. "I really know I shouldn't be driving right now," he calls out sheepishly as the trooper marches back towards his patrol car with the identification card.

While he awaits the verdict he remembers, like most people do when there is no other option, to pray. Watching in the rearview mirror, he prepares himself for incarceration as the officer returns from his vehicle after running his ID through the network of information shot digitally through a satellite in space to the computer brain of the ONE squad car.

"Please step out of the car," the cop tells John in a direct command upon returning to his car, his hand no longer resting, but poised over the pistol on his hip.

The apprehensive trooper steps back a few feet as John emerges from the car in careful, controlled motions, and stands with his hands straight down along his body on the side of the busy highway.

"Come around here to the back of the car," the trooper tells him.

John walks to the back of the car at the officer's command, ready to place his hands on the trunk, expecting to be frisked and then handcuffed.

Before the man has a chance to tell him to assume the position, John leans casually back against the hood of his car and looks into the cop's eyes as he has just taken his Sunglasses off.

"I know I shouldn't be driving," John repeats, holding a peaceful stare into the man's eyes. "I'm not a bad guy. I don't abuse drugs. I don't steal from people. My only crime is being broke."

John sees the blood boiling within the trooper's reddening cheeks and the tiny capillaries bulging in his eyes as he tries to control his response.

"You are driving around with no insurance. You have outstanding warrants and you are driving on a suspended driver's license. Do you see any way you are not going to jail!?" the infuriated cop asks in a credulous yell. His eyes flash down to John's hands as he thinks about cuffing them.

'Just stay with me,' John thinks to himself as he tries to bring the man's gaze back to his eyes by a swift, controlled twitch in his stare. The cop instinctively darts his eyes back to John's, trying to detect any sign of a threat.

"If you let me go, you'd probably be saving my life." John tells him, evenly, calmly.

"You are driving around here with no insurance!" the officer repeats in a drill sergeant's yell. "You could get in an accident and you wouldn't be able to pay! Then what would the other people do?! It does not necessarily even have to be your fault. It could be an accident; you might have a tire blowout. Then what would the other guy do?"

The officer begins swaying gently to John's unnoticeable, insinuating body movements, his eyes held still by John's stare. The cop realizes his emotional outburst is out of place and doubt enters his decision making process as his emotions take over.

"I can't even read your damned license plate because it's so damned covered in filth. What in the holly *fuck* is that!" he yells as he points to the license plate.

John knows he has done his job, now, the trooper's hazing joke telling him he has turned the tide. Purposefully releasing the trooper's gaze, he turns to look at the filmed over metal plate on the back of his car and picks at it with his finger nail saying,

"What the hell... damned, that's pretty messed up," agreeing with the trooper.

After a strong scolding, the cop hands him a ticket with three offenses and three warnings scratched across it and let's him go. John puts it in the glove box with the rest. The ONE vehicle rolls past him in a silent stalk as he waits and pretends to shuffle things around within his car. They've arrested him four times for these fines, this time they let him go. He looks at the tickets in his glove box as he crams the new one into it. He knows he'll never pay it. He'll just have to continue driving to his job and hope they don't take him the next time.

Before he begins to finish his journey to the carwash, he breaks out into tears of despair, wondering what unseen sequence of events could possibly lift him from this maze. His skin turns hot on his arms as he grips the steering wheel and bangs his head against it. The water flushes his eyes as he begs the cosmos for an answer.

People passing by on the highway catch brief glimpses of the strange scene: a young man in a car on the side of the highway, crying, with his forehead pushed against his steering wheel as they continue their commutes to work. John raises his head to wipe the tears from his face, wedging his wrist bones into his eye sockets to absorb the flowing moisture from his eyes. He bellows another groan of pain as he pushes his car into gear, then he goes to the car wash to work his shift. He tries not to think about it anymore, but his stomach feels as if it's full of battery acid.

Upon arriving at work, he feels slightly better joining his comrades. Medial work is done with expert's precision as they serve the servants. The people line up in their cars to have them washed, staring blankly into their cell phones as they wait in the lines for their turn to hand over their keys to him. Walking a circle around each car as it reaches the end of the line, he kicks the tires, probing the customers for weakness as he tries to squeeze a few more dollars from each one. Of the fees for extra services, he earns 10%.

300 people a day will be treated to the same agenda. This one is a cop; his tab is paid for by the city. There is no use in getting him to spend money; the city only pays a set amount. Better luck on the next one. Here comes a lawyer. Nice car, I bet that sporty Japanese import cost tens of thousands. He'll give you some cash under the table to get it done cheap. He thinks that underhand dealing will get him ahead, so let him think it. The truth is that the 50 dollar bill he slid you was more than you would have charged to have the guys gloss his dash board. How about this guy pulling up with the government plates? He must need something; we know he's got money to spend.

"Come on, mister, we'll hand clean your rims, just a dollar a wheel. No? Are you just leasing this thing? Oh, because if you owned it, you might want to take care of it. How about a spray wax for ten bucks and you get the wheels cleaned for free?"

John hustles them all, the gangster with his weed to trade, the plumber whose car will leave cleaner than his clothes, and the politician, all alike.

"Serves them right," he thinks, "they could wash their own cars and it would be free."

When ladies go in to complain to his boss, the man comes out to yell at him a bit about his pushy ways. The Manager and the Ticket Writer both know it's just for show. If he doesn't piss off at least one person a day, then he's not doing his job. He looks through his book of tickets as customers drive up, calculating the average dollar amount of the hundreds of receipts in his hand abstractly and only raising his glance towards them for a moment. They pull up beside him and he remains silent.

The young couple in the luxury sedan are happy and showing it, as they pretend not to notice him while laughing at some secret joke in their BMW. Her blonde hair is carelessly falling over her baby doll face. The guy is reveling in his virility as he nonchalantly blows her off. His practiced look of disappointment is veiling something as he looks off to the right and curls his upper lip ever so mockingly at her, at everything around him. He doesn't need anyone, doesn't need her.

She has caught John in her eye. As her boyfriend pretends to be pretentious, she is raising her eye to the guy standing in front of the car counting his tickets by the gas pump, and noticing his stone face set by a hard jaw above a strong, tan neck, which was still soft in youth. She has practiced her look, too. She turns her head in another direction, appearing to be looking some other way as her eyes sneak up and to the side in mischief. A slight smile raises her lips as she rolls her eyes slowly under her long, teased eyelashes which swoop down as if to wash her stare away. Delicately, she raises and flutters them like butterflies under her command, sending secret messages flying out to the attendant from the passenger's seat of her boyfriend's car.

The annoyed boyfriend now rolls down his window, tired of waiting for the older boy to come take his order.

"Welcome to Magic Car Wash, how can I help you?" asks John, courteously resting his reddish brown eyes on him. The guy tries to avoid the stare, getting out of his car and turning around to stick his head back down into the cab, pretending to look for something inside and ignoring his question. John waits patiently, poised with his pen resting on the pad of tickets, ready to write. When the customer finally emerges from the car, he purposefully looks the other way and starts talking to his girlfriend as he reaches his hand out for the ticket. John just looks at him, saying nothing until the boy is forced to look towards him and say,

"I'll just have a car wash."

"You want to have your car washed?" John repeats back to him.

An awkward silence ensues as he stares at the customer quizzically.

"Yeah, just a car wash," he responds, his hand still outstretched for the ticket which, he must bring inside in order to pay for his wash.

"Ok."

John sticks his head into the guy's car, surveying the carpet for spills. The young thirty-thousand-aire has kept it pretty clean, there are no stains on the carpet for the detail shop. There is the typical dried up coffee around the shifter and cup holders with cigarette ashes stuck to it.

"You should have us clean that." John states, pointing the back of his pen towards the mess.

"Yeah, whatever, clean it," the customer responds, as if he

didn't know it was there.

"Ok. I'll send it to the detail shop, They'll clean up your dash and console and I'll have them clean your wheels," he tells him.

"How much is that?" the customer asks.

"Just fifty bucks."

"Fifty dollars! You've got to be kidding me. No way," the guy responds, indignantly.

"Ok."

John is surveying the exterior now. He wipes his finger down the hood, smearing the last coat of wax, which appears to be only weeks old, in a streak with the light film of road grime.

"You ever wax this thing?" he asks.

Then, in a final insult, he reaches his foot out and rubs the wheel with the bottom of his shoe in a downward stroke. The black brake soot comes off easily, revealing the shiny aluminum beneath it.

"You should have us clean those wheels."

"How much is that?"

"Do you want Armoral on your tires? We'll get down there and hand clean your wheels, it's just a dollar a wheel. Now, I don't know about you, but I'd pay some poor bastard a dollar a wheel to clean my rims, any day. The Armoral on the tires is just another buck a wheel. You want some wax?" he asks, turning his head as he looks at him seriously.

"No, I don't need no damn wax. I just had it waxed," he says, then follows up with, "How much does it cost?"

"We have two kinds. The cheaper stuff is 8 bucks. The good one is a spray polymer that they spray on your entire car. It's really good. It makes the water bead up on your windshield; you don't even have to use your wipers! I'll tell you what, let me have my guys in the back clean up that dash, and we'll do your wheels and wax for free. Ok?" Again he stops and listens, focused on the silver spoon fed boy as he nods his head slowly in a subliminal message.

John rips the ticket from the pad and extends his arm out to the confused boy, holding it before him and waiting for him to take it. As he does, he looks down to see that his car wash will cost him fifty nine dollars and ninety nine cents, plus tax. The blonde is still standing on the other side of the car, waiting for the boys to work it out as if she is afraid to enter the fracas. John shoots her a direct look and smiles, a quick look practiced and perfected to be both insincere and professional. As they walk into the lobby, he writes the order on the windshield with a bar of soap.

"Got one coming back to detail," he yells across the parking lot to Magic, who is smoking a cigarette.

Upon hearing this, he immediately puts out his smoke on the pavement and walks briskly from across the lot.

"I got it, I got it. Which one? This one?" asks Magic as he points to the dark blue BMW.

As he walks up on the car, he immediately begins inspecting it. Stooping over, looking closely at the paint, his eyes narrow. His nose crinkles up as he runs his hands over the bumper, brushing off some unseen blemish with his fingers. He opens the door and looks inside the cockpit at the tan leather interior.

"What you want us to do wid it?" he asked, his head rising quizzically towards John as he rested up against the open door.

"Just clean that shit around the cup holder, fix it up a little bit, and throw some Armoral on it," he tells him, patting him on the back. "It's a fifty dollar detail."

Magic hops in quickly and drives the car back to the shop. John looks up to see the other Ticket Writer finishing up on another few cars under the metal canopy. It is getting dark and there are no more customers right now, so John decides to walk back to the detail shop. Lighting a cigarette as he walks up, he finds Magic purposefully examining the row of different colored spray bottles hanging from the handle of a cart in his shop. He lifts one up to his eye level, swooshing the green liquid around as he examines the mixture like an unseen chemist perfecting alchemy in a dark, secret laboratory.

"Here. Take that now and go in there and clean up that dash," he says, as he hands one of the young workers the bottle. "Flint! What up, baby!" He greets him with a big slap on the hand.

55 years old, maybe 65, his active personality and proud posture never surprises John anymore. His dirty hands push the long fingernails into his jean pockets and he produces half of a Black and Mild cigar which he lights.

"Whatchew got going on these days?" he asks, as if they have not spoken in years.

"Oh, nothing, same old shit, just trying to make a buck. Toothache was killing me this morning." Just as he says it, he regrets having said it, but it is too late as the muscles in Magic's puzzled face push his eyebrows together. His look is practiced, too. His look says,

"You white boys really think you got it that bad?"

The shop's lights accentuate the wrinkles in his face, revealing his sincerity as he opens his eyes up all the way to look at you.

"You just gotta believe in God, put your faith in the Lord," he says in all seriousness.

His skin is not black, but nothing is. It is Purple, Red, deep Eggplant and light Yellow in the incandescent lights which highlight his happy cheeks and raised brow.

"I know, man, I know," John assures him.

"Naw. Lookit here," he tells him, in a new tone of heightened gravity.

He points his strong finger into John's chest as he begins to iterate his point.

"You got to put your faith in God. You understand me?"

"Yeah, I got you. You know I do," he says.

He knows where this is going. The old Black man grabs his hand in his, clasping it within his leathery palms and squeezing tightly. He lowers his head.

"Dear Lord, please show us the way. We just ask of you, Lord, that you keep showing us your mercy, allowing us to live and eat and do all the things, Lord. We want to live for you." He pauses for a moment, his eyes still closed and still grasping John's hand tightly. "We just ask for your forgiveness tonight, Lord. We are here to tell you; You are the all mighty power my Lord, and we are honored everyday just to worship you."

"Amen!" John exclaims as he grabs Magic's shoulders and gives him a hug. A brief hug, a gangster's hug, affirms them to each other in solidarity.

"Hey man, you do good." Magic tells him as he holds his fist out as a duke for daps.

"I will," John responds enthusiastically over his shoulder, heading back over to the service lines to greet the car which is just pulling up for a carwash.

At the end of the day, John inventories the gas, recording the tally from each pump on a sheet of paper. After that, he goes back to the detail shop to help them finish the remaining cars. The Beamer is still parked there in the shop. Upon examination, John sees that the job has been done. The dash is glowing in its shiny wetness and paper mats have been placed on the floor.

John asks Magic," Why didn't you tell me it was done?"

"It been done. I didn't know he wanted it. He wants it now? Send him back here."

John hears crickets beginning to chirp their violin legs as he walks to the lobby of the carwash to find the couple waiting. They look as if they were waiting in a hospital to hear the fate of their newborn baby. He held a rolled up ten dollar bill to tip the detail workers tightly in his hand.

"Hey, great news, your car is ready," he tells them. "Right this way." They follow him out and he points them in the right direction to retrieve their car.

It's a pretty uneventful end to another uneventful day. John drives home in the dark to his place, which is 20 miles away. He pulls up, goes into the house and grabs a beer from the refrigerator. The solitude is bringing strange thoughts out of him as he finally enters his home. Shadow raises his head, alerted by his presence. The dog's mouth is hanging open as he pants. Broken teeth from his fights no longer hold his tongue in his mouth, and it hangs loosely from his smile.

"What do you want? Did you have a good day?"

Talking to the dog may sound futile to some people, but the tempo of the dog's tail slapping on the side of the couch tells him he is on the right path. Despite all the stresses of John's world, the dog just continues to pant, slowly moving his head to the side and enjoying the attention.

"Oh! You had a good day? Well that's nice, because my day sucked! You lucky fugin' dog, you. You don't have to do anything!"

His face is soft. As John pets him and presses the animal's fur against his stooped head, he feels the elasticity of the dog's warm skin. So tough, so abundant in its ability to resist puncture are the rolled up layers beneath his black hair. The scars are stripes in better sights, revealed as the dog smiles on another day.

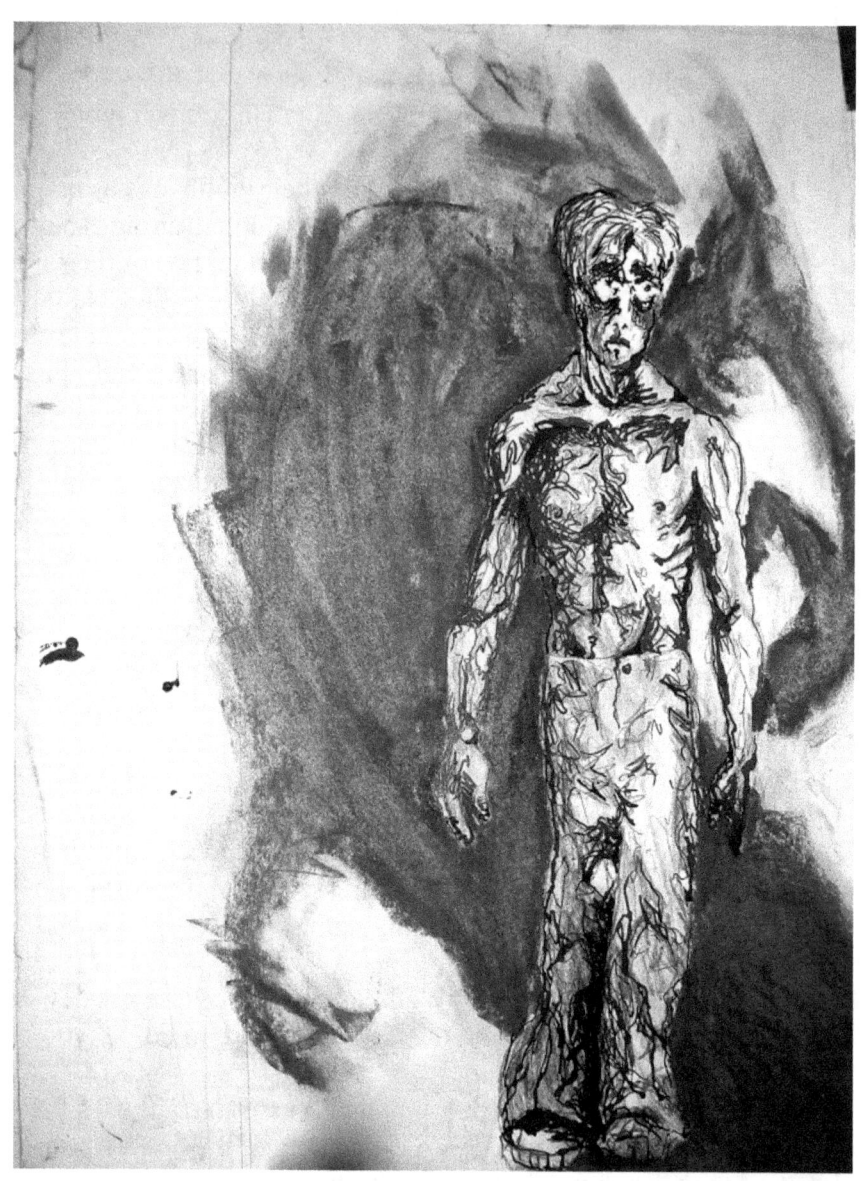

6. PETTING DEAD DOGS

The mother bitch works very hard. She chases them around, carries them in her mouth. She makes sure to eat their excrement every time they drink her milk and dig their little needles of claws into her breasts. With eyes shut they, the fortunate dependents, wiggle around, squirm and squeal. The mother pants softly and gazes blankly into the distance. The same stoic look still holds to her face as she sleeps and they continue to muscle for position on her nipples.

She is dreaming. You can see her running over in her mind all the actions of the last three days as they flash through her head in vivid images: the puppies falling out, eating the placentas, finding them still beneath the litter, trying to revive them, and running around trying to find their bodies. As she discovers one going cold, she licks it forcefully, trying to keep it warm and stimulate its breathing. So tiny, they struggle feebly to hold on to life, but their effort is in vain. The heart beats faint, each pulse weaker and farther in-between, until the mother can no longer hear it. She lays her head over the puppy, letting the warm, abundant roles of her neck envelop the dog, warming it and hoping to feel the slightest hint of another heartbeat. When she finally removes her head, it is obvious that the tiny animal has gone cold and she has lost another one.

In her mind she searches for reasons why, wondering how she can try to do better next time, in line with her latest dead daughter laying behind her, back to back. It's as if they're sharing the same dream. Find the heart to take the dead body away from her. So much emotion vested in it, so sad to see her go. The mother sleeps with her dead daughter lying up against the back of her neck. She grunts and seems to be trying hard for something as she dreams.

All night the little one with white socks tried to die. Like many of her littermates who had only known one or two days out of the womb before perishing, she was premature, dehydrated, and not feeding well. The tiny puppy must have been forced from the teat by her blind, bigger siblings and not gotten the vital antibodies from her mother's first milk. Could it be parvovirus? A horrible death. It eats at her intestines as thick, yellow bile comes from both ends of the dog. She loses all of her fluids; the seemingly minute amounts of nutrients holding the only chance of her continued survival are there on the carpet. Each time she did eat, she would begin convulsing within minutes. Her head would go back as rigormortis set in, her back becoming stiff in your hands where you could feel the constricting muscles pulling her tight like a kite. Her little feet poke out in a final stretch, freezing her outstretched limbs like sticks.

In this case; you must put your finger in the dog's mouth and pull her tongue out from the back of her throat. The tongue sucks back in convulsions, restricting the passage of air. Now that you have freed the windpipe with your finger by suppressing the tongue, pump her heart and lungs by pressing in a rhythmic motion under her tiny arms with your thumbs, trying to mimic a heartbeat. As you do this, keep your finger in her mouth and make sure her tongue is suppressed. If you feel her start sucking on your finger and spitting out some mucus, congratulations. You've just escaped death.

If not, her lungs will be suppressed and still by now. Never mind the mucus, cover her mouth with yours, and inflate her lungs with your breath until you feel her chest is fully expanded. After inflating her lungs, press on her chest with your hands until the air is forced out. The vacuum created in her lungs will naturally pull air back in as her chest expands. Repeat the process of manually activating the respiratory system until she begins to breathe again.

Over the next 48 hours, you hold her for every minute. She fits easily in the palm of your hand. When she sleeps, she is so still that you frequently hold your finger over her nostrils to feel the miniature and delicate breath barely tickle the tips of your fingers to make sure she is alive. Each time she freezes up, you feel the life go out of her and again begin the process of reviving her. You've put so much into this one.

"Please come back!" You beg her. "Come on, you got it, just

breath, ok!'"

It's not hard to understand what it's all about, it's natural. It's like the first breath from a baby; it's like trees growing leafs, the mother's unconditional love. The poor girl, she would save them all if she could. It seems she will have to pick and choose but she doesn't know how. She never could have prepared for this. All the energy that went into creating their frail little bodies, arriving complete with fur, feet, four legs and two ears, has depleted the mother bitch. They need to be warm and she pants in the heat. She has become boney and is near death, herself, but she will still fight with all her power for their lives.

It's natural and you can count on it. You can count on the leafs budding in the spring, the rise and fall of the ocean's waves, the spinning of the earth, the setting of the Sun. You can count on these immutable tendencies and write songs about them, but if it doesn't rain, the trees won't grow. When the lungs don't pump, the heart doesn't beat. When the baby is premature and there are too many of them, it may not get that first vital, ever important meal. Only in that stage of infancy, before breathing too much oxygen from the air into their lungs changes the chemical makeup of their bodies and closes the intercellular spaces where antibodies are allowed to flow through, can she receive her mother's salvation in the form of immunity passed on through antigens in the mother's milk. She depends on the love from the mother for any chance to survive. The love is there, but there is not enough to go around. It is all she can do to eat away the purple placenta sac from around them and stimulate their breathing by vigorously licking them until they breathe by their own volition.

The dozen of them, all black with few white markings, are only distinguishable by their size. Who can tell them apart? For 24 hours she labors, producing ten pups with almost identical black coats and white feet and chests. Over the next two days, four more pups appear, all dead on arrival. She is exhausted now. She breaths heavily and pants as croaking, grumbling sounds are emitted from somewhere inside of her. Four days later, there are only four left. Now that they are happily breathing, she rests and eats and tries to put some weight back on. It is very important that she lives. 10 stiff bodies await burial in a plastic bag on the front porch, and without her there to feed them, the other four will surly die as well.

Outside, the weather is hot. Children look out the window in a wistful way as they begin to dream of rainy days, in reminiscence of when the sweet water would come down gently, adding mist to the summer sky and beading down their windows as they looked out at the wet day, wishing that they could go and play. John's garden turns brown and dry given a single day without watering. He is starting to wonder what he would do, heaven forbid, without a gardening hose.

The Agricultural Commissioner of Texas has just announced that Texans should begin gardening again. This rich soil has gone 100 years without cultivation. The soil is called bottom soil. It runs off from the hills and gathers in the lower lands with its nutrients accumulating over thousands of years in the rich, black dirt. You can virtually garden all year round with little intervention besides watering and weeding here. Also, the land produces a variety of natural foods on its own. Come to find out those annoying vines that crept up the fence each year were actually Tomatillos, a tangy green pepper. "A man who eats tomatoes lives forever." That's what they say.

John gets on his big, heavy, metal handled garden hoe, swinging it in rhythm now. Ol' John Frone used to amaze him with that thing. Here he was, a 77 year old man, war veteran with a colostomy sack, swinging that 20 pound hoe and raking through the untilled land like butter. At first, John would feel a bit silly, barely making progress with the morning Sun beginning to reach its vantage point over him, as Old Man John's rows formed neatly and quickly right beside him.

Now, in the setting Sun behind his house, he works in a dedicated rhythm with the crude yet ingenious instrument. He heaves it high above his head, then swings the momentum of his body backwards, merely directing the fall of the swinging blade. Without a pause of rhythm, the end of the gardening till ascends from the earth where he has Sunk it, yanking up another chunk of weeds and dirt from the ground and exposing the rich, black soil. He switches sides of his body every few minutes as his muscles begin to burn and his intensity grows.

From behind closed windows, curtains are moved to the side ever so slightly without his notice as he grunts, growls, and yells:

"Yes you son of a bitch, yeah! Get your ass up! Get up! Come on! Yah! Urgh!"

They are looking at him, but he doesn't care. They're feeling pretty safe in there; with their cable TV and cold flowing air. But the price of food keeps going up...

The tomatoes are botched, the meat is green on the bottom of the red dyed packages along the grocer's cooler and the price keeps going up. There are talks of rationing, talks of gas vouchers and a scanning chip in your wrist required to operate all vehicles. Talks of violence prone children in schools alternatively shipped to remote government military academies for proper discipline and isolation are becoming common, light discussion on the nightly news.

Talks today all paint him. He is red in the Sun, red from the blood surging through him, and he thinks of this world spinning apart around him like chunks of dirt as he heaves, grunts, and yells at the flying ground now under the mercy of the heavy gardening hoe swinging over his head. He's been painted out; they're going to try to get him now, and he knows it. He sees clear signs in his mind, as obvious as the ground cracking underneath him.

Every day in the yard there is another gaping crack in the land where the lack of rain has caused mother's skin to crack like blistered lips in the cold dampness, her epidermis is exposed as she makes her closest pass to the scorching Sun.

Oh, the Mother Bitch. Licking her own wounds while trying to salvage those remnants of life she still has a chance of supporting, of saving. Somewhere something, some force we fail to understand, looks down on us. The love is there.

"I've started you on the path, now it's up to you." she says in the still, small voice we fail to hear. She loves us, but can only save so many of us. She sighs in the finality that only she knows, and does not know how to deal with it.

Meanwhile, the fat ones born drive in their shiny new cars, shop at new malls, and spend their days in an utter daze of unimagined ease and softness with no idea, no way to know what's coming. The days pass, the tilled earth becomes sprouts of vegetables, and the people go about their business, finding trivial ways to pass hours which become days, and days which become weeks and months.

Having survived against all odds, the resilient little dog is nearly half her full size now. A disgusting smell rises from the pink meat in the fleshy gash upon her shoulder. Eight months old, the little dog has lived through worse than this unexplained wound. Having gotten out of the fence, she returned home with the gaping gash in her side, wagging her tail and dripping blood. She is a little *too* unafraid of the world and has, apparently, gotten too close to a big, mean dog somewhere in the neighborhood.

When she first came home with the wound, she walked slowly across the white tile floor of the living room, leaving a trail of deep red drops beneath her. The opening was deep and wide, past the epidermis and into the muscles of her shoulder. John cleaned it up and she laid around on the couch for the next few days, licking her wounds. Now, three days later, she wags her tail and smiles up at her master, happy and unfazed. She keeps walking, like a tank through a wall.

Long ago, before this every man for himself mentality prevailed, there were common laws for the common cause: If you need that, we'll find a way to get that. No one had anything, but they still got it done. They got it done through the belief that they would get it done, that they would never let anything kick their ass.

One of them, who could fix anything and rig a shimmy from a beer can, was invaluable when your car broke down. They all called him Killer, though he wouldn't kill a thing under any normal circumstances. Long black hair hanging down his face was striped with two symmetrical white streaks running down his long beard. Problems that made most people raise their eyebrows and shake their heads, giving up to their inability to solve the questions in their heads before they even tried, caused his brow to furrow and his eyes to turn intense as fire burned within his brain, which was racing through a million possibilities and angles of reason. He refused to have his ass kicked by anything, including a question. Hardened hands from working on machines stroked the wise beard as he rationalized equations and drew out diagrams in his head. He had invented flying machines and self propelled motors from magnets and light sensors from electrodes and diodes, he would figure out anything.

Another, who could do little to make your car run, could speak as eloquently to a crowd as a silver tongued lawyer, and was the only one who could help you when the collectors were at your door. Some said Brian had once sold a cracked furnace to the devil. Crockett, the tree trunk of a young man, couldn't really talk you out of a foreclosure or fix your car, but he could beat a person's head into the ground like the stump of an old tree and yank a fish from a lake with the best of them. Killer brought the flame, Brian brought the whiskey, and they all ate fish.

Brian was the salesman, and when everyone argued about the best way to get it done, he could help each see the other's point of view. Carlie cooked and Kaylee cleaned. Mike could pick up a tree and carry it any place. John yielded an axe like a scalpel, dissecting the trunk of the tee into logs like a machine. Tom Emory taught him to shoot a pistol, simply, as if he were pointing his finger. Mister Mason taught him not to jerk as he squeezed, not pulled, the trigger. Mr. Mason was an expert at those things; he could also mix the gun powder and load the shells perfectly.

The artist was the mystic, putting a spiritual touch on all that they did at the end of the day, making it seem worthwhile. The preacher helped them see their relation to one another, helping to congeal the parts into their whole. The machine grew. You did not have to know the person to know that they were a functioning part of the machinery. One piston, one wheel, one belt... which part was that? The crazy guy was a loose nut, but he was bouncing around in there for some purpose.

The orchestrators so titled themselves. Not really being in the machine anymore, they fancied themselves as its operator. They were in other worlds, in the presence of hired help who cleaned their houses, wiped the remnants of their dribbling piss from their toilets and prepared their food. The small people were but pieces of the mechanisms which produced their easy spoils for them and they would begin to choose the useful parts for themselves.

The machine's wheel was huge. It used unseen, mysterious methods to turn organic matter into combustible fuel which pumped its pistons and turned the wheel in time. It used infinite variables of tiny parts fitting seamlessly together like intricate jigsaw puzzles to get the job done. They did not know how it worked and, hastily, began weeding out the parts they deemed unnecessary. This one goes, that one stays...

Their systems were in place, refined and redefined through the years. Weeding them out, the undesirables, had become a routine procedure that would start at an early age. 'We don't need any monkey wrenches in our system,' was their internal proclamation, and population control was their silent agenda to weed out the oddly shaped and seemingly useless tools, those that didn't fit in. World governance had been their ambition for hundreds of years, and now that it was finally coming to fruition, they knew where their problems where likely to lie.

Those monkey wrenches could be hard nuts to crack. In order to flush them out, there were chemicals placed into the public water to cause illness and death amongst certain gene sets. Historically rebellious, God fearing and freedom loving clans were stealthily targeted through metals insidiously lacing the water, plastic food containers, Styrofoam, and everyday objects including toys and dishes. Genetic codes were surgically identified and tested for weaknesses, all in the name of science.

Then there were prevailing toxins in the readily available diets that killed others through artery decomposition and anemia within the blood cells. There were cancerous toxins in the air, invisibly and insidiously culling out the population indiscriminately. There seemed to be no escaping or fighting it, and a prevailing apathy took over the thought process of those who began to grasp it. They hid it away from their own conscious thoughts, although they knew subconsciously it was there all along, eating them slowly as they managed their daily tasks of feeding themselves and providing for the simple necessities in their daily lives.

Paralleling those complex schemes to thin the herd were the institutions set in place to file these surviving members into their roles in the machine. The curators, perfect in their infinite wisdom, even knew that they would be needing a second class of citizens for their dirty work as well as an elite class to keep them in line. They tested them through various scientific experiments including multiple choice tests examining their problem solving capabilities and physical tests of will, stamina, and aggression.

It was not an exact science, but many parts fell into place themselves: The father's line of work became the natural progression for some, be it law or medicine, or taking up the family name at the tire repair shop. Some found their role in enforcement, finding their place in society to be living as a class slightly above the trivial laws they enforced. The willingness to blindly obey was required, and they found these to be loyal servants of the privileged class in the way of street police and incarceration workers. They did not question why, they only exerted the brutal force on those in noncompliance. They could find these small minded bullies anywhere, readily. The numb minded propensity towards dominance was a gene set made abundant now through natural selection.

The ones with writing and artistic skills were necessary, but potentially dangerous, and were sifted carefully. For them, they would have to know the difference but pretend they didn't as they expressed the views they knew they were supposed to, without being told to. Trendy intuition was vital to feel and direct the pulse of the public, particularly the youth. Propaganda needed to be bright, colorful, original in its presentation, and almost surreal. The music needed to match; the artist of this production must understand the emotion we are trying to arouse in our audience. Just like the enforcement officers, the artists did their surgical incursions into the public's eye without asking 'why?'

Of course, there were those odd ones out: They didn't seem to get it, they argued with the things that did not make sense to them. They expounded upon every idea, as if it were a new one, not knowing that these theories and facts had been known and disregarded for years, systematically, intentionally. These stubborn ones took a lot of work, at first. Day one: stand in line. Day two: turn a blind eye. Day 3: Now it's your turn. They would be broken down, or sifted out.

As the systems for organizing the youth into functioning members of the machine became more and more standardized, they began to grow onto one another in over lapping layers. The layer of standing in lines would eventually be combined with those concerning organizing subjects by means of alphabetization, numeration, and serial codes. Then, to simplify the categorization, they began giving the students color identifications. Supposedly random, these helped to sort them out, and served to take away the sense of identity based on one's self perception from day one. You were John Glenn. Now you are color red, number seven.

The nonfunctioning members of the machine would surface

quickly in this organized structure. Now we could see them from an early stage of development. Combined with the mental aptitude tests and games organized to show will and force during the play ground activities, we could see clearly which one might pose a problem. There were many options in place for us to sort them, such as prescription pills and alternative schools. Places removed from the functioning members adored with padded walls and Plexiglas windows made convenient homes for them. Some would resist the microchips placed beneath the fleshy skin of the bottom of their forearm, just as some dogs would. For these primitive few who refused to understand that it was for their own safety, their own good, it would not be easy. Euthanasia could only get you so far. The bad dogs could simply be put to sleep by a shot, but it was not so simple for these simple asses of children. It seemed as if they were driven by an internal anger, primal in its irrationality, but human none the less in their glaring eyes.

There was a place for them. It was a place where knowledge was not taught, and in fact frowned upon just as much as critical thinking. The students were required to take psychotropic drugs which made them more manageable and hindered their will to think, speak out, or fight. There, in their 'Alternative Schools,' they learned not about the history of mankind and applications of knowledge, but to conform, to obey, and to be punished. Few of these would end up making a difference now, as most would end up financially destitute, without the means to do much more than spout their incoherent beliefs to fellow crack brains or random passers by on the street. Statistically, they would usually end up jailed, 'institutionalized,' or dead before long. Their chance of reproducing, of passing on their ingrained will to fight through their genes, was greatly reduced. The addictive drugs administered by neo doctors of the machine would soon be replaced with soothing illegal and legal substitutes, which would continue the cycle of depression and non functionality, both in the brain and physically, separating them from the normal society for years to come. They had it all figured out, the makers of the machine, but there was an intangible: God was in it.

The popular media expounded the people's God as mysticism and foolish tradition through various outlets. Reality of everyday life, of everything they needed and every policy they had to adhere to on a daily basis, kept them busy. When the price of gasoline became a major story in the media, it was clear to those looking through the watchful glass eye of a vulture that they had them right where they wanted them.

If for some reason the public opinion, carefully guided and gauged by polls and television ratings, began to turn against them, there was an all too easy fix for that. All that was needed was rumor of a foreign attack or, better still, a new strand of disease to send the masses flocking back into lines to get their shots or turn suspecting eyes on any of their non conforming neighbors. The poor herd's routine was so established, so dependent upon the interworking of conformity, that the foul smelling fuel which they pumped into their vehicles, the nectar which propelled them to traffic licensing offices and immunization clinics on their way to the grocery store, dictated their daily lives by stretching their meager budgets. The masses living paycheck to paycheck could not survive beyond the web of illusion and dependence on the order of things, they never hoped to.

Tiny, insidious incisions into minds were injected through wide eyes staring at TV sets. The glass lens looked back at them like a vulture's eye, waiting for the brain to die so it could devour it at will. Insane pundits of a crazy philosophy were put forth as the messengers of a higher faith. Every movie or television show featuring a religious character would portray them as crazy or secretly evil, all persecution was made acceptable by faith in god.

The spiritual void created a want and need for something deeper, something higher. The void was filled by strange, foreign mysticism, as religious symbols from different continents and cultures were made into t-shirt logos and little plastic dolls. The people's need for something more was met by philosophical speakers who took hours talking themselves in a circle, leaving people either mislead by a false premise, or left contently confused with no sense of direction at all. The shelves would be stocked, the checks would be docked, and the machine would run consistently and smoothly.

All seemed to be accounted for, but God was in it. Life fed on life, the organization continued in every direction. The tree's roots grew down and out as the branches divided off into sub-segments of twigs. Within the organized pattern of leafs, the veins broke into mathematical patterns of fractals, the cells within them divided into smaller orders of organization. The atoms that composed them bonded predictably even still, as the smaller particles came into science's spectrum of awareness and wide eyed humans found more order within it. Through studious evaluation, they found the mass of the particle, yet could not identify the force in-between it that made it rotate at such a constant speed and predictable distance from its invisible nucleus. They could never understand what held it together in its tiny orbit or why the force between the particles was stronger and harder to divide between smaller particles, what the distance was between the quark and the electrode, where the energy came from and what it all meant. They saw that the Moon was held in orbit of the Earth, the planets of the Sun, the solar system loosely rotating around an imagined center of the Milky Way galaxy, which they even knew was rotating around something much bigger. It was all there, on the tip of their finger.

With each new discovery, they thought they almost had figured it out. With each new genetic phylum and medical classification, they felt themselves coming closer to complete understanding and mastery of the essence of life. They cloned men, grew human ears on the backs of rats, produced livestock in a rainbow of colors, and deemed themselves orchestrators of a new order, of the order of life, of the cosmos. They deemed themselves creators, but continued to leave out the one simple variable, the one simple force. Had only they known that God was in it.

They never should have taken it so far. As the trees swayed and grew towards the light, the survivors of the simple class unknowingly began to adapt. The carcinogens they were exposed to began to make them stronger and less susceptible to other toxins rather than kill them. They began to speak to those swaying trees, hearing God in the voice of their breeze blown leafs and developing their own brand of religion. Just when they had the strange outcasts and irrational fighters right where they wanted them, they started forming personal bonds based on love and a faith only in humanity, in the spirit. Their walk became personal; they locked out the prepackaged ideas. It was not a movement; it just began happening everywhere, simultaneously. They heard a voice telling them to come out of her, that fat bellied beast, and to find their own will. They started making gardens and seeking out remote locations to live. They began teaching their children their own values and keeping them home from public schools, subconsciously sensing the danger it imposed on their beloved offspring.

Meanwhile, back in the real world, acceptably conforming children were being culled into hateful, self serving little heathens of high class sexual vanity and pride. They were being formed as perfect fuel for the machine. The atoms were being accelerated faster, the march for disaster, as they served themselves, they served their master. Even as they marched on through the weaponization of proton acceleration, their enemies were finding ways to turn their machines against them. The gears were turning; the lubrication was in the workings of all that they did. All the things they had to have, from slimmer TVs to bigger SUV's, were fueling their appetite for consumption while depleting their reserves and fueling the fire burning everything around them.

The world, strewn with famine and riots, was literarily burning around them, but they were able to ignore the fire through the imagined distance created by their own vanity. Their sky was turning darker with each Sunday trip to the mall, their minds bleaker with every commercial they saw. Their spirits grew anemic, their bellies grew fatter. Their enemies assembled, gathered their power and waited for the coming day. They were perfecting their methods; they were planning to put a stop to the great marching machine.

John stoops over in his garden. It is a beautiful day, mid April after a few days of rain, and the Sun is beaming out, subtlety warming and drying the top soil. He is hunched over, balanced on the balls of his feet and pulling new vines and weeds up from around the vegetables just pushing through the moist soil. His legs burn as he hunches down on them, meticulously working his way down the rows of planted seeds and pulling the weeds. The Okra is not coming up. He had planted the Okra from the left over seeds in the pods which had grown too large and tough to eat the previous year. Why weren't they growing?

Hybrid seeds engineered for maximum produce output were what he had used the year before. Just recently on the AM radio, he had heard an advertisement for 'non hybrid' seeds. The crackling voice on the radio claimed that they would be the ultimate commodity in the coming days. The problem with hybrid seeds, was that they were engineered to only grow once. Purposefully, the scientists had designed them to produce seeds which would not grow again the following year. They were even engineered to kill similar, non hybrid crops around them. The seeds from them were not supposed to grow, however, some of them still did. There were always those few who had resisted the genetic programming, and when watered and tended, they would grow. Maybe the survivors from the various seasons of replanting the genetically altered seeds would produce a tougher, more resilient seed? Why did they want to live, what made these few seeds that still rose from the dirt and climbed towards the Sun so different?

The oil rationing is really starting to show its ugly side now. Assurance of necessary goods and services being available was the rationalization behind the government's complete nationalization of the Oil industry. An unsuspecting public had begged for it, imagining an alternative to the soaring price of automobile fuel and energy costs. Instead, the solution came in the form of harsh reality when the regulated fuel was easy to afford yet totally unavailable. The deal with Brazil for import of oil was a positive step, though the Russian made war crafts in the hands of Venezuela prevented any of it from reaching the states. The regulations and fines levied on almost every automobile prevented most people from driving, legally, anyway. However, people still drove in the face of going to jail, spurred on by the necessity to go to work and pick up their kids. There were always stories of people getting arrested, but there just weren't enough cops to stop it. Now that most fuel purchases had to be pre-approved and done through the issued fuel rationing cards along with a matching ID, it didn't much matter anymore. Of course, the gas stations still accepting cash due to some loophole were enjoying a line of customers.

Grocery stores once filled with people and goods seemed vast and vacant. The size of the supermarket building now seemed unnecessary, as all the shelves were less than half stocked. Looking at the back of an empty milk cooler into the stock room once completely concealed by goods was so surreal. He remembered the days of pushing the cart alongside his mother, taking for granted all the easy access to a never ending variety of flavors and foods. Cream cheese came in onion, plain, low fat, strawberry, low fat strawberry, and organic. The brightly colored plastic containers lined the shelves, making a colorful pattern down the refrigerated rows of the dairy shelves.

Now, looking at them through sadness at the memory, seeing instead the grey concrete walls of the dairy cooler behind the rows of empty metal racks and glass shelves, he realizes what a luxury it was to have such a variety of food abundantly available to him in the past years. The racks once holding a variety of goods were now almost completely empty. His biggest concern in those blissful days had been persuading his mother to buy the strawberry flavored variety of cream cheese instead of the onion flavor. They were poor and he did not always get all he wanted, but there was always plenty of food. He would stay up late at night gorging himself on strawberry cream cheese spread across bread and bagels, sometimes eating it straight off of his finger. Now, with the rust on the metallic grating exposed and the cooler smelling dank from mildew forming within it, he wished he could get cream cheese at all, or some fresh milk for that matter.

At the election of a new president, a new leader of the free world was declared. The people had chosen decisively through an overwhelming turnout in inner cities, the likes of which none had ever seen. Although local reporting across the country told stories of voter fraud in the election, the president was enormously popular throughout the international community, according to national media outlets. He was handsome, he was young, and he was so eloquent that even when he did not know the answer to a question posed to him in public, his mastery of language and confident proclamation of improvable facts left people thinking he had answered their questions with a level of intelligence that was so much higher than their own, that they didn't even understand it and that they were best to pretend they did. All they could do was accept his answers as truth for fear of being found foolish.

He was a great politician, a great salesman. The twisted twinkle in his eyes, the way they seemed slightly dampened by the humor of his own brevity keeping him close to tears, made him seem sincere. The air that none of it mattered to him because he already had all he needed felt familiar to the lower middle class, who always thought of themselves the same way when buying gas from a clerk or demanding ketchup from a fast food worker. They identified with the handsome young president's wit, his swagger.

Sweet, intoxicating television. It held the power to change global warming into global cooling almost overnight. The threat of drought ridden famine could be replaced with the threat of another ice age with the flip of the switch. Whatever happened to acid rain? The nightly news told them as children the rain had toxic chemicals in it, but it did not seem to melt the plants. Kids would still play in it, running around in the mud and chasing each other in what seemed like a surreal, wet bliss. None of them ever seemed to have died, and eventually 'acid rain' went away.

But the threat never went away. The news was always predictable: If it wasn't a drought, it was a flood. The threat of a new millennium crashing all computers compelled millions of citizens worldwide to stock their shelves with canned goods. The threat of poisons dripping into the water supply made them buy bottled water, and the threat of salmonella in food packaging plants made them throw away their canned food. It was a vicious cycle, continually played out through coordinated media nationwide. There was always something to be worried about. Disappearing bumble bees and genetically engineered vegetable seeds were sure to spawn the destruction of all trees and life as we knew it, as long as the ever errant gigantic meteor did not crash into our planet first. If the public's attention span was not so short, there would be no swimming or playing in the Sun, no digging in the dirt and nowhere to run from a maze of prescription drugs and psychotropic remedies.

Of course, the trees kept budding. Those of them who ran around barefoot in the grass, shirtless through the woods and headfirst into the brown rivers, amazingly seemed to survive at a higher rate than those cautious ones who's mother's caked them down in Sunscreen cream and pumped them chockfull of vaccinations. The heathens roamed the earth all day in the Sun and got tans rather than skin cancers. It didn't seem that you could make them sick if you tried. The media's newest dangers were but a background sound to the wind whizzing through their ears.

There were those who would continually find a way to put their talents to use, who would continually see things as they saw them, who continued to pray. They were not trapped by the consolidation of ideals and intellect by the main stream. To them, the new president was humorous, and handsome, but not the demigod people around them made him out to be. To those whose thoughts had found their own paths, who had been in the practice of making up their own mind since their upbringing, he was just another salesman, a face for the same current they had been drowning out all their lives.

Secretly, the people living in spite's world knew what people outside of their dimension thought of them. Secretly, they feared the tenacious independence of people who didn't think they needed mandatory health insurance or a guarantee of civil order and protection in order to survive. They shuddered at the sight of their children running through the wet ditches barefooted in chase of a snake, and thought something should be done to bring them into reality.

"The lust for power, that's what it is, son." His father's words from ten years past rang in his ears with new meaning as he lounged on his couch, watching the evening news.

It was Decoration Day, the festivities were great and they showed video footage of memorial commemorations from all over the world.

The president walked alongside the decorated military Generals to lay a giant wreath on a tripod near the grave of thousands of dead soldiers. Walking beside the sturdy defense men, the president appeared frail and weak. The camera was not flattering from the awkward angle, perhaps. The way he walked, with his head slight to the ground, you could almost see him getting shoved in a middle school hall way. Bullies liked attention; they knew that being perceived as powerful attracted the girls. Nobody is pushing him now...

In his first few weeks of power, the new president laid out 'bold, sweeping reforms' to fix the ailing economy. The economy, not so much ailing as being priced out of five dollar cups of coffee, never needed 'fixing.' However, the 'fixing' would be done. The fresh young president outlined his bold new reforms on national television in the ultimate bid to sell his deal.

Part 1: Banks. Lending of money was paramount to the institutions of society. After all, the majority of all profits gained were formed by accruing interest and this was, clearly, a pillar of industrialized society.

"We will make sure these institutions are in place by regulating how they spend their money, and if they don't lend the way they're supposed to, we'll put different people in their places who will. We will no longer let rich banking executives fly off on their private airplanes to some exotic island resort to drink their martinis. Not while, mean while, millions of children in this country are without health insurance. We are too great of a nation, and I do not find it acceptable, I will not accept corporate greed to continue to make millions while thriving off the sweat of the poor!" The crowd stood and gave him a thunderous applause.

John cracked another cold beer as he watched the man on his TV screen.

"Step 2, will be the reform of health care," said the man on the screen. "Millions of people have had to go without health care over the last two years. My plan will put a stop to that. We will make sure once and for all that Americans who need health care will get it!"

As the orator finishes his line, the crowd of seated senators rises to applaud him. John angrily throws his can of beer across the room.

"What if I don't need your health care," he yells emphatically.

"For too long now, the current establishment has taken its profits out from the backs of the poor. We will make sure this is no more."

The droning voice of the new president continues through the cool night in his living room, blending out and in to the prevailing atmosphere of the night. John dazed off into thought again, spurred on by the increasingly intoxicating effects of the beers he was drinking, not listening to the trite rhetoric of the politician anymore.

"The third step I am outlining here tonight is the right for every child to have an education. A federally approved education is no longer a chance for further progression in today's society, it is a *condition*. Dropping out of high school is no longer an option."

Again, the crowd leapt to clapping approval of the new president's thoughts.

"If you serve your community, serve in the armed forces, or volunteer with local outreach groups, you will be guaranteed a college diploma. These policies will open up doors for our children; it is our job to make sure they walk through them."

"What if I don't want your damned education!" Yelled John, hurling yet another beer at the television screen.

He then turned the channel to a local newscast of a chirpy woman saying the exact same thing, at the exact same time. The newscaster was trying to smile, a tear glimmering in the corner of her eye as she tasted the flavor of the shit coming from her mouth. It was all the same. Two heads of the same beast fought for power every four years, wrestling yet another privilege of freedom from its citizens with each persuasion of fear and of malice used to gain the political clout the frightened citizenry gave them. Their message was outlined specifically in the innuendos of every talking point.

"Someone will kill you," they said as they showed the burning buildings behind the soothing voice of the even newscaster. "Think of all that power you're holding, your privileged life of driving cars and ordering food at drive-throughs," she said in undertones and innuendos as images of marooned automobiles lined up on highways flashed on the screen. "Do you think those less fortunate around the globe are not conspiring to kill you, to knock you off your high horse?" The rallying, ragged clans from far away desserts waved their weapons on the screen. "Think of all those tacos you're flipping. Do you think the man who is at the top of the mammoth corporation is flipping tacos? Do you think he cares about you while he's getting rich off of your efforts to barely feed yourself and depend on government rations to feed your family? He doesn't care about you, just flip the damn tacos."

The turbaned faces' wide white eyes gleamed with an unmistakable look upon their Suntanned skin. They were up to something. The underlying messages in the newscast were enough to make him turn the channel back to the silver tongued politician who was still droning on.

"It's time to make sure all people in this great nation are in the same boat," the robotically enthusiastic voice droned on. "No more will we shun in disregard as our fellow countrymen drown in despair, no more will we let Wall street executives fly around in their fancy jets while hard working countrymen struggle to make ends meat."

The coffee table was strewn with cigarette butts which had missed the targeted ash tray amongst half smashed blue and silver aluminum beer cans. The remote control was sitting right next to the ash tray, decorated by a few cigarette ashes which had fallen onto it. Grabbing the remote, John mashes the buttons but finds it no use as the speech is on every channel and the president's convincing pitch rolled on.

He was 'calling on all nations' to unite while continuing wars on different battle grounds, and nations from across the globe began to open their concourses of dialogue with him. He made his first trip as 'The Leader of the Free World' to formerly dissident countries and bowed to their kings, polished apples and ran down reporters. Within eight short years, he was prepared to give up his post as President to become the first ever head of the newly formed world government which had stemmed from the International Earth Preservation Council. It was hailed as a huge relinquishment of power, a grand display of humility in face of an electorate at home that was ready to give him a third term in office. He promised to continue fighting for change, to continue showering the people with rice and shiny plastic, and assured the public that he was still "right there with them." They knew he was just one of them, even as they watched him board his private jet and fly away for a three week long island vacation.

It had begun, under the guide of the newly elected international sensation, as a means of regulating bio-carbon emissions in industrialized nations. He was the least powerful man on earth, the chosen face for their big pitch. Their overwhelming support, as well as bribery and extortion, had allowed them to stop trade for any international company in a heartbeat if their regulations were not met under the legislation they passed. The power they created rested on the fact that they could stop any commerce they choose with the swipe of a legislative pen, as they set the standards and regulatory limits of production byproducts for each company quarterly.

That they would take over your company was no idle threat. They were open about flaunting their ownership of the fallen industry giants on international media channels. They wanted everyone to know, it served as a threat. There was no governing body with authority over the organization enforcing these new regulations to which one could protest the fairness or consistency of their findings and assessments, and through a fine which they collected from offending companies and dispersed to non offending ones, they reshaped the landscape of the emerging global economy.

Then, moving on from the barely protested persecution of the powerful few, they moved into the consumer sector by beginning to regulate, internationally, the emissions of automobiles. For this, a new global policing agency was needed, an enforcement arm for the newly formed global governance agency. The Organized Nations for the Environment, or O.N.E., was formed. The authorities they placed in every county of every country answered to no one except the central agency. They had but one objective: to remove offending vehicles and drivers from the roads.

The list of offenses warranting incarceration became long and confusing; they were frequently changing and varied according to makes and models of vehicles. Exceptions were made for driver's license classes including Alpha Red and Beta Blue, the carried over classifications from the public school days of the privileged class. Since none of the law enforcement or military vehicles met the 'average standard' in any consumer class, people processing ID's indicating government(GV) or law enforcement (PO) status were automatically exempt, as well.

The confusion of the laws was compounded by the fact that in each nation, armed enforcement officials in charge of carrying out compliance with these laws were always brought from foreign countries in this newly formed global pact. It was not long before "ONE" was a household name and accepted by most as a governing body with authority. It was not to be questioned. The soldiers who enforced it never asked any questions, and did not even speak the local dialect. To them, your protests sounded like a monkey chattering, a dog squealing, or a person crying. They had assumed the role of responsibility under of the title of "Organized Nations for the Environment Volunteer", but were not volunteers at all. They were mercenaries, paid soldiers with a specific mission and objective.

Those years proved to be widely considered as boom years in the most powerful, industrialized nations of the era. The call to move all electrical energy sources to nuclear fusion started as a chorus then became a law. With the ONE volunteers enforcing the new laws, ensuring order and crushing dissent, the construction of nuclear facilities, transport infrastructure, applications, sub stations, and regulations seemed to march on as unstoppable progress. The streets of New York were uprooted and even skyscrapers demolished in a symbolic show of the commitment to uproot the disgusting and primitive sources of power that lay beneath by destroying the pipes laid there so many years before. The march to energy independence became a sprint, a blind footrace towards an imaginary goal. It was a goal which propelled the runner's mind, through self deception, to fight for his life towards a symbolically taped line, safely away from an imaginary foe. Gasoline burning automobiles were banned from production. The shutting down and converting of every national automobile plant also created work, temporarily, and the economy boomed.

The boom was short lived, however. The machines the men created took their own places once the plants were built, and manufactured the standard issue automobiles in a level of automation never before seen or even imagined. The machine simply had to be fed raw materials and could virtually spit out the small, electronically propelled transportation modules referred to as 'pods.' Once the huge reactors had been built and the infrastructure had been established, the plant jobs in the energy sector dried up, too. There was no more building of refineries to be done; the energy infrastructure had been centralized and needed little input to run on its own.

The hunt for work by once proud laborers, once confident in the necessity of their trades, was exasperated by the limited range of the new vehicles and their general unreliability. The lack of qualified workers and transportation were magnets in the knees of conventional businesses in a metallic world, as qualified workers sat stranded in the humiliation of their immobility. In random and constant precision the major industries fell, however the necessity for the services and products they provided remained as the international government, the elites fronted by banks with household names, began assuming operative control of them in their downfall. Soon, every major facet of commerce had been centralized under the banner of the "ONE."

Now all the businesses were owned by the same small sect,

and they were perfectly content. There was no need for improving, there was no pesky interference from competition. Every medial job paid the same medial rate, everyone conformed to the same requirements, and quitting one job just meant working for the same people somewhere else. Every employer was nothing more than lower management for the parental government.

Medical services fostered dysfunction, they found it statistically more efficient. Explaining to patients and their loved one's symptoms and treatments, effectively meant the hassle and expense of making sure the treatment was done. Lost in a pile of paperwork, the nurses had no idea what the patient's illness was, and could only respond to questions with the drugs they had been directed to administer.

"Oh, I'm sorry Mrs. Ramirez, it just says here that you are supposed to take Biavlcan and Throwzine, with a new drip of Procoteen. You have to ask the doctor. He comes in at 2 tonight, and I'll be gone, so I'll leave him a note and see if he can come talk to you."

A nurse would be paid a nurse wage and a doctor would be paid a doctor wage, but just like the janitor, it was as far as they would ever get. There would be one nurse to every 15 patients, and one doctor to ever 6 nurses.

Every industry was the same. The ticket counter at the airport didn't care if the customers were happy, they knew they had no choice but to file onto the airplane and accept it. There was no incentive to deliver good quality meat on the hamburgers. If the customers wanted to buy the hamburgers somewhere else, it was of no concern to them. They owned the other place, too. There was no need to pay a competitive wage, either. Everyone knew well that there was nowhere else to go.

The previous attempts of classification become more and more useful as the progression continued, selecting the desirables of the progressive society while leaving those who were not part of the big act financially destitute. They were second class citizens. Never to be perceived as inhumane, the propaganda commercials showed the ONE soldiers as bright eyed idealists from other lands, concerned about the well being of others and making the great sacrifice to leave their homelands and travel abroad to help "O" class citizens. They were shown as handsome men with wavy hair, sub machine guns hanging by the side of their clean uniforms as they handed toys to children. 'O Class' stood for 'Opportunity Class.' They were the ones who had not been able to keep up with this rapidly evolving economy and job base, the administrators said. They must be helped, and through organization and coordination, the Organized Nations for the Environment, would do that.

"I'm confident we can do it," said the politician's smooth voice on the television, "We are the shining light in the world, and it is our duty to identify and help these citizens unable to keep up with the rapid progression of this great new, international society."

Marking them with invisible inscriptions was the first step. Unlike a chip, which could be removed and even switched, the photo phosphorus 'tag' was applied within 3 seconds, and with only a slight burning sensation of pain. The randomized patterns of the bar codes were chosen by computers and were as distinguishably unique to their database as a person's fingerprints. The great roundup of those unwilling to come in for their inscriptions was the first major act of policing by the new ONE forces. Even some of those who willingly went to get inscribed, fearing what would happen to their families were they taken by force, would never be seen again.

The inner city railcars that used to always be empty now made sense, as they were used daily to commute people out of the cities to unknown destinations in the country side. Detention camps set up at docks near waterways quickly ferried the detained to huge boats set closely offshore. As the soldiers ferried their prisoners like bounty and sent them off across the foreboding expanse of the ocean, new troops came in their places from returning boats, unloading prisoners from other countries who were supposedly captives of war, but more likely undesirable citizens of the O class from other ONE member nations.

The ones rounded up were often regular men who felt they had nothing to fear or hide. Sitting around meager meals with their families at dinner tables, their TV's showing the standard fair of transsexual men selling their decrepit bodies to unsuspecting college johns, or almost athletes running insane obstacle courses and inevitably falling into pools of slime and jello, they had no idea the trucks were in their yard until the door busted open to the bang of a battering ram and the blue suited ONE troops filed into their homes. Blue collared fathers had no answer to the question as to "why," while they were hogtied and drug off, helplessly watching their children's wide, terrorized eyes, as they looked at their father for the last time in utter humiliation.

They had accepted the filing classifications in their schools, they had accepted the un-bending authority of the international troops, and they had watched and even laughed at the calamity of the poor bastards chastised on their televisions for being different. They had always thought that they were one of them, one of the ruling class.

'Eat the rich' was the prevailing mantra which had led to the downfall of the men who had employed them. On television screens, they watched them escorted from buildings with their heads huddled into the collars of their big coats looking down, their hands behind their backs, handcuffed. It seemed they would never run out of villains, but, they eventually did. Then the 'rich' became the working class as the poverty increased. More and more of them depended on the government for their daily needs, so those who could get by through saving and hard work became the villains. Once considered the pillars of working class communities, their homes were openly looted and they were forced to stand constant guard.

Eventually, the increasing percentage of the population living off the government became the targets. They were the ones who could not fit in, who needed opportunity. Their opportunity came in the form of distant work camps where labor easily done by machines, the breaking of rocks, the fabrication of fencing, was done by underfed workers living in "Opportunity Camps."

They had turned the blind eye to the grabbing of everyone's freedom, justifying their complacency, constantly arguing to convince themselves that it was not them they were after. It was always those on the other side of some imaginary line, they deserved it, the worker bees had thought as they sat affront the droning cathode light with their families. Now, after being drug across a pier to a boat and piled into a dark hull, they felt the sting as their chickens came to roost. There was no reward for their quiet obedience, no shelter from the storm that had engulfed them as they watched.

They were not people, they were Fuel. They were the only fuel for the onward marching machine, the forward march of progress.

The weapons created through science's onward march were secretive. Tesla's work in antimatter became the main focus, as the unnamed force between element's particles was manipulated. That tiny force, that invisible thing holding the balance of everything in place, was being noticed. Giant proton accelerators were being built around the globe, in the name of science, as they searched for ways to weaponize the force. Few curious minds privately questioned ONE's commitment to further knowledge, and their feeble protests were as unknown to the public as the rapidly advancing science in antimatter.

A grid of coordinates crisscrossed around the globe, serving as a way to aim the beams of the machines through intersecting pulses. Ion waves from proton accelerators in different spots around the world could be aimed to coincide anywhere around the globe, or in space. No one really knew what exactly they could do. Did they produce anti-matter? Some said the ionization made by intersecting them at specific coordinates could effectively 'cook' the brains of entire populations. Some said they could be used to shift tectonic plates under the oceans and create massive earthquakes and tidal waves. Some said they could shoot holes in the Sun. The science was simple, just not readily understood: They learned to create the void; the energy just flowed into it.

Smaller versions of the machines were dispatched to law enforcement forces around the world. A single, silent emission from them could stop the workings of electronics up to miles away. Some people blamed the deaths of entertainment and political figures on them as planes sometimes fell from the sky with no apparent reason. The money and resources poured into the development of these super weapons, which were craftily positioned around the homogenized globe, was mind numbing. Average people continued to work, to do their share, burning their life force away at meaningless jobs, content in their insignificant existence as long as the numbing light would wash away their fears as they sat in front of it nightly on their couches. The soothing voice of the well groomed people on the evening news told them to laugh at it all, made them feel normal as numbers rolled out to which they could never count. What exactly is 13 trillion? Is it as much as a bazillion million? The masses never stopped to realize they were only feeding the machine with every dollar they earned, lever they pulled, and wheel they turned.

There was no war; there was no rumor of war. The controlled information they received through the consolidated media outlets told stories of renewed jubilation and wealth around the world thorough pictures of people shopping in stocked grocery stores and trying out the latest fashions. That was all they saw, never stopping to consider the harsh contrast it would be had a camera came into their own lives and seen their own desolate conditions. They were trained to hide it, to do anything to hide the despair of their financial positions.

Meanwhile, giants of private industry were being squeezed out of existence by increasingly growing demands to meet irrational expectations of efficiency and care which piled onto their costs. As the manufacturers shut their doors, more and more people got their pink slips. Engineers talked over beers at the pub about their 25 year tenure as they considered taking jobs in door to door sales. Trained mechanics began working under the shade of trees. The strain to fill the gas tank was paramount to the silent discussion of a new world bank, and a new world tax on energy. They did not need to notice the fact that every business squeezed out by their agenda was bought up by the capitol generated by the taxes imposed on those very businesses and workers, and that power was being consolidated.

They struggled like mad to drive the newest cars, to wear the newest clothes, to paint their faces and hide their souls. Few and far in between were the ones who arose and awoke in the dream, to find their soul burning for steam, their life only fuel for the marching machine. There seemed to be no way, but God was in it.

7. MIMOSA DAY

She is so excited. Now she is allowed to play with the big dogs. She has learned by now to approach with caution and she walks up behind the big Buster where he eats his food from the forty pound dog food sack on the floor in the laundry room.

He is orange like inner fire and tattered up with frayed ears and bald patches of gum in parts of his mouth where teeth should be. All of the scars that pronounce themselves as bald patches in the fur covering his body just make him look tough, not defeated or old. He stands forebodingly over his food, looking back at times with the blank, black eyes of a shark. The scars form stripes of white flesh running across the short red hair of his rigid forearms. Muscular shoulders grip onto the sturdy body, still proud through the numerous battles he has carried it into. His teeth are broken and many are missing due to the violent clashes they were at the end of, they are the hands and hammer's head of his combat. The loose skin, so hard to penetrate in its flaccidity and toughness, is rolled up in abundant lumps above his shoulders as he rears his head and emits a low, sinister growl directed at the curious puppy coming up behind him.

There is no way to keep him from being a big, mean dog, and there is no chance of curbing her curiosity as she inches up behind him, her head stooped low, her tail pointed back in a slight but evident apprehension.

"NO," she hears yelled by her master. Although she has been allowed to play with the big dogs, John is still a bit unprepared to let them argue over food. She does not need to eat his food; she just follows the big dog anywhere he goes, instinctively. This time, it may get her into trouble.

She was that one that lived against the odds. Of the 14 who had slid from their mother's womb, only four would live to see the third day. The others, too frail or unfortunate to grasp the vessels of their mother's milk soon enough, had perished in John's hands as he resuscitating them time and time again. The strong antigen in their mother's milk would protect their delicate immune systems from the looming threat of Parvo and other viruses, but they would not drink it in time.

Four lived. He found good homes for them all, farming them out carefully to friends as the emotional toll of ten precious puppies dying in his hands brought him inseparably close to the remaining four. Two of them would later be lost by the people who had chosen to keep them, and the only surviving boy of the litter six would be her only known sibling. Brett took him in after his house got broken into, and he grew into a huge brute of a guard dog. The rest were unaccounted for.

"Maybe that's why dogs produce litters of ten, because the majority of them are sure to die?" He thought.

She could have died, and in fact, had more reasons to than her littermates. At three weeks old, she was smaller, but braver than her littermates. She befriended Buster, cuddling up against his flapping rolls as he slept and yapping and nipping at him as he plodded around the house non deliberately. However, as he slept in the spare bathroom, she stumbled into him carelessly and he awoke startled in a snorting growl. He jumped up as his paw came down over her and his mouth pulled her head in the other direction in one, unconscious action. John heard the snarl, followed by the yelps and ran in to see her dragging her head around on the bathroom floor.

His first order of business was straightening out her neck. From his own experiences with broken bones, he knew the best thing to do was to hyperextend the joints, letting the fragments find their own places to settle back into. The mother dog watches as he pulls at the pup's neck amidst her screams. The little dog seems to be asking, "Why!? Why! Why?" in her yelps as the blood drips from her mouth. The tiny stream of dark red blood is barely visible over her shiny black nose. He feels her vertebrae popping back into place beneath his hand. His thumb and index finger is wrapped around her neck, making a hook behind her ears to pull outward on her head. As the baby dog's vertebrae are pulled into a straight line by the stretching of her body, they nestle into their natural crevices. Her head is back on straight.

He had rushed into the bathroom at the sound of the yelps and Buster's quick, snarling snap. She lay in the middle of the narrow bathroom floor, pushing herself around in a circle pivoted by her loosely hanging head as she lay on her side and her legs tried to run away. Pin sized drops of deep red blood spotted the floor beneath her as she yelped in pain. The mother dog had ran in at the same time and snarled at Buster in a questioning, angry look.

"Buster, how could you!?" exclaimed John as he gathered up the pup and tried pushing the rest of the puppies out of the big dog's domain. Her littermates had heard the yelps and were there to defend their sister, barking and growling in all twelve pounds of their combined intensity.

The following days prove hard as vets and friends tell John to put it down, that she's sure to die in pain, that it's the humane thing to do.

Shannon watches the people coming in and out of the house. As she washes the dishes, she fields small come-ons and sweet compliments from the men and women she encounters. She has claimed her spot, like a leaf temporarily halted by a stone in a stream.

She is a pit-bull, reared from honoree genes and cracked out, mean spirited dwellings where she learned to thrive and grasp onto the little morsels of love they dropped for her. She is worthy of their adoration, displaying her sweet spirit readily, both afraid of and indifferent to the pain of rejection she puts herself up for with every sincere smile she offers and beautiful word she drops from her mouth. She is a little thin, a little stout, obviously strong while still fragile and petite. She cooks the best eggs. She is the kind of woman men grasp for, then attain, and then go looking for other women again as her trusting nature leaves them to their own devices. Then, just as easily as she drifts into their lives, she floats off again with the slightest inclination wafting her lofting winds.

He held the injured puppy day and night, propping her limp neck straight and gently cooing her as he hoped for some miracle to grant her survival. He tried everything from eyedroppers to force feeding, but she just wouldn't swallow anything. On the third day, sure that euthanasia is the only way; John prepares a smoked salmon sandwich with one hand as he holds the dying dog in his other, mentally preparing himself for the trip to the vet to have the puppy put to sleep. The puppy lies on her back in the crevice of his arm as she has now for three days, squinting her eyes and stretching out for rest. She is weak from starvation. The dog showed so much will to live over the past three days. She seemed to be determinedly fighting, barking at blindness and raging headlong into walls after her convulsions, then pushing her soft head against John's arms as he cradled her. Had not she displayed such a strong will to live, to fight, he never would have stuck the small piece of smoked salmon into her mouth.

It was a last ditch effort, really a grasp at something he had hoped for, prayed for, and already accepted as impossible. Feebly, she licked at the meat, then swallowed it down hungrily in a quick gulp. When John saw her consume the soft fish, he might as well have seen Jesus himself walking across a tumultuous sea. For the past several days, she had not eaten anything. Her attempts so suckle at the nipple of her mother ended in frustration due to the broken bones in her jaw and a crushed nasal cavity that prevented her from forming the strong suction needed to extract milk from her mother's teets. Being only three weeks old, she had not been weaned and was only accustomed to drinking her mother's milk. Over the next week, her three litter mates grew to nearly twice her size as they gorged on milk while the little puppy survived on eyedroppers full of condensed milk and tiny morsels of soft food. It was a miracle.

Shannon expects no happy ending. The early death of her father had shown her the harshness of reality. Her father was one of those; content in his domicile while the world corrupted and disintegrated around him. He kept his time filled with gadgets and guitars, television shows and rented movies, pornography and methamphetamines. The rest of the family followed suit, occupying their happy days with shopping and TV watching, bongs and fish tanks. Nothing had prepared any of them for the quick disbandment of their family's life.

She left a note on lined paper torn from a notebook pinned to the wall which read,

'I'M WASHING YOUR CAR IS THAT COOL!'

He sat up in his bed and looked out the window beside it to her in shorts and a bikini top in the front yard, working diligently with a rag as the water hose hung from her hand. They were good times. His bed was never empty; his refrigerator was stocked with orange juice and Champaign. He had a list in his pocket of 500 friends he could contact with the push of a button on his cellular phone to declare a holiday like a king.

"Yo, Q."

"Yo, what up?"

"Man, I've got some girls over here on the couch. They're all off today, it's Sunny outside, and nobody wants to put on their shoes. We're going to end up running around barefoot in the yard as soon as I pop a couple of bottles of this Champaign. Come on over, it's Mimosa day."

"Word? All right, let me do this thing I got to do with my cousin, and then I'll swing through there."

The people came in and out of his house. They stayed when they had nowhere else to go, they left when they did. Jarrod was one, Shannon was another, and she would leave whenever she caught a ride. The two spare bedrooms served as temporary shelter for a variety of people. Sometimes for a month, sometimes for a day.

Zarina and Christina were kind of passersby, but they passed by frequently. They seemed cemented in circles of the same situations as the rest of the children of the Peopocalypse, although they came up in a completely different city. One of them knew their dad, possibly. The two adventurous girls, running through the world in a soiree of bars and clubs, easy loves and free drugs, weren't sure exactly what they knew. When they came by Flint's, they got a free breakfast and some coffee, at least. It was a *God-damn* good free breakfast, the hairy troglodyte would tell them. He was a happy, bare footed and bare-chested man who seemed to be good for advice, and that was how they saw him. Maple sausage was squeezed from the plastic tube onto the hot griddle for the special guests, emitting a sweet smell into the air of the kitchen as the eggs were pulled from the fridge with the cheese, breakfast tacos being the standard fair for the pair.

A good meal is paramount, and breakfast, they say, is the most important meal of the day. Lots of energy will be needed for your growing body, especially with all the activities we have planned for this special day. Mimosa day is the new holiday. It has surpassed Thanksgiving in order of importance, as the gas money to get home is spent on cheap Champaign, orange juice, beer and whiskey. Even Christmas could be Mimosa day, or Christmas Eve. Why not today? The two beautiful girls, each a fine representation of the great state in their natural forms, were stopping by for the holiday. It required *Thanksgiving,* and we would much oblige.

Breakfast was a mere formality. Although they all know the name of this game is bottoms up, they procrastinate and wait.

"Oh, I have some whiskey" John remembers, slyly.

"Oh, really? I love whiskey!" replies Christina.

"Who's that old man walking up your driveway?" asks Zarina.

The dogs bark as if they were the first to notice as John hushes them.

"It's just old man John. Shut-up, you stinkin' animals!"

The dogs continue yapping excitedly as Zarina remembers out loud,

"Hey, that's the guy who got you to do the garden!"

"Yep, that's him. Watch, he's going to ask if I have any beer. That old guy loves beer!"

They all hush as the old man reaches the door, thinking he must be able to hear them through the open window. The screenless gap is emitting the cool Texas breeze warmed by the autumn Sunlight of a crisp November day.

Old man John is handsome in his windbreaker and matching 'Purple Heart' hat topping his pressed pants. He shaved before 6 AM daily, although he had no pressing engagements besides walking around the neighborhood, and wore the Purple Heart lapel on his front shirt pocket consistently. He was a proud codger of 78 years old. A mess hall sergeant of many wars, he always knew how to get along with everybody. In a social setting, nothing was really a problem to him.

"You're a Democrat?! I'm a Democrat!" he would tell John was his mantra. "You're a Republican?! I'm a Republican! See John, that's how you get along, alright?" the old man told him. He hated drugs but loved beer. He could get along with whom ever, over a couple of beers.

"No, John, I don't. But I do have some whiskey," said the host as he raised his eyebrows in an inviting grin, responding to his question while simultaneously inviting the old man into some mischief and the two young girls along with them.

The shots would be poured in fours, as they were the only four there today. Black-Tooths, which consisted of three parts whiskey and one part cola, could get it done, eventually.

Old man John would tell stories of his war days, of hookers

he'd known in far-away lands, while changing parts of the stories to suit the ladies, talking over everything while the two young girls ignored movies and music to listen to him speak. He loved it there, at Flint's little house. The young people there clung to his words. He ignored their partaking in illicit behavior, which he despised, and found people he came to love. He tolerated their ways because they listened to him. They listened to him because they had never had a wise old man try to tell them something old and wise. His grandkids were spoiled. Unlike them, these kids never tasted the knowledge he dropped so casually, except occasionally from old drunks outside of gas stations who still hung to the wise old sayings and dropped them carelessly from their lips to justify begging and a life of neglect. They had never known an upright old man like John.

These kids were as hungry for wisdom as Old man John was hungry to be listened to. So, he came and he talked, he spoke and they listened, and they played music he liked. The old Country stuff, it brought him back to his wild times. He listened to that song when it came out in the 40's, he would say, and you could almost feel the dank, drafty air in the honky-tonk that he took you back to while describing it in simple terms.

"Boy, I tell you John, those Southeast Texas women are something else! Lined in that bar there, boy…"

You knew the bar was dark and dank, with black wooden planks adorning the entire place as women lined up at the bar. A fat man in a leather vest and cowboy hat was buying drinks for the one trying to sit on his lap as he leans on the barstool, which is adorned with fresh red glittery plastic covering. The redneck smacks his tongue against the roof of his mouth beneath his thick black moustache as he talks, reveling in his own vitality and power. His awkward days of being ignored and belittled by women for being a bit over weight are now only a justification for his open womanizing and domineering sex with bar-flys bought as cheaply as a few drinks. John Frone, a strapping young army sergeant, approaches the pompous man and all the ladies at the bar, unafraid of the large, brash cowboy. He was a few inches over six feet in those days.

"Boy, I was a hell of a man, too, until Ol' Charlie started shooting holes in me. Seems Ol' Charlie didn't like me too much."

His green suit pants were sweetly creased in those days,

forming a distinct line down to the reflective polish of his black leather shoes. His army hat hung down over his forehead, the back of it cocked up like a roster's tail, proudly. His dark, connecting eyebrows held steady over his wide, collecting eyes until he raised them for a laugh, which he was always able to provide. He walked with his thumbs turned inward towards his body and the points of his fingers curled loosely into his palms, ready to make a fist and fight at any moment's notice. The young military-man was strong and strapping from working on that farm, out there in Southeast Texas.

"It was a different world in those days. A man was lucky to do good enough to go down to the lumber yard and get a job for a few years. If you made it to eighth grade, you had really achieved something, and everybody *hated* picking cotton. Boy, the blacks, whew, they didn't stand a chance in those days. Naw, it's not like it is now. And you know, Hitler, he was going to take over the world...

"I was in the mess hall there, and Charlie started firing, bwoooy, and they had those mortars honed right in on us. See, in the previous nights, they had done some attacks, but nothing really happened, okay? Well, what they were doing was just honing in on us, getting our positions, okay?" His hand moved in front of him while he held John Flint's gaze and told the story through un-verbalized sentences coming through his eyes as he captivated the young man's stare. His eyes widened and the young man could feel the fear. "Okay, so I ran out there,' he said, his eyes raising up now to make sure everyone was paying close attention before he continued, "and the gunner was injured, shot to all hell." Again he paused, allowing the sentence time to stimulate graphic images of bodies whirling apart amidst mortar explosions before he continued. "You know those big guns they use for shootin up tanks and planes and shit like that?" Again he paused to insure complete attention by his audience.

"Yeah, those big ones with the strings of bullets hanging out?" the younger man asks perceptively.

A slow shift comes over the old man's face as if he is trying to discern whether the young man is twisting his mind.

"You know what shrapnel is?" the old man asks. "Yeah? Well okay. Most people think it's when the shrapnel explodes and it blows out and gets ya that you have to worry about. They think it's all the little pieces of metal and nails blowing out from the explosive that gets you, as it bursts out. But they're wrong, okay? It's the pieces that fall down from the sky that get you, see? They go up," he twiddles his fingers over his head, "then they come down. Just little pieces of metal, about yea big," he said as he held his thumb and finger about an inch apart. "But they were jagged and spinning, they would really mess you up. Well I had one come through my shoulder, right here, and it also came through my arm. I got some in my stomach, and, oh, it took some off of my face."

"Really," replies the young man.

"Oh yeah, they took off some of my face. I've got a titanium metal plate they cut out to form my mandible right here." He lifts his head back and opens his mouth to show them the place where the plate is, and his pink gums are revealed around the sporadic teeth still intact. "Yeah, Ol' Charlie got me pretty good, but all I could see was that 50 cal. machine gun."

The old man leans forward on his cane, leaning over John to make sure he listens.

"Bwoy, the machine gunner, I mean he was bloodied, blowed all to hail. I was a mess hall Sergeant, I was primarily there to cook, but I had still been trained to fight. So I had to grab that magazine and man that gun. Bwoy, and I could see em' runnin through the woods there, hiding behind the trees. But that 50 caliber round... You know about a fifty caliber? Well a fifty caliber will cut through about anything, I mean, it'll cut through a building. Oh yeah. I had those rolls of bullets hanging there down beside me, and man, it would go through em'. Cutting down a tree aint no problem, not with one of them things, I tell you what." His story faded off into a distant look on his face as images of blood spraying Vietnamese soldiers being cut in half ran through the minds of his audience, then he changed the subject.

"Boy, as a soldier, a man in uniform, those ladies knew you had some change in your pocket, see? I told her, 'hey, you wana drink?' She said she did, but she wanted a 'Lady's Drink!' A *Lady's drink,* ok? A Lady's Drink, back then, see, a beer would cost you 50 cents, ok? But a *Lady's Drink!* Oh man, that could cost you TWO DOLLARS! Oh man..." The story would continue and blend into a thousand others as the drinks went down. "*TEXANS,* a pair of Texans... Even in Germany, *nobody* wanted to mess with a pair of Texans. You get two Texans together, and they could really tear

122

a place up. Then we'd have to pay a little extra money to the bar, to pay for their broken tables, chairs, and what-not."

"We wanna drill. Will you drill us, please, John?" Zarina asked as she leaned over the old soldier where he sat on the couch in her very convincing way.

She was beautiful, long and lean, six feet tall with wispy, blonde hair. She had changed into her little-bitty shorts and form fitting shirt; to be comfortable. Her legs shone out beneath the tiny shorts as long tributes to the strength and grace of American women. She was happy and proud, always smiling. Old Man John's face glazed over, and you could feel the breeze of all the cool bars of his youth in spite his noticeable silence. It was as if the young girl's most convincingly persuasive manner of asking the question, which was usually reserved for and practiced to perfection by getting guys to buy her drinks at bars, brought him back to all the women who had approached him in his youthful days of world travel and had asked him to buy them a drink. For moments he stared blankly at the sexual vixen, considering the question.

"Come on, John, they want you to drill them!" yells John, excitedly laughing as he rolled on the couch in an intoxicated bliss of self amusement.

Old Man John just sits with a blank look as they stand up in the middle of the living room and begin their regiments alone, drilling each other. They had both had short stints in the military.

"Mine's Navy, yours is Army!" quirks Christina. They seem a little confused.

"About face!" commands Zarina, as they poke their proud little breasts out and turn forward, presenting their sexy young forms outright. They begin a dismal, yet admirable attempt at forming ranks.

"Left face!" she yells, as one turns to the left and the other to the right, in perfect unison.

"Oh, my other left!" laughs Christina.

"ALRIGHT, PRIVATE! Give me an about face!" Old Man John suddenly shouts in a large voice, which fills the room like a sonic boom.

Startled, they spin in his direction and show full attention as he demands it, giggling only occasionally as they confuse their rights and lefts in a drunken, delightful stupor.

"That's pretty good, you've got the idea. That's some pretty good soldiers you got there, John," he says now, that he's satisfied himself with having them march in place and do pushups for 10 minutes straight.

"Hell yeah, I know. I'd hate to be the guy to mess with them!" he responds enthusiastically.

They really were tough, a great representation. All of the kids who came around here were pretty tough, John would think, as the Mimosa Days passed and blurred into one another. The drilling became like a ritual on those fun filled days. The first time Jarrod had come in and caught them doing their routines, he joined in. Then he got the other kids who followed him around the neighborhood involved. It became a Yoga-like exercise for the men who stopped by John's place, too. John was staying fit digging in the back yard, usually alone, as his buddies learned fine points on life and marching from the wise old man over beers in the living room.

Between his lessons on drilling, and within them, the old man taught them other things, telling them stories of surprise in character, of despicable self indulgence eating fine young men. He told stories of valor, of fighting with broken, burning shrapnel in his body. He told stories of grit and patience, how to hold form and fire to kill. He taught them aim and maintenance of the rifles and pistols around the little house on the prairie, while the paper gangsters and drifting riff raffs watched in solemn reverence. He was making great soldiers of all of them.

Zarina and Christina kept a light hearted eye on it all when they stopped by to grace the whole scene.

"That's right, about face!" they would yell mockingly when they surprised the young men drilling with Ol' Man John as they plopped up on the couch with cold beverages. The intimidatingly pretty girls would laugh, but then continue to encourage the boys in their work.

"I used to do that; I can do it better than you!" Zarina would shout as they both jumped up to join the ranks of the marching squad practicing form in John's living room. They were like cheerleaders for a team without a name. Soon the wooden floor was thudding like a big bass drum under the feet stomping in unison.

They could shoot a gun as well as any Russian soldier. Some thanks to the military, but like most of their true Texan siblings in spirit, they were raised with guns in their hands. They had always been able to shoot them, as long as they remembered. It must have been something that was taught to them long ago, at a young age. B.B. guns were awarded to their brothers on their 11th Christmas and the games of puncturing aluminum cans began. Some showing of pride for a girl to shoot better than a boy came to those enthralled by the thrill of competition. To aim a weapon was as simple as tying a shoe. They could really squirm at a cricket, acting all girly and squeamishly afraid. Pretty weak, one might think, but there was some strength there, too.

When the fish were brought from the lake the first time, they watched John slice a line down one's belly, then begin gutting the beautiful animal as it still sucked for air. The adult bass heaved for breath as the fillet knife slid through his stomach. Its shinny skin was patterned in green and black brilliance atop its white belly as it was peeled from the pink meat. Its bulging eyes rolled back, as if trying to get a good look at the mad man holding his head firmly down on a cutting board while dissecting his body. It seemed he knew that the butcher could see himself in his eye's reflection as he watched it die.

A short time after squirming at the sight of its entrails sliding from its belly, the girls helped in breading the large filets. They ate the white fish with potatoes happily that night and the next time they saw a fish brought into the kitchen, they snatched it up from the fisher's hand. Aggressively, as if attacking some fear, they slapped it down on the cutting board and took joy in finding the proper knife, giggling and joking as they went through the blades looking for the best one.

"This is the sharp one," says John, pulling the slender, silver instrument from its harness. He hands them the filet knife and they go to work on the poor meal to be, stabbing straight into her distended stomach.

Inside are minnows and a crawfish, as well as some indistinguishable items of sludge and mud which drip out slowly onto the cutting board over the sink before the animal's still moving eyes. Zarina discards the remnants in a trash sack then overzealously begins cutting the meat from the skin as John rushes in.

"No, no! You're wasting all that meat!" John exclaimes as he narrowly escapes death, dodging the blade whipping towards him.

Zarina had thrown her hands up in disgust as he jumped in, pushing the blade behind her head in the gesture which nearly stabbed him in the face.

"But we're cutting this fish up for you," she whimpered.

He gently removed the knife from the frustrated girl's hand as he grasped the slimy fish in his other hand. The bass was full of roe and she was still breathing as the bright yellow eggs spilled from her slowly.

"Well, first you've got to cut her head off", he said.

He looked back to see the further disappointment on their faces. "Well, I guess you don't really *have* to cut her head off first..." He slides the blade in just behind the poor animal's head. "This is how I like to do it. Put the blade in just behind the ear here. See all that? That's all good meat."

He puts his fingers between the ribs and the thick back muscle as he patiently works the blade down her side, pulling the meat back in small segments as he feels for the bones with the finger tips of his other hand which are inside of her cool body, between her muscles and her bones. The sharp blade simply slides between the meat and bone, effortlessly removing the meal and exposing the internal workings of the fish with its shiny, sharp edge.

"Now, you try this side." he says once he's removed the meaty filet.

"But you did it so good!" they respond, "do the other one!"

"Here," he says, handing the girl the knife. "You can do it."

The cutting of the fish, the plowing of the dirt, the practicing military drills, they all serve the purpose of yanking the drifters from a world of functionality. As the people come and go, they take with them the strange, un-reality they have experienced and walk with a different demeanor through the plastic streets of flashing lights. They come in and go out, some staying for days at a time and others only for an afternoon. No matter how long they stay, they are all witness to it; they are all affected by it.

The tile is swept daily, collecting discarded black hairs of the watching dog. He and his brother circle the premises under foot and find places to plop down. The two of them witness the whole spectacle with their tongues hanging lazily from their panting mouths. The black pit is unimpressed as he collapses down on the floor and feels the coolness of the tiles on his belly while watching the young boys lift one knee and turn right face in perfect unison to

126

Old Man John's command. The black dog looks back at them, passively, his eyes rising slightly to wrinkle the loose skin between them as the little survivor who now calls this home prances across the room before him to greet a guest.

Shannon has returned with her mother, who needs a place to stay, too, only she won't admit it. She says she'll sleep in her car somewhere, but John won't allow it. Instead, they all drink until driving is out of the question and she sleeps on the sofa. As John watches her there, he begins to think that these survival skills may come in handy someday, maybe soon. More and more of them need it, more and more people are lost in the world with no good place to go and more and more of them seem to be ending up here. He remembered when he had met her in a bar downtown. She had the look of eternal sweetness in a world of shit. Her angry eyes could not disguise her baby face. She was no match for the world, he wanted to take care of her. She was happy to trade cooking and cleaning for a safe place to stay.

Soon she was intertwined in the daze of Mimosa Days, spreading her wings and flapping her eyelids at all of John's friends. She even captivated Jarrod's heart to the point that he couldn't take it anymore. In a fit of jealousy, he tried to fight John, and had to move out. John didn't care. He was having fun, living free, and doing as he pleased.

From the spot at the bar where you are standing you can clearly see his face. He looks like anyone else, blonde hair, thin but not too thin, tall but not too tall, and he is looking at you intently. His green jacket is casual, he sips an expensive beer. What does he want from you? His eyes probe you for a sign of weakness, calmly, rationally. He definitely knows you, and you know him, although you've never seen his face before. You've got it now, he's the Devil. His eyes are asking you a question. He does not want you to do something for him; he is more concerned with what you may do to him, although it seems that he is indifferent to the pain you may cause him. He is searching you. He knows your side, he knows you have him here now, right where you've always wanted him, and he wants to know what you will do about it. You look into his eyes, knowing what you are facing, but you are unafraid. You think of grabbing the physical form in your powerful feeling hands, of ripping him apart. Then you notice something: He's just like you.

Like a distorted mirror image that shows what you could be in a different light, only backwards. It *is* evil! It is everything bad, yet you find some relation with the figure, the old telling eyes of the young preppy man. You tell him silently that you will let him go, from pity, you have just made a deal with the devil.

He awakes in his bed at the dawn of early morning and shakes off the dream before going back to sleep.

The morning fog is rising like mist over the water of the old industrial bay. You have traveled endless miles of peril to reach this far away destination. From the low skiff which you are floating on, you see the rusty metallic sides of the man-made shore rising from the brown and frothy water. The structure's jagged walls are Orange and Red from oxidation and flaking off like dying skin.

A giant barge is pulling up to it in front of you and there is a soldier directing you to dock in a strange language, probably Russian. He sees that you do not understand and speaks English to you;

"You go here." He points to the dock and you jump from your skiff which has carried you through rivers and oceans to arrive at this strange, unknown place.

On the dock you meet Vladimir Putin, the king of the evil empire in a bejeweled golden crown, and you join him on his boat. He is cordial but menacing in his silent, dead stare. Some form of negotiation is taking place as you size him up and he stands like a statue, allowing you to do it. He just stands there, unashamed of what and who he is. A hard man, an honest man, you decide you like him but keep your hard demeanor as well, to avoid showing any weakness.

On the journey you lighten up, lighten him up with a smile and drink some mixed drinks. You get him back to your country, deep in the woods and bring him to your art studio where he adores the work and offers to buy it for any sum. Although he is far from his element in your deep wooden cabin, he still seems in command and confident in his presence. This one, he says, is the crown piece of your collection, as he looks at the abstract painting of chaos and out-bursting lines of color illustrating a will to rise above the calamity around you. You do not recognize the piece, but you know you have done it. He will pay you any sum.

His long petticoat is simple but fine, his posture is pronounced in its uprightness. He is hiding no secrets. It's a deal.

8. GRANDIOSE

It was a clear, Sunny day. The light was coming through the leafs in the Pine trees swaying overhead and everything was green. Megan and John followed Billy through the yard of trodden grass and sandy patches between it to the front of the brick house where he lived. Billy had taken them to find a snapping turtle for John's fish tank in the murky waters of the Southeast Texas bayou's swamps and marshes. Megan and John were far from their little efficiency apartment back in the congested city now, tromping around in mud while following their rubber boot clad tour guide. Amongst the trees and across the streams they climbed muddy embankments and shared stories, finding almost every creature imaginable *but* snapping turtles.

Upon arriving back at his home in the woods, they cross the front yard and enter through the front door of the little house. They pass through the living room, around the dining area, and through a side door into a built on room in the back. The dim room may have once been a back patio that has been closed in with naked plywood, and they exit the building through a swinging screen door. On the back porch, Billy pokes at a live alligator in a metal tub with a mop handle as they continue talking and the four foot long reptile thrashes around.

Billy was a country boy. He wore light blue Dickie's overalls over a white t-shirt and his red skin rose above its collar line to curly locks of blonde hair hanging out from under a red baseball hat. The hat, faded to nearly pink and frayed from constant use, sat slightly upwards and to the side. It was not a pre-worn, trendy hat from the mall; the well worn look was authentic. It was a perfect off center in that it did not convey premeditation of style, there was no way it could have been off center on purpose. It was an honest hat-cock that told of his honest disregard for 'civilized' society. Strong, round forearms frosted with light blonde hair reached down into his pockets as he spoke. His Texan accent had a thick Creole glaze.

"We were down there in the middle of the night; your brother was with us, over by the cut? And, enyway, Travis never told you? We would go out at night and catch Alligators."

They were standing next to a big metal tub in his yard now, looking down at a four foot long live alligator.

"So we got this big one, right? I'mean, it was huge. Twelve feet long, fourteen, easy! Just teeth flashin, we were trying to pull him onto the boat. I usually like to tie em' up, you can sell him. But, I mean, this thing was huge! It was like, we were gona *hafta* shoot it for sure, it was just too dangerous. Then, out of nowhere, this light comes up, and we hear the, what's that thing called?" He mimics someone speaking through a megaphone.

"A megaphone," says Megan.

"Is that what it is?" he retorts.

"A bullhorn," says John.

"Yeah, a megaphone, I mean, a bullhorn! Well anyway, we knew they was comin for us, inthen…" In mid sentence Billy's speech is interrupted by an abrupt question.

"Wait, it's illegal to catch alligators?" asks John.

"Well shit yeah! You gotta have permits for that stuff. They are a protected species. Well, enyway, we could see the flood lights of the Game Warden's boat coming around the bend. We knew we had to get rid of him and he was all in our boat, I mean he was spinnin around n shit, big jaws snappin everywhere. 'Snap! Snap!' So I just shot him." Billy makes the shape of a gun with his right hand and illustrates the shots as he tells his story. "Boom."

"So, ya'll got away?" asks John.

"Yeah, but get this: The next day they had in the front page of the paper, right across the top, '*ELSIE MURDERED*!' It was that *gadamn famous alligator* that everybody pays to feed when they go over the bridge! Down there by the state line! Is that shit crazy, or what?" Billy exclaims as he bursts into laughter, raising his hand above his head and slapping his thigh through his tight jeans.

"Who the hell would want to feed a *gadam* damned alligator? I mean, they pretty, I guess." The archaic creature in the metal vat sloshed around as if on command to prove just how pretty he wasn't when Billy slapped its head.

"You want to see them dogs?"

They walk back to where the wooden doghouse sits in the back yard and the mother dog gets up to come towards them. She is shiny black, her muscles ripple under her short hair as she approaches with a curious look made sinister by her short clipped ears. A solitary white diamond on her chest exaggerated her broad shoulders. She was like a sinister submarine methodically moving towards you across the yard. Her torso was round in its muscular figure; her head was rounded out by powerful jaws and a gaping mouth that spread from end to end with a row of jagged white teeth.

Her yellow eyes set un-flinching on you as she slowly, steadily, walked towards you with her head lowered only slightly, the perfect amount. Her look conveyed a tactical menace, showing she did not care what the civilized world could do to her in trying to keep her from defending her young. Her cocked head was the perfect threatening omen: you would never know if it was on purpose. It was just instinct to her.

"Check this out!" says Billy.

He walks across the well worn yard to the rubber tire swing that is wrapped around a big tree and frees it. It seems like a weird swing, the tire is nearly five feet off the ground. John is looking up at the tree branch to see if it the rope has been wrapped around it too many times, trying to figure out why a swing would be so high. The dog follows him over, pulling her chain with her, Billy restraining the dog by her collar. He commands her to sit and to stay. She sits on her haunches and watches him expectantly as he backs over to the hanging tire.

"Watch it girl, waaaatch it, watch it," Billy tells the dog, holding the tire out in front of her. She braces slightly in a moment of silence.

"Now *get it*!"

She explodes like a spring towards the tire and leaps for it, stretching at the heavy chain around her neck. Although the thick linked chain seems fully extended, she is stopped short of her target and the tire continues to sway on its rope. With less momentum, she continually tries to reach the tire, pulling and leaping impossibly towards it. Her teeth are snapping with each near miss as the chain sways behind her and the tire swings back again, just before her face.

"Here ya go, girl!" says Billy as he holds the tire closer to her reach. She lunges for the car tire in undaunted determination and latches on. The sway of the chain pulls her back and her feet are suspended in the air as the tension between the tire and her chain lifts her. She still holds on, the chain and the rope suspended across the yard, one attached to a tight collar around her neck and the other to the tire in her jaw's concrete grip. She growls as she yanks at it, convulsing her body into controlled contractions with her toes hanging just off the ground.

"I had to get a new tire just last week," Billy marvels.

The puppies are running out to greet them. Now that they have put the big dog put up, they walk over to the wooden dog house in the yard to make their pick.

"You should have seen the one. Oh, I gave it to T-ray, he got the first pick. Huh? Oh, well, not anymore. An Owl ate it. Yeah, an Owl, he said he saw it himself. Just came down from the tree and…"

"T-Ray *saw* the Owl come down, right out of the tree and, what, just grab the dog?"

"Hell yeah, man, that's what he said. Or maybe a Raccoon ate it, or something, I don't know… Enyway, this is the one for your brother," he points towards the Orange one. "That's the biggest one; he's got the best coat, too."

The puppies all prance around their guests, frolicking around and fighting with each other, their intensity made cute by their miniature growls and snarls. Megan is picking them up and flipping them over as she gives them all baby talk.

"You don't have any black ones?" asks John.

"Go look behind the dog house," Billy tells him, "but you don't want that one, he's retarded."

Behind the house the Black sits alone. He is anxious and nervously pats his tail while lowering his head below his shoulders. He lowers his head even more as he approaches his new boy, swaying it slowly and low to the ground as he inches towards John's feet. He is not rambunctious like the other ones, but quiet and apparently sick. The vulnerable puppy gently rolls the top of his head into John's palms as he scoops him up.

Holding the dog like a baby under his front arms and lifting him up to his face, John touches his nose to the tiny, wet nose of the puppy and looks into his eyes. The little dog returns the stare, unflinching. Their worlds collide in chemical reactions; a whole spirit is passed through the eternity of molecular energy combusting at controlled precision as they spurn reactions within each other. A tunnel from some distant time passes through the little black eyes, sending out that eternal energy back spinning into John's brain, creating a permanent, physical bond.

"You will be a good dog," John tells him, I will take good care of you."

Most of the dog's front teeth are missing now. The years have been hard on him. Back then, John had grand and noble visions of his rescue of the dog. He had taken the Black dog and the big Buster which had been groomed for his brother. At the time, Travis Crockett Flint had been living with him. When his brother moved out, he had no place to keep the dog and John won it by default. Eventually, the big Buster would be his dog and the Black, Shadow, would be Megan's. When she left, John also won that dog by default. He would later learn that they were the only two survivors of their litter.

Puppies are a numbers game. Who's to say which one lives? The odds were against them. On the night they took them, their stomachs had been so distended from worms that the skin was stretched tight about their bellies.

John had heard that farmers sometimes fed handfuls of tobacco to farm animals to de-worm them, because tobacco contained a natural form of Arsenic. Before ever taking the dogs from the wooded yard of the house, John force fed the two of them half of a pack of cigarettes on the front porch. Within minutes, strands of worms began spilling from both ends of the puppies and piles of angel hair pasta looking parasites continued to appear behind them throughout the night.

From then on, the pups led a healthy, active life. He and Megan had fed them well, groomed them well, brought them on trips, and loved them well. They became the most affectionate and protecting dogs they had ever seen, rolling up next to them or flopping their warm, soft rolls of skin over them on cold nights.

Even as puppies, their bark was a menacing deterrent when they were riled.

The Black was more easily riled than the other, he also seemed more emotional. Both of the dogs were prone to getting their feelings hurt and had developed extremely interpersonal skills of communicating without words. Shadow would 'shake,' Buster would 'speak.' The one refused to do the other's trick, although they both would sit on command.

Other things came natural to their breeding. Sitting and staying put by their master's side was easy to train them on. John would train them to be obedient with the cats which put them into a frenzy every time they entered the arborous corridor between the two apartment buildings where he walked them. As they turned the corner of the courtyard and saw the cats, their ears would pop up and turn forward and their tails would turn straight, pointing back.

"Wait for it... not now, stay, stay," he would whisper to them.

"Sit, stay," he would tell them. The dogs would sit and emit low whimpers. He then unleashed their chains.

"Stay. Now, watch em." With that command, the dogs would rise from their sitting position and slightly crouch, hunching their necks into their shoulders to lower their heads, as if trying not to be seen by a prey in the tall grass fields of some primal hunt.

"Whatch em.' Whaaaatch em," he would say. They were stalking slowly together now, keeping their eyes on the cat 40 yards ahead as they crept forward.

"Now, *get em*!" Upon hearing that command, the dogs break into an open run at the wide eyed cat which scrambles for a tree and runs up it. They bark at the base of the tree, jumping high on the trunk and grabbing the bark with their teeth, hanging from the side of the tree and trying to pull themselves up it with their powerful necks. Silly dogs.

"Enough!" With this command, they drop from the tree, their snarls stop and they trot back over to their master.

The attack training came almost instinctively. With the words, 'get em,' preceded by the command, 'watch em,' they were set loose. Other things also came naturally, such as barking at strangers and running through the streets and woods with their master like they were warriors on a raid. They trotted alongside him, increasing speed as he sped up and never getting under foot as he maneuvered them through alleyways, up and down concrete stairs, through rocky trails and thick underbrush. He had found new running buddies as they ran open-out, imagining themselves on some great hunt as he had done in his childhood days with his friends.

The Black was Megan's dog. It was her who had held him through those first sickly days, petting and consoling him constantly. Now, if together, he would not leave her side. No one dared make a quick move towards her with the big dog by her side. His muscles rippled under his shiny black fur which seemed to reflect blue light, like a crow's feathers.

In puberty, the puppy's head grew two ridges of powerful muscles that formed domes over his skull, wrinkling the loose skin between his ears which flopped forward. His face was rounded by powerful jaws that gave the impression of tennis balls in his cheeks as his mouth hung open to reveal gator-like teeth.

"Oh, Shadow!" she would tell him upon returning home as he excitedly crossed back and forth between her legs, under and around her.

"Good boy!" she says as she reaches down to pet him and he rolls onto his back, extending his legs out into the air in glee.

He had thought he was doing them good, they were happy dogs.

His reputation was growing in his new terrain. None of his childhood stories were known, but he began to show his colors in various ways and make a lot of friends. Fearlessness translated into an outgoing personality, he approached strangers all the time and engaged almost anyone is his vicinity. As he made his own place in society through the bonds he formed, he felt less and less like an outsider; he no longer felt the primal drive for survival consuming him.

A wide variety of people came by their place all the time in those days. Hidden deep in a maze of apartment buildings and strip malls in the central city, their place was ideal to party at and they always had something to drink. When people would come over, he would fancy himself a great counselor as he gave them personal advice. He championed Drug use and told himself he would lighten the world up as if life were a high dollar Pepsi commercial. He told people to quit school and to say to hell with their job, to just have fun while they could. When he started to cheat on Megan, he told himself he was doing a favor for the other girls by making them feel good.

"I am worth it," he would tell himself, "I deserve it."

He began to see himself as a higher stature than the young people in pot induced dazes which he surrounded himself with. The dogs began to fight each other more frequently; Megan began to stay gone for days at a time. That just meant more time for him in his diluted maze of thoughts and justifications. He saw the wonders of the kingdom from the top of the mountain as people came by with drugs and gifts. Women seemed to be automatically drawn to him as he surfed through his days with ease and simple luxury.

The dogs were like identical twins when they peed, he thought, watching the two dogs rising opposite legs over a fire hydrant. They held their tail in the same awkward curve, they rose opposite legs and they faced opposite directions, nose to nose. Synchronized swimmers, their bodies held in relation to each other to form a symmetrical image with their contorted limbs, would be envious of the spectacle. Even their muscle tone was the same as they formed a statuesque fountain head, the only thing incongruous was the color of their coats.

They were like two sides of a mind or spirit. The Black, quiet and vindictive, was the fiercer of the two. He proceeded with caution and attacked with decision. The fawn colored dog was happy-go-lucky and clamorous. He frequently tripped over his own feet from excitement during his formative years. He always smiled and his ears flopped forward as he ran to you, his long lagging tongue hanging out from his gaping mouth, the grin reaching from ear to ear.

It was the day after he strayed from her for the first time that the dogs first fought each other. Megan and John continued to grow distantly apart. Although breaking up had become a routine between them, this time would be different.

That night, he picked up from a bar a pretty girl who was completely smashed at 1:45 AM. No true crime of passion, he had planned this mission carefully. He had talked to the girl on the phone, gotten to know her through a circle of friends, and waited until the fifty cent drinks would have taken their toll. Then, he showed up, bought a few more rounds, and offered her a ride. He felt defiantly vindictive while sneaking out of the house where his girlfriend slept.

He took the girl back to her apartment where she stripped down before the mirrored sliding glass closet door spanning from the ceiling to the floor. She had spread herself out before him on the bed, unashamed of her long, shapely legs and natural in her nudity. She enthusiastically let him do whatever he wanted to her. Afterwards, she immediately got dressed and left him there to go see her own estranged boyfriend, who, it was then revealed, lived two buildings away, in the same apartment complex. As she ran across the parking lot, drunk and half dressed, John washed himself in her sink and drove home confused.

'I would hate to be her boyfriend,' he thinks to himself. Then, he begins to rationalize his actions which would become habitual on his way back home before crawling into bed next to his own girlfriend. That night, he refrained from curling up to her soft, warm body in fear of her smelling something strange on him as he went to sleep.

The next day, he brought the dogs to the pool of their apartment complex to let them get a bath. While spraying them with the water hose, they ripped into each other abruptly. Shadow attacked Buster, charging through his brother's neck with an intense, rolling snarl. The sound was frightening in itself. Buster responded by grabbing Shadow's leg in his powerful mouth. You could hear the popping of skin as Shadow's teeth Sunk into Buster's muscles, and the cracking of bones as Buster gripped down on the narrow bones of Shadow's leg. His teeth were like a saw as he jerked his head back and forth.

Blood slung from them as they yanked and shook, speckling John's skin as he yelled for them to stop. The usually obedient dogs were deafened by anger and pain as they growled, occasionally releasing each other, only to latch back onto one another in different positions. John yells in despair as he watches the two dogs he loves destroying each other. Their eyes have rolled back into their heads, as if turning off their brains to the pain as they mangle each other's flesh.

The aftermath left shinny red streaks of raw meat down Shadow's arms. Clumpy scabs formed around the wounds to their ears and over the deep lacerations about their faces and heads. They both stayed docile and limped around the house as they recuperated for the following days. The broken teeth which he noticed for the first time the next day became a regular occurrence as they fought more and more in the coming months and years.

It became a regular sight; the dogs reared up on their hind legs, facing each other and snarling. They pulled back their lips and displayed their jagged teeth to one another in savage warrior's faces, with their tongues poking out slightly between their front teeth. Then, like antlers of warring bucks, they would bang their teeth on one another until one of them succumbed and went for a leg or a shoulder.

Upon inspecting their mouths by pulling up their lips after the fight, John winced in empathetic pain while looking at the broken teeth. He thought about how bad that must hurt, then left the house to continue in the root of its cause by searching for fuel for his burning lust and food for his growing ego.

Years later, he looks back as he considers the past and his role in the debacle, alone and far from his previous self proclaimed state of grace. The delusions of grandeur were so great; he thought he was helping everyone around him simply by shedding his luminous aura on them with his presence. What was he thinking? Perhaps he thought that his condescending patronization would be a great way to follow punching them in the face? That using their insecurities so slyly to lift them up would make them feel much better about being left in the gutter? Did he think that his triumphantly smashing walk through a field of daisies had made the world a better place?

He had fallen for the great lie, the same lie that brought movie stars and governors to their knees while thinking that the allure of their own immediate satisfaction was the most important thing in the world. He had become the center of his own universe, the light of his own world, a legend in his own mind.

He and Megan grew further apart until they finally broke up officially. She had found pictures of him with other women. The women had come to him like servants, attending his every need and carnal lust as he viewed them as royal bathers sent to fulfill his needs. On their last day, crying on the couch, he told her about every one of them. They were girls who had befriended her, girls who had sneered at her, all girls who he had introduced to her, which had unwittingly shared with her the carnal knowledge of his body and urges. Once she left, he reveled in his new found independence, chasing joy to hide the new grim irony that he was alone. His soul was on the back burner as he continued down his path.

Eventually he lost the lease on their downtown apartment. He sold his belongings on the driveway, packed the two dogs with all his worldly belongings into his sports coupe, and headed for Houston to stay with an old love who had recently been divorced. He had not known where he was going until he sat in his car in his driveway with the animals and called her.

"Hey, what are you doing? Me? I'm just sitting here in my car with my two dogs and everything I own. What are you doing?"

"I've got a big empty house and a big back yard, come bring them over here," she responded.

The next few years proved a blur as he went from female to female, staying with women who would keep him. His mother and father both were able to take him in, but not with the big mean dogs. Everyone told him to commit the dogs to the pound, but he knew they would be killed. They were not desirable, labeled as dangerous and unpredictable.

He adopted Shadow out to a guy who he met on the internet and made him promise to call him if he ever had to part with the animal. Shadow watched him and his brother drive away while whimpering profusely. John was just happy that it looked like at least one of them had a good home. He had burned all his bridges, there was only one place left for him to go. Jaime was the last person he could turn to.

Jaime and his father, Jaime, lived together in a rundown trailer outside of the city. He did not have a number to call them, but remembered slightly where they lived. It was down a lost country road behind a truck station. The drive through the rolling plain's fields curved gently and gave great views of the waves of golden grass before ducking into an enclave of swaying willow trees overhanging the road. After turning left on a road he almost missed, he found their place and explained his predicament after waiting outside for them for a few hours and then letting himself in.

They told him they did not want the dog around, but upon pleading, they allowed him to keep Buster in his room. The room was a wooden built-on unit to the dilapidated trailer where they had kept their dog, Bear, while they were out. Bear was a mixture of a Chow and a Coyote, his long red hair matted from dirt and his purple tongue held in his strong canine jaws. The animal had relieved himself in the room where they would lock him over and over again; leaving the mattress stained with his urine and dried up lumps of feces intertwined with matted red hair everywhere. 50 bucks a week, that was the rent.

Choices are easy when there are no alternatives. He began cleaning his new room, first removing all the dog's mess, then meticulously sweeping and cleaning plywood floor. He bought some cheap linoleum tiles at the hardware store and put them down. The mattress was a loss, but it was all that he had, so he took it in the yard with dish soap, a brush, and the water hose. He scrubbed it and soaked it and left it in the yard to dry in the Texas Sun. He found himself dismayed when the mildew from the water drying too slowly within the layers of foam sewn into the mattress left a horrible smell and the smell of urine remained as well. He cleaned the dog stained sheets and blankets he found around the house and piled them high over his new bed. It was a far stretch from the fancy poly-foam mattresses of the rooms he was accustomed to being a guest in.

Eventually he found a job. He returned at nights to the room where his dog was confined and swept the dog hair and dander from his sheets before laying down for sleep.

Jaime and his father had a keen routine. They worked as plumbers in the day and hung out at their favorite bar in the evenings. They came home and treated him to long conversations about nothing until they all passed out in their clothes then got up to go to work after two hours rest, still rank from the previous day's sweat and dirt. It was machine-like how they kept going.

Tough as nails, they drifted quickly through days of fun and carelessness. A perpetual smile nearly always covered the father's face. The ability to tell a joke, even badly, in the face of dire straits, was a skill John wished he possessed himself.

"Agghhhh! HA HA!" Senior's back arched as he gruffly laughed at the ceiling. "You thought you was gona get to keep it! Stupid white boy!"

Words were shared in the kitchen in such a preposterous way that it sent beer sloshing around from their blue cans as they convulsed with laughter. John took the uppers and the downs with it, hiding from himself his situation of utter despair.

He met a nice girl one day at a bar while job hunting. He had applied for two jobs, and 2 PM was a fine time to escape the Sun in the dark pub. In short shorts and a tank top over her bikini, the gorgeous blonde entered the room with an overweight friend. What a lush... She played hard to get while shooting pinball, then gave up her number.

"Hey, you got a boyfriend?" he asked her as she concentrated on the pinball machine.

"No," she responded, her eyes never leaving the shiny ball rolling around and bouncing off of bumpers within the pinball machine. He could see the glare on the metal ball reflected through her clear, bluish grey eyes. Blonde hair hung in lumped waves around her smooth, tan face, and the delicate white fuzz on her skin looked like velvet in the dim light.

"Well, do you want one?" he asked.

They exchanged numbers and he called her the same night. Surprised to learn she was a college graduate with a master's degree, they scheduled a first date. He knew this must be a girl of manners and refinement. The date lasted for three days. He marveled at her free spirit as she spent days on end in the small room of the trailer, fulfilling his every sexual desire. He thought she was *the one*, undoubtedly destined by the stars to be his soul mate. She was living out a fantasy in which she was captured by a sex crazed caveman and forced to live on Busch Beer and Doritos, perhaps. When it was over, she was gone, knowing well that she'd be back.

Soon after, he landed a sales job and began bringing home more than just women. Before long, his weekly paychecks equaled a month's pay of his host's. With money in his pocket, he soon fell back into his old routine. The Barbie doll blondes who came by his room in the rank dwelling fueled his ego, he was proud he could get women to succumb to him and drive their shiny cars to such a crude habitat. He bragged about their devotion and divulged the details to his new housemates over cold beers cracked constantly. He thought the whole thing was like a blissful haze.

In the middle of one hot day in the summer, he awoke stone sober and alone. It was an off day and he walked out into the dirty house alone. The matted carpet stared up at him from the floor as he paced from room to room, then back again, aimlessly. A strong sense of futility overcame him. He thought about the black dog and hopefully wandered if his new life was any better. His phone was ringing so he went back into his room to answer it. It was his dad. His deep voice drawled out slowly through the phone.

"Well, hey! How are you, son?" his voice came into John's ear like an old reminder.

"You doing okay?'

"Yeah, I'm fine", he responds.

"Yeah, well how's your soul? How's your spirit?" he counters, knowing instinctively his precious son's life is daily slipping away.

"It's fine."

"It's fine? Well, you don't sound 'fine."

"Listen, son, don't do like me. Don't be all idealistic. You're mother is a strong woman, you're lucky you have her genes. Be more like her. Son, I've seen the error of my ways. A daddy's supposed to be able to help you. Just to send you a couple hundred bucks, it's such a shame that I can't do that," he is interrupted by John's protesting voice.

"Man, don't worry about it. I'm fine," he responds. He doesn't want to brag, but tells him anyway,

"I just got a 4,000 dollar paycheck. He feels proud as he exaggerates, as all salesmen do about their commissions.

"Well, that's good," the wise father responds, skirting the statement and continuing, "Son, I've been talking to God… And I *know* what is *the important thing*. Son, how's your ministry?"

His question hits John like bricks as he ponders it in his silence. He thinks about a girl named Jenny, of her boyfriend who had looked up to him so much until he found out that he and his love were lovers. He thinks of the hurt the younger man must have felt. The young man was an inspiration to him, remembering the words he had said, openly touched by them. He felt like such a traitor thinking of the way the would-be disciple now hated him secretly.

"Your ministry is all that matters. You have to build that son, daily. When you get the spirit, you mount up with wings as eagles and fly. You run and don't get tired. But it's that walk, son, that daily walk that keeps you in fellowship." His dad's words are slow and concise, perfectly aimed and timed to penetrate deep into John's consciousness.

"Let's pray." he states. "Heavenly Father, we come to you

with John right now..." His prayer continues, asking for his son's return to discernment and peace.

A strange daze overcomes John in his solitude that day as he busies himself drinking beers and smoking cigarettes. That day, alone at the trailer, he ponders his life, wondering what he has done to help anyone. He remembers his days of ring leading and his prior delusions of grandeur, wandering what he now has to show for it. The matted carpet is caked with layers of dirt and moisture. As he opens the door into the back yard, he is again reminded of his soiled life by the piles of trash stacked up around the porch. He thinks about his old dog, Shadow, and wonders how his life might be alone. 'It's probably better than it was with me,' he thinks. Just then, in chorus, the phone rings again.

"Hey, it's me, Dusty. Yeah, well, you know how you said to call you if I ever had to get rid of Shadow? Well, I can't keep him. I got a new place over 6th street, and they don't allow dogs. Yeah, I tried, but no one can keep him," said the young man over the phone.

"I'm on my way," John responds and gets dressed, hopping in his car and driving into town. When he arrives at the apartment, he finds it empty. The boy has completely moved out and all that remains is the dog who is pushing aside mini-blinds in the window desperately. The door is locked, but a John finds an unlocked window and lets his old companion out.

"Aw, good boy! Yes, it's me, I missed you." He says as he pats his head.

Dogs are supposed to be able to recognize over 700 words, but he is sure that his dog could orate like Shakespeare if he had been given the appropriate tongue for it. On the ride home, he is overcome with a state of Zen looking at the old companion he'd thought he would never see again. Shadow is smiling with his head hanging out of the window on the passenger's seat, his pink tongue dangling in the wind. John feels a great spirit of redemption, as if a second chance for goodness has been afforded to him.

Once back at the house, he watches as the two dogs reacquaint themselves, surprised to find they are not fighting as they sniff each other and chase each other around. It's as if doing the right thing and getting the old dog back has erased years of wrongdoing and their careless frolicking is evidence that they are not hurt anymore.

The feeling of renewal overwhelms him, and he decides to take them for a walk in the cool evening air of the country side. Small homes with big lawns on both sides of the road seem silent, and he doesn't notice the people on their porches as he watches the castles in the clouds. The dogs are roaming back and forth on their tether, trying to sniff out every scent in the crisp air. As they both pull at the leash like a sled, he follows them and enjoys the grand landscape of the sky. God is speaking to him in imagery as purple stretches out above him, painting true pictures of grandeur in the Sunburst pattern formed by the castles of clouds extending out from the orange, setting Sun. John looks to the skies as he explores the spread out plains community of mobile homes parked on the sloping, open hill country.

"Please God, just let me serve you," he says aloud to the quiet skies.

"I know I have done wrong," he says as he walks. The waves of guilt overcome him with thoughts of the people he has trusted and who have trusted him, of people who had let him down and people who he had betrayed.

"Please let me try again, let me serve you."

As he is pulled around the corner of a old country road by the leashes in his hand, a house for sale catches his eye. The dogs pull him eagerly into the open backyard flowing into an overgrown field and he lets them off of their leashes. The field behind the house seems to slope up to a line of trees and he hikes into them, watching his shoes navigate over the black, rocky dirt beneath. As the weeds and Sunflowers get thicker, the slope inclines and the twisting Sugarberry trees are before him. He climbs the incline to the top, where he is overcome in surprise to find a big lake reflecting the orange streaks of the setting Sun across its water.

Looking back at the little house, he knows he has found their home. The overgrown weeds will become the garden, the little house will become the drilling grounds for lost boys, and this is the place where she will be born, the resilient little black dog with white socks.

9. WASHED

The bug banging on the window is trying to get into the light. Beneath the rotating, slightly wobbling ceiling fan, three of four electric lights shine from behind impassable glass as the bugs strive for its luminosity, valiant to their deaths.

A caterpillar stays cocooned for a season, then emerges to

become a decoratively adorned avionic Butterfly. From the sluggish composition of a worm it transforms, through various stages of metamorphism, into a creature capable of navigating aerospace via wings pulsing at 600 flaps per minute.

Around posts and other seemingly unsurpassable objects he whirls with daft maneuvers in the air. The world seems slow as he whips around people's heads and in and out of their soda pop cans without notice. Wow, the fly really is quicker than the eye. Upon the slightest impulse of thought, his speedy wings lift him high from the ground, pulling his legs down below him in rapid accent. He has achieved self actualization.

But, amid his glorious revelation of being able to fly, he knows not that his triumph is short lived. Within three passing days of his transformation from worm to aviator, he will die.

Why in three days? How do the millions of new flyers know how to die after three days, right on time, every time? The revolving planet's relation to the Sun tells them so. The dark of night and beaming Sun bring out mixtures of chemicals within its body, telling the moth that it is time to change, to age.

The Sun light, bright and as dependable as day, awakens the bug with stimulation and turns the dreaded clock one more tic. Once the light has come and passed three times, its body knows it is time to die. No more does it fly joyously around our heads; no more does it rest on flower's petals and show off its pretty wings. No wonder it strives for the light in the window.

John finds that his days are limited, the hours are short. Working at clearing the land around his new house and repairing the home itself are laced with incursions to work at real jobs, Mimosa days, and a little sleep. Shannon had left and taken with her the wildest of times. The Sun was again the beacon that rose him in the mornings and the flowering rows in the garden were evidence of his refocused energy. Through the work and play, his father's words echoed in his mind. 'Son, remember to build your ministry.'

At the time, he thought of his 'ministry' as a group of people who he showed kindness to, who he tried to help in any way he could, and who would return the favor. An offering of friendship was placed up before all of them, the mean, the dim, the bright and all the like. He spent time endeavoring to make friends, to build relationships, and to help people.

It was never hard to sleep in those days, for sleep only came when his mind was exhausted and his eyelids refused to stay up. The sleep that came was deep and welcomed. He burned his days and nights, racing to keep time from catching up with him. After three years of living in his home, he was gaining stride. He felt as if he had finally emerged from his cocoon and as if his own wings were those infamous ones swilling the matter around them, spinning off little cyclones of energy which snowballed together to affect global weather patterns.

A Butterfly flaps its wings, a small group of molecules swill to intertwine their paths with their surroundings, setting off a chain reaction that could become an entire pressure system, twisting tunneling clouds collecting the sea beneath them. The effect of the butterfly's flapping wings could, theoretically, evolve into a vortex of clouds and rain, much like the giant hurricane looming in the Gulf of Mexico. The storm, aiming at Southeast Texas, gave John's father a fair reason to come visit his little house for the first time, in the midst of an unusually hot Texas summer.

Watching the weather on TV with his dad seemed like a surreal luxury. There was a satellite orbiting the earth. Many miles made it invisible, but its keen eye twisted mechanical wheels to focus its vision. The vulture seemed to hover as it peered down from space. On his head were a hundred cameras, with lenses so magnifying that they could count the hairs on your head. The vulture stares down patiently and transmits the images of the storm from an always open infrared eye.

"You better go back." he tells his father.

"I know," the white haired senior responds calmly.

He will be heading straight into the path of the new storm. The last one gave him reason to come visit as it was advertised as the *doozy of the century*, but it fizzled out before it ever hit shore. The gigantic storm miraculously dissipated on the radar screen before hitting landfall. But behind it, another storm was following its path in the Atlantic. Thousands of Southeast Texans, who had taken off of work and spent all of their money on gasoline for their cars, were faced with returning home as another hurricane quietly gained steam in the Gulf of Mexico.

The trip was hard on older automobiles, now depended upon to shelter families from the oppressive Sun over the several days long creep down the congested evacuation routes. In teary eyed departures, dogs and cats had been left behind or stored with friends or even in hotel rooms, which were booked to capacity in every city. The down turning economy had left many of them broke before the added expense of evacuating was piled on, and they faced a tough decision in heading back to their homes in the face of another, stronger storm looming in the gulf.

The trip was perilous in itself. Cars could only be counted on so much as shelter from the blistering heat. Water and fuel may be scarce for miles, there was the chance of being stranded on a fenced-in highway without moving for any amount of hours. Upon returning home, they may be faced with leaving again. Adding to the complication was the new law recently announced stating that during a 'mandated evacuation,' remaining behind was grounds for imprisonment.

The laws were becoming ridiculous. Amongst the chaos of their lives, people had no time to protest them at all. Citizens with time to be concerned had now been selected through a careful process and had learned to brush new regulations off as insignificant. They knew there was an elite class that the laws did not really apply to; they knew they were a part of it. 'Don't you think we're on that side of it?' they would say in the company of their own, on the way to a shopping mall.

John and his father spent the week together in his small cabin painting and eating tomatoes from the garden. It was the first time his father had come to see his home and they both reveled in the joy of each other's company. John soaked up the love of his father like a sponge, growing stronger with his encouraging words. Now, upon time to return to his home, this new storm was aimed directly for his destination.

That morning they had sat in the front yard amidst the beautiful Sunshine. They walked circles and paced as they spoke, then found relaxation in yard chairs or on the steps of the porch as they wasted the time away talking about loose and easy subjects. The threat of the storm seemed far away as they watched the branches sway in the horizon of distant and near trees moved by the breeze. The light was coming down bright, casting dramatic shadows in the leaf's canopies and blasting the green scenery everywhere.

They really enjoyed each other's company. The dogs ran

around in a few big circles before plopping down on their bellies in the front yard. Fiona, the baby girl, ran off after a small dog across the street and John called to her.

"Hey, girl, get back over here!" He was delighted when the eight month old puppy turned and ran back to him, showing amazing discipline against her curiosity for such a young being.

"Good girl!" He looked down at her as she sat in front of him, looking up and smiling proudly. The Sun reflected off her eyes, creating a piercing gleam as she smiled up and he patted the dog on her head. She then went back to rolling around on the lawn, twisting around with her legs up to rub the grass against her back with her tongue hanging out happily.

Old man John came walking by, as usual, and upon seeing them in the front yard, decided to have a few beers, too.

"Ol' Mr. Tom, I sure do enjoy talking with you," he told John's father.

They told a few stories, some by now familiar, and said their goodbyes. When he left, Fiona followed Ol' man John home, sneaking away from John and his dad as they went inside. It was almost an hour before they realized she was missing. Eventually, John put on tennis shoes and went out looking for her. She seemed to have mysteriously disappeared. The neighbor who was outside collaborated the story which Old man John had told him, that she followed him half way home and then turned around to come back. After that, no one had seen her.

It wasn't the first time a dog had run away, Buster had once been gone for two days, he thought. Although, he did find it strange that the young pup would stay gone for so long. He felt worried about her, but let it go. He had bigger fish to fry.

"It's probably going to fizzle out," says John. "I wouldn't worry about it; it's probably just like the last one."

The storm which every television and radio station had warned would be catastrophic, the one which had prompted John's father and so many others to evacuate, had fizzled and died just before reaching land fall. After the devastating storms of the last couple years and their increasing frequency, people had begun to take the hurricanes more seriously in the wake of their destruction.

"Yeah, we'll just have to wait and see," replies his father.

The fact is that there is no reason for him to be running from a storm. Short of being washed away in a flood, his home is safe. The windows may need to be boarded, but the chickens in the yard will still lay eggs. The well will still produce clean water and the tank will still hold fish. He knows he will be ok.

They are not sure when they will see each other again. The last of the sporadic gas stations had shut down over the last week, causing lines of panic from the storm which never came. Two weeks ago, the sweeping reform of public transportation was just another thing being talked about in the news paper and on rogue radio shows. But during the chaos of the storm which gripped the stare of a concerned public's eye, changes began to be made. Fuel dispensers had begun to be fitted with terminals which only allowed them to operate with a new fuel rationing card. As a matter of opportunity, the refugees and locals alike snatched up the free 'emergency' fuel cards being handed out at fueling stations and thought little about the change that was happening. The cards were worth 100 dollars in fuel and welcomed by the strained people who received them.

The change was unexpected by confused customers who were told by clerks that they would need to visit the Public Transportation Office before they could buy gas in locations where there were no gas cards to give out. Now that it is time to return home, the final stages of the new regulations have just officially been enacted. No one knows what will happen next as people across the country scramble for electric cars and refugees plead with social workers along evacuation routes for more fuel cards. There was a tense feeling of uncertainty looming in the air.

"Son, you sure do need to be mighty careful." The father's voice is laced with a deep concern, and it rumbles out of his throat in a low and gentle tone.

"Don't worry about me," replies his boy, "if there's one thing I've learned about myself, it's that I'm going to be okay."

They embrace in a hug as the father prays for his boy. Standing there in his front yard as he leans up against his dad's hairy chest, John thinks about the things he is praying for as the wind rustles the thin hairs of his forearms grasped around his father's neck.

"Please just guard John's heart, God, and please just show him the right things to do," he began in prayer as he held his first born son in his arms like a child who still needed his protection.

His Dad's words had built him up over that week, fortifying

him in mind and spirit against some dark chapter that seemed to be looming just around the corner.

"I'm so proud of you, son," he would tell him, "so very proud. People are what matter. Don't worry about that stuff! So what?"

The friends and neighbors who continued showing up at his house over that week had frustrated John. He wanted all of his father's time to himself on that short visit, but his friends were intrigued by the bright eyed old artist and they stopped by everyday to spend some time with him. In spite of all the frequent interruptions, they found plenty of time to spend together. Deep into the nights they would talk.

"That momma of yours, she's just a great, great, great woman. You're lucky you got some of her genes, or else you wouldn't stand a chance. I'm so very thankful that you kids got some of your momma's genes."

"Boy, she was really something else. She was really wild. I'll bet you wouldn't believe your momma was a free spirit? Man, her parents thought about having her committed because she would hitchhike across the country to go to some rock concert. If she wanted to go, man, she just went!" he exclaimed emphatically, his arms waving up in the air above him as he acted out a gesture of not caring by circling his hands over his head as he talked.

It was late, their eyes were getting glassy and the beer was starting to talk as he continued,

"That momma of yours, boy I tell ya, she's really tough..."

In the morning they pack up his things, preparing him for the journey across the state and back into the deep, low lying woods of Southeast Texas. The trip from there had cost him a tire and nearly his life. As he swerved to miss a car broken down in the middle of the highway, he nearly flipped his vehicle and shredded his tire. Turning hard while slamming on the brakes pulled the wheel at a wild fulcrum, and as the car hurled forward on the congruently aimed wheel, the rubber tire had been stripped from the alloy rim. He was lucky to be alive as his midsized SUV slid out of control into the grass on the side of the road. He got out and changed his tire and now he was riding on a spare, there was no backup tire for the long trip back home.

A slipknot, pulled firm by John in its twine rope twang, holds down his dad's big steel easel to the top of the white Ford SUV.

"Are you sure you don't want to just go ahead and wait it out," the son asks hopefully.

"No," his father says assuredly, "I need to get back in case that storm knocks out the windows, to protect the paintings."

The radar image on the television shows the massive cyclone figure of hurricane Kyle looming over the gulf. There is no doubt; it's going to land head on. The island is right in its way. The satellite orbiting in space gives a glimpse through a needle's eye down into the gulf, relaying images of the circular formation seeming to suck in everything around it as it twirled. Watching the time lapse aim the path of the storm directly at Galveston turns his thoughts to Francis.

The thoughts of his old friend conjured a deep tide of feelings. The bond they shared, from growing together and sharing so many experiences, was like a bounding oath in his heart. He decided to call her on the phone.

"Hello, hey! Are you okay? You think you're going to stay? No, you have to go! There's no choice, it's going to hit you. Uh-huh. Really? No, I'm just hanging out lately. How many cats do you have? You'll have to leave him there. Yeah, he will be okay."

He doesn't know why, but he knows that this one will not fizzle out; it's going to be big. Maybe it's the way that the radar images seem to show a circling vortex pulling in everything around it as the spiral appeared to become more compact and well formed as it raced for land. Maybe his subconscious clock is telling him that the coast is a little overdue for a '100 year storm.'

Any fool could see that she sees it coming, too, but she hates to see it go. She has embraced the beach life, her fair skin absorbing the ocean wind and her soul becoming adept to the island mentality. As a bartender on the strip, serving drinks and a wink for a tip was good and constant pay. She had money to spend and time to lend, she had two wheel motion in Sunshine filled days pedaling around the island to a taqueria for breakfast or to a good friend's home for dinner. The island air replenished her and she became its essence, her face like Sun, smiling at everyone. Her downtown loft was the only place to stay when in town, and she adorned the walls with paintings by her favorite friends, including John.

She was his unicorn, and he needed her now. She needed him. He knew anyone could go get her, but he fancied himself bringing her back to his dwelling which she had never seen, keeping her safe for the time being, while permitted. In no impure fashion, he relished the thought of having her in his midst, of watching every sentence wisped from her lips.

The world was falling apart around him. His paranoid delusions all too often proved to be true. There was no sincerity anywhere anymore. The expectations of virtue had died like a memory, buried somewhere deep. Now, he just wanted a friend. She had been gone from his life for so long, him chasing women and her chasing song. They had stayed in touch over the phone but rarely, on occasion, did they see each other anymore.

The old car sat in the front yard; it had not been driven in months. Patrolling ONE vehicles had kept it dormant and it sat sadly like a neglected puppy. The risk of getting pulled over outweighed the challenge of getting gasoline and the burden of finding rides or walking in those months. When he gently pulled at the lever beneath his finger tips and the car door opened, a familiar smell from the cockpit wafted out into his nostrils like the breath of an old friend, bringing back old memories in a swirl of déjà vu.

The air set into his lungs as he gripped the steering wheel and turned the key in the ignition. A whinny, ratcheting sound failed to turn the motor over. He tried again, hopefully twisting the key. This time the motor turned once, sputtered, and kicked to life. He could hear the lifters and pulleys moving within the motor in sequence as it caught its breath and began to gain a consistent rhythm. The gas needle sat at empty for a second, then, as if awoken abruptly, shot up to nearly full.

Looking over at the empty passenger's seat, he began to think about the last time he saw her. They had stood together and looked down at the picturesque city of Galveston from the patio roof of the old education building, a towering high-rise downtown. They could see all four corners of the island connecting to water. The eighteenth century architecture rose up beneath them in the form of old mansions from every conceived style that the old world's building materials would allow. Flying Buttresses, arches and trusses of aged stone stare at the passing sky amongst swaying palms.

Looking towards The Strand, they could see the Historic District's old Commerce Building. Five stories of stoic, square bricks contrasted the water, standing before the bay where a brightly colored red and blue cruise liner sat awaiting departure. The centuries old palm trees swayed below them like green balls of wispy cotton to the wind carrying the soft edged clouds across the blue sky. Her hair was gently moving across her face in the warm Sunshine as she smiled. On the ledge of the rooftop, she pointed out the carcasses of many dead birds scattered about.

"The hawk brings them up here every day and eats them, then just leaves their bodies here," she told him in wondrous awe. "Can you see the old light house on Crystal beach?"

Holding the rail, he looked far into the distance, straining his eyes to see the lighthouse across the water on the peninsula to which she pointed. Directly below them, across the street, the white walls of Saint Mary's Basilica reached up to the sky in ornate designs. Atop it is a statue of Mary, her hands opened palm out below her, her head looking down over the island city piously.

Now he sped through wet paved intersections and maximized his average speed on the highway, the passing lights flashing off of his eyes as he stared at the desolate highway above the speedometer's needle stretched over the 120 mark. Taking off the governor apparatus which kept his vehicle from traveling over 120 miles per hour had gotten him into enough trouble in the past, but right now, he didn't care. Of course, he slowed down when he thought he might see a cop, but the majority of the sparse cars traveling in his direction flew by behind him like a mere imagination of stretched red light from their tail lights glaring in the moisture on his windshield for brief seconds.

Everyone on the road was going the other way, lined up in a stagnant line on the opposite side of the highway, separated from him by a cement barrier. Normally, both sides would be opened to evacuating traffic, but this storm had caught them all by surprise as they had just converted the roads back to two way travel after the disappointment of the last storm. This storm was different. The last one had caused virtually no problems, but this storm was miles from the coast and already flood surges were being reported over the AM dial.

The giant structures of highways rose up before him as he flew through the heart of downtown Houston, endless paths that led millions of drivers from one highway to another on concrete ramps passed him by in a blur as he navigated the freeway and fly-bys as if on tracks. There was only one destination for him, and he felt fine to leave all these people behind.

A tack spins upon a smooth wooden tabletop in a dim, quiet room. In the silence of the room, the rhythmic hum sounds soothing in its constancy. 'Whrirr,' it hums with a steady vibration as it spins there on the surface. The tiny head is teetering so fast around the edges of the contact point that it seems like a steady motion as it glides across the table, a controlled bouncing held in rotation by the balanced weights spinning around the fulcrum. Tiny variations in the pattern of the bounces roll together like instant algorithms to cause the top to begin circling as it spins, whirling around in little loops that form figure '8's. As the momentum slows, the rhythm becomes less steady and the top begins wavering. The ball weights at the end of its spinning arms begin to hover up and down as they spin, as if pulling at each other or bouncing on a teeter totter.

The earth spins around its axis, whirling through space at 18 miles per second as it rotates the Sun, slung like a giant rock in the star's gravitational sling. It spins like a top, compounding the ground speed by thousands of miles per hour. It spins to unknown winds, as its entire constellation is but a spec in another swish of rotation. The speed is calculated, minus the unknown variable, through deduction and logic. A spot deducted through inference of an imaginary point is measured through the distorted lenses' constant variable for the speed of light, which itself is distorted by the time used as a measurement for its distance traveled between two points.

How is the time bent by alternating densities of matter and antimatter which the light travels through? Let me tell you how shots in the dark, guesses and educated inferences stand as common logic when deducting the realm with assumed clarity. A little to the left, a little to the right, it all goes on in its rotation at a scale so grand we can't even ponder on, or feel it's speed while clung by gravity to its velocity.

As the axis tilts a bit, the ellipse is slightly longer, the pull is softer. The summer becomes hotter, the winters become shorter, the lakes evaporate as the ice becomes water. The water collects steam in coalescing streams which wind down and find their ways into oceans to make waves. Away the shore erodes while people build their homes along the coasts so seemingly assured to disappear. It all made perfect sense.

He drove through to the mass of land lying over the causeway bridge to retrieve her. He passed the old mansions and the statue adorned cemetery of Galveston's Broadway, turning left at the familiar landmark of Lady Justice, who's scales seemed tipped just a little bit in his favor. Pulling up in front of her downtown loft was surreal in its serenity. There were no cars around, no vacationers, and the usually busy Strand was desolate. After ducking into an indiscrete door on the corner, he runs up the wood plank stairs and through the old halls to bang on her door.

She lived in the old Commerce Building. The old hallways were wooden and seeping with history. Crisscrossed stairways ran up each end of the building and were connected by narrow halls on each floor. Between the rows of doors leading to converted apartments in the halls were heavy old steel doors from the building's operating days, left open to allow passage between what was once a safe separating one side of the building from the other on each floor in the middle of the hallway. The doors had been painted slate blue and revealed their mechanical workings as they stood open. Looking at the huge doors from the side, you could see the gears of the locking mechanism and tell that they were twelve inches thick.

Inside of the old safe connecting each side of the building were various compartments and wooden boxes making shelves up the wall where important documents, valuables and large stacks of money had once been stored. A chill passes up one's neck as he walks through these corridors and thinks of the ancient hands sorting papers into the boxes, or the jewels and heirlooms once stored there by a well dressed, older lady with an ornate golden handled cane.

Her blouse was velvety purple, giant diamonds hung from her wrist and her neck was adorned with giant buttery perils as she stowed away her precious belongings some time before dying.

$40,000. That was how much money was in the deep freezer underneath Francis's mom's beach house. Gambling, although accepted, wasn't really legal there yet, so the money from the slot machines at their bar was all kept in cash. Pitt's had hid it there under a bunch of frozen fish he had caught while passing a nice days away fishing in the bay.

Many men who love to fish would admire Pitts's life. He owned a bar, had a beautiful wife in Francis's mom, Doreen, and was well respected in the local community. He had a good golf cart for the beach side of the peninsula which was painted in the logo of his favorite football team, the Pittsburg Steelers, and a flat bottomed boat for the bay side. The large bay behind the peninsula stretched out for miles, but was nearly all more than four feet shallow. The abundance of fish swimming in the shallow waters meant great fishing, your bait almost guaranteed to spin past lots of fish. Wading around in the bay would be the more adventurous way, but next to a cooler on a boat was cooler. So, naturally, he hid his money under his fish, in the deep freezer which was now surely defrosted due to the probable lack of electricity on the peninsula.

"Yum! You know with the power all out, that probably smells real gowd," Francis tells him, conveying the horror of a cooler full of decaying fish through her lit up eyes. "I know there's at least 40 thousand in there, and 20 thousand in the other one. I know because they told me, they want me to go get it."
Big beaming eyes encompass him in that old familiar way as they open the tunnel of thought between them. Considering the ideas, consequences, and rewards; rolling them over and looking for the angles, they strategized together without speaking a word.

"Is it even possible to get out there?"

"The last ferry is about to run. I know because Jim, you remember Jim, Right? He's running it. It's just for the last couple of workers so that they can get out. I don't think they're going to let anyone else on it. We'd hafta go now. I mean like *right now*."

Bundled firmly against her, the big green nap sack hangs from her shoulder and he carries her other bags as they rush down the old wooden stairs and onto the Strand. Water is pouring down now, rushing down the stony street. The bricks give good traction to the back tires of the old Ford Mustang as he lets the clutch up and whips around the corner of the historic district, squinting through the windshield. Whipping winds splash sheets of rain across the glass as if thrown from buckets. Gusts of wind momentarily bend the palm trees along the road down until their plumes nearly touch the ground. The island is a ghost town as they speed down Ferry Road.

Jim is at the end of Ferry Road, just as advertised. He is

waving them forward with an orange wand in the rain. Water is dripping off of his blue cowboy hat, down his white mustache, and running down the bright yellow plastic parka in little streams. The Mustang pulls up and lowers the window. The white car with black tinted windows seems vaguely familiar to the veteran Sheriff as he tilts his head down into the window. Frances greets him with a smile, and he soon remembers John, as well.

"Frances, you better go and keep going. Don't you stop by someplace and start thinking you want to stay for some stupid 'hurricane party.' You get on that highway and keep driving once you get to the other side. Do you understand me?"

The adventurous pair quickly agrees with him and they are on the boat. They stay in the car on the way over, holding hands and resting their heads together on the rocky trip across, seeing only the pouring rain on the windshield. The sea was tumultuous, tossing the vessel high and low in its sway and they felt the car rising up before descending again as the boat toppled the crests of giant waves. Just as the lights of the opposite dock came into view through the blinding rain, the clouds opened up over the peninsula.

The sight was stunning. Wisps of the coming hurricane's circling arms were stretched out across each side of the long strip of land, leaving blue fingers in between their white wisps through the giant sky. Sun came through it in a clean, orange light which shone off the white side of the old light house and off of the wet, glistening streets.

A moment passed, and they were off the ferry and onto the open road. An endless landscape of strange, twisted plants atop lush, rolling landscapes seems to pass before her eyes as she watches from the window of his speeding car until, from the view out of her passenger's window, she finds herself turning off the highway onto a side road lined with old beach houses leading towards the bay. The old wooden houses stood high upon their stilts, overlooking brushy yards, broken down cars and boats. There were no people to be seen anywhere. The familiar road brought back distant memories of the one thousand other times in the past they had whipped around that same corner together.

A giant hull of a boat still sat in the adjacent lot as they pulled into the drive of the beach house. Ancient rust reddened the two story hull of the old commercial freighter which was strangely out of its place in line with a row of bay houses standing on stilts.

A million times he had wondered why someone would want to haul a big iron boat out here and leave it in a place where it looked like a house should be. But there it sat, a giant ocean vessel from 95 years ago, parked in the St. Augustine grass next to Francis's mom's beach house.

The freezers were there, at least one of them were.

"Someone must have gotten that other one. The small one probably just fit in the back of Pitts's truck. Or maybe someone just took it? I don't know. Oh well. Let's take a look in this thing. Kinda stinks."

A primal instinct tells them to disregard the source of the putrid stench and shut the lid to the cooler. The grotesque image and smell of the decaying fish beg them both to turn around and walk away. Deciding to knock the cooler and its contents over instead, they have other plans.

A slosh of carcasses and money spills out. They hastily scrape aside the wet stacks of money from the slime of decaying fish and stuff it into a knapsack. Looking at the remaining pile of money on the concrete below the beach house, again the survival instincts grabbed them by their guts as they fought off vomiting at the thought of separating the bills from the gelatinous guts they were intertwined with. Again, the allure gets the best of them as they wash away the rotting fish with the water hose while trying not to breath.

They load up on cash, stuffing it all into the trunk of the car. A baseball size roll of 100 dollar bills in the slime had caught John's eye while they had cleaned the money, the money they almost had decided to disregard. He grabs it from the wet cement and shoves it into the front pocket of his blue jeans just before they leave. After hastily surveying the driveway to make sure they had not forgotten anything and grabbing the gas can for Pitts's lawn mower, they jump in the car and are out of sight of the beach house within 20 minutes of arriving.

It is a 30 minute drive to High Island, then another 30 or 40 minutes to the major highway. It is five o' clock; they expect the storm to arrive at around midnight. They have a trunk full of cash and half a tank of gas and are well on their way.

Feeling good, staring out at the old neighborhoods rolling by beside him on the two lane highway and thinking about all the good times he had growing up spending summer breaks and spring vacations in them, he notices something alarming. The water is rising up in the residential areas along the highway, over the streets in the neighborhoods on the beach side. 'I guess that's why they put them on sticks,' he thinks to himself.

The further they travel, the closer the water is to the highway. The frothy ocean is now underneath the stilted homes, covering yards and driveways and running into the shallow ditch along the highway. Approaching the cut, the line between the water and the road has begun to disappear. As they cross the narrow bridge connecting the ocean side to the bay side, water from the ocean lashes out across it and onto the car. The huge gush lapping up over the bridge slaps the side of the car and pushes it over a few feet as they speed through the wall of water. As they cross onto the other side, they look ahead and see that water is on the road and they slow down. Boundaries of the road become hard to distinguish under the murky water and debris flowing back and forth in it. They push forward for a few hundred more yards until brown waves of the ocean finally lap over the hood of the car and the motor sputters to a stop. 10 minutes of driving would have put them on High Island. They almost made it.

John got out and looked at his old faithful companion, standing in water up to his knees and watching it lap up over the hood. He tries starting her up a few more times, but knows it is futile. There is no choice, they must forge on. Grabbing a few parcels from the trunk and filling one of the overnight bags with cash, they began to wade through the water towards the next town.

Moving was slow as they pushed through the knee deep water. The sky started to grow darker as they pushed harder to move through the murky mess, racing against time. Through the windy rain, they saw another car parked in the rising water. A woman was perched on the top of the old baby blue station wagon and she rocked a baby which she gripped in her arms.

"Hey, you can't stay here," John shouted out to her. She looked at him through determined eyes with curiosity. "The water's going to come up way worse than this over the night. Your car will be washed into the bay. Come with us, if you want, it's probably your only hope."

For a moment, he could see the ferocity of her flashing glare in the black eyes under her wet hair. A ravenous bear would not take the baby from the grip of her arms were it a hot honey glazed ham.

Her suspicion was evident in her stance, she was ready to fight.

"You should really come," said Francis in a reasoning voice.

Her matted hair was plastered over her face as she stood still for a moment. Making her decision, the soaking wet mother reaches into the open window of her car with one arm, while clinging to her baby in the other, and pulls out another child. The boy seems to be about three years old. Dumbfounded, Francis and John watch wide eyed as yet another child, a girl of around eight, follows her little brother out the window of the marooned vehicle. Her black bangs were matted over her freckled face by the water as she took the three year old from her mother and followed her towards John and Francis.

Herding the young in front of them, the group forges forward through the knee deep tide water. The despairing sight ahead of them is only of brown gulf water and the only reminders of land are the buildings and billboards who's pillars emerge from the frothy salt water. Their will to survive and determination keeps them pushing on as their legs begin to burn in exhaustion and the water rises to their chests, then their shoulders, and up to their chins. By the time they bump into another group of people, they are swimming and watching the last signs of light disappearing from the sky.

Ferocity begins spiking the water into stinging pellets with whipping wind. The elderly couple, the young married couple, the single mom with three kids, they were all caught off guard. No one had expected it to be so big or to swallow the entire land mass so quickly.

During the final minutes of grayish light, the loosely formed band had held together well. The things brushing up against their legs were definitely not minnows nibbling at their toes; they were not swimming in a clear pebbled stream. Sometimes they could see the jagged fragments of structures rolling through the water, sometimes they knew the debris rubbing against their legs under the murky water was an inanimate object. Other times, it was evident that it wasn't. Scales of animals that seemed five feet long sometimes twisted around their legs, causing them to jump and push harder into the water.

The group was strong, some of them were holding hands so they didn't lose each other ahead of Francis and John. They quickened their pace, trying get around the slow moving group.

When one of the girls in the group reached out and tried to grab her hand, Francis retracted. As the girl turned to give a credulous look at Francis, she missed the sight of a giant roof frame rolling up over the water and tumbling across the front of her circle. The four people caught under the structure disappeared into the water. Splashing around frantically, the remaining members of the group pulls one boy up from the water. His arm and shoulder are almost completely ripped from his torso as he bleeds out into the water. The purples prevailing over the grayish blue of the sky, John and Francis trudge forward into the night. They cannot help him, or any of them, anymore.

The silhouette of High Island briefly appears in flashes as lightning occasionally strikes in the night. Wooden debris bobs around you, bumping your side from under the black water as you shudder. You have one hand on her shirt as you swim through the water. Against the arm that is reached back, gripping her shirt, you feel course hair and a giant body come between you as the shirt rips in your hands. The cow passing by in the water is swimming for its life and kicks downwards with its hooves as it pushes you under the water. You feel the hoof bang into your face as you struggle to reach the top.

A common phenomenon associated with unconsciousness is the elongating effect it has on one's time perception. Time slows down as the thoughts race through your mind in the form of vivid dreams.

He is standing naked in the locker room. Before him, Kevin Jax, furious over being knocked into the locker where his bad knee banged the edge of the open metal door, punches him in the face. A black white comes over him. Every instinct in his body tells him to fall down, but he does not. He stands up, then is told by Coach T that he must run but one more lap around the field to win his medal. He is running, effortlessly, across the green grass on a warm, Sunny day. He hears his father's voice,

"You'd better toughen up, boy."

A fighter's best asset is his chin, his temerity for a punch. What defines a great chin? Is it the ability to keep swinging once you've been rendered unconscious? It is a decision not to go down, ingrained beneath any conscious comprehension. Within the endless sea of dark water, deep within the dark recess of his brain, a tiny light glows, a tiny ember wills him on and his body begins to move.

Through a temporary state of unconsciousness, you keep fighting for the top in a disoriented state as your hands reach out around you, trying to determine which end is up. Flailing around blindly in the mucky water, you realize a car is rolling over you as it floats through the water. You grab it and fight for the other side of it, feeling debris brushing against your feet below. Your fingers grasp at the opened window of the automobile and pull your body upward. Reaching to pull at the water, cold air rushes over your hand and know you have found the surface.

He perches atop the floating car. Panic grips him as he jerks himself around looking for her; all he sees is the gleam in the black pupils of cattle swimming around him. Thunderous lightning briefly illuminates an apocalyptic scene as it arcs. The light exposes a still flash of wreckage in an unending sea, a surreal scene of cartoonish houses floating amidst the hoards of swimming cattle and piles of debris floating in the water. As quickly as it illuminates the sky, it goes out, leaving the image burned in his memory.

He studies the image in his mind once the light has passed and he sees something floating, briefly. It is the swirl of auburn hair and the tattered remnants of her shirt. He closes his eyes, points to the spot where the image in his mind seemed to be, and dives into the water head first from the side of the floating car. The broken boards and nails tear at his arms as he frantically swings them in the water, searching for her blindly. Diving below himself, he grasps for a miracle amongst the debris in the dark water, running out of breath and being pushed around by the broken carcasses of structures. He sees nothing, but he feels her unmistakable skin brush against his outreached fingers. Swimming in the direction he thinks is up, he grabs her by her shoulder and pulls her up to him.

Finding the surface, he squeezes her around the waist, remembering the CPR he had performed on the puppies, and pushes her diaphragm open by completely suppressing her lungs within his encircled arms. Water gushes from her mouth and the suction created in her lungs pulls the air back in as he loosens the grip around her and feels her flattened body begin to expand. She coughs and spits as the oxygen entering her body awakens her and the muscles around her lungs contract, continuing to expel the water within them.

Her arms rest around him as he begins to swim for the ever closer island before them through seemingly impassable mazes he only sees in the strobe of lightning flashes. As he swims for the land mass, the sky is circling around him and, again, the rain has stopped. A perfect circle is formed in the opening of the clouds above, swilling out in giant rings encompassing the sky, temporarily letting through the moon's reflected light. They are in the eye of the storm and the whipping winds are now but a soft breeze. Swimming through the obstacle course of broken boards gives way to climbing past and maneuvering around them.

Increasingly, he finds debris beneath his feet and continues pushing until he can walk, ascending the slope of ruble in the water leading up to land. Walking away from the water, arm in arm, they trod through the muddy field and thicket quickly, knowing that the ferocious winds of the storm will soon be throwing everything in the open around. Giant trees uprooted and cracked like pencils are everywhere, warning of the destruction coming with the back side of the spiral shaped storm. Pushing through the dense shrubbery at the end of the pasture, they find themselves in the back yard of a house facing the highway.

Compared to the nightmare behind them in the water, the back yard seems safe and normal as they hop the twisted barbed wire fence. The wooden house upon sturdy pillars has held, and looks like reasonable shelter. They consider it briefly to stay in, but the stairs have been ripped from beneath the stilted home, so they move through the front yard and up the old highway.

One block up the highway, people have gathered in the second story of the public school. The 1950's era brick fortress of a structure looks safe and durable, they get inside and upstairs. The old man from the elderly couple is there. He tells a story of he and his wife hanging onto a house post until the house fell around them, breaking up and floating away. He held on to her as long as he could and she gripped the post with all her might, but the water was too strong, it took her away. In despair, he eventually let go, as well, to be taken by the water. He does not know how he ended up there. A far, distant look comes over his eyes as he is asked if he wants to talk about it.

"No, I'd rather not," he replies distantly as the wind is picking back up, the sky seems to have harnessed his tears.

Booming winds hurl trees and light posts into the building throughout the night, destroying them while slowly chipping away at the brick fortress. John is bare-chested, huddling next to Francis where she sits with his shirt wrapped around her. They are both soaked to the bone and badly bruised. In the dark, the numerous abrasions look like black splotches about their bodies. A bloody leg extends from the tattered edge of his torn pants to his bare foot. Slashing debris in the water had ripped everything from them like greedy fingers, tearing their clothes and claiming their shoes.

Now they had time to fully appreciate the foolish risk they had taken for what had seemed like a huge pile of money. The sack with the money which they had almost died for was gone, along with everything else they had salvaged from the water logged car before abandoning it. He nestled his forehead down into her hairline as he clinched her steadily throughout the clamorous night.

The morning dawn brings contrasting serenity. Emerging from the school, the refugees find a scene of total devastation. Particle remnants of homes are strewn about the branches of broken trees and automobiles protrude awkwardly from sand where they are partially buried. The sand has been piled high over the remaining cars and fallen trees by the ocean's surge, creating a surreal landscape. Survivors walk in groups up the highway inland, detouring around a huge barge which has been left across the road by the receding water like a small child's toy. The cool, wet air of the morning subsides to the heat of the blistering Sun making a hazy steam of the moisture all around them.

By mid afternoon, mirages of mirrors glimmer off of the highway in the distance. Wounds and exhaustion drag at his body as he walks beside her. They have been walking north from the shore along the road for nine hours without food or water as they approach the outskirts of Winnie, the town along the major interstate.

Flashing lights grow brighter in the distance with the dimming of daylight as the evening approaches. Twisting his oculars like focusing telescopes, John discerns the unmistakable slate blue of the large transport vehicles beneath the blue and red beacons of rotating strobe lights ahead. People are being loaded into the trucks behind a parameter where, in the minuteness of far away distance, people appear to be struggling.

As if being seen, a Blue vehicle's lights click on and it begins approaching down the road from ahead where the refugees are being herded into the transport trucks. A glimpse of rescue shines like a birthday cake in his mind at the approach of the ONE authority vehicle, glimmering as the easy end to his aching joints and dehydration.

As the vehicle approaches, an ominous feeling over takes him. Looking at Francis from the corner of his eye, trying not to let her notice, he begins questioning their approaching rescue. The ONE troops had proven themselves brash and vindictive in their dealings with the local peoples in the past, treating them as stock while processing them into jails and through security terminals at concourses. The ONE volunteers were an idealistic bunch, trained from a young age on their elitism and the superiority of their dogmas. He thought about the certain way in which they were processing the refugees ahead, undoubtedly dividing families as they sorted them into the vehicles through various classifications, primarily gender.

'They are pretty self righteous,' he thought as he looked at his fierce companion, 'but not too self righteous to have a go at someone as pretty as her. Someone who would never be missed after the events of the previous night, someone who would be considered lost.' He considered that they would probably be stored in a warehouse or stadium and located into a nearby metroplex within a few months, and that they would definitely be separated, while the sweet taste of rescue became bitter in his mouth.

To the left of the highway is an open field for grazing pasture, thick wooded Forrest lines the other side. The warm feeling of the inside of her palm sends a calming strength though him before he realizes he has grasped her hand, never removing his gaze from the oncoming vehicle.

"Come on!" she tells him as she pulls him towards the barbed wire fence at the edge of a field. They traverse the fence and sprint for the trees. Once within the tree line, the light of the outside world becomes distant and the dense thicket becomes a world unto its own. John remembers the strange yard in the neighborhood from that first day of kindergarten and the feeling of entering an unknown world where one step separated him from another dimension of reality.

As they slowed to a walk, they began to notice the stark change in the environment. The light passing through in sharp rays within the small openings of the branches was soft and it contrasted the surreal carnage and destruction they had witnessed all along the highway on their day long walk.

Evening shadows gave way to night's darkness in the thick woods as they walked East, following the course of the moon across the indigo sky between the canopy above them. Instinctively, they remained quiet, touching each other frequently, not wanting to risk losing one another in the dark. Gentle breezes set the leafs rustling in motion above and around them, arousing their imaginations as some critter would scamper off in the night at their approach.

Maybe one could be caught in the day time, they needed food. It had been over 24 hours since they had eaten. John tries to think of creative ways to catch a rabbit once the Sun comes up tomorrow. Calculating how long they may be stuck out here in this wilderness and how he will ever get home leads him to thoughts of broken sticks and how he will sharpen them with rocks. Images replaying in his mind of the old loyal Mustang being overwhelmed by the rising waters lead him to wonder where the old car is now and he imagines it at the bottom of the bay.

"It will make a good place for fish to hide," he thinks out loud.

"Your car? That's funny. Maybe they can fix it up with all that cash," she responds. "Hey, what is that?"

Ahead there is a light shining through the gaps in the trees, appearing as only a small dot in the distance. Quieter now, they edge towards it through the thicket until it is evident that it is a porch light revealing an open yard at the edge of the woods. There doesn't seem to be any other houses around it, so they draw closer in silent caution.

Crushing leafs and Pine needles are barely audible under their feet as they hold their breathing in their anxiousness until they cannot even feel it coming out of their noses anymore. Every sound is magnified in their heightened alertness as they approach the edge of the thicket. Old washing machines and pieces of motorcycles are littered about the side of the wooden building. Wooden stairs lead up to a small metal door with a metal sign attached beside it reading:

"Hippies, please use the side door."

"I guess that means us," says John, as they emerge from their hiding.

The low growling of a dog hits their ears as they hear the giant animal rushing across the yard towards them. John jumps in front of Francis and hunches down to take on the animal, which jerks backwards as it reaches the end of its long, heavy chain, just feet from his face. Another light turns on within the house just before the door slowly opens. The light behind it casts a silhouetting shadow in front of the heavy set man in the doorway. He held a shotgun by his side, letting the barrel hang down towards the ground as the ferocious animal continued to snarl and pull at his chain three feet away from the unexpected visitors.

"Can I help you?" he says in a thick Southeast Texas accent.

John and Frances turn their eyes to each other and smile at their tattered appearance in response to the question. Her clothes were torn and his torn shirt barley covered her. Cuts from the rubbish crashing into them in the water had formed black scabs from their heads to their bare feet. John was still shirtless and his remnants of blue jeans barely coved anything of the bottom half of his body.

"Yes, I'm pretty sure you can, man, I'm pretty sure you can definitely help us!"

The joke spurred the Southeast Texas boy in the door way into a booming laughter as he clinched his knee and asked,

"What the hell are you two doing way out here?!"

"We survived the hurricane, you don't even want to know," says John, almost ready to completely break down from both the physical and the mental exhaustion he was only now feeling. "You don't even want to know. I'm John, this is Francis."

"I'm Ben. Ben Decobe. My friends just call me Big Ben. Come on in."

Words of universal kindness and southern hospitality let them know instantly that they were temporarily safe, sheltered by one of their own kind.

"Trisha, get some of them leftovers heated up, we got company!"

They followed him into the house, which was surprisingly tidy compared to the yard, and smelled of southern cooking and Lilac candles. They collapsed onto the living room floor, sitting back and resting as they reached up to acknowledge Trisha, who came in from the back hallway in a nightgown.

"This is John, this is Francis. They were in the storm," he tells his wife in a direct way, as if explaining something simple.

"Hi," said Francis, mustering a sincere smile at her hostess, "sorry we showed up unannounced!"

"Oh, you poor thing! You must need something to wear! Let me give you some clothes!" replied Trisha, graciously. "Ben, go get them some clothes! Let John borrow one of your shirts.

"You want some pants, too," he asks John.

"Naw, just let me cut off the rest of these," John replies, knowing the pants that fit Ben would be huge on him.

While relishing the reheated red beans and rice on cornbread and drinking cold beers, they relate the story of the previous night to their interested new friends in great detail. They tell them about the car being submerged, the cows stomping them in the dark, the houses floating around in the tumultuous waters around them in the night, and of straying from the ONE vehicle's oncoming approach on the highway. Only the mention of the cash is left out of the story.

Stories and jokes are passed between the brothers in spirit deep into the night as they pass the small metal pipe back and forth and Francis falls asleep on John's arm as the two men talk. Ben tells him that the water surprised a lot of people when it overcame the peninsula so quickly, because underwater currents had filled the bay side and actually came over the land from behind, not from the ocean side. John looks back to his memory of the ancient boat in Frances's yard and now realizes how it must have gotten there, in the '100 year storm' that came 100 years ago. He replays his foolish decision to get the money in his head over and over again as if somehow he could change the past by repeating it in his head until his eyes close and he falls asleep sitting upright on the couch.

The big boat is talking to him as he drifts in and out of consciousness. But a rusted out shell of some former vessel of things and people, it was once a mighty traveler of the great open seas. It sits marauded, now, and speaks to him softly as he drifts off.

"I'm here because something put me here. I was drifting along on the calm open waters when it came and picked me up. It tossed me about as it wished and then left me here, stranded on land with no way back to my familiar waters where I was allowed to drift and float as I was meant to do."

Gaping holes in the ship's hull form a mouth with giant, jagged teeth as it raises its voice to a roar.

"Get out of her way. She will destroy you!"

Just then, a giant wave of water rushes up from behind the boat and engulfs you, tumbling you around like a rag in the sheer force of its rushing water and washing you far out into the deep, gloomy bay. You are far from the shoreline, and you can only strain to see land in the distance. Water all around you is brown in the murky night which has now overcome the sky in its darkness, you turn and splash at the surface for something to grasp onto. Nothing is there. You scream, but no one hears. The far looming shore is unattainable, too far for swimming, and no one is there to help you.

Sizzling bacon and the smell of cooking eggs wakes the two refugees, who find themselves wrapped in each other's arms on the sofa. A big, snuggly blanket has been placed over them in their sleep and they squeeze each other firmly beneath it. All the mornings of their youth when he held her but could not sleep came to him as he looked down at her in his arms and kissed her automatically, simply.

The morning haze is a bliss, an in-between dream that fades with the shadows as the Sun's light squeezes through the tiny cracks in the mini-blinds and the pair starts to remember where they are.

Getting up, he stumbles a bit, still buzzed from the night's beers and weary from their perilous travel. Naturally, he pulls up at the remnants of his pants as he stumbles towards the kitchen and Trisha in front of a warm stove.

"Damn! That looks good! You guys sure are nice. Where's Big Ben?"

As if on command, Ben walks steadily and smoothly from the back hall of the narrow building, scratching his belly button beneath the t-shirt which was raised up over his ample stomach as he stretched his other arm over his head.

"Hey, you guys up?" he says, brushing the sleep from his kind, discerning eyes.

Hot coffee brings reality to the forefront as they enjoy the meal together. Ben's life is simple on the outside. He and his woman live out in the woods, they grow most of their own food or catch it in the yard as it runs away and clucks a prayer to some unseen power. They seem to have everything worked out on their own.

ONE troops don't even know how to follow the old dirt roads through the path to their self sufficient cottage. They always get lost at an obscured turn off into the woods from the main dirt road and end up dead ending at the water's edge, assuming it is just another dirt road to the river. But there is one spot, the spot where the road curves hard to the left, which you can turn off into the overhanging trees onto another dirt road which drops off quickly and leads winding its way to their house, to the right.

"How do you go to town?" John asks.

"Come on, fool, I'm going to show you something."

Ben leads him towards a narrow hall at the side of the living room. Walking down the hall, Ben tells him about the tenacity of his pit bull, turned around and hunched over as if ducking under the low ceiling of the dark corridor. As he speaks, he rolls his hand around in explanation, distracting from the fact that he has swiveled what seemed to be a panel in the wall at the end of the hall, exposing a steel door which they enter through.

They walk together through a dark hall built onto the end of the house sloping downward. The construction is reminiscent of an underground mine, with bare wood framing the rippled tin walls. 20 feet down, the tunnel breaks 90 degrees to the left, descending further into darkness until Ben flips on the light. Florescent lights sputter to a glow sequentially down the large corridor, exposing vehicles draped in covers and all manners of tools and machines about the shelved wooden walls.

"I get the tags from a buddy of mine who works for the state. They are fresh and clean, straight up, government tags. With these tags, we can go where ever we want, homeboy."

A big red pickup truck holds John up as he becomes silent to listen to Ben's story and leans back on its solid steel side.

"Man, when they see those tags, boy, they don't even bother messin' with us."

Shiny gold colored wheels glare out from under the white sheet draped over the car behind Ben and beg for John's curiosity every time the glimmer hits his eye.

"So, how are you going to get back?"

The question is more than a question. It is a branch extended in caring. It is known now, who they both are, what they both stand for, and the code that they will engage each other by.

"I don't know. I have some family out here, in Mauriceville, on Flint Road. It's probably, oh, about 60 miles from here. I don't know, I guess we'll walk."

Instinctively fidgeting for something, John reaches his hand down into his front jeans pockets where he feels a moist lump of money folded in a tight roll of damp paper. His hand stops in surprise as his fingers probe the unmistakable texture of the bills he had stuffed into his pocket and forgotten about. The memory of stuffing it into his pocket before the nightmare began rang in his head as he held it out before himself in disbelief.

"I guess I forgot about that."

A wide grin comes over Ben's face as his head cocks to one side and he looks at the big roll of one hundred dollar bills.

"You like Camaros?" Ben smiles openly, one arm slightly in front of him as he leans over towards John.

His front hand is turned palm back, accentuating his stalky forearms as he poses the question in a manner that cannot be refused. Blonde haired and silly as hell, he had a very simple but effective manner of persuasion: He would just tell you how it was going to be, and you would understand that it would only be for your own good.

Once, a Buddhist practitioner from Brazil had traveled to Texas and somehow found himself at Ben's house with a bag of records and a backpack. Enrique was his name, but everyone called him, 'Fish.'

Fish was a brave soul, devout to his beliefs and disciplined as he rose every morning to meditate and chant towards the East. He lit incense and candles, he hated violence, and he did not, *absolutely not*, eat red meat.

"No, no, I do not eat. I do not eat meat, man, that is no good."

The man named Fish was convincing in his conviction and thick Portuguese accent as he waived off the offer of southern home-cooked goodness from his host's kitchen, not knowing what he was missing.

"You gona eat some of that Chicken Fried Steak and gravy that my ol' lady cooked, mother fucker."

Ben's smile spread from ear to ear as he only slightly leaned forward with the steaming plate heaped with chicken fried steak, homemade mashed potatoes, and green beans all covered in thick white gravy in his extended hand. Fish swore it was the best thing he'd ever eaten.

Southern hospitality was a weak description of what was at hand. Just like the bud bringing leafs and the bees bringing pollen to the flowering trees, the love spread simultaneously, springing up in wells throughout. Faith in human spirit, the propensity towards love, kindness, and understanding, were the golden keys to mercies they had become accustomed to and survived upon for such a long time.

Close encounters and tight fits requiring perfect alignment of the stars for their very survival were counted on by so many and the still small voice blew through the breeze as rustling leafs into a million ears at once. It was a subculture, sub spirit, hardly ever talked about any more, yet living on like a recessive gene in the space between matter of human beings. It was in trees that sing, in everything, seen or unseen. It was shining in brightly reflected lights off of the mirror polished purple paint of the 1983 Camaro as Ben rolled the sheet back from it, wafting it through the air in slow-motion.

Every inch of the car was straight. No blemishes in its smooth body, not a single ding or dent marred its flowing lines. Black, thick tires held its staunch stance squarely. Its nose was angled just slightly down; the perfect amount that made it look like it was not done on purpose. The paint job was royally authentic, glitter reflecting in its princely purple hue. Walking around it slowly, crutched over to peer down the length of the car from different angles, John revels over the vehicle.

"It's got a 350, four bolt main," said Ben, adding, "and a turbo 350 transmission."

Classic muscle cars, all but extinct, aroused a certain nostalgia among many. Valves emitting explosions from carbon steel cylinders, through aluminum headers and into exhaust pipes from the simple solution of a spark igniting gasoline, turned the big cam in the motor determinedly, the sound speaking loudly to the craftsmanship and power of the engine. The thudding, pulling sound, combined with the smell of gasoline fumes, caused euphoric flames in the brains of passers-by as a familiar aroma and view hit them like déjà vu. It woke up that sleeping thing within them, that warrior's spirit. John pictured it rolling by on the sunny street of an old, white picket fence neighborhood as he stood behind it, looking at the white cursive letters forming the title across the back of the car: "*Bigg Ben*"

"Damn! That's gangster!"

John is truly amazed by the beautiful machine. "How long did it take you to make it like this?"

He is peering through the window at the immaculate interior, imagining his hands on the polished aluminum "T" shaped shifter and the leather bound steering wheel.

"Yeah! You like that? Ha-Ha! I knew you would. I always had it, it was my momma's. I just worked on it, took care of it."

Big Ben runs his hand over the hood slowly, as if reminiscing as he speaks. John can imagine him bent over the hood, peering closely at fiber glass filler as he sands it smoothly into the contours of the chassis with his bare fingertips.

"When's the last time you got to drive it?"

Gas is a tough commodity to find, even for the well connected, so John assumes it will have been a long time.

"Last week," replies Ben, "I drove it to the store last week." Ben sees the suspicious look on John's face. "Come here, let me show you something else about us east Texas swamp boys," he says.

John follows him around a maze of stacked up tires, stepping over floor jacks and tools towards the far side of the shop. Ben leads him to a large wooden set of shelves, constructed of standard lumber which was turning brown with age. The plywood shelves, stacked with rusty coffee cans and a few old metal gasoline containers, looked like they had been used for years from the stains of oil and grease.

"I told you I had some gas!" said Ben.

"Yeah, that's a lot gas Ben, maybe 5, 10 gallons?" John said, trying not to show that he was unimpressed by the small amount of petrol on the shelves.

At that, Ben smiles and reaches his hand behind a coffee can full of old rusty screws, stretching his arm deep into the cabinets until John hears what sounds like a car door when the handle is pulled. The entire wall of shelves swings back. The room on the other side is low; the ceiling barely over their heads, and it seemed to go on forever in the dark with the round tops of fifty gallon drums reflecting the dim light.

"See, back in the day, this here was the main industry in these parts. We wanted to get a job, we'd go down to the local refinery," said Ben.

"I know, I used to work in them," responds John.

"Good. So you know how it is. Well, when we all heard that everything was getting shut down; we started sneaking this stuff out in the spare tanks of our trucks. Most of my buddies, they're in jail now, but this is where we kept it."

Thousands of gallons of petrol line the deep room in perfectly aligned steel drums. Ben looks over at his new friend's face as John's mouth hangs loosely open and his eyes glaze over for a moment before Ben tells him, matter-of-factly,

"This whole thing is under the ground."

They end up hanging out in the shop for hours, drinking cold beers and smoking while listening to music played through classic, direct drive turn tables. The relics of modern music still spun the records smoothly with their magnetically driven tempo and the sound stirred memories of old times as they enjoyed the relaxation and comradery. Eventually, John had the idea to count the money which he had stuffed back into his front pants pocket. There were two hundred one hundred dollar bills.

"How much for that Camaro," asks John as he puts on his car wash face.

Ben had never considered selling the car. Never, that is, until very recently. Friends had come to him about it over the years, but none of them ever had enough money to make an offer that wouldn't insult him and he knew it, so he always just said it wasn't for sale. The need of money had recently reminded him that he only took the car from his mom's yard and fixed the non running motor up so he could sell it in the first place. Hours of meticulous work with his hands and in searching and bartering for parts kindled a keen affection for the character filled car.

"I'll give you 10 thousand dollars for it."

"Shit, make that 20."

"I'll give you 12 thousand dollars for it, right now," he says, counting out the money in his hand. They are both a little drunk and happy from their day of bonding as they barter.

"20."

"13 thousand, or else just sell me that van for 25. Twenty five hundred, that is."

John holds out one hundred and thirty one 100 dollar bills out in front of him, thickly stacked and fanned out. "Thirteen thousand and one hundred dollars, final offer."

"Alight, you got you a deal. On the van."

"What! You're kidding me! Come on, man," pleads John.

"Ha-Ha, I'm just kidding! Hell, I was gona give it to ya, but I'll take that 13 thousand, if you insist!"

Backing the car up and out of the trap door Ben has opened for them, they wave good bye to their new friends. The driveway out of the hidden structure is like the mouth of a dark cave, sloping up in a steep twist behind them. Francis holds the vinyl seats to brace herself against the backwards incline as they emerge into the Sunlight. After making a "U" shape backing around, John drops the gear shifter two clicks down into drive.

Seemingly endless power from the old V8 engine propels them forward into the Sunny day as they spring forth down the country road at the command of the accelerator beneath his heavy foot. Endless joy seeps through the enveloping trees on the paved road as they emerge from the dirt road leading back to Ben's and open the throttle of the big motor, lifting the car up as it accelerates down the road. They take the back roads, as Ben had indicated they ought to, for many miles until they reach a link to the major interstate highway far outside of town.

It is not the side of the highway with a ramp to lead back home, however. There was no indirect route to the west that would keep them from passing through the badly ravished town where ONE troops were undoubtedly still rounding people up, so they were going east. Demolished cities had been routinely cleared of inhabitants and rebuilt as government property in past events in other states, so he made his decision to go east on the back roads, instead. He knew that there was a good chance of getting on the highway and escaping the town if he took the back roads far enough outside of town before entering the major transit route. He was heading back to his place of origin, to the murky hidden recesses of Southeast Texas.

They enter the highway cautiously but quickly, turning their heads around in both directions as they shoot from the wooded side road and onto the feeder, then speed onto the main concourse. The road is completely empty except for one blue vehicle far in the distance ahead of them which they squint their eyes at, trying to determine what kind of vehicle it is. They ride slowly for miles, trying not to approach the vehicle miles ahead of them too quickly as it vanishes around curves and reappears in the distance on long, straight stretches of the highway.

Tall pine trees are snapped like toothpicks and littering the forests along the highway in cut trails formed by twisting cyclones which carved their way through the sturdy trees like a surgeon's scalpel on the night of the big storm. It was the same highway he had traveled on for so many years, but it seemed so different. They daze in imagination as they watch the scenery roll by them, not noticing the boxy vehicle of the ONE convoy gaining up behind them.

By the time they notice, the armored vehicle is close behind them. John slowly suppresses the accelerator pedal and gains momentum, bringing the speed up to the maximum 70 miles per hour limit. The giant truck behind him accelerates as well, blowing out a cloud of black smoke from its upward facing exhaust pipes and staying just behind the sports car.

"We're just ten miles from the exit," says John. They hold their breath and say nothing for the next five minutes, peering from the side of their eyes into the rear view mirrors at the beastly vehicle looming behind them on the desolate highway. As they pass the only other vehicle on the road, the one which had been far ahead of them, they can barely muster a smile at the old black man in the beat up blue pick-up truck. Just then, the lights begin flashing atop the big vehicle behind them in their mirrors.

"Stop and pull over," say's the calm, ominous, computerized voice of a woman through the megaphones atop the vehicle.

"That big thing can't possibly go much fast than seventy," John thinks out loud as he grip's Francis's leg and looks over to her. She looks back and says nothing as he wheels his foot forward onto the accelerator.

Opening up the motor on an old hot rod is an art which requires finesse, just like anything else. If you press it down too hard, too quickly, like an inexperienced lover, you run the risk of bogging it out. Before you dump all that gasoline into the intake, you need to feel the revving motor work up to that tempo which creates a steady hum before you can fully open the air intakes of the carburetor and really run it all out.

The giant motor begins to hum as it reaches synergy in its peak production and the car rises from the ground as the speedometer rushes past the 100 miles per hour mark still gaining momentum. The hum becomes a roar as the needle pushes towards its maximum, 140 mph, and continues to twist past the mark.

The flashing lights disappear from sight in the setting Sun behind them, vanishing over the horizon just a few miles before they slow down quickly and take a short, bumpy exit off of the highway and swing left under the overpass. The engine again howls and before they know it, they are speeding down a winding country road. About ten miles later, they turn left into an unmarked dirt road through a canopy of Pine trees which opens up to a wooden fenced horse pasture.

"Welcome to Flint Road," he tells her.

They drive slowly down the long dirt road, carefully maneuvering the street machine over the ridges and holes in the road with the wooden horse fence along the side of it. No need to drive fast now, amongst the wilderness. They are safely out of sight from the outside world. Trees in the grazing pasture are leaning over and snapped like splintery twigs from the storm while others stand unharmed. Down towards the end of the rocky road, they turn off into a narrow opening which sneaks up in the wall of the woods to the left side of the road a few yards after the horse fence stopped.

Together, they strain their eyes as they turn into the dark, wooded canopy. Two houses stand in the yard which opens up a little ways past the trees, one in the front and one way in the back. They walk up to the bigger house in front along the brown wooden deck to the side door where a metallic sign, which looks 50 years old reads, "*Hippies, please use the side door*," in cursive.

They do not knock, just walk right in. They know damn well the two old brothers who lived there would never expect them. In their rubber rain boots, muddy upon the plywood kitchen floor, they had not expected to see anyone for days, even weeks. Surprise would have overcome them at that moment, if anything could surprise them at all after the last two days.

As the two youthful adventurers busted into his door, Killer was over in the kitchen, his leg raised up on a stool as he stood and leaned on his knee, smoking a cigarette. Lying back on the couch, directly in front of them, was no other than Justin Peoples.

"Hey, buuuudy, how you doing?"

Justin does not seem surprised at all, and unexpectedly, John is the one who is surprised by his surprise entry.

"What the hell!?"

As they slap hands, he pulls him up off the couch. They grab each other in a firm embrace and pat each other's backs with tightly clenched fists. They have not seen each other now in many years. As Francis and Peoples stand at distance and say "hi" to one another, John walks over to his uncle and grabs him for a hug.

"What are you doing here, you little piss ant?"

Killer's long hair hangs in a ponytail behind his back under the "Reliable" hat logo and onto his faded black biker T-shirt. His long beard goes out below him, still virile yet totally white. The old codger's strong, tanned arm reaches out for a hand shake, then slides around to jab John in the side as he extends his hand for the shake.

"Gotcha!" Killer yells gleefully.

Killer had taught him how to change oil in a car. He had taught him how diodes and resistors worked by storing and squeezing electric energy. Looking down at him in his adolescence, years before, he had also taught him the meaning of life.

"Do you want to know what the meaning of life is?"

The first time John Flint had been told that he was a man was by his uncle, 'Killer,' as he cracked a cool Blue can of brew. The way Killer had peered down at him in those days, focusing his sharp laser scalpel of a glare through his eyes to impart something he could make him understand, made little John Flint feel special. In all his wisdom, Killer felt that the young boy was someone worthy of understanding, of trying to pass it on to. The pubescent boy stood silently in honest reverence, trying with every part of his being to be ready for the wisdom which was about to spill out.

"The secret of life, boy," say's Killer, as he raises his hand in a theatric wave, "is to love life."

He points his iron finger deep into the young John's chest as his eyes open fully and his head cocks back, captivating the boy's eyes in his stare.

"Just love life. The good and the bad, just the same. That's all you've got to do."

Years later, the whole scene sticks to him in memory. Killer's place is adorned with a million gadgets on the shelves built along the top of the wall and around the desk at the front of the living room, now, like always. Accumulated over the years, like the photographs on the walls of old friends passed, each trinket brought John intimately into a childhood memory upon close inspection.

John had always admired Killer. His mind was capable to bear a flight worthy airplane from the rugged trunks of pine trees and his mightily loud stereo could rise the birds from their branches in alarm. His mentor had taught him so many things over the years. He taught him about negotiating pay and polishing aluminum, about how to crash a motorcycle and how to deal with 'gadam women.' His buddy taught him a little knife play, Bubba taught him some footwork. Killer taught him how to pop a pistol from an attacker's hand by snapping his hands in a crossing motion to twist the gun from an attacker's hand:

The hand is quicker than the eye. Simultaneously punching the wrist and the back of the attacker's hand pushes the weapon's barrel into another direction. The gun spins around in the wielder's hand, the leverage too strong for his grip, and the handle of the pistol comes to rest in your palm.

"Now, if that happens, you've got him really screwed up. You have to really act pissed, as if you're going to shoot him. Say, 'hey, mother fucker, weren't you just pointing this at me'? But you've got to be serious. Don't point a gun at someone if you're not ready to use it."

John stored every word Killer had ever told him in indestructible vaults in his mind.

Cold beers are again cracked and the refugees feel as if they have taken on a vacation instead of a flight for their lives as now, out in the deep piney woods, they are amongst friends. The power is all out, but electric generators keep the music running. Chickens still run around the yard laying eggs and catfish still swim in the tank. Clean water still sits at the bottom of the deep water well and all is fine. There is no store to drive to after the storm, so there is plenty of room for stories as they tell of their wild adventure and of how they came to own the fine car in the yard. After that, they hear of how People's had ended up there.

"I had gone to the beach to see Pickle, and we all got too drunk and got into a fight. Pickle took off the other way, and I went wandering down the Sea Wall… Over there by the McDonald's? Hell, I was so drunk, I didn't even know where I was. You know me; I'm not scared to stand in the rain."

The old Peoples they had remembered from ten years ago still shone in his energetic mannerisms as he spoke.

"So I'm walking up Seawall Boulevard when these Mexcins' come up to me in front of the McDonalds. You know the type, all gangstered out, pressed slacks and flat brimmed hats, mad because I was asking his girlfriend if she wanted to be with me…

Anyway, they beat the shit out of me, all ten of them, and then they took my shoes. My wallet, my shoes, they even took my shirt. I was all bloodied up and drunk, so somehow I found my way to the ferry. I met some people from Orange, and I got a ride back to where Killer's house was. At least where it used to be, where I remembered it being."

Francis sits back and laughs invisibly in the corner at his story.

Killer interjects with,

"They found him, you won't believe this, wrapped up in an American flag, sleeping on the trampoline."

"I was thinking, 'I don't remember a trampoline back here, but I just figured they had gotten a trampoline. Those people woke up and found my ass wrapped up in the American flag, half naked, sleeping in their back yard on their kid's trampoline!"

"Well, what did they say?"

"I was like, 'I'm here to see Killer! And they were like, 'Killer don't live here no more!"

Again, Killer interjects with,

"When they dropped him off here, they were so nice. They said it wasn't the first time! Apparently, it wasn't the first time some riffraff had showed up there looking for me! Poor people! Can you imagine buying a house and always having a bunch of crazy people coming around looking for a guy named 'Killer'?"

Southern hospitality was again an expected grace when the strangers had brought Peoples to Flint road, where he had been staying ever since.

Finally, after getting the primary stories of how they had arrived there out of the way, John say's,

"I'm going to go to the back, see what my old man is doing," and waves goodbye to his friends. He walks out of the side door and through the yard, which has now grown pitch black, following the trail to the cabin in the back. The only light is that reflected off of the Moon, barely squeezing between the dense leafs of Pine trees onto the Pineneedle littered path. Upon the wide trunk of a sloping Pine tree at the end of the path is a wooden sign reading: *'Tom Flint Studios.'*

John opens the door slowly and peers his head in. The old smell of Oil Paints and Turpentine invites him as he looks to see his father looking up from his notes and a bible at the desk in the center of the one room cabin.

"Well, hey, son!" Tom says in surprise, "What are you doing here?"

The question is answered slowly, in phases between his own questions about how his dad is doing, as John examines the new painting forming on the canvas which sits on the large easel. He marvels at the canvass as he tells the story of the last few days, of all that transpired since they last saw each other back in central Texas, hundreds of miles away.

Exploding lines of fire and radical light slash down the canvas on the easel in the one room studio, forming the features of a face in the night time sky of a ferocious storm. Trees beneath it are twisting wildly in the wind, which is depicted by flying debris and water exploding out at you as you get sucked into the scene. The image seems horrifically realistic, although not a single line of the painting is defined.

The easel on which the painting in progress sits is custom made. A one-of-a-kind masterpiece of square steel tubes welded in perfect congruency and bolted to Red Oak rods which supported the painting. The whole thing had been crafted for him entirely by hand. All along the walls of the wooden cabin hang paintings and more of them are stacked all around, leaning against every wall. The artist's life is plainly displayed in the image created by his domicile, his dedication, his simplicity.

Tom is researching. The master artist sits amongst several stacks of plain white paper piled upon the long table, each evenly stacked with notes and references written on them. He organizes his thoughts and expounds them daily, constantly, until he stands before the easel and lets the pondering come to fruition through his paints. When he mixes them, he lowers his thick glasses and looks over them at the pallet. Like riding a bike, the quick and delicate strokes of the brush have become second nature to him.

His arm holds steady as his wrist swings back and forth. Frances and Peoples eventually come over to the cabin and sit in as the father and son talk for hours and drink beer together. They pass around a fine, hand carved briar pipe with an ebony mouthpiece and laugh as they all become more and more intoxicated and blissful together. Eventually, Peoples and Francis wander back to Killer's house to get some sleep on the couches. Now dazed and in the spiritual world between dream and consciousness, the Flint's begin an open line of concourse as the spirits start to flow.

"I tell ya what, son. After all of this, I'm not afraid of anything, of anyone. I'm serious. You could have a gun and pointing it right at me, and I wouldn't back up an inch. Just nothing scares me anymore. Because if God is real... And I was talking to my brother the other day and he tells me, he says I ought not say, 'If God is real,' but I mean it in a rhetorical kind of way. But *IF God is real*, then we will be okay. If not, then none of this *shit* matters, anyway."

Tom admires his own set jaw in his son's face. He is proud of the boy, as the boy is proud of his father. They have kept their tenacious trait and cultivated it together. The world spits in their face a thousand times, their buddies get good jobs and fish on bass boats, but they keep painting and drawing, writing and pondering. Ex wives and girlfriends would lament and beg them to submit to a normal regiment, to get a real job, but they would have none of it.

In forceful letters, agencies would demand payments, government agencies would demand fees with the threat of captivity, and all one had to do to escape the doom was to get a job at the hardware store, it could all be so easy. But they couldn't, they weren't wired for it, it smelled too much like surrender. Never was one bent to back down and, in each other's presence, they reaffirmed and sharpened one another like red hot iron striking iron.

"But you know what, son? God *is* real!"

"You remember that Pit Bull that used to always be behind Buchinno's house? Yeah, the Red one? Yeah, it had a red nose, red body. Came up to the house one day and it had been shot. Had a bullet hole going in one side of him," say's Peeps as he points to one side of his chest, "and out the side, like this. He was just wagging his tail and bouncing around like everything was fine."

Peeps relays the story with a faraway look from the back seat as he leans forward between the two reclined seats of the coup and talks to them.

"Then Brandon was like, 'Damn, that's the fourth time them bastards have shot my dog!' Them dogs are tough, they don't really care what you do to them, they just keep on coming."

He looked real tough. He was a big man now, well over 250 pounds. He was fat around the belly, but he held his big shoulders back and stood erect, anyway. A long black beard twisted to a point down below his chin, ending above his sideburns abruptly at the spot where his shaved head began. Greek style wings were tattooed over each ear on his bald scalp. They had had their bouts, Peoples and John. They had tested each other enough times to learn.

One thing to learn about Peoples was to never let him get his hands around you in a fight. Not very effectual as a puncher, you would do well to keep him at bay with your hands. If he gets his arms around you, chances are good that he'll take you to the ground. Once there, you're sure to be in for an elbow popping arm-bar, or a demoralizing 'rear naked choke hold.'

In a 'rear naked choke hold,' you will feel the despair of utter hopelessness as your back arches up backwards from where he is sitting at the bottom of your waist, with is right arm around your neck. His left arm is pulling at the wrist of the arm around your neck, forming a lever and squeezing you terrifically. He's going to make you tap. The only problem is, when you tap, he's not going to quit.

"Fuck it, John, Jesus never tapped." Sailor's wisdom is rare and precious.

He is enjoying the free ride to central Texas as he talks. He had been out there for three months before the storm, brushing horses and watching trees softly sway in the breeze from Killer's porch on Flint Road, with time standing still in the wooded hollow. Now, while zooming down the interstate highway, the hours pass quickly in conversation and remembrance. He sits in the back and hands out beverages, sharing stories and reliving old memories with his two old buddies. They relish their long drive back to the little cottage on the prairie, where John had left so long ago to go pick up Francis and bring her back. Riding in the vintage machine, austere in its meticulous refurbishing and government tags, they light heartedly enjoy their trip home.

Peoples is a drifter, and he will be put to good use in the garden. The garden grows its produce: food and seeds for further crops. Anything that has to do with food should interest Peoples. He has shown an affinity towards it.

"It's water weight," he would say, "all you skinny people are going to be hating it when the apocalypse comes. You'll all die of famine and I'll pick your bones." The garden grows plants, but the cultivating of minds grows warriors. Peoples will be good in the garden, thinks John.

Francis is officially a refuge, her former home on the island being unreachable after the storm. She wants to get back to her cat, but the reality of survival has put her poor pet at the back of her mind. Cats are extremely resourceful, she thinks.

John is just excited to get back to his dogs and see how things have been going back at home. His mind turns back to Fiona as he remembers his last image of her in his mind, where her deep orange eyes are reflecting the bright Sunlight as she smiles up at him, her asymmetrical bottom jaw hanging loosely as her tongue wags out.

With a beautiful woman sitting beside him, her gorgeous auburn hair rising up behind her pleasant smile to the wafting winds of the open window, he stares into space for the love of the lost dog, and speeds towards home.

10. SAPIENCE

Have you ever tried to corporally punish a Pit Bull? You need to be a master of psychology to do so effectively. It's a game of brinksmanship that would make Stalinist Soviet soldiers shudder.

A mixture of ingrained determination and stubbornness, strong emotions, and unlikely intelligence, make punishing the animal a precarious task, easily fouled into making the dog behave worse rather than better. The Pit Bull will allow you to punish it, but only to an extent. There are some qualities which will never be corrected. Ashamed, sorry, and confused about the nature of what it has done wrong, the loyal dog will take a good spanking. But at the point where punishment becomes irrational, unreasonable; when the dog finally becomes afraid, it will do something strange, something only understood at a primal level.

When it has no more options, when it has had all it can take, it finds a corner and backs itself into it. You will stand over it with a belt or a newspaper rolled up and you will see a look that says,

"Okay, I've submitted, but I cannot back up any more."

You may realize you have gone too far in your punishment and take a deep breath, step back, and say something to the dog in a nice voice like, 'Dangit you danged ol' dog, why did you chew up my furniture; don't do that anymore, okay?' then bend down to pat his head as his tail begins a nervous, wiggling wag and he inches towards you on his belly, tilting his ear up in the way he asks you to pat him, yearning for your approval.

Or, you may be so consumed by anger from coming home and finding your favorite chair spread into white fluffy pieces across your apartment, that you fail to tame your raging temper and strike the dog again. As much as the dog knows he is your inferior, he will not let you punish him anymore. Eventually, the dog will bite back.

As she lays there on the couch, he wanders if she's asleep. All the things running through his mind; the mortgage, the water leak, the warrants, the bills; all he can really think about is her. How did he come to be here, constantly one step behind every obligation? When did he become accustomed to feeling like everything he had, from his car to his house, even his freedom, were only a breath away from being taken away? How is it so easy for everyone else? They seem to have no problems, no money worries; it seems it should be easy to take care of these things. As he lies awake in the darkness, he can hear his thoughts aloud in the room.

'There has to be a way.'

He knows he has to make a way. No use lying down and being awake. Make this time mean something. He gets up to tend to menial tasks: laundry, dishes, chores, bills, and tallying up the sum of money he needs to come up with.

The little voice nags at him to set these things right. That same voice tells him to forget it, not to strive to be right with them, to put it behind himself. Put it behind the important things; right now was a time for survival. Beyond all reason, something keeps telling him that the vegetable plants in the back yard are more important than his financial obligations. The nagging, yet strangely logical voice, continues to fill his ears in every moment spent in silence. He hears it when he lies awake in the dark and under the hard bearing Sun where he works in the garden. The modest plot of Okra and Tomatoes has quietly grown into a vast field of neatly separated mounds forming long rows across the plot behind his house.

'The prince of Dubai doesn't pay his debts, why should you? Is your choice death and taxes? Those plants will keep you alive. You need a better system to keep the varmints out. A well, you must have a well. And that windmill, have you forgotten about that windmill? You must start drawing the designs for that. Figure it out.' The little voice nags him to get it right.

'What equipment will you need? What materials will it require?'

He starts drawing on his plans but his thoughts turn to the day when they will come to get him.

'Then what will you do? You need to start planning for that.'

He draws the map out of the wilderness behind his house in his head. He sees the enclaves and slopes in the terrain. He starts to think of ways and designs to out maneuver them, to get away and survive if they ever try to come for him the way they have come for so many others. The voice in his head grows louder.

'If they were chasing me,' he thinks, 'I'd jump behind this rooted pit, behind the wall of weed-ferns and disappear. But they'd search for me. They'd pass by and track their way back, eventually... I'll track them! As they pass me by, I'll creep up behind, and hide one spot behind them!'

He courses out the path in his mind, he draws it out.

The next day, he walks the path in the woods behind his house that he had run through the night before in his imagination. He starts digging out the holes he had hidden in and forging the trails through the dense reeves and weeds. The bush is like a maze laid over sloping terrain ranging from deep, soft dirt to jagged, odd shaped boulders.

You must be careful walking; it would be easy to twist an ankle on this terrain. Trying to go around the thick weeds will keep you walking in a circle and you can't go through them, they're too thick. The dogs go under them; they push down between the bases of the weeds on all fours, so you do the same and enter the canopy beneath the dense brush. It's clear in here. You can see everything out side, but no light comes in and there is no way of knowing that there is a dwelling inside from as close as three feet away, even in the stark Sun. Tall reeves completely hide the enshrouded hole.

'If they go around the other way, they'll be walking through nails and boards of broken up old pallets and fencing from the neighbor's private landfill,' he thinks. 'They'll have to backtrack and come around this way. I can make another pit here... They will walk over it, over me. Then I can just follow them down this ravine. They will be walking along the top; I will be on the bottom. Under these exposed roots and foliage, they will never see me.'

As his brain boils in the Texas heat, the deep conversation with his subconscious bonds him to his new friend. Like the uncounted millions who have come before him over the past 10,000 years, here by this natural lake, he feels comforting reliance in the land.

The Indians have left him weapons. They've stored for him in the soft soil where he digs a rock shaped like a crescent moon, about the size of a baby's head. It is evident that some ancient hand worked the stone by the way it is symmetrically chiseled into a sharp edge. The bottom of the rock is smooth and flat, diamond shaped where it had attached to its handle ages ago. In the coming days, he ties it between the 'V' of a split stick, which he has dried and sanded. He weaves the wet straps of an old baseball mitt around the end to secure his axe head and ties it tightly. Letting the axe dry in the Sun, the leather stretches tight, securing the chiseled stone in the handle. The weapon's weight feels assuring in his hand and he imagines it crushing a skull in a long ago battle.

'Leave it here for later, get back to work,' the voice continued. He has to prepare, to protect her and to provide for her.

'Remember where you put those sharpened nails protruding from the board just under the dirt.'

Daily walking the dogs to make sure the spots he will hide in have been marked several times to mask his scent from tracking dogs as he formulates his plan, he imagines being chased through his maze in the dark. The imaginary voice of her tells him he is going crazy, a little paranoid, as she speaks into his head.

"Maybe so, but I'm no use to you dead," he answers back to himself out loud.

'Huh?'

'This conversation is becoming a little too crowded, there's only room for one of me in here,' he tells himself.

The fight between his super-ego, his paranoia, and the last remnants of domestication carries on in his head. Tie, dig, work, sweat. Think.

'The guns will be the first thing they'll take,' he thinks.

"I need a wooden crate buried in the sand with some bullets and a gun. I need to make sure no one knows I have it," he thinks aloud, alone in his living room at 4 AM.

Guns are people food. A gun is traded for a TV, then for 50 dollars, then for a tattoo. It sits around an apartment unused, only flashed occasionally for show, waiting for the day when some emotionally charged reaction will bring it to bear the intimidating force it was designed for. Like a secret lover, once it has done its nasty job, it is hidden from sight and tried to be forgotten. Sexy in its form following function, in its strong, straight curves, the pretty weapon worries not. She knows she will always have a place, she has her appeal.

He gathers the guns he has collected at his place from behind the couch, from under the bed, and from the buried spot in the closet under piles of dirty clothes. Secretly they are carted from the little house, hidden in sacks, to the spot where he has already dug a hole in the soft sand below the lake's runoff slope. He places them in a crate and buries them there, half thinking to himself that he is crazy and the other half thinking he will be glad later.

The system devised for getting water from the lowland lake and into the garden was a simple one: Five gallon buckets were dipped in and poured into the troughs of dirt between his neatly planted rows of plants. Food was becoming more and more of a commodity. Laws had been passed banning keeping chickens due to health codes, and anyone who grew enough food to feed more than one person was now subject to prosecution if their garden was not properly licensed and inspected for bacteria and pesticides.

"Rules," he thought out loud, then laughed heartedly to himself. He had stopped caring about rules long ago.

Although the specific laws of how much food you were allowed to grow were muddy and undefined to the common person, the fear of prosecution was enough persuasion to amount to the final death nail to the dying tradition of growing one's own food. Every piece of fruit was carefully accounted for now. There was no more letting the half rodent eaten gourds rot in the field. Now, instead, they would be collected and dried on the arid wood of the front porch under the beaming Sun, the seeds extracted and used for the next planting season.

Neighbors started coming around the house into the hidden

field of rich, black bottom soil. At first, they came for some okra or tomatoes, which he gave readily. There was far too much for him to eat. He only wished one of them had a cow so they could trade him some milk. An older man down a ways had some goats, but he refused to speak English and seemed far from letting any of them go. He and others would show up there in the morning hours and help with the growing garden effort behind John's little house. They would talk about the state of things in a nostalgic scene of old timers giving advice on the gardening and young people shifting their eyes about alertly under a brow furrowed by constant anger they could not explain. That the anger of the youth had become like an old cavity was more evident in the crisp midmorning Sunlight.

From daily aching of being poor, to the sharp pain when a nerve was struck in realization that there was not much they could do about it, it was their own cross to bear. Though some of the older ones who could see it all in their set faces wished they were able to, no one could feel the pain for them, and removing the root was the only way to make it go away. It was a dull pain they would tend to forget, finding the only way to cure it to be hitting themselves with a rock as the Black Plains Indians who once roamed this land had done. A stark reality was the name of the game. They could accept their pain, learn to live with it and move on. They could continue finding a way to put food into their sore mouths, or they could die in hunger. It was the naked definition of angst.

Before long, work began around the deep end of the pond. The elders helped map out an irrigation system which would easily allow water from the basin to seep down into the lower field and keep it moist. Daily they found that the youth came and worked, as if the digging and sweating somehow dulled their aching pain, as if the dirt under their nails was the only pill for the sickness of an incurable anger.

Now they were doing something. No more standing in line for a reward of cleaning someone's yard or washing some rich man's son's car, only to be screwed out of the agreed pay. Now they were doing something that would produce food for them and their families, and they had seen the fruit already when bringing home a few tomatoes, squash, or cucumbers John had offered from his patch.

Hard work is a cohesive. They began listening to the stories of the elders during breaks. Although no one told them to work, they worked often to the point where John would have to stop them to drink water.

"Here man, take a break, have a smoke or something. Come over here and sit down with us for a bit."

Although he was not their boss, they frequently asked him for guidance and permission.

"Hey, is it okay if I dig this trench around this way? There's a rock down here that I can't get out..."

The last big roundup had netted many of their fathers in this neighborhood of hardy hold outs, and many of them had never known the feeling of earning a man's approval through hard work.

Their gardening area at the back end of a twelve acre lake was behind the houses at the bend in the road, so it had gone unnoticed by the authorities who rarely drove down the road which only led back further into the sparse community and, eventually, to a dead end. Because the majority of refugees had not been allowed to return home, the authorities were having enough of a time keeping up with the sudden rash of violent crime in metropolitan areas.

There were even a few rumors of bands of business owners and workers staging violent stands against the ONE troops in some smaller towns across the state where the authorities had been sent in to seize and shut down establishments that failed to conform to inspection standards. They had been informed by official looking letters that were to cease and desist, but they kept making their BBQ, anyway. Violent crime was exploding everywhere, who would care to look for one little vegetable patch in this rural community? But now the group was growing...

There was an intangible, unforeseen growth developing there. As the water came down periodically, soaking the barren ground, and the Sun continued to rise daily, providing a photo-energy that the plants strove up against gravity to meet at the closest point in the sky possible, the gardeners almost felt the earth spinning. A euphoric ringing blurred their minds while the spinning of their planet moved them at one thousand miles per hour, and the centrifugal force felt as if it would pull them off the ground. They were of the light, of the heavens, but earth bound. The cards were stacked against them, but God was in it.

God was in it, so the plants kept growing. The schools stopped teaching, but the youth kept learning. The people ate well and developed a new sense of self worth. It began showing in small ways. First one would decide to tell his boss to screw off after being treated unfairly, then another would speak out, flapping their wing's like a butterfly to begin the winds of all out revolt.

"I won't work for this, what's the point." Said the disgusted young man as he received a lesser wage than had been negotiated, at the end of a week spent slaving in the oppressive Sun.

"Something is better than nothing." he was told.

This was the negotiation tactic they all began to use, the bosses, being that the workers had no choice. They had them right where they wanted them, they owned every job available. Routinely, hungry workers were told a different wage than they were actually paid, but they were so deep in holes of debt and poverty, that looking for new work, even taking one day off, was impossible. They usually settled for whatever wage they could get.

"You have to work somewhere, don't ya? I'll see you in here at 6 o'clock."

"No you won't, I won't work for this."

Another one went to school after reading a book he had borrowed from one of the older men and asked his teacher if she thought the current situation in class resembled the Gulag of the Bolshevik takeover in Russia.

"Where do you think that came from?" the teacher later asked the school's administrator.

A preacher, who was preaching the standard message of personal pain and happy feelings that only came from a life of sacrifice, was confronted with the ideal of a personal walk with God in front of his congregation after his sermon. Then what really tore it, was when a cop was told he had no right to cut in line by a disenfranchised mother of four in line at a movie theatre. Normally, no one would contest him, but the intense eyes of the others at the marquee told him that he was best served by backing down. The audacity of the woman was so preposterous, she actually made it onto the evening news.

Something was going on, and it wasn't only in John's neighborhood. It seemed to be starting everywhere. Perhaps it was like the flap of the butterfly's wings, moving one molecule here, which altered the course of two others that also influenced the path of four others in their turn, slowly changing the course of events in the air, until it emerged as a great weather system halfway around the world. Perhaps it was just the positive flow of energy being put forth and radiating through space and beyond, changing the minds and hearts of all that it touched. Perhaps it was the work of a higher power. Perhaps God was in it.

Before John had ever left to the beach, local cops began patrolling the neighborhood more slowly, peering into back yards and stopping the people that they saw, asking questions and making blank allegations. They began to feel uneasy about the boys they saw walking the streets who looked down as they passed, but shot peering looks of hate at them from under their brows in the rear view mirrors. They were curious as to where the plastic grocery bags full of vegetables that they observed people carrying down the street were coming from.

In the wake of the devastating storm, the atmosphere was different. Although the weather hadn't affected the central Texas lands, refugees had been diverted there, and police actions had been heightened.

For John, the worst part of it all was that when he returned, he was devastated to find that no one had been able to find his lost dog. They looked for her, they said, but roaming the streets had become but impossible. It seemed as every car that turned down the street was sure to be a ONE vehicle coming to check your compliance. The disaster had given them an excuse to institute an undeclared form of martial law. The streets were not safe, but they swore they had looked for her.

He thought about her every day when he woke up. Joining back into the regular routine, he rose daily to walk back into the garden with the others. Thoughts of what may have become of her consume him as the motions of a gardening hoe yank up the ground beneath him mechanically. Could she have died? Maybe the big dogs in the neighborhood had killed her and she was somewhere rotting in a ditch. Maybe a young child had found her and took her in; sneaking her table scraps amidst her parents telling her that she could not keep her. Maybe the local authorities picked her up and took her to the pound, although no records had been registered there. He had scoured their data base for her. He had talked to every neighbor he could find as he walked around looking for her.

When one of the patrolling officers came around the corner of

John's garden one hot summer day, he stopped dead in his tracks. He was dumbfounded by what looked to him like an army of men with shovels and metal rakes, cultivating land amidst rows of tomatoes and beautiful okra flowers along the rolling terrain. He instinctively rested his hand on his holstered gun at his hip as he surveyed the scene and began walking backwards, as if he had entered the lair of a mother bear protecting her young. He retreated to his car and called for backup.

The sergeant who met John in the front yard was stern.

"What the hell have you got going on here?"

"Just a garden."

"Is this licensed?'

"What do you mean?"

He takes on the form of a Marine Drill Sergeant as he yells into John's nose.

"Are these rations subject to the Freedom From Famine departmental approval, tested and distributed with the proper authorities, is what I mean, boy, and don't play dumb with me."

"We're just growing some food, it's natural."

"This is an unlawful gathering according to the People Against Mob Violence act. We cannot have you gathering in this way."

"We've done nothing wrong."

"Are you arguing with me?" The cop's shoulder inched back, as if about to raise his baton in a striking manor.

John remained calm, not flinching a bit. He knew that raising his hand to cover his head in anticipation of the blow could be labeled as a threat and would mean a sure beating, but that he probably would not strike without cause in front of all these people.

"*I'm* not *going* to destroy this garden. *You* are. You have 24 hours to make sure this is gone."

He turned and left. As he walked away, he heard a word from under the breath of the wiry young Jarred.

Jarrod had never known his father. When he was 12, his mother's boyfriend had him hold the baggies of white powder rocks he was selling on a street corner in the 5th ward of Houston. At 14, he was caught breaking into a house with some older, mislead boys, and placed into juvenile detention center. Meant to be a slap on the wrist, he was supposed to leave after six weeks. All he needed was for his mother to come sign him out. He had sat and waited for her for four long years. While his mother found ways to feed her drug addiction by manipulating people around her, his childhood had passed him by in padded rooms, institutionalized.

At the age of 18, the state could no longer keep him in juvenile detention, as he was not a legally a youth anymore. Confused and possessing the social development of a 14 year old boy, they put him out on the street. He had come to John one day in total despair. While living with some people across the pond, he had been learning how to load clips and speak like a true stereo type of a southern racist redneck. He came from the back one day while they were working, asking if there was any work to be done. When John noticed the fresh tattoo on the boy's wrist, he began asking some questions of his own. The prison style tattoo was that of an Arian circle.

"Where are you staying?" asked John.

"Across the pond. I get to sleep on the couch, unless someone comes over, then they let me sleep out behind the barn," he said in a rich, low voice. He looked to the ground by John's feet as he spoke.

"So, they're pretty nice to you?"

"Yeah, but I don't like the way they talk to me."

"What do you mean?"

"Well, when I said something they didn't like, Bud just punched me right in the face, out of nowhere. Then he did it again the other day. I don't know, I guess that's what I get for being stupid, for saying something stupid."

"What did you say?"

"I don't know, something stupid. I don't remember. Something about black people, one's that I liked. They don't like black people very much. They get mad if I don't call them 'niggers,' but I got some black friends back in Juvi and..."

It was obvious to John that the tall boy had nowhere to go, that these people were taking complete advantage of the thin, brown haired juvenile.

"Please don't ask me this," John pleaded to the voice he knew he must obey. It was too late, he was already being asked.

'This is the last thing I need, some stupid kid who doesn't know his way around anything,' he thought.

It was too late. God's insistent voice had laid it on him.

After a few minutes of hoping his mind would change, John asked the boy if he needed a place to stay. He was met with a reaction so enthusiastic, it was evident the kid really needed it. Over the next few days, they worked together on making the spare room his own. Cleaning the carpet, hanging up pictures, and painting the walls, transformed the room as it transformed the boy's spirits. As they worked together, Jarrod's story began to unfold. John began to appreciate just how easy he had it growing up as he learned more about young man's upbringing.

Although John never had much in comparison with those around him, he always knew one thing: his parents loved him. His mother had always shown him the love that told him that he was important. She had always taken the time and patience to answer all of his naive questions, to help him understand and to gently coax him away from trouble and danger wherever she could. She did her best in guiding him in a direction of love, of kindness. His father had done nothing but build him up, telling him constantly that he would be great, that the only person who could ever have any chance of defeating him was he himself. All the little proverbs he instilled in him:

"Never speak without thinking first."

"You only get one chance at a first impression."

"It's the holes we shoot in our feet that keep us from walking on water."

Jarred had gotten none of that. He knew only the law of watching out for number one, no one else was going to do it for him. Honesty was an ideal superseded by the necessity to eat and survive, in his world. Telling what was expected to be heard had become his second nature. Stealing was wrong, but it didn't matter in his world of survival. Trust was a weakness, mercy a mistake. His life's story summed up in one sentence on John's consciousness as he told himself:

"Your ideals are a luxury of your privilege."

He would teach the boy some honor, he was determined. In hard lessons, he taught him these ideals one by one. The privilege backing them was only contained in John's mercy towards the boy. When he caught him stealing from the jar of change on his desk, he decided not to kick him out. Instead, he spent the next few days reminding the boy of what it meant, how he had helped him, and how stealing from him had hurt his trust. His goal was to break down his walls of indifference, to make him care.

Once Shannon had gone, Jarrod returned, and they never mentioned it again. He struggled with the boy to make him want to work, even after their fight. The boy agreed to every task, but then performed the chores dismally, showing his lack of truly wanting to do anything. John would break him down like Socrates and then lead him to the spot of the poorly done chore.

"Don't tell me you can't do better than this."

The battles raged on as a work ethic was slowly installed in the boy, until he learned to have pride in the things he had done from the contrast of the shame he began to feel for doing them poorly. He hated John, he wanted to kill him. But in John's patience with the boy with everything from his ruined clothes from the boy jumping into muddy creeks after snakes, to losing his fishing tackle box, to nearly killing him when they finally came to blows, he became the closest thing to a father the boy had ever known. Now that Shannon had left, he was back and looked at the whole thing as a lesson. Jarrod had learned many lessons while living with John, now he was going to learn one about keeping his mouth shut.

The cop stopped in his tracks. He knew exactly where the word had come from when he heard it.

"Pig" had been muttered under the boy's breath, in protesting defense of his friend.

The cop's eyes turned on him in intense rage of wide open insanity, his brushy eyebrows set high over his maniacal snarl. His face took the focus away from his hands as he drove the end of his Billy Club into Jarrod's stomach, sending air forced from his lungs out in a gasp as he then dropped his club across the side of the boy's face. It landed just between his jaw bone hinging his wide open mouth and his skull, dislocating his bones and cracking them expertly with a blow the man had executed many times before.

Within half a second, the beating was over and the boy lay quivering on the grassy ground. Blood spotted the blades of grass and trodden dirt beneath him as he wrenched in pain, holding his stomach. He bled from his mouth, nose, and from the hole in his ear; a clear sign of brain trauma. John stood in a rigid silence, holding his hands as steady as possible through their quivering rage as he said a silent prayer for the boy, watching the cop walk away. The others did the same.

The Sun was beginning to set. It made an array of colors as it shone its final light through the clouds over the lake. In Oranges and Reds, it sent its final beams down on them. The clouds rolled out over the sky, twisting outwardly in a pattern that seemed to encompass the crowd of people in the yard. As John looked up at the sky, he was reminded of God's mercy and grace, of the words of his father telling him that he could never be defeated, that 'in all things, we were more than conquerors through him.'

His resolve was set, the time was coming, it had come. There was no reversing the chain of events now set into place. Seeing them vividly, he set his face in stone, in silence. The sky turned purple, brilliant, ominous and foreboding in the final lights of the Sun. The men looked at each other standing in that field and nothing was said as two of them raised Jarrod onto their shoulders and brought him into the house, laying him on the couch.

"I'll be okay, I'm fine. What is that bright light? Aw man, it's hurting my eyes. I hear this 'wha-jamp wha-jamp wha-jamp' sound all around me."

John turned the overhead light off as he began wiping some of the blood from Jarrod's face with a cool, damp washcloth.

"You'll be alright, just get some rest."

This was no time for lectures about 'keeping your damned mouth shut,' but that would come later. For right now, he had words burning the tip of his tongue and he quietly walked out the front door.

John walked out to the patrol car still parked at the end of the patchy caliche driveway on the street. He walked straight to where the trooper sat within. He approached the window, where he saw the Sergeant looking down at a clip board smugly, and rapped on the window. As the window came down smoothly at the command of the electric motor, he felt the gust of cold air escaping from the air-conditioned cab and saw the sociopathic cop looking up at him, unconcerned.

"This garden is going nowhere. You can go get whatever order from whatever judge you like, but this garden will not be going anywhere. Mark my words. I'll be here when you get back. Take your time, take all the time you need."

With that he turned his back on the dangerous criminal in the dark blue uniform and walked back to his house. He felt the man thinking of shooting him from behind, but had no fear.

'Though a thousand arrows fall to the left of me, and a thousand to the right, not one shall pierce me,' he heard in his head. His mind was sound, his heart was calm, he knew that God was in it.

11. TOO FAR

Motionless in darkened woodlands

(Deep within, the raging war)

Ghostly faces in deepened shadows

For he's gone one step too far

Is this just?

Cloaked in twilight, he keeps seeking

Just one sign he seeks to see

To the death in silence struggled

He regrets it has to be

It's just another step

The ball point is worn so slightly, ever so subtly. The smoothed indentions are small and barley noticeable, but upon inspection, it is evident that the hammer is worn well, that it took years of striking very hard objects to produce the tiny, almost indistinguishable indentions in its head.

The tiny holes drilled into John's teeth have grown cavernous. The small lumps in his head, the indelible scars about his cranium, are hidden by his growing hair. As he intimately strokes his face with the sharp claw side of the hammer's head, he remembers where he got each of the battle scars. He hooks the hammer behind his neck, catching the skin around his bones with the curved metal hooks made for removing nails from wood and tugs, ever so slightly, feeling how simply the bones could be removed from their delicate placement within his body as the jagged edge pulls at his skin.

He practices the stroke a few times in the air, focusing on the subtle twist of the wrist it would require, the fulcrum point and balance needed to keep the device in his hand in the instance of removing one's head. 'If one swipe doesn't do it, one more at this angle to drive it through the skull will work,' he thinks. He looks at the hammer and knows it will never come down on him. His place is to deliver, not to receive.

A glazed look comes over his eyes as he gently taps the flat side of the hammer's head against his temple. He remembers his hazing, the attempts to rectify him. The bullies who chastised him were the authority figures of his youth. He remembers the time they pulled him aside to question him about a rumor of a fight off of the grounds. The two has-been football coaches locked themselves in a small room with him and began their interrogation. They stood over him as he sat in the chair at the conference table, their veins bulged from their fat faces as their skin burned red in mimicking rage. They just needed him to react once; just one excuse would be all they needed to bounce him from normal society and into a maze of institutions and prescription drugs.

Although he would not give them a reason, the two principals would pound him with insults and accusations until the boy's tendons tightened within his skin in an effort to hold back his

204

own hands, until his facial muscles quivered, until he felt the hot, salty tears running down his face as he cried like the child he still was. Even in his foolish youth, he knew he must not react. He knew what they wanted and he refused to give it to them.

The jagged feel of the hammer's claw against his skin riles distant memories as it scrapes across his cheek. Memories reveal themselves in quiet references of feel and smell, not so much based on tangible events. That feeling of the long lost lover, finding her finally happy, the smell of her which remains the same, the emotions that ran so strong, it all comes back. The people and places are gone, but the memory remains in a nostalgia left behind by her passing aroma. Remembering all, he scratches the hook of the hammer across his back over his shoulder.

The police that entered his mother's home at the age of 12 walked straight into the downstairs living room where he stood in front of the sofa. With one shove, they sent him toppling over the back of the couch, flipping him over the furniture to a square landing on his head.

"You are worthless!" they told him.

The rest became a blur as he went into a secret, inward place. The hammer swung, the dents began to show on its steel head as he remembered the day for the first time in many years.

He stares blankly into the darkness from his window. He knows they will be coming. He examines the hammer. It is hard, it is integral. It will serve him well. The head of the hammer banged seemingly unbreakable rocks, it held its form.

The hammer was a perfect symbol of his own life, he thought, of his own character shaped through banging and striking, molded and dented but still unbroken after all these years. 'The grown men,' he thought, 'the child I was. I would like to meet them now.'

He had seen blind rage turn to fear; he knew that it was not a human that he had confronted all those years, but a spirit. It was a spirit of fear. Years of decisions based on that fear formed layers of easy patterns, accumulating like silt on a river bed until they became as tangible as stones, fossilized in the thought patterns of those he battled.

As he watched electric flashes strobe in the not so distant sky out of the window in the dark room and the thunder rolled in sequence not so far behind it, he knew he would soon get his chance. Those coming for him were the same manifestations of the same spirit working within those men, and he decided at that moment that he would have no mercy on them for their foolish lack of judgment.

He knew his story may never be told, that he may not even crack the invisible mold or break the machine's steadfast hold on any of them. He knew his actions would never be able to inspire dissent amongst the population, for it would be buried in stories of Christmas shopping and dog walking. It did not matter; he had to make a stand. They had gone too far.

Crawling through his hidden tunnel

(Deep within, he feels the blame)

Fortifies his weakened fortress

(Fueled with fire, his heart aflame)

He watches the caravan of headlights coming down the long road to his house as he laces tight his thick soled boots.

"What shall I do?" He stops to ponder

"What can I say to save the day?

Give me courage not to waiver

Teach me wisdom, words to say'

'Blaze me a trail, a path untrodden

Open eyes to your one hint

Give me strength to fight unstumbling

And set my face like flint"

(Some would run

Some would pray

Some would pray for strength to stay)

Peoples had taken Jarrod with him across the road to Mary's to eat some of her famous tacos and they would probably not walk back until the pouring rain of the storm subsided. He was alone in his house as he turned off all the lights and crept out the back door, across the yard and garden and into the woods. Memories of childhood bouts ring through him as he locks Buster onto a chain in the pounding and blinding rain. He wanders what came of Fiona and for the first time is happy that someone may have abducted her.

'If they shoot my dog now that he's chained up, they're just evil bastards,' he thinks to himself walking out the gate. The solitude of the rainy night brings him back into a vortex of memories as the crashing water from the sky blanks out the black night. He hears car doors slamming in the front yard.

Gangster as a white boy could be, Michael Carmichael was equipped to play basketball with M. J. himself in his matching blue sweatbands on each arm and leg. A magical sheen bounced off of the polyester shorts and matching light blue jersey as he came into the outside daylight's splendor from the front door of his mother's house. Michael had been raised by one too many rap videos and ghetto gangster movies, and although he was not very large in stature, he fancied himself a menacing figure. To make extra money, he would stop young boys riding bikes or walking home from school and take it from them. One of the boy's had been John's little brother. Michael had stopped him and he and his friend held him there by holding onto his handlebars and demanded money.

"Yeah, right," said Crockett, "I'm not giving you shit!"

He said that, and then the bully started shaking his handle bars and spat on him.

"My big brother will whip your ass,"

"Who's your big brother?"

"John Flint."

"I never heard of him, he's probably a wimp."

That was how the story was relayed to him.

After asking around, it turned out that a lot of people did know Michael. A lot of people, it turned out, didn't like him. One guy said he had caught him breaking into his house, another said he had bullied his kid brother, too.

"That guy really thinks he's tough. Yeah, I know him. He's always got that dew rag on his head and he walks around the neighborhood, strutting like a chicken with that friend of his. Yeah, Michael… he lives right across from Chunks."

Chunks was the neighborhood pot dealer. He sold skinny Swisher Sweets for five dollars and John knew him well, so he decided to go see him. His house had a basketball goal in the driveway where people frequently converged for games of Horse or Two on Two between smoking weed in the garage.

"Yeah, Michael, he always wants to play basketball wit us, but we never let him, Flint. Why, are you looking for him? Oh… He lives right there, across the street." Chunks told him after he had heard the whole story.

"That's perfect. Go tell him you guys need an extra man for a game."

He had taken his time getting ready and was fully geared up when he emerged from his mother's front door. As he finished crossing the suburban street and entered the driveway, John approached him and extended his hand.

"What's up, I'm Michael," he said as he grabbed his hand. John gripped him firmly and yanked him towards himself.

"I'm John Flint!" he yelled, as he swung his other arm out and smashed his fist into the side of his face.

The cocky youngster reeled back and threw up his hands in defense as John began circling him with his clenched fists down by his waist.

"You're the one who stopped my little brother on his bike and Spit on him, aren't you?"

"No! NO! It wasn't me; I don't know anything about it!" Michael pointed at his friend who was just coasting up from down the street on his bike and said, "Ask him!"

Michael continued edging backwards as he tried to talk his way out of it.

"I don't know anything about it," his friend said.

"Oh, no, I heard about you. You're the fat one, you were in on it, too. Don't think you're getting off scott-free," John told him.

As he continued circling his prey, he watched the outside step of his retreat through the corner of his eye. Each time Michael would step back in one direction, John would open his gate to make sure his outside foot was outside of his opponent's, thus keeping him within his circle, like a bunny in the glare of a stalking cougar. The two argued amongst themselves over who did or said what as Michael unwittingly backed himself up into a corner between two houses where a tall wooden fence met a brick wall.

"I'm not the one who spit on him," he said frantically shaking his head.

"I thought you said you didn't know anything about it!"

With no further warning, John bashes him in the face with his fist, crushing it down into his palate as another blow came instantly up to sink into the boy's stomach, doubling him over and forcing a spurt of blood to spew from his mouth as he went down. As he crumpled, John kicked him squarely once in the face. Within two seconds, the boy was utterly wrecked. Standing over the sobbing boy he glared down and said,

"Don't ever mess with my family again."

Those robotic motions of slinging fists with hooked arms had been practiced so many times since then. Microcosmically legendary feats had been recreated a thousand times over for the hundreds of battles he had waged. It was a game he felt confident in; although his talent had no use in the post modern world he had grown up in. Mechanical were the motions of attack from his spring loaded arms, automatic were his circling movements as he side stepped confrontations to gain advantageous positioning. He remembered the day he took it too far.

Drifting through memories of hundreds of bouts in his mind, he begins to feel the tense feeling of his shoulder bringing his knuckles through their target, recreated in muscle memory as he methodically swings his hands at air in the night. He remembers the day he vowed never to fight again, when he swore he would never hurt another person.

Waves of guilt rush over him thinking about his foolish actions of the past. His thoughts ride him while slapping him like a monkey clamped on his back. He begs for release from the weight of his guilt as he recreates the situations over and over, examining every angle, wondering how the people must have felt to be punched, to be embarrassed and demoralized.

Oh sapience.

I wish I was sapient enough for you.

But time has proven me otherwise. I have seen the error in my ways, told to me before my days of reckoning and understanding. Yes! The two go one in one. Their words now like fleas jumping at my feet, just trying to get past my low spun socks. If I had their wisdom now, if I now had the chance to understand their elder knowledge before this impending doom came to pass; before it comes down on me.

If I knew their words,

"You better do this," or, "you better do that."

'If only Ol' Man John were here now to give me his wise words. He would know what to do now. My dad would know what to do. So many around me falling to frail frustration, so many sinking into depression's abyss,' he thinks.

As he enters the woods and the strobe lights come to rest in front of his house behind him, he lets out a howling yell. The growl becomes a roar as he clinches his fists and squeezes his arms tight. Indistinguishable words are uttered forth as he bears his teeth.

"Walacino bagin daagan fruuden! Rhahyokiean fuder slabgden!"

As his defiant battle cry rages out, he feels invincible. The cold rain seems to steam off his burning skin; he feels as safe as a fish in water and melts into the rainy night.

John's clothes are porcelain now; the mud has caked up and stands as a shield to some tiny force, something that could not hurt him anyway, like the pelting rain. The mud is in his socks, his shoes, his hair, and his teeth. He's been running through these woods for quite some time, breathing through gritted teeth as he slides into another muddy pit to hide beneath the running water and standing mud. They make one more pass for him, then one more, then one more. Each time the gang of troops passes sufficiently, he edges up behind them a little more, picking another hiding spot for them to easily miss on their way back, as they hardly search the ground where they've already searched before. They end up back at the edge of the lake where they started. Some want to call off the search, but the captain does not want him to get away. He is right there beneath them and could reach up and pull one down each time they pass. His black knife would gut them without a sound to breach the tumbling rain.

"Now it rains." He thinks.

"He may have never come this way," one hopeful, wet tutor yells through the rain, piecing together the map of the black terrain they seem to be circling in his adrenaline doped mind. The rain bounces off of his raincoat like bee bees on a battleship, but he still feels miserable as the water pounds at his face and fills his heavy boots. Holding his hand up to shield his eyes from the water, he thinks he sees a flash of movement behind the others. Shining his flashlight in the direction, he sees nothing but black shadows beneath the thick foliage. The sound of water rushing over the natural damn of the nearby lake washes out his voice as he yells,

"It's nothing."

He realizes that none of his partners can hear him as he speaks. An irrational blanket of fear envelops him and he feels his skin become instantly hot and the hair stands up on his arms in goose bumps at the thought of being watched. Deciding he wants to go, he shouts up to his comrades over the rain,

"He must not be back here."

"He's gone", says another, not wanting to say that he's just ready to go home.

His wife is there, probably watching TV with the kids. They all wish they could go home. Some directive had placed this search as top priority and unable to be postponed due to weather.

They had been told to expect resistance, and had assembled a well armed squad. To their General, it was as if a personal motive was involved in the capture of this particular subject, and they all knew the search would not be called off any time soon.

The Head Captain of this search is a proud man. He's been here, seen that. Although the times now facing him seem strange, he obeys his orders with a hefty zeal usually reserved for those taking in on the bounty of the kill. It's his chance to tell himself that he is one of the elite, the privileged, the untouchables. As a child, he used to wonder what it was like to be one of them. The young boys with outstanding confidence would run around the playground kicking at the ball and laughing light heartedly. They could juggle it on their legs, kick it in the air, and bounce it off of their heads as effortlessly as trained seals. Life was but a toy to them. As he hunted down these infidels, the criminals, he fancied himself as one of them: the royal lot, casting down the undesirables, putting them in their place, in a rotting jail.

"There's your place, you inferiors!"

His demeaning never makes him the man they were, their royal prestige emanating from them as their confidence shown cool to all, to the teachers, to the girls, the ones he liked; everyone saw their greatness! How would he ever be on the other side, the loser's side, after being a witness to all this spectacle?

This captain's father was one. Cast off to the side, he was. While the others played their football and drank together on weekends, while they bullied each other in a show of invincible toughness, his father had shunned away. They rode together on busses and did their conquering at opponent's fields clad in plastic armor and matching uniforms. His father never saw how a man could be so emblazoned as to go to another's school and fight for victory on their own foiled turf. He could never. He grew a hatred of those with the fortitude to do so. He later saw them going abroad to fight an enemy on foreign soil, to "fight the battle on their turf", to "take it to the enemy."

He never had that boldness, so he found ways to fight them. A passive resistance, an inward glare, and a forward stare would get him over.

'What, you think I'm not a man?' he thought.

He would find bumper stickers to put on his gold Toyota minivan to mutely state his point. He would support the enemy by demonizing his compatriots:

"Liberation? Occupation!" read the bold red letters on his back bumper, referring to the unpopular foreign war his fellow countrymen were fighting at the time.

The war was draining the economy, making the five dollar cups of coffee fewer and further in-between, so he felt safe knowing he was not the only person jeering them. They were those same souls who had made him feel so bad with their boastful arrogance, flaunting their irrational bravery back in the school yard.

He had another sticker with the initials of his country's leader simply crossed out, displaying shame in his unruly, pompous government. He would get them somehow; fight his battle in his own way, on his own turf. As obvious war veterans drove past him on the highway, he would see their stickers proclaiming their pride loudly and quietly sink behind his steering wheel, without the guts to even look at them or expound his radical "beliefs." He was afraid that his cowardly eyes would betray him if he looked them in the face. As they drove by him without an apparent thought or even sometimes with a bewildered, sympathetic look, his father would sneer privately in his own little revenge and revel in his own moral superiority.

'Some courage, the old man had real grit,' thought the captain sarcastically to himself in the rain.

Not this captain. He had chosen his side, he was one of them: a winner. But he was wiser than that. The years of booking riff raffs for fighting and hard working builders on the way home from construction sites for unpaid fines had taught him something: These people didn't care about any of that.

The western front had gone a lot smoother. After the massive round of tidal waves washed as far ashore as North Hollywood, a police state was the natural progression on the coast and it worked inland. Unprepared for the disruptions to the disposable goods pipeline, the people asked for it, almost. You couldn't really say anyone was fighting it, at least. As broadcasts continued of looters and protesters burning cars and being raked down by machine gun fire from armor masked infantrymen, general consensus prevailed that Marshall Law was the only way.

Very few stories leaked from the distant coast about the small resistance which seemed to be in small, private outbursts of expressions of frustration: A man had been burned alive, a law abiding citizen in a suburban house who refused to turn over his collection of hand guns and rifles to the local authority. He was a solid figure in his community, even active in local government, but he was burned alive in his home like a witch on a steak just the same. The story was quickly blotched out by the bombing of a sky scraper in the North East and it was even impossible to find any mention of it on the state censored internet. The only thing being talked about was the dirty bomb that had unleashed some illness in New York, and what symptoms to look for. It was different there: although official control of information had not been publicly declared, it had been seized.

The public forums had been regulated out of existence. Syndicated talk shows, featuring "citizens" calling in to discuss social and political statements were still around, only now all the callers were actors. The hosts pretended to be people's advocates, bold and defiant, while skirting the issues they knew they were not allowed to touch.

The art stream in the media had been utterly blocked. Every movie, book, or song produced would bear their stamp, in the form of a UPC code verifying license of distribution. Possession of non licensed media was highly illegal, as it was regulated by the central government for means of protecting national security from the harms of subversive enemy propaganda.

Artists painted their protests in radiant outbursts of random symbolism in their abject view of the world around them, but it was almost guaranteed no one would ever see these. Anyone who had enough money or resources to get an independent message out had been assimilated by that point in time. For those seeking something more refined, deeper, in their entertainment wishes, they could enjoy licensed movies with a maze of elaborate plot twists and deep sub plots ending in a way that left them thinking, wondering what happened while leaving no semblance of a point or moral.

There on the southwestern coast, they were plain stoned, dumbfounded, walking around without a cohesive sense of what to think, who to trust, or which opinion was a good one to have. The ONE squadrons walked through the streets relatively unchallenged. Their weapons casually hanging from a strap on their shoulder, smiling with a poor child playing in a fire hydrant or offering them cookies in front of the TV cameras, they were accepted as the authorities.

Any one not driving a car was considered non threatening; and in reality, any one driving a car had to be a thief to obtain any gasoline, anyway. All of it had been deemed public property to be used only for the good of the society. Like owning a gun, driving was a privilege reserved exclusively for the police and the ONE troops and government officials. There was really very little for normal occurrences, and obtaining gas vouchers was something common men simply did not do. The electric cars had also been deemed illegal in most counties after being listed as a cause of the rolling black-outs effecting cities across the sea board.

The captain's limited understanding now seemed to be heightened by the cold water running down his face. He stopped moving and felt the numbness begin to tingle in the back of his head. In the roar of the water banging onto him, he thought he heard a wet 'crunch.' The pounding rain felt like tiny explosions on the citadel of his thick blue jacket. He stared blankly into the darkness before him as he lowered his flashlight to his side. In the darkness he recounted the years past, the people he had caught, beaten, and fought. The women he had raped on the back of his cruiser on the side of dark highways, the fathers he had drug away from crying children, and the boy he had beaten to within an inch of his life with his baton just a day before, were all there with him. He felt differently about all of them now that he began to realize that he was becoming the hunted one. His partners who followed him into the woods were all lost, it seemed, and he felt alone as only static answered his beckons on the walkie-talkie.

"Seems like Bill went off the other way while the rest of us walked along that ravine," he yelled into the walkie-talkie.

Bill had been in back. Hanging onto the roots that were exposed with his body pressed against the side of the deep enclave, John had hooked Bill's ankle with the claw of his hammer as he walked by above. In the pouring rain, no one heard him fall backwards into the rushing water below, landing awkwardly on his head. As he fell upside down through the air, John had jumped from his hanging perch and landed on him at nearly the same instant that his head smashed into the basketball sized rocks at the bottom. His neck was broken by the fall, and all he saw was the faint silhouette of a dark figure landing on his chest as the hammer's claw ripped through his skull.

He did not even have time to scream. The others had only walked ten yards before they realized he was no longer behind them, but they did not know where he had gone. They shone their lights down the gully briefly, seeing nothing below the rushing, muddy water, and continued on.

When they reached the tall weeds that made up the overflow basin, they saw two distinct trails cutting through the dense mass of reeds and bushes. Two of the searchers went one way, two went the other. As the captain followed the trail, he held his pistol up by his flash light and followed the illuminated path with its aim. In every shadow he thought he saw something. He even fired a few shots into a shadowy canopy of weeds, only to find that his heart's pumping for the kill was spurned by nothing more than a hollowed out stump in the darkness resembling a squatting figure.

He continued to follow the trail cautiously, suspicious of every swaying branch in the rainy night. As he emerged into an opening in the foliage, he began to feel as if he had been there before. Then it came to him: he was in the same spot where he and his partner had split off from the others. The trail was nothing more than a circle. Where were the other two? As he turned to query his companion, he found him to be missing, as well. Now he thought back to the calls for helicopter assistance.

"No way we can fly in this mess," they had told him.

His two partners who had been sent their own way were not responding to their radios. Maybe they had caught up with Bill someplace and decided to wait back near the edge of the pond, he thought. There was no way to see through the sheets of rain and he began to feel he had lost his sense of direction. There were no stars to guide him, no people beside him.

When the two who came the other way passed by John's entrenchment in the reeds, he waited calmly. He saw the chain of events unfold before him as if he was a third party, an invisible bystander.

The path was narrower than they knew, as under the matted grass lay a trap: the trench dug there was laced with sharpened bamboo shoots, nine feet deep and covered by a bridge of matted foliage. It was the first one in the pair who found it, his ankle twisting inward as he lost his balance and slid down the slippery clay side of the muddy hole.

He hollered and squealed like an ensnared pig as he went into the deep pit and was hung up on the sharpened barbs. One spike slid smoothly through his lungs from just under his armpit from behind, hanging him there like a soppy rag doll. His eyes glazed over as he gagged and gargled on his own blood coming up through his throat into his mouth, then flowed back down into his wind pipe, suffocating him.

His partner had heard his final scream through the hissing, growling rain, and turned his light into the seemingly natural hole. By the time he saw his partner gagging on his last breaths and realized the immediate danger of the situation, it was far too late. John was behind him, poised with the sharpened bolt of his knife at the side of his neck. As it thrust through his wind pipe and the blood shot out through the dark air, the wind of his scream was let out the new hole in his neck and never made it to his voice box. The second stroke plunged the blade deep into his temple and he fell in place, gently rolling into the hole. He tumbled down into the darkness amidst the protruding bamboo spikes. John stood over the hole, looking down. Water was rushing over the edge from the rain, nothing seemed to be moving inside the pit.

He cut through the winding trail made invisible by its zigzag path towards the other side of the circle, where the other two troopers were unknowingly moving towards their partners. He crawled on his belly, inch by inch, as they came towards him. He stood up behind them as they passed, now confident that nothing could destroy him.

And so what if they did? To live as a hunted man, not free to live his life his way, was not a life for him. Death would be a fine substitute for the life they had been trying to force him into. It would be a suitable substitute for the jail he would sit it, a grand release from the chains of a prisoner's life.

As his thoughts became louder, his fury grew hotter. It seemed as though the drenching rain was rising back off his soaked shirt in the form of steam. The last guard turned around and saw him in the dark. He raised his gun from ten feet away towards the dark figure. The guard had him dead to rights, he paused in pulling the trigger to relish the moment.

John looked like a demon to him as he pounced like a Black

Cat, covering the short span in one leap and plunging the black blade directly into his eye. He was conscious, crossing one eye to see the shaft in his face, just before the hammer crushed through the side of his skull. His mouth was left agape as he hung by the hinge of the hammer nestled into its new home amidst his spongy brain, his finger still poised over the trigger of his pistol.

No sound was emitted, no breath was breathed. His wide, open eye seemed to see everything as his body, unable to respond to any of the commands of his still functioning brain, began to slowly fall sideways in the exact position he had died in. His muscles held his now useless frame perfectly in place in an instant state of rigormortis. His partner, having just fired on the hollowed out log and feeling embarrassed, had already moved on beyond the turn of the path and was moving quickly towards what he was sure was the path of his prey.

'Drop this body here, no time to hide it; I've got to move on,' John thought to himself.

Now looking blankly into the darkness before him and calling helplessly into his radio, the captain knew chillingly that he was prey, and he had not the slightest idea what to do, besides to repent.

It's like the times when there is nothing to do but to pray, and non religious people begin to ask god for concession and mercy in hospital rooms or natural disasters promising impending doom. It's in these times we turn to God. It's not as if the eternal spirit was not there in all the other times, the good times; it's not that he found us now because we are alone in the dark. He was always there, but in these times we look for him and become surprised when we find him. The wisdom was there all along, the clear voice of understanding had been calling to him his entire life, he just never heard it. Now, sure he will die alone, miserable and wet in these woods, a voice is telling him what to do in the form of an "I told you so." He hears the small voice and finally asks for its forgiveness.

He thought then to the countless girls he had consensually raped on the side of dark highways and the soft feeling of crushed cartilage at the tip of his boot as he drove it into people's ribs. As he conjured the memories, the pain became his. The captain stares deeply into the dark, in a trance, feeling the tingle of awareness climb up the back of his neck like a hot wind from a furnace. His eyes are open, but he is not seeing anything, until the whites of two eyes appear directly before him. He is unable to move as he feels a sharpened rock crash into the side of his head. The lights go out.

Morning light on misty woodlands

Needed rest he tries to claim

Yet tomorrow brings a battle

One more raid from guilt and shame

A fist and a battle scar!

It's just another step

Another step

Too far.

The Captain awakes to the roar of a huge fire, the heat tightening the skin on his face, and he imagines for a moment that he is being cooked like a chicken on a spit over the flame. He feels the cool dampness on his legs as he begins to come to, and realizes that he is sitting about ten feet away from a burning mass. Horrified at the sight of what looks like blue uniforms in the blaze, he finds himself sitting in wet grass, his hands bound behind him as he cooks slowly. Contrasting the dew wetting his clothes on the ground where he sits and the dampness of the morning air, he can feel the heat of licking flames and smell hair and flesh burning within them. The smell of burning hair and bones is undeniably carnal, heightened by the sounds of liquids boiling out of unnatural holes in charred carcasses. Popping bubbles indicate the boiling innards within the hardened, crispy exteriors of the bodies burning on the embers. The contorted bodies were frozen in charcoal.

'A fitting burial for a warrior,' thinks the captain.

It may be the only glory their bodies have ever known as they are abruptly separated from their earthly form at the molecular level and join the atmosphere around them.

The morning dawn is purple; the chill of the air brings him around in welcomed gusts of coolness caressing his matted face and hair. The blood dried on his face is cracking and pulling his skin tight, like long worn Halloween face paint. He feels the tightness in his mustache from the caked up blood holding the hairs matted together, pulled from the contractions as he grimaces at the horrid sight and smell of what is around him. He knows it is not a dream, as surreal as it seems.

John rounds the burning heap with a long poking stick and sees the captain has come around. He walks slowly and deliberately towards him. A cracked layer of dried up mud still hangs on John's skin as he bends over and looks the captain square in the face, staring into his brain, forcing him to return the stare.

As John makes another round around the fire, prodding and turning the burning mass with his stick, the captain strains his neck to look around himself over his shoulder. There are trails of smoke everywhere. The great rain has made the perfect opportunity, and the people of the region are finally allowed to burn their waste. That must be it, he thinks to himself. Next to him, not more than three feet away, are a pile of guns, belt buckles, badges, and other metallic objects. He wanders if his captive would be so emblazoned as to leave the guns loaded. He dares not move for them, to push his extended mercy any further. He knows he has been left to live for a reason. He looks up to see John looking at him, leaning on his stick.

"I've got a nifty hole for all of those", he says, "no one will ever find them."

He leaves and returns with a bucket of water. He lifts it up before the captain's thirsty, gritty mouth, letting him take one sip, then turning its contents over on his head.

"You awake?"

He leans down in the captain's face with his head cocked to the side.

"Good." he says.

Then he punches him in the face. The hooked arm comes from the side, crunching the boney knuckles through his teeth.

The captive feels the loose, broken teeth's jagged edges cutting into the soft flesh within his mouth like broken glass. The blood trickles out over his lips as his jaw hangs loosely. He tries to grip consciousness amid the flash of blank white and black as his eyelids flutter. As he regains consciousness, he sees John has sat down before him. His arms look heavy and his face is tired as he leans over his crossed legs, pondering a twig in his fingertips.

"I was a good natured kid," he begins.

Then, in a long monologue, John begins to tell him the story of his life. As the captain watches with a dumbfounded look, he chronicles the first day of school; the constant moves from city to city, the struggle to make ends meet, to pay the fines, the pain of eating with broken teeth. He even tells him about the cops in his living room and not remembering what happened after he blacked out from rage when he was 12 years old. John's scene of the cops in his living room sparks a distant memory in the trooper's mind. His aching mind is tingling, he fails to suppress the thought that he may know the boy.

John seems to slip into a dream as he talks, feeling a surreal gratitude in his captive audience's attentiveness. He speaks, eating up minutes that become an hour, then continues for another hour as the captain listens.

Something touches the officer, be it in the despair of a certain impending death, or his realization that he may have had a role in its orchestration, and he begins to silently cry. He can remember the confusion in the innocent face of the child looking up at him as he shoved him around and belittled him. The gruff face of the man becomes sincere as the tears roll down and he begins to audibly sob. He closes his eyes and feels John's hand on his shoulder.

He looks up to see a new look. The crazed eyes of the killer have become understanding. In helplessness, in realization that his options are few and his last card has been played, in the realization that he is at the mercy of another and that the only one who can help him is an unseen force somewhere in the sky, he has become a sympathizer of the enemy who would take his life. He feels the tense muscles in his abdomen pulling at his guts, his stomach aching from the angst of knowing he is very near his rope's end with almost nothing he can do to affect his outcome. He now knows the despair the boy has felt nearly every day of his troubled existence, for he is feeling it now.

Hours later, the fire is dying into red embers among white ashes. There remains the skeletons of the bodies in the hot ashes. They seem like hard bones, unburned by the flames, until John reaches down to touch the skull of one with his finger and watches it dissipate into dust. Just then, as if on cue, a strong wind blows the skeletons outlined in ash around, and they are gone. There are no remains of their bodies. Their worldly vessels have been strewn to the wind in particles as fine as wind itself. John Flint looks in the direction of the wind, holding his jaw square and gazes far off as if saying a silent prayer.

He then walks to the captain, picks him up by his tied hands and leads him through the field towards the house, expecting to make his last stand with his hostage in tow as he emerges from the patch of wilderness. He contemplates his fate and how he wants it to end, but decides now that the matter is out of his hands. He says one last prayer to his merciful God as he emerges from the woods into the vegetable gardens behind his house. There he sees not a force of police, but an little army made up of his fellow garden workers, neighbors, and friends yielding shovels and rifles, circling each other nervously. They seem relieved by his arrival.

"What the hell is this?" they ask.

"A hostage" he replies. "What the hell is going on?"

"We've been attacked," Jarrod tells him in hurried words blending into one another.

His face is obviously bruising, but he seems remarkably chipper for the blows he has sustained.

"The town square is on fire and they say it's everywhere. We don't know what to do. I tried to tell everyone to wait for you, but they said some cops came and took you in the night. I guess that's where those abandoned cop cars came from, huh? Peoples said you were dead. I knew they couldn't get you, with your crazy ass! So, you got you a captive, huh? What happened to the rest of them? You killed them didn't you?" Jarrod asks with a mischievous, sly grin.

"I don't know where they went. Maybe they fell in the lake."

John looks at his captive, then at the faces looking to him. Not knowing what to say, he drags his captive into the house and the others follow. John's eyes are glazed over, he seems separated from the room as the others teem with questions of what had happened.

Mysteriously, all the power is out. Eventually, someone produces a wind-up radio. They sift through the noise and dial in on a signal coming through on the AM dial. It was a continuous humming, high pitched beep. They scanned through the entire dial, but found only the monotonous electric whine. After a few minutes, the sound was interrupted by a series of breaks and pitch variations, and then the voice began:

"You are being asked to stay in your homes. There is currently no contact with local authorities. The Coastal United States is under occupation. All local authorities are being asked to organize at local levels. There is currently no communication from the following cities: Washington DC, New York, San Francisco, Los Angeles, Houston, Austin, San Antonio, Oklahoma City, Kansas City, Dallas-Fort Worth,..." the list continued on from the mechanical drawl of the computerized voice.

"There are currently no flights, please avoid airports and major metropolitan hubs. Local law enforcement and military bases are asked not to act without orders, please await directives from your local ONE outpost. These broadcasts are being sent via emergency generator operation and will continue once every hour on this frequency. Again, please remain in your homes and avoid any major metropolitan areas."

Everyone piles into the front room of the little house looking confused, formulating theories and trying to figure out what is going on. The younger teenagers and children go in and out, bringing word from their friends back to one another and comparing clues. Mothers hold their babies straddled on their hips and talk to one another with concerned eyes. Men compare notes and nod their heads in blank bewilderment. The light switches flick up and down with no response in every home down the block, all the phones are out, and even the cars wont start. Gathered in John's living room, the people of the neighborhood feel isolated, encapsulated together in opposition to some unknown force against them.

On a large dry erase board, a map is drawn out of their neighborhood and the surrounding terrain. There are only two streets leading into their area and they are surrounded by forest, fields, and a lake on all sides. Together, they formulate a plan on how to best defend their homes.

"Outposts. Glenn, take the three of you to the end of the road, but cut across the pond to get there. If you see anything coming, get the word here pronto. I mean, *as fast* as you can get here. You, go to the other side of Dove Hill. Take them with you. If you see anyone coming, send word pronto. Mr. Mason, get your ammo loading supplies and bring them here. No, I take that back. Take someone to help and go home and start making bullets there, send someone back with what you can send right now. And guns. Everyone, let's get our guns together. If you have extra, share. Let's make sure every man has a gun. I want men with hunting rifles positioned at the corners of the area. Who wants to go? You? If anyone gets into this area, you are to pick them off from outside. Manuel, Jackson, take camping supplies. You guys are our runners. You can have guns, too, but your job is to move between the out camps and keep everyone informed. Everyone else, stay here. These houses around the food and well will be our central post. We need to do this now."

"Some of you girls can come with me. Bring your kids over here across the street if you want to help, we can make some food for these guys," Mary chimed in.

The captain looks around him as the people begin to move in perfect timing, going their separate ways and returning with supplies from their own houses. The machine was in operation.

John goes into his room to get his lever action 30-30. He looks around himself, at his walls covered in years of artwork depicting a struggle against an unnamed force. He sits back in his chair and realizes that he is still fighting one. Buster has been let off the chain and now comes to his side. He looks up at him, then over to the window and emits a low, rumbling growl. The dog then looks back at his master as his mouth opens and his eyebrows rise. He can feel the tenseness in the air. John sets his mouth square and looks at the dog who breaks into a smile. He was made for this.

12. THE FACE OF THE BLUE BEAST

Transmissions from surrounding areas have been carried in the new means, the old means reinvented. People escaping the city tell their relatives the stories of the ONE troops centralizing in police headquarters and government buildings when they huddle down in dark dens. They exchange the stories with those they meet in passing while walking down the misty streets. The international troop's sub machine guns and heavy weaponry proved to be the deciding factor in who now ran the law enforcement efforts in this new reality of anarchy.

As global was the iron grip of the Organized Nations for the Environment, so was the attack that crippled the whole structure allowing their fabricated power to exist. Bewildered bandits in burkas were banding with slant eyed scientist who knew western European men in black leather suits. They slid stealthily down walls and silently overcame resistance with deadly force, simultaneously in several spots around the globe. Their targets were mile long proton accelerators manned by scientists in mostly remote locations. They had learned of them, smuggled manuscripts on their operation, and carefully planned to coordinate their attack. They had watched their wrists as the clocks winded down and they had pulled the lever.

When the lights went out, few thought it would ever last for long. The steady routine of heading to the grocery store, turning on the television, or flipping on a light, was as ingrained in them as eating grass is to cattle. The first inclination of inner city opportunist when the power grid failed was towards looting. With no electricity, their devotion to repetition drove them to steal television sets and cases of beer, the bottles sweating condensation as they were still cool for the very last time. They had no inclination that the fancy electronics would never be useful to them again.

Incidents seemed isolated. Accustomed to a constant stream of information and pictures assuring them that the world was okay, many began to panic simply from not knowing. A dozen days later, when necessities such as food and water had become scarce, their worst nightmares were beginning to manifest. Hard working, beer sipping people who had watched riots in other cities on their television sets, now found themselves caught in the middle of what seemed like a bad dream, waiting to wake up.

Within a few days, bands of neighbors had formed to protect each other from the packs of unabated criminals roaming their streets. The day the lights went out was a day no one would ever forget. Farmers manned their rifles and families in the suburbs locked their doors, waiting for the television to come back on and tell them something. As the day became a week, the reality became as apparent as the rotting meat piled in the parking lots of grocery stores and restaurants everywhere.

Confusion had led to panic; panic had led to irrational and hasty action. "O" class citizens had now become suspects of the ONE forces at the highest levels, the highest levels being made up of those most obedient and basic minded people within the organized levels of crime prevention. No one, at least no one around there, really knew the cause of the destruction of the infrastructure, how the lights had been turned off overnight or how every avenue of communication had been disabled. The enemy could be Muslim extremists from a sandy third world, secretive Russian scientists, or little green space aliens, for all they knew.

It could be the radically thinking internal opposition of the country they occupied who hated the presence of the international forces, many of which were the law enforcement officers who had been forced to use only small caliber handguns and electronic tazing devices since the arrival of the ONE forces. The international troops were cornered and confused, they were determined to question and disarm all citizens one by one and to occupy all police structures and government buildings.

Their questioning tactics consisted of physical attacks on people within their homes and on the streets. Doors were kicked in without warning, rooms were 'cleared' by flash grenades and indiscriminate machine gun fire upon any movement inside the acted upon dwellings. A lifted arm to cover one's face during the beating, a raised voice of protest, an angry look in their direction; all were considered signs of dissent which constituted resistance. Resistance constituted live action, and in live action all things were forgivable.

Then those labeled as insurgents were listed as casualties of conflict, COCs, and left in their lumped, lifeless forms. Whole neighborhoods of peaceful suburban dwellings were being swept. The order of who was taken and who was passed by seemed to be random.

The 'volunteer' force of ONE was conscripting youth as it marched on, offering a choice to the indiscriminate beatings and killings, guarantying safety in return for unquestioning service. Many of the strapping local youth were actually helping them in the whole hearted belief that the attack which had shut down every power grid in the country simultaneously had been carried out by these lowly citizens of their own country. Many just went along with it to save their own skins.

They were spreading from the city; they had even taken over the local courthouses in the outlying town as an area of operation. There were reports from a courthouse worker who told her daughter that they had asked for records of all criminal offenders in the area. She claimed that they were planning to locate every home schooling family, community organizer, church leader, gun owner, preacher, and food producing land owner, as she told her secondhand story to the old man she had always seen walking around on the street. Old man John told a few people, and soon the word was out that they were to leave no stone unturned as they worked out from the inner city looking for 'O' class citizens.

The reports kept growing. The girl from down the road, her mom had told her, that's how her boyfriend's little brother found out and was able to tell the man who had a few old cars for sale at the end of Jim's road. Jim had passed the story on to a few other people, who, like bees spreading pollen, had planted the seeds of the stories in the minds of the people they met walking aimlessly down roads who were looking for some food or shelter, picking up and passing along other stories of the new invasion.

Word of it was everywhere. The disillusioned, 'upper middle' class could no longer deny it; no one could claim to be safe from it, as no one knew the prerequisites anymore. Things that used to insure their survival seemed useless now: the rare shade of their new shoes did not take them any farther down the steamy paved street, the shiny plastic emblems on their cars lost the power to ferry them past imaginary social boundaries. Even those who had once felt safe enough sticking to the rank and file felt insecure looking out from a single, sneakily raised blind in their living room windows. The people who always thought they had nothing to gain were even out in the streets now. They felt they had nothing to lose.

The invading forces now moving on citizens was there by invite, invited by the people of a nation who had before held the idea they were invincible. The Trojan horse of safety had been pulled into the land by binding ropes; ropes of security, ropes of indulgence. The things they had clung to and depended on had bound them to bring the assassins into their midst by their own labor, the sweat off of their own backs. The troops had not asked to be escorted into the battle so sneakily, but now that they were here, within the walls of the city, their only choice was to fight their way out.

The ONE forces were carrying out their own communications in similar ways as the peasants around them now, but they were no longer looking for guidance in the foot carried messages. Their primary motive was now a primitive one: survival.

The troops were lost in a world where they had no more communication with their superiors. They had no more backing of the international forces. There were no planes to take them home, no wires to send their orders, no televisions to outline their rules and offer the reasoning tone of guidance to the confused masses. There were no more helicopters to hover over their prey with infrared eyes and relay their hiding spots back to them on the ground.

They were now the strangers in the world, outnumbered by a distrusting native population who felt that the new invasion was nothing more than a takeover bid by them. To seize control and establish their authority was the only option they perceived to being overrun by the hoards of mongrels they had been sent to this strange, seemingly barbaric land to oversee.

Pitiful was their force, in reality. Organization of more than 20 people would be able to turn them back at any juncture, it seemed to John Flint. The stories of the takeover found their way from little girls on distant corners, through ears of their peers, to his bedroom. From what he gathered, the troops had never been seen in groups of more than ten, they seemed to get lost and turned around in the unfamiliar terrain easily without the aid of GPS. They were forced to meet back up in centralized locations daily.

They had no way of knowing who had perished, or who had simply not made it back when they took tally of their men at the end of a day. They did not know exactly where the other one was going or who was their enemy, so they wore their cobalt blue one piece suits where ever they went to avoid being mistaken as ordinary citizens and mowed down by their own. Their lack of discipline was evident by the reported detours to rape and pillage, none having the authority to stop the other from doing whatever he wanted.

If they needed reinforcements from neighboring brigades, they would have to send word with a person manually, by horseback, or even by foot. They had limited horses and even more limited horse riding skills. They also had limited supplies of food; everything they ate was commandeered from citizens and hoarded as the lack of refrigeration left giant piles of rotting food strewn along parking lots in its wake. Their ammunition supplies were also limited, and they used whatever guns they could confiscate during their raids. They were seizing power, but their grip was a weak one, and the handle was becoming increasingly slipperier with the sweat of their nervous hands.

"Now the mission is becoming clear, now I see what you must need from me," thinks John as he gently runs the tips of his fingers down the hair on his dog's back, not looking up from the board where he lays his plans and organizes the information he receives.

His arm hangs loosely by his side, his mouth drips slightly open, his lips like loosely filled water balloons hanging off his face. He settles into a deep stare into nothing as his mind formulates the equation. Some part of his mind knows he is in a microcosm as he formulates his plan for the Battle of Dove Hill .

Death and dismemberment are a factor. Those who will fight with him, X, equals greater than 50, minus the unknown variable of those lost in the first stand, the sum added to the unknown variable, Y, being those who will join him afterwards. Of those, an unknown number will have access to an unknown amount of resources, food being Z, ammo being X to the Y degree, dependent upon how many weapons are available for which ammo is available and the rate at which the rounds are expended. A certain percentage of those will use their ammunition wisely, many will be able to disarm multiple ONE troops alone, while others will disarm none before perishing or retreating. This Y variable is deducted through a chaotic, abstract equation. XY is greater than Z. The word will have to come in time, ten minutes from the east road and eight minutes from the west, leaving 20 to 22 minutes for final preparation and positioning. Operational time is less than or equal to 10 minutes.

The time of day will be an important factor in strategy. Nighttime offers optimum advantage to the defender in the wooded areas. That factor can be ruled out. It would have to be day; he must plan for the worst case. If they are met at the entrance and are able to push through into the neighborhood, what are the chances that the file holds ranks and continues to fight without guidance or word from the others? Where are the weakest links? Who can keep them together? The whole of the parts is cemented by the unknown variable; he feels the underwater tree reaching up to him, growing up beneath his foot to steady his balance.

"Move Zach over to A1 point with James and Jeff," he yells from the opened door of his bedroom to the woman handing out supplies and relaying messages to runners as she turns to mark the changes on the dry erase board on the wall of the living room.

"Bring Jarrod back here for direct words with me. And where

the hell is Peoples? Send word to the Hernandez's to hold their footing and stay alert. I want points C and D on ready for fighting at the front of the entrance to our street, and I want them to join in battle through cross fire tactics if so much as one shot is fired. Be sure they know, they need to be ready."

"Got it." she says confidently.

Francis has picked up the role with the zeal of a scribe, and John is quietly amazed at the fortitude of the young woman. She displays the strength only a woman can have in her cheeriness amidst the looming uncertainty. She does not ask for concession or surrender. Her instincts tell her that this is the way to survive, that any chance of continued existence depends on her ability to fight now, to assist in the process of those preparing to give their own lives in her defense, in the defense of those around her. She knows they are only taking the men, that distancing herself from all of this would be more pragmatic for her immediate survival. But her instincts tell her that she would serve a horrible existence without the men now coming together to defend their own in one last stand. The decision has been made and she follows it whole heartedly.

"And send word that I want every person available here for a meeting half an hour before Sunset, I think we're going to need a pep talk."

He sees it coming. The equation has added up for him, he sees the answer in his mind. His drawings now are not of melting breasts and flexed arms of comic book heroes, but map outlines and movement charts, lines drawn between points with numbers signifying distances and approximate travel times from one point to the next.

Triangles represent force variables in ammunition and weapons stock, rectangles of those who are to remain in place and arrows for those that are to move. Like linebackers filling gaps and defensive ends reading run vs. pass in a game of football, they are to execute their actions based on variables represented by fire symbols, smoke, or lightening. Their tasks are drawn out. Unknown variables are asterisked and stars signal the important holds to fall back to and defend in cases of being overrun. Friendly fire is to be minimized by geographic coordination, aimed by aligning two land marks in the direction of your neighboring posts. Lists of directives are written out on the side of each paper, and a different chart is hand drawn on a personalized handout for each person as they arrive for the meeting.

"We are probably in for a fight" he begins, "and we all know why we must do it. I think that their ability to communicate and bring in support is very limited. We only have to defend against this small force that will arrive here, I believe, tomorrow sometime in the morning. People are being crushed right now, people are dying. But people are fighting. People will rise up and this tyranny will not last forever. We can stand down and be crushed, or we can be a part of the solution."

The people in the room begin to sway a little as they say things like,

"Tomorrow,… wow," and

"I didn't know that."

"They took Paintbrush yesterday, and we are the natural progression." he continues. "Some families holed up inside their homes and were burned alive. From what we've been able to gather, they leveled the community within half an hour, left very few survivors and took very few prisoners. They are moving with a purpose, and as far as I can see, they will be here waiting for the next Sunrise. They are expecting to march through here quickly and move on to the next slip by mid day. But that's not what is going to happen to us. Once we defeat them here on our turf, they will try to send for their closest support in Red Valley. Because we are in the best position to defeat them, we will let the runner pass to bring them back here to us. Once he spreads word to them, they will send another runner back to the town square and the courthouse. He must not pass that point. We must not allow that second runner to get to the next wave of backups. We can beat them here, gain steam, and bring the battle to them before they can assemble.

"Over the course of tonight, Glenn and Able will cut through the woods, around the ponds to the other side of Red Valley. When you see a messenger leave there, you are to kill him. Period. It is imperative that they do not get word into downtown before we do, before we begin to attack. We will defeat all of them from the immediate area we encounter. You will have to be confident of that as you try to spread the word towards the square that we are coming, that we will need help."

He continues to outlay the plan for the battle in the morning, never stopping to think how crazy it is. Occasionally, he swings a glance in the direction of the bound captain in his chair. He is listening intently.

"We won't have time to deal with you. If he gets crazy, one of you is to shoot him, immediately, no questions asked." he says, never looking away from the captive.

The captain responds unexpectedly.

"I'm on your side. Trust me; I've had to take orders from those guys since they got here. There is no love lost between me and those international forces, the last thing I need is for someone speaking Italian to me to be in control."

"I'm sure we all trust you, you're a blue blooded American, just like the rest of us." John responds sarcastically, rousing a laugh from the men around him, though he senses that the man is telling the truth.

He has noticed a change in his demeanor since that long talk by the burning fire. The original resolve to gather weapons and organize for battle had been initiated by this captain's demand to destroy the garden, before the generators of the world had shut down over night and before the ONE troops instituted their own band of martial law. Had not that fateful act taken place, bringing as many men together for this resistance would have been almost impossible.

It was that garden, that simple display of mercy which brought food from the ground, and the water from the sky that brought them together in a display of what all was really possible. That was what had formed this unit.

The factors of the equation add up in his mind. One part this, one part other. He has it all figured out, the chaotic pattern makes perfect sense to him. He counts on the value of the unnamed variable, he depends on intercessions of the spirit at every turn. He knows the equation will stand up to proof based on the factor he cannot quantify. He knows it will work without doubt, for although he does not understand the complete workings of it, he sees the answer in his mind; he knows the value of the unknown variable. God is in it.

The darkness follows a quiet sky at Sunset. The cold air is crisp as the cloudless sky leaves its mood on display in a blue grey. With his arm around his rifle, John lies in his warm bed and goes directly to sleep.

His dreams are laced with Indian counsels of sitting warriors and old men whose flaccid testicles hang exposed from beneath their leather flaps as they sit around a fire in a teepee passing around a long wooden pipe. Their words are indistinguishable, but their message is clear. They bellow out giant clouds of ascending smoke as they ask the elements for intercession in battle in a growing chant. As he walks out of the tent, he is confronted by a red dawn. There is a giant black horse carrying an armored knight towards him. His armor is that of a machine. It is not like the old middle ages armor, but smooth edged, modern. Behind his iron mask, eyes burn orange with fire and heat is emitted through his jaw piece as light bending steam.

He will hear no pleas, he will speak no peace. There is only one way to confront this beast. John's hands become like stone weapons as he feels the power in them and decides to attack the mounted figure. He confidently hurls his new appendages at the monster, and recoils in self doubt as they bounce off of the steely armor with no effect. At the point of impact, the creature does not flinch. It seems to be smiling under its mask, griping the reins of its horse with boney fingers clad with long, steely spikes clinched around chains holding the huge beast at his command beneath him.

John trains his mind for a way to defeat it. In his violent dream, he sees children being crushed beneath clawed feet. He sees Francis being raped by the monster who has now taken the form of many beastly men, laughing and spewing flames from their gapping mouths. John runs towards them and hurls his body through the air, lunging at the monster and wrapping himself around it. They fall to the ground together. The helmet has come off of the beast. He looks into its indifferent eyes to find the same face he had seen years before, the preppy boy from the dim bar who had asked for his mercy in another dream, and was here to visit him again. It must understand, John thinks. He pleads with him for peace, asking the many manifestations why they are hurting these people, what is wrong with him.

"What the hell is wrong with you? Why the hell can't you see, why do you do this!?"

The blue eyes look back indifferently, as if deaf to the panicked screams of John's voice. John grabs the head in both hands and turns it sideways to yell into its ear, but finds it has no ears. The flesh there where ears should be is smooth and without holes.

He then begins to bang its head against the rocky ground, but he feels as helpless as an infant fighting a grown man, as there is no effect. There is no reaction from the cold, dead look in the eyes of the beast as its head mutely bounces off the ground. The eyes are pale black as they look up at him amidst the head being repeatedly smashed. John feels the back of its head break into wet softness with each bone crushing blow of his skull. He does not flinch, the eyes are cold. He cannot die, he is already dead. John stands up, takes a few steps back and breathes heavily.

Then, from out of nowhere, his brother, Crockett, appears beside him. Big and calm, with his jaw set in that famous pose of non defeat, he walks over to John.

"What are you doing?" he asks mockingly "Are you trying to kill that thing? Ha. It's nothing, it's just a thing. They can't even fight. Here, you want me to show you how?"

He produces a rifle, an old World War One relic, and pulls the gun up to his shoulder. Nodding his head over, he removes his glasses and quietly looks down the sights at the immobilized beast. His upper lip flexes as he squeezes the trigger, and the explosion in the chamber jerks his shoulder back in recoil. Then he cocks his head up and squints his eyes into the distance, looking for his assured result. They both already know it worked, of course it would.

"There, the thing is dead," he says as he hands the riffle over to John, "Now take care of the rest of them. I've got to show you how to do everything, boy?"

The dream continues with twisted visions of demons and monsters, laced with memories in the form of his hand slashing out before him yielding a knife. Jaggedly ripped flesh and intestines flow out before him.

Once the deed is done, the brothers crawl on their bellies into a opening in the walls of the building from the rooftop on which they are fighting. They crawl downward through a confined space. In between pipes and industrial fittings, squeezing between the two foot gap for what seems like an eternity in almost utter darkness, they descend into the building. Then, as they emerge at the other end, they see daylight.

They are looking down on an old town square. Golden light illuminates fresh trees adorning the grass between gardens dividing a paved street. The walkways are set in red bricks and follow stairs up to ornamental wooden doors in front of the buildings on the square. A woman is pushing a stroller; a little girl is playing, watching a balloon bounce at the end of a string as she holds her mother's hand.

As he awakes in the pre-dawn of morning, he thinks of his brother and his father out on Flint road. They are in the deep swampy areas of Southeast Texas, surrounded by fierce individualists 500 miles away. Their terrain is different, more secluded. They have the well for fresh water, the 30 foot deep tank full of fish, the chickens, and the horses.

For the first time, he has a moment to think that he may not be the only person leading a charge against this new enemy, the deregulated army of the ONE. They may already be in a similar battle back home and everywhere in between, he thinks, remembering the heightened levels of ONE forces at the ports and passes of that area. The character of people lining that corridor towards the Southeast Texas coast are fierce by nature. Imagining their faces, Sun worn and lined with character, he prays for them, and is filled with a calm feeling that everything is okay. They will find a way. The equation yet grows. He sees the multipliers that start the domino effect from his victory today towards the fight working its way towards him from the coastline of the state as he visualizes the immediate future.

"We can take it all," he thinks out loud.

He dresses and gears up, lacing up his lightest boots last. Wearing his favorite pants, he picks a beige t-shirt and covers it with his black leather jacket for armor. In the lining of the biker jacket, he has stitched pockets holding pieces of iron and steel from various sources, including barbeque pits and the base from an old swiveling boat seat in his back yard. Around his waist is an ammo belt with a holster holding a semi automatic 9mm pistol. Under his arm hangs another pistol, a 357 revolver. Its weight seems calming, grounding, real. He swings the nylon strap attached to the Winchester lever action 30-30 rifle over his shoulder. His black marine combat knife rests in his belt, he places another large pocket knife in his pocket, and a smaller combat knife into the strap at the back of his calf before stuffing the bottom of the pant legs into his boots.

As the sky begins to turn purple, hinting at the coming of day, he walks out into the dewy yard and rekindles the fire in the pit behind the house. The crickets have stopped chirping for the night, everything is dead quiet as the fire begins to crackle a bit from being prodded by the stick and moved gently by the cold breeze temporarily picking up. It raises the hair on John's neck as he peers around himself at the dark tree line. The cobalt black of the swaying shadows mesmerize him for a moment, and he stares into the darkness. Something seems to move in the canopy of the mesquites.

The wind again picks up, whirling burning embers within the fire and pulling the low lying branches of the willows with them, bringing the trees to life as their shadows take the forms of many screaming old men. The swaying branches of the trees became long beards and moustaches outlining furious mouths. In a trance, he hears them speaking to him in words of intercession he cannot understand. He raises his arms up and utters summons of their wisdom in a prayer of words he'd never pronounced, pronouncing his unity with them. An outline of his up-stretched hands forms a shadow towards the trees as the growing fire, whipped by the winds, silhouettes him from behind.

Jarrod is sleeping in a chair next to the fire, keeping watch. Turning away, John lets him sleep. The children sleeping around him have taken Jarrod as their personal leader, looking up to him as an authority of age who is still one of them. 20 or more of the children and prepubescent young men are bundled together in the cold, huddled like a fresh litter of puppies, relying on each other's warmth and sleeping soundly as their faces move slightly in reaction to their dreams. Next to them are the weapons they have gathered so proudly: a few twenty-twos, swords and self made spears, and other war contraptions. They sleep so soundly; they must know that the clamorous trees are keeping watch of them.

John pours the last of the coffee grounds into a t-shirt which is wrapped around another coffee can, heats up water in a pot, and pours it slowly through the grounds. The weather now on them would have spurned a great deal of local news coverage and road closures in the old world, the world that did not matter now. It would have been such a big deal, but the warm fire and his clothes give him ample protection from the light frost on the plant's leafs. In the old leather biker jacket that Killer gave him, he found an ancient, beat up package of 'Parliament' cigarettes. Upon inspection, one last cigarette sits bent within the pack. Gently, he straightens it out in his fingers then lights it on a glowing stick from the fire. Watching the dim orange creeping into the grey sky, he pulls the smoke deep into his lungs in a long breath then slowly blows it out. The tobacco taste lingers in his mouth as he relishes the smoke smoothly lining his throat.

As he sips his coffee, the others begin to wake up. He stands on the back porch and waits for the reflective mirrors to beam their okay signal from each post in the first rays of morning light. Blink, blink, blink, they come from each post around the pond, up in the woods that separate the area from the main road, over in the low land descending back to the other side of the neighborhood.

The Hernandez's, father and son, are the last to signal. He pictures them there in the woods, starting their fire back up and cooking some eggs. They are the deepest in the woods and have run their mirror up a tree with a rope which they simply tug to flash the signal. Upon seeing the last signal, John knows they are all there.

Back inside, he sees the police captain is awake. Reeling in his simple happiness to be alive for what may be the last day of his life, John decides to confide in the man who peers at him quizzically.

"I don't know what the hell I'm doing," he says, "I really hope I'm not leading these people to an early death. I'm not sure I know exactly what I'm doing."

"Oh, I believe you do," the old man says, looking quizzically at the battle clad young man before him. "From the way you're dressed, I'd say you're about to kill some people. After the way you did that night, you may just be gifted at it."

The captain scans the floor in the apparent stupidity of his own statement, and then looks up with a flash of a bulb above his head.

"Back in the war, it seemed like some people just lived through it. Some, you knew would go. Whether it be their incompetence, their brashness, or their lack of concentration in the way they looked all around during the battle, you just knew they would not make it. But others, you knew they would never die. They seemed to be able to walk into any firefight, any enemy village, any situation, and come out OK. You would think they had an unseen shield of protection by the way the bullets whizzed around them. They knew it, too. I think you're one of those types.

"You're old school, like me. It's not like the old days. In the old days, the General would lead the charge. Men were led by warriors so fierce that they themselves could take on the king's work of breaking the front lines and killing the most of the enemies single handedly. It was as if some divine intervention allowed them to lead the battle to the place it was supposed to end anyway, as if they were characters in a book they had already read the end of. Histories of our culture have been preserved by such great feats: 300 Spartans and long-hammer wielding Germans and mythical, monster slaying heroes in the storied years of eld. It's not like that anymore, only, with what you're facing, it kind of really is."

"Yeah, that's what I'm counting on," he says, alluding to his unknown variable, his secret weapon.

"I only wish I could join you" say's the captain in a defeated air of great hope.

"A dead soldier is of no use. You should think about God."

The Captain is the other variable floating around in John's congested mind as the day begins and the people around the house rise and go out to their posts. He knows it has some importance, but can't see trusting the man. He grapples with the idea of executing him. The way the captain has dealt with the new reality has surprised him. He expected more of a revolt, a vulgar outburst. Instead, it seems as though the big cookout and dose of anti reality has changed his mind, renewing it as a cleaned slate, a new backdrop to all he has seen. John wonders if it's all just an act. 'No time to think about this now,' he thinks, and turns from the bound man.

Francis stands silently in the threshold of the kitchen, obviously thinking the same thoughts, rationalizing the man's life. Just taking a moment to notice her, his gaze is ripped away by distraction. Through the window, Jarrod catches the corner of John's eye as he runs full out around the corner of shrubbery at the end of the driveway in giant strides through the front yard towards the house.

"They're here," he says bursting into the front door, "They're almost at the end of the road!"

Grabbing Francis with one hand behind her neck, he kisses her and quickly pulls himself away from her magnetic gravity before rushing out the front door. A cool fog shrouds the long road as they leave the yard and begin to walk down the rock driveway in the misty morning. At the end of the road, a large shadow lurks in the fog. It is a giant ONE urban combat vehicle. It turns the corner and begins its slow drive down the country road. 20 or more soldier's silhouettes come into view through the dense fog as the convoy slowly approaches. Seeing their shadows as well, the vehicle stops and the men begin to run towards them.

With his eyes open wide in intensity, John grab's Jarrod's shoulder to get his attention and motions towards the ditch on the side of the road, then darts for the opposite side of the street, sliding on his belly into position in the shallow recess amongst the tall grass and weeds.

Rising up on one knee, John brings his rifle to his shoulder, aims for the foremost soldier and cocks the handle of his lever action rifle. He hones in on his target 40 yards ahead of him, then, guided by some propensity for randomness, turns his sights to the soldier directly to the right of the one he had been aiming at. His finger rests on the cool metal trigger curved beneath it. Breath slowly expels from his mouth as the world slows down around him and he gently squeezes the trigger.

'Bang!'

The gun's shot rings out loudly across the terrain as the soldier drops to the ground in the distance. Ducking down, John cocks his lever and moves forward 10 feet, crawling on his belly in the wet ditch along the side of the road. Cracking from the troop's automatic weapons is intertwined with the sounds of bullets bouncing off of the close by pavement and the sounds of tall grasses shredding at the whiz of passing projectiles above his head. He hears three rapid shots fired from a few feet back, across the road, and knows that Jarrod is firing on the troops. John again rises onto one knee as he raises the rifle to his shoulder in one fluid motion and picks out another target. In the second it takes him to drop another soldier, he notices that there are less than half of the troops on the road now. They have spread out.

"Jarrod, break off the other way," he yells across the road.

He rolls over and crawls up the side of the ditch on his belly until he is level with the paved road, and aims from the ground at the four troops who are within 30 feet of him now. He fires off one more round at the one on the left, spinning him around as the fast moving bullet rips through his chest. The other two guards kneel down and begin firing in the team's direction as Jarrod fires off another round of shots, wounding another soldier who kneels down with his hand over his shoulder before falling forward onto the ground.

The rapid fire of their machine guns eats the terrain around John as he breaks for the wooded field beside the road and keeps running through the thorny mesquite trees as if he were a bullet himself. Reaching a low wooded canopy, he turns and dives for his stomach to look behind him. He sees and hears a twenty two caliber rifle popping across the road through the fog. The flash of light from its barrel is followed by a round of rapid machine gun fire in its direction. They are too close to miss him, this time. This time, Jarrod's stubborn refusal to back down has cost him the ultimate price.

John's dismay is interrupted by the sound of boots crunching through the woods behind him. Carefully turning around in his hiding spot where he lies, he can see the figures coming through the woods towards him just twenty feet away. There is no time to run; they will just shoot him down.

"We all must go," he thinks aloud as he springs from his belly with both pistols in front of him and begins firing at the encroaching troops.

As the other five raise their guns, it as if the misty woods come alive with gun fire from beside them, and the soldiers slowly fall to the invisible projectiles passing through their bodies.

Manuel and the other neighborhood kids come running through the trees towards the troops behind the array of gunfire and pounce on the wounded bodies like swarms of ants, stabbing them and smashing them with knives and hammers. The Hernandez's creep slowly and cautiously up behind them with their hunting rifles held up beside them.

"They went up around that way," say's the senior as he points around the pond towards the back of John's house.

Breaking into a sprint, John runs as fast as he can towards the house where Francis is waiting. Emotionally charged, he runs through the branches and weeds towards the house with total disregard for anything but arriving there.

The short burst of shots from the field of tall reeves surrounding the garden was loud, but John never heard them. He did not even feel the one that hit him as it passed through his fleshy arm and into his abdomen. The next sensation he remembered was of his body hanging loosely beneath him as the guards drug him face down up the wooden stairs of his own back porch by his arms. The wooden steps banging his knees were but a haze, and even his head banging into the end of the door as they opened it didn't seem real. He felt like an old TV when the corner of the metal door clanged against his skull.

In a trauma induced dream, he finds himself standing in his pajamas, holding a teddy bear and looking up at his bearded uncle Killer in his long johns, befuddled by the digital snow on the television screen.

"Just hit it, like this!"

Killer whops the old Television set hard with his clenched hand right on top and the picture jumps back onto the screen.

As he is drug through the back door into the small laundry room, he fully regains consciousness and pulls himself up by his arms, which the two men are grasping, and raises up his legs beneath him. The ripped muscles where the bullet passed through his abdomen scream at him in pain as he strains to suspend his legs, but he does not hear them. He is twisting his body to free an arm as the guard behind him smacks him with the butt of his riffle in the back of his head. The crack leaves hot blood dripping down the back of his scalp, but he does not feel it, either, and snarls as he twists around to punch the man squarely in the face. His fist rips through the muscular, red face with the blonde moustache and crushes into the delicate facial bones, flattening them beneath his stony knuckles. The texture is that of a giant rice crispy, crackling lightly, and he can feel it.

As the trooper behind him raises his pistol to fire, the small room erupts into an explosion of energy as Peoples bursts into the back door and hurls the soldier into and over the washing machine, which clangs and folds beneath the force like a toy as the trooper flies through the shelving on the wall. Peoples is like an angry mother bear as he growls and raises his arms for battle. At the same time, as if on cue, the big dog springs from the back room where Francis and the others have been hiding and attacks the other guard from behind, jumping up to grip his shirt and trying to pull him down.

The soldiers turn their drawn pistols onto the dog ripping savagely at their partner with powerful jaws. As they are busy firing into the animal whose eyes are rolled back as he pulls at the man, impervious to the slugs ripping through him, the soldiers are momentarily distracted from the fracas in the laundry room.

Taking the opportunity, Peoples lunges past John through the corridor, into the kitchen where the troopers are wrestling with the big dog. With both arms extended in his charge, growling with his eyes open in full intensity, he loops both men around their necks as he barrels in between them. Raising his legs off the ground as he lunges at the two guards and grabbing their throats in his arms, Justin brings both men down with his weight and momentum pulling them backwards as he attacks in an animal's growl.

One of the soldiers is carried into the corner of a countertop by the force and falls to the ground. Justin lets go of him and quickly pivots to swing his legs around the back of the ONE soldier who has managed to land in a sitting position. Justin slides his thick arms under the soldier's arms and around his neck like two powerful snakes. John sees a maniacal stare in Justin's eyes as he constricts his strong arms across the soldier's neck and arches his back in a mechanically practiced rear naked choke hold.

In that instant, John jumped heel first onto the other soldier's chest and lunged down on him with a straight punch to his face, leaving him temporarily stunned. His feet astride of the young man, John turns behind him to see the other soldier who had been thrown through the shelving now reaching down for his gun on the laundry room floor. John grabs his knife from his boot as he lunges towards him, pulling the blade outward with is arm, propelling it upwards from his leg with one motion as it penetrates the soldier's tan head, just below his chin.

The blade, bolt-like and sharpened on both ends, easily Sunk the eight inches to its handle through the fleshy matter in the man's head and punched the top of his skull out just a little bit, allowing a flow of blood to wet a portion of his short brown hair and mat it down. The blood trickled down his face from beneath his helmet. Justin had the last of the three soldiers' windpipe clutched in his scissored arms and was very near to killing him as John removed the knife from his own victim's head and turned to watch. The trooper's face, green and purple with suffocation, looked blankly into John's eyes as he ceased struggling to get his fingers between his neck and Justin's arms, and his hands instead begin to hang limply in front of him as if he were pointing to his face in his sleep.

The Captain watches all of this, still bound to a wooden chair and muffled by a sock tied around his head and in his mouth. Peoples, finally rising from the slow death of his choke hold's victim, turns to the bound man and walks towards him.

"I'll show you!" he yells. He is about to knock him over in his chair with a swift slap of retribution when something from the bound man's eyes catches him and he stops, his hand pulled back over his head as he stands over him, ready to strike. The captain's eye refuses to twitch as his eyebrows ask for mercy and Justin recognizes the emotion and stubbornness displayed in his face. Amidst the battle between the foreign ONE troops and the surreal events of the last hour, the two realize they are not so different, after all.

Watching the whole scene, John finally understands his previous feelings of compassion for the old police captain. Together, Justin and John untie him and help him to stand. His bones are stiff from being tied onto the rigid wooden chair for so long, and the older man shows it as he stands up.

"Listen, I'm on your side. I knew it would come to this. I don't care what may have been before, but I want to see my daughters grow up speaking American, and I'm on your side."

A distant memory of the man's face finally pecks at John's subconscious as he looks at him in a new light. He still does not realize that it is the same cop who pushed him over his couch and onto his head as a child. Mysterious, unexplained emotions running through him are interrupted when thunderous machine gun fire abruptly rings from the front of the house. Justin and John run to the front window and look out to see the giant assault vehicle on the road at the end of the driveway.

Three giant wheels, four feet tall each, lined each side of the dark Blue vehicle. ONE was cheaply stenciled across its industrial metal side over the protruding rivets along the steel sheets making up its body. Tiny window slits were the black eyes to the outside world, squinting as if annoyed by the growing Sunlight of the passing day. It's thick armor had actually been designed to resist an electromagnetic attack. Atop it, a machine gun torrent revolved around and fired into the house across the street.

The 'Mini Gun' is anything but 'mini,' firing 170 rounds per second. Its line of fire emits a glow from the stream of bullets like a laser cutting through the air. The vehicle is eight feet tall and the automatic machine gun swivels atop it like a robot controlled by some unseen lever within. Tiny windows show no signs of life within the seemingly impenetrable iron assault vehicle. A hatch for entering the crew cabin is evident on the flat top of the vehicle, but there is no way of reaching it.

Bullets from rifles bounce off of the hard shell of the vehicle with little sparks as they ricochet. Small caliber rounds pop from behind tall reeves across the street, and the Mini Gun rips through the grass like a lawn mower, shooting chunks of flesh flipping through the air as it paints the shredded green foliage red.

As John watches out the window of his living room at a sight he never thought he would see, he feels as if he is watching a movie and that the window is only a giant screen when he sees Peoples running across the yard towards the great beast with a tire iron. His hands feel numb on his rifle, his legs clench at the sight of the barrel turning towards him. He realizes his hope now rests in the battle between the modern machine gun and the tire iron.

As the torrent swivels atop the metal skinned machine and fires upon John's house, Justin jumps onto the vehicles and pulls himself up onto the top of it. The rounds rip through the walls of John's house like paper. Like a slow moving mechanical saw, they move across the house from the far side and cut the wall down into splinters as the stream of bullets moves through the structure effortlessly.

The hatch on the top of the iron hull of the ONE vehicle opens and a soldier pops his head up. He begins firing his pistol into Justin's back, just as he plunges the tire iron into the spinning mechanism of the automatic gun torrent. The strong iron rod wedges in between the gears of the spindle, causing the gun to be stuck in one direction and rendering it impossible to aim from the controls within, just before the spray of bullets reaches the spot where Francis and John are ducking together. A loud grating sound rips through the air as the gears of the spindle grind to a halt while Justin watches defiantly.

He grins at the man who is sticking his head and shoulders out of the hatch and firing on him. The bullets seem to be passing through him unnoticed as he releases the tire iron and lunges onto his belly towards the soldier, gripping the trooper's arm in his grasp as he tries to shut the hatch. Justin holds his wrist firmly and reaches his other arm under it to form an inescapable figure four around the soldier's arm, undaunted by the pistol which is still firing rounds into him. The other soldiers inside are pulling at their crewmate, frantic to shut the hatch which is currently blocked by their compatriot's entangled arm.

The firing stops as the pistol runs out of ammo and Peoples closes his eyes as if going to sleep. Lying on his stomach, he is nearly nose to nose with the soldier in the hatch as his face becomes serene, the blood dripping into his still defiantly shaped mouth. The soldier jerks his arm to see if it can finally be released. Instead of getting his arm, he sees the alarming sight of Justin's eye opening in sheer determination. He feels the grip of the man who should be dead grow even tighter, as Justin lunges forward and snaps his jaws onto the soldier's nose.

Emboldened, the others who had been fighting futilely against the armored vehicle along the side of the street rush from their cover and climb the sides of it to where Justin still holds the hatch open as his blood runs into pools on the slate blue steel. The police Captain yanks the hatch open and the others swarm into the cockpit, firing weapons down into the soldiers below as they descend inside and finally overcome the beast from within.

Once inside, the carnage was terrible. At close range, confined in a tiny cockpit, the soldiers were smashed and stabbed, mauled and mutilated by the furious youth invading them like Piranha. The agile youngsters sinuously squeezed between them and swiveled around their necks with knives and axes.

Too late to stop the second runner, the battle had begun, there was no stopping them.

13. A NEW BEGINING

As quickly as the invasion of the United States of America began, it had ended. Just as a red sea swells to kill the life within it simultaneously around the world, the pipelines and infrastructure of the superpowers had been brought to its knees. The super weapons they created in the name of science, giant proton accelerators capable of creating antimatter and shooting holes in the Sun, had been seized in one coordinated, global attack. They had been activated to stop the workings of the machine that created them.

The radicals who activated them counted on the complete breakdown of the weak western world once the lights went out. They claimed that there was no moral fiber to hold them together. They envisioned an easy takeover in a short time, once they had let the panicked violence die out.

The insurgency of the international ONE troops spawned in the chaos had nothing behind it, though. It had no manpower to try to overcome the gun wielding citizens in Texas who were raised shooting them, no tanks to patrol the now vacant streets of the Empire State. In Europe, the outcome was the same. Citizens overcame the international forces and those of the extremists like angry Soccer mobs. They could do nothing to control the people; they had only destroyed the infrastructure of the powers who kept them in their place. Whatever powers had orchestrated the debacle, they had counted on the tendency towards conformance which had been bred and nurtured in the civilized modern societies of powerful countries to make it work, but they had miscalculated.

Just as the flowers bloom to signify the changing of the season, forgotten remnants of fighting souls had shown their colors across the countryside. Fighting from the outside in, warriors in the barrios and in the rural back woods had risen up to the international troops and encouraged those around them through their actions until the surviving ONE forces disbanded and tried to merge into society.

There was to be no more driving to the mall, but clothes would still be made. They would be made from cotton grown on farms by foot pedal spindles operated by women in wooden homes under candle light. There would be no more driving to the grocery store to buy greens from seven seas, but food would be eaten. It would be grown by men tilling soil with plows swung overhead by back muscles instead of diesel driven machines. There would be no more suited men representing the turning wheels of giant corporations and government bureaucracies taking a piece of all that was earned through interest and taxation, but there would be trade. The tomatoes would be traded for beef, the clothes would be traded for shovels, and the work would be traded for shelter.

Windmills were erected quickly; wells were dug as community projects coordinated by elders of the neighborhoods. Horses, once considered a pesky indulgence, became a commodity overnight, and horse thieves became villains again. They were gunned down by citizens of the neighborhood the next day. The destitution that had formed these tight organizations quickly translated into a bond of camaraderie amongst the people.

The military men had gone back to their families and began organizing the people in their neighborhoods into loose law enforcement bodies. Fellowships were formed and people gathered weekly to sing and praise. People pulled together and many found their quality of life improved. Cooking of meals became a social event, and life slowed to a peaceful pace around the globe.

Justin's death was a hard one on John. Just as the others who had perished that day, he had given his life in a manner befitting a warrior. Once the others had infiltrated the ONE vehicle's hatch, he released his grip on the arm of the soldier which had prevented the hatch from closing, and simply laid his head down in his own blood to rest. He sighed a content sigh, as if he were a child going to sleep in his mother's arms as his body relaxed onto the cool metal roof of the armored vehicle. John climbed up and tried to rouse him.

"Goodbye Flint, I'll see you next time," were his last words.

The spot where they buried him is marked by a young oak tree now. John looks out the back window of his house at the blooming garden. White flowers of okra stalks blow in the gentle breeze with the long swaying grass behind them. Francis's arm is wrapped around his waist as they gaze off in silence.

After overcoming the assault vehicle on that dreadful day, Manuel and the other young men of the neighborhood took it for a little joy ride. They drove it straight to Paintbrush, the next neighborhood down the Farm to Market road. The band of teenagers and adolescents piled on top of the vehicle, encouraging others to follow the vehicle and try to hop on. The Minigun was easy for them to use, it was just like playing a video game and they racked up points anytime a ONE trooper could be tracked down. It was like driving a real Corvette in the arcade. They told their story and encouraged others to take up arms as they worked closer to the central square of the nearest city. By the time they had gotten there, the parade had become a mob. The sinister blue ONE vehicle had now become a pied piper for resolute warriors in hiding as it led them through the streets.

Similar uprisings last over the next few days, but overall, the battle is finished quickly. Thousands of similar battles complete with one of a kind heroics rage on during the coming weeks. But their fires, like the one on John road, are eventually extinguished and the proud surviving residents of the areas eventually quell the spreading embers before they can reach out and influence his life. The battles rage on, but he can't feel them.

The familiar street still seems surreal in the aftermath. While surveying damage and searching for survivors, he finds the lost puppy, nervously patting her tail in an old wooden shed, surrounded by oil and vats of chemicals. She doesn't recognize him at first, but runs towards him once she hears his voice, jumping, yelping, and trying to lick his face as she runs circles around him. She is brought home just in time to rub her nose for one last time with her dying father.

True to his nature, he had survived the bullet wounds, but only for a few days. He was old, his breath came slow until they eventually stopped and he passed in peace as a hero in his house.

The seasons change, the spring buds burst forth in their vibrant greens. Weeds and wild vines emerge in the gardening areas, their little white and pink flowers catch the morning dew and it is time to go to work. There is plenty of work to be done, plenty of things to do. By the time of the next freeze, smelting pots for metal works had been built, houses had been re erected, and an incredibly deep well had been dug.

The house is chilly but much warmer than outside from the smoldering stove and the body heat within. Buckets line the counters, over heaping with fruits and vegetables. Having picked all of the remaining produce from the garden ahead of the season's first freeze, John enjoys a home-brewed ale in the kitchen of his silent house. Frequently, he paces over to the slightly cracked door of the second room and casts in a joyous eye.

The pit bull looks just like her daddy as she lays guard over the foot of the crib. She stays there anytime sweet Melissa sleeps. Eyebrows slightly jumping in her sleep, no one knows if her memory holds the events of the past or if the qualities of her father will ever be needed again.

There was no radiance to compare to the sapience of her swinging tail, the child slept soundly and all was well.

The end

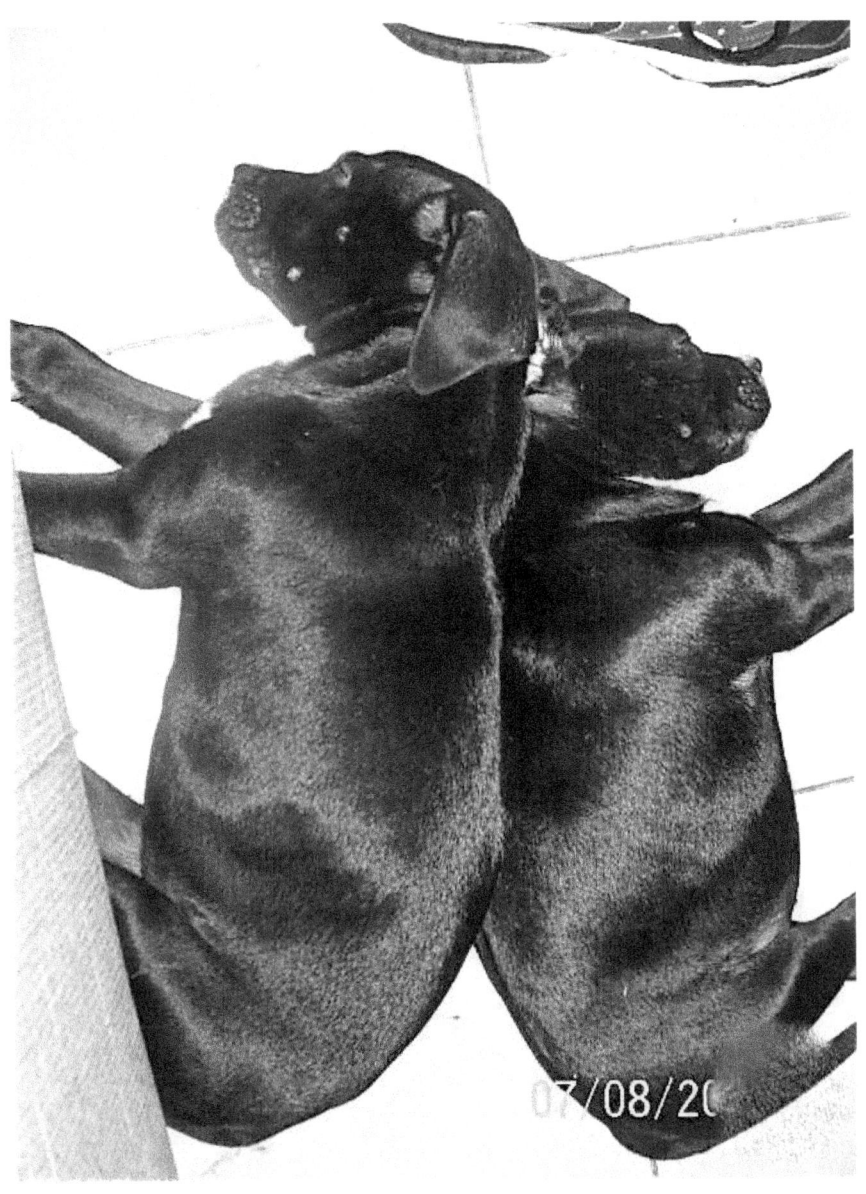

www.ingramcontent.com/pod-product-compliance
Lightning Source LLC
Chambersburg PA
CBHW070816180626
46818CB00001B/292